THE PROMISE BEHIND THE PROMISE

or

PRIDE AND PREJUDICE AND REINSURANCE

Mark MacGougan

Also by Mark MacGougan:

NEWSPAPER BOY

For Linda,
of course.

DISCLAIMER

The characters in this book aren't intended to represent any real people, living or dead, but are, in fact, modeled on characters from a novel published in 1813. Similarly, the companies depicted in this book aren't intended to represent any real companies, operating or defunct.

The reader is also cautioned against drawing any connection between the characters' qualities - good or bad - and their job functions, titles, or departments. We bring to our jobs our own virtues and vices.

Table of Contents

CHAPTER 1

One can wholeheartedly agree with the famous statement about a single man of means being in want of a wife without necessarily agreeing that every story involving such a figure needs to end with a marriage. Take, for the sake of argument, a story set in a large business establishment. In such a setting, a romance – particularly one between individuals of unequal stature within the organization – is rightly viewed with suspicion and concern.

A more satisfactory ending for a story in such a setting could be the firm establishment of a mutually beneficial business friendship. If the principals have unequal status within the organization, the nature of such a friendship might be characterized as one between a mentor and a protégée. In place of a ring might be a particularly attractive job offer. Such a conclusion may strike some readers as cold and bloodless, possibly unworthy of the investment of time needed to reach it. Still, it may be noted that the marital arrangements reached in many fine traditional novels could be fairly characterized as mutually beneficial business friendships.

"I'm worried about the girls," said Ms. Nebbit to Mr. Bennet as he appeared at her desk to submit some paperwork. He would have preferred to drop the material off in her in-basket without troubling her. Over his many years of working in the same department as Ms. Nebbit, he had consistently been so eager to avoid interrupting her important work that he had attempted many various times and days of the week for submitting documents to her without ever yet having discovered any option when she would be reliably absent from her post.

By "the girls", Ms. Nebbit was referring to the five young women Mr. Bennet had hired and currently oversaw under what was known as the Pride Team - a corporate hire program of the Juniper

Reinsurance Company intended to bring promising and diversity-assisting young people into the organization and provide them with a year of rotational background experiences on the expectation that they would be hired for permanent jobs within the company by the time their training year had expired. In fairness to Juniper Re, it should be noted that the organization – while it may have been patriarchal in its history and might continue to be principally led by male executives – was not a place where those male executives would think to refer to a group of young female employees as girls. This was a liberty that Ms. Nebbit felt justified in taking, being female herself, and feeling no small amount of motherly interest and concern for them.

"Oh?" said Mr. Bennet, dropping his papers in Ms. Nebbit's basket and eyeing the hallway back to his office.

"Very worried indeed. I don't know what you were thinking, hiring all those girls when jobs are so tight. Half of them will be let go or end up being forced-placed into some shameful mailroom position."

Mr. Bennet was briefly distracted by the thought that Ms. Nebbit's own position was a sort of mailroom, with the disadvantage that one was obliged to do the delivering oneself. She had touched a nerve as well – there was no guaranteed path out of the Pride Team, and those who weren't able to secure their desired full-time positions faced the prospect of having to settle for options that were less and less desirable.

"There's no shame in any honest work, and I'm sure the young women, whatever their faults, will all find good ends. Heaven knows there are plenty of places in this organization that could use some youth and energy."

Ms. Nebbit tilted her head in his direction and lowered her voice. "They're about to announce a new Head of Claims. Someone from the outside."

"Oh?"

"His name is Bingley. Charles Bingley. He's from Cornwallis Re."

"Is he bringing anyone with him?"

"Not that I've heard of."

Mr. Bennet pondered this. A new senior officer, unencumbered with any staff or connections, would need assistance and trusted

2

associates. Someone like that could benefit greatly from an able and congenial protégée.

"He starts next week. You should look in on him. Put in a good word for your girls."

"Yes, thank you."

"Yes – you'll look in on him?"

"Yes – I appreciate your suggestion and will give it the same consideration I give all your good advice."

"So that's it, is it?" Ms. Nebbit lifted her head and raised her volume. "Ms. Cullis has probably already booked a slot on Monday for the entire Surge Team to go down and meet him as some kind of a field trip. Meanwhile, you'll just sit in your office, minding your p's and q's, while every other officer in the building rolls out the red carpet and gets the new Claims Head to hire whatever deadwood they want to get rid of!"

"Yes, thank you. Also an excellent suggestion. Here's an additional thought. What if I sit in my office – minding, as you say, my letters and my own business – while you go look in on Mr. Charles Bingley? That way, I'll remain untroubled, the Claims Department will be free of everyone else's terrible deadwood, and you can exert your full force and charm to entice him to take on the entire Pride Team."

"Really. I wonder sometimes why I even bother."

"So do we all. So do we all."

Despite their many years of familiarity, Ms. Nebbit had never learned when to leave off pressing a case with Mr. Bennet. She was apparently doomed to a kind of rhetorical Peter Principle, where any position must be promoted to its point of ineffectiveness.

CHAPTER 1b

The reader is asked to forgive a Moby-Dick-like chapter here regarding the business of reinsurance. Much as we're all anxious to get on with the whale chase, it's sometimes necessary to acquire the background information that will enable us to understand the setting, words, and actions of the protagonists.

Insurance companies receive money for taking risk. Any large, successful insurance company will, of necessity, accumulate quite a considerable amount of risk. Insurance companies are very happy to build up large stores of money, but are less fond of collecting so much risk. So they look around for a solution to this problem, and they do what any of us do when we are worried about risk: they buy insurance.

The insurance that an insurance company buys is called reinsurance. There are many kinds of reinsurance. There is facultative reinsurance and treaty reinsurance. There is excess reinsurance and proportional reinsurance. There is per-risk reinsurance and catastrophe reinsurance. There is reinsurance purchased directly and reinsurance purchased through brokers. There is reinsurance on personal lines business and reinsurance on commercial lines business. There is reinsurance on property and casualty insurance and reinsurance on life and health insurance.

The reinsurance company, of course, ends up with the same problem as an insurance company. It likes to accumulate money, but worries about accumulating risk. So the reinsurance company buys insurance. This is called a retrocession. And what happens to the risk accumulating on the books of the retrocessionaire? We will stop here to consider the eternal voyage of risk. The picture in our mind's eye might be compared to the hint of infinity one glimpses when two mirrors face one another.

Any insurer or reinsurer is, by design, an army at war with itself. It's a cold war, to be sure, marked by smiles and civility and team-building exercises, but a war nonetheless. The chief axis of the conflict is between the company's Marketing staff and its Underwriting staff. The Marketers want to write business and aren't inclined to be overly fastidious regarding the projected long-term profitability of such business. The Underwriters want to maintain profit margins and aren't inclined to reduce prices or improve terms just for the sake of writing more business.

The distinction many businesses make between Marketing and Sales doesn't exist in this context. An insurance or reinsurance company typically doesn't have a Sales department. People responsible for the sales function are known as Marketers – or sometimes Field Underwriters.

The Marketer is typically an extrovert, impatient in the office, attentive to the moods, needs, and vanities of customers, and similarly attuned to any personal slight or loss of favor within the organization. The great advantage to the Marketer is that the department is able to take credit for all revenue coming into the company, and there is an implicit threat that – if the Marketer were to defect to another company – the business written by that Marketer might follow. Consequently, the Marketer is typically well compensated.

The Underwriter, by contrast, is typically an introvert, dispassionately weighing pros and cons and – rightly or wrongly – more attuned to the outcome of a spreadsheet than the emotions of a customer. The Underwriter's role is to act as the restraining Superego to the Marketer's Id. In theory, this serves to protect the interests of the company. The advantage to the Underwriter is that the department is viewed as having a particularly high and strategic perspective. Consequently, the Underwriter may have a better opportunity than some others to ascend to the heights of Senior Management.

One challenge for many Underwriters is the ability to say *No* in person. Your pensive, bookish introvert has little difficulty saying *No* to a Marketer by email or phone, but may flinch eye to eye and – put face to face with an unhappy customer – may, in fact, collapse like a house of cards.

The conflict between Marketing and Underwriting proceeds cyclically. Marketing is typically in ascendancy during what are known as Soft Markets, when business is generally unprofitable. Underwriting tends to hold sway during Hard Markets, when business is generally quite profitable. To the novice, it might appear that it would make more sense for these periods of ascendancy to be reversed, but clearly there must be a good reason for the pattern to be as it is, since it has been universally observed within insurance and reinsurance companies for as long as anyone can remember.

Other departments that are tangentially drawn into this conflict include Claims, Financial, and - when it exists - Actuarial.

Claims handling is very different in reinsurance than it is in insurance. Insurance claims adjustment is perhaps the most thankless job in any financial business. The insurance adjuster must interact with people who have suffered some terrible calamity and who are almost certainly not familiar with the exclusions and limitations of their coverage. In a reinsurance setting, the claims process is much more comfortable for all concerned. Here the claimant is an official of an insurance company – someone who has not suffered any personal calamity, and who is entirely conversant with the normal exclusions and limitations of coverage. The process is therefore more akin to paying off the holder of a winning lottery ticket.

The Claims Department tends to attract people who would have been judges if they could have done so without having to be lawyers first. They are happiest adjudicating contracts and mediating disputes. Still, as they pay losses that could perhaps have been anticipated or avoided, some otherwise fair-minded Claims people may fall prey to that sense of grievance that often afflicts people whose work springs from the mistakes of others. That is to say, they may become resentful of the Marketers who pursued the loss-prone business and dismissive of the Underwriters who approved it. Fortunately, this unhappy possibility only exists with respect to Marketers and Underwriters who make mistakes.

The Financial Department tends to be a world unto itself. Its members function something like the translators at the United Nations. The consumers of their services must simply trust that the messages being received are a fair representation of reality. Members of the Financial Department tend to work long and sometimes unusual hours, driven by the many deadlines in their own odd and unforgiving calendar. The general temptation for Financial people is to think that – because they have booked results in the company's financial records – they have themselves achieved those results.

Scattered among Underwriting, Claims, and Financial - or sometimes a department unto themselves - are the Actuaries. They are a sort of priesthood of mathematics whose role is to augur the future. The Actuaries and the Underwriters might seem like natural allies, but the separateness of their traditions and the nearness of their functions make them uneasy allies at best.

Other functional departments have their distinctive qualities and cultures. Operations is very good at making lists and flowcharts, and quite steadfast at avoiding any knowledge of – or possibly feigning ignorance of – the company's actual business. IT requires two parallel staffs - one to do the work and the other to communicate with the outside world. Human Resources is clearly very important, but no one outside of that department understands what they do. Still, they are in the happy position of being able to take credit for any company result or accomplishment achieved by a human being. They aren't aligned with or against any other department, and its members wield a circumscribed but considerable power over the other employees, which they like to assert through the imposition of minor indignities, such as forms that must be filled out and training programs that must be consumed. They decree such requirements with impunity, as there are very few employees looking to pick a fight with the people who administer payroll and benefits.

If insurance is a white collar business, then reinsurance is a starched white collar business. By long tradition, the industry has been staffed and managed by people from the right schools and the right families - a place where a diversity hire might be a fellow who attended Choate and then Princeton as a scholarship student.

Such generalizations tend to be particularly apt with respect to certain small, specialty reinsurers headquartered in town - such as Mr. Bingley's former employer, Cornwallis Re. As a large reinsurer headquartered in the suburbs, Juniper Re might have appeared to be somewhat less inbred, but it was certainly not a showplace of diversity. Mr. Bennet's Pride program represented a modest attempt to widen the company's talent pool.

The term Pride was understood to be a convenient acronym - although few people would have been able to tell you that it stood for *Professionals Recruited to Increase Diversity and Excellence*.

Some people viewed the team as providing a helpful inoculation against the demonstrable tendency of the company to be culturally homogenous by introducing a diverse group of young employees hand-picked to have the skills and temperament needed to succeed in the organization. Other people viewed the team as an awkward social experiment whose members, if they were valued at all, were valued for their demographics rather than their skills and abilities. Consequently, and perhaps ironically, it wasn't unusual for Pride Team members to find their association with the group somewhat embarrassing.

Mr. Bennet never liked the term Pride. Some corner of his thoughts continued to list Pride as a deadly sin, but another and possibly stronger reason was that he associated cheerleading self-regard with low expectations. He took to referring to the group sometimes as the AHT - the Acceptable Hygiene Team.

The Pride program represented an impressive commitment to diversity by the organization. The fact that team members sometimes struggled to secure permanent positions commensurate with their talents should in no way be taken to suggest that anyone in the company preferred a lack of diversity, or that anyone allowed their judgment to be clouded by inter-departmental jealousy over the fact that the program was operated out of the Underwriting Department. Certainly, everyone in the organization had the highest regard for Mr. Bennet himself, whose impressive knowledge and good sense were universally held to atone for an occasional lack of enthusiasm that some might otherwise interpret as failure to be a team player.

CHAPTER 2

The Juniper Re Home Office was a suburban campus with one large three-story building connected by walkways to two smaller buildings. Scattered throughout the complex were conference rooms named for past company presidents. The south end of the second floor of the Main Building, which is the locus of the Underwriting Department, featured rooms known as Longbourn 1, 2 and 3. These rooms were divided from one another by movable walls that could be retracted to create a large space for special events.

On this particular morning, the walls were in place. Arrayed around a table in Longbourn 2 were Mr. Bennet and the current Pride Team: Jane, Elizabeth (sometimes known as Lizzy), Mary, Catherine (usually known as Kitty) and Lydia. As junior members of the organization, it was normal for them to be known by their first names. It required a certain stature to become known as *Mr. This* or *Ms. That*, and only a handful of the most powerful and senior officers could attain the distinction of being known by their initials.

Mr. Bennet hadn't intended this year's Pride Team to be exclusively female. Offers and inquiries had been made to male candidates. Still, he wasn't sorry at the outcome. He believed Juniper Re needed more women in positions of authority, and he was enough of a statistician to calculate that – if he maintained a normal balance in the Pride Team's composition – its ability to change the balance of the overall organization would be considerably diluted. In addition to their femininity, various members of the team ticked off some other diversity boxes for the organization. These elements aren't germane to the story at hand, so we'll attempt to be as blind as the organization itself aspires to be regarding topics such as their ethnicity, national origin, sexual orientation, neurodiversity, and degree of able-bodiedness.

Also present in the room was Ms. Nebbit - for reasons having less to do with any formal relationship she had with the team than with her maternal interest in its members and her control over the conference room scheduling.

Mr. Bennet scanned the room. "Do we all have the Idea Fair on our calendars?" he asked. "This Wednesday, two o'clock in Meryton."

The careful observer might have detected some slight eye rolling at this. The Idea Fairs were an important opportunity for them to make personal contacts across the organization, and the team members were as conscious of an upcoming Idea Fair as any debutante was ever conscious of an upcoming ball.

The Idea Fairs were such pleasant and useful gatherings that many people assumed they were a longstanding tradition at Juniper Re. In fact, they were an innovation introduced by Mr. Bennet five years prior to our current story, in the face of what was then a daunting combination of opposition and indifference. That no one now recognized the events as his invention did not bother Mr. Bennet in the least. He took it as a sign of success.

"Do you have any notes for us?" asked Elizabeth. "Any suggestions for the Round Robin?"

While each Idea Fair included one or two presentations about topics of interest within the company, the highlight was always held to be the Round Robin, which was a kind of speed dating of corporate problem solving. Officers from various departments would come to the Round Robin and bring with them summaries of two or three very specific problems or challenges they were then facing. Less senior employees - including but by no means limited to the Pride Team members - would rotate from officer to officer, hearing a problem from each and offering thoughts about how to attack it. A bell for the next rotation would ring every ten minutes.

The Round Robin provided promising young employees with elusive Face Time with company executives and an opportunity to demonstrate creativity and ingenuity. The exercise was not, however, without risks. An off day at the Round Robin could hurt one's prospects just as surely as a brilliant day could help them.

Mr. Bennet nodded. "Good question, well asked Lizzy. I'll go around the circle. Jane - you generally have good answers to the questions, but you put them forward tentatively, almost apologetically. There's no reason to apologize for having a good

10

idea! Elizabeth - you have the best answers of anyone, but too often that's not enough for you. You must improve on the question or substitute a better question. This is the opposite of Jane's issue. It is perhaps too forward. I've been told that half our participating officers are afraid to meet with you. Mary - you go into a trance and come up with the most wonderful answers two hours after the Idea Fair is over. That isn't the point of the exercise. You need to be willing to put forward something right then, even if it isn't fully worked out yet. Catherine - you are often funny, which people enjoy, but sometimes also sarcastic, which makes our participants fear you almost as much as they fear Lizzy. Lose the edge if you can. Lydia - your issue is the opposite of Kitty's. You have no edge whatsoever. You are all smiles and charm and everyone has a great time visiting with you and they only realize much later that you have provided no answer to the question at all. I ask you not to lose your charm but to add some substance to it. Those are my notes. Ms. Nebbit, would you add anything?"

"Why, you haven't addressed the most important topic of all, Mr. Bennet! Being well spoken is fine as far as it goes, but the critical thing is to be well dressed. You want to be attractive and feminine without being flirty or inappropriate. Jane and Elizabeth are neither of them fashion plates, but at least they understand how to place themselves in that reasonable middle ground. Mary, I'm afraid you are quite insensible to being attractive - and Kitty, I'm afraid you are quite insensible to being feminine. Lydia, meanwhile, has a tendency to show more of her person than is strictly necessary for any reinsurance purposes."

These comments drew a raft of groans and objections from the team members. Mr. Bennet held up his hands to ask for quiet. "I do not and will not comment on this topic. You may take or leave Ms. Nebbit's opinions on this issue as you see fit. As far as I'm concerned, I simply expect you all to be there on time and mentally ready. I think we'd all like to make a good impression if Mr. Bingley, our new Claims Head, happens to be in attendance."

"Oh, sure!" said Ms. Nebbit, with a theatrical roll of her eyes. "Or the Pope or our country's President - since they have each been given the same cordial welcome from our group that Mr. Bingley has received!"

Mr. Bennet remained focused on the team members. "It will perhaps not surprise you to hear that your great champion here, Ms. Nebbit, has been urging me to intercede with Mr. Bingley on your behalf."

At this point, Kitty gave a short laugh that drew a sharp look from Ms. Nebbit.

"Kitty!" said she. "I don't know if you mean to laugh at Mr. Bennet or at me, but I can assure you that either one would be Completely Inappropriate."

"Yes," said Mr. Bennet. "Let us all remember to laugh as little as humanly possible."

"Speaking for myself," said Elizabeth, "I would hate for us to be thought of as some charity case, requiring you to go hat in hand to every person of influence you can find."

"Of course," said Jane, "we would like to meet Mr. Bingley."

"Of course!" exclaimed Ms. Nebbit. "One would have to be an idiot to think otherwise! But I advise you all not to hold your breaths. The Christmas Party is just a few months away. I expect we'll probably all have the chance to meet Mr. Bingley then."

Mr. Bennet scanned the room. "Mary. You have a talent for building models to predict an outcome. Could you calculate for us the likelihood of Mr. Bingley attending our upcoming Idea Fair?"

Mary paused rather longer than she probably would have preferred. "I'm sorry, but I'm not sure I can right now."

Mr. Bennet nodded at this. "And what about you, Ms. Nebbit? What's your calculation?"

"No calculation, just experience. I'm not saying it's impossible for Mr. Bingley to appear at the Fair. Just highly, highly unlikely."

"I respect your opinion, Ms. Nebbit, but I don't think it reflects well on Mr. Bingley's reliability. For he has told me himself that he plans to be there."

This statement created a stir of excitement and a volley of questions, which Mr. Bennet answered as he was able. He had paid a visit to Mr. Bingley first thing Monday morning and found him a very personable and sensible-sounding addition to the company. Mr. Bingley was intrigued by the Idea Fair and had entered it into his calendar on the spot.

"But why didn't you tell us right off?" asked Lydia.

"I thought of it as a kind of joke," said Mr. Bennet. "But I had some second thoughts when I saw how Kitty got in trouble for laughing."

"Kitty, you may laugh now," instructed Ms. Nebbit. "We may all laugh quite happily when Mr. Bennet listens to good advice and does the right thing for you girls!"

"I think," said Mary, "that the chances of Mr. Bingley attending the Idea Fair could be expressed as 100% minus a factor for his unknown reliability and minus another factor for unforeseen circumstances interfering with his schedule or with the Fair itself."

CHAPTER 3

As it happened, Mr. Bingley was completely reliable and no unforeseen circumstances interfered with him or the Fair. Initially there was some confusion among the team members because he arrived at Meryton as part of a group that included two men unknown to them. Which was Bingley? Eventually, word circulated that the man with the open collar, navy blazer, and easy smile was Mr. Bingley, while the tall man with the tie, dark jacket, and appraising eye was Mr. Darcy, another new addition to the company.

This in turn provided some additional frisson to the proceedings. Who is Mr. Darcy? Where did he come from? What's his position?

While Mr. Bingley seemed entirely approachable and comfortable with whatever company or situation he found himself in, Mr. Darcy appeared to be something both more and less. Mr. Darcy looked, in fact, like the Platonic ideal of a business executive. He was tall and solid and serious – his face a judicious balance of handsomeness, athleticism, and studiousness. The mere sight of him at a meeting would be enough to give heart and confidence to any employee – unless such employee had actually worked for a company run by such a Central Casting executive. For the unhappy truth is that executives with such unimpeachable appearance are often looking impressive while they announce bad luck and disappointing results – or looking doubly impressive standing next to some uninspiring specimen who runs the conglomerate that has just bought his company out.

It was the tradition for Idea Fairs to be hosted on a rotating basis and this particular event was hosted by Mr. Litchgate, the Head of IT. His department had recently relocated to Building Three, which was admirably modern but lacked an appropriate space for an Idea Fair. Meryton - which when partitioned was actually four conference rooms - was on the third floor of the Main Building in the area that

IT had vacated. The Idea Fair was duly called to order by Mr. Litchgate. There ensued a brief presentation on Bayesian updates for earthquake coverage that Mary found quite delightful, and then the Round Robin began.

In the first round, there were ten executives with questions ready. All of the Pride Team members except Elizabeth were able to secure a partner. Jane was pleased to be matched with Mr. Bingley.

After a friendly exchange of pleasantries, Mr. Bingley showed Jane a chart of elapsed time required to settle claims. The chart was divided by type of claim and year submitted.

"I just received this data and am wondering what you think it says and what, if anything, I should do about it."

Jane appreciated such an open-ended question, was a dab hand at interpreting charts, and had some considered opinions about the company's claims-handling procedures and how they affected its customers. When the bell rang to signal the end of the first rotation, Mr. Bingley asked if the rules allowed for them to decline to rotate and continue their discussion. The rules did in fact allow for this and their discussion continued.

Elizabeth meanwhile, looking for some way to redeem her time, wandered over to where Mr. Darcy was seated and watching the proceedings.

"Don't get up, please," she said, although he had made no move to rise. "I just wanted to introduce myself. I don't believe we've met."

"No," replied Mr. Darcy. "I'm sure not. I'm new here."

"I'm Elizabeth Austen. I'm part of a rotational training group called the Pride Team."

"I see. You do training or you get trained?"

"We get trained."

"Very good. I wish you well with that."

"Thank you." She waited a moment. "And you are?" she asked.

"Oh, sorry," he said. "F. William Darcy." And he shook her hand.

"And what is your position?"

"Special Assistant to the President."

"I see. And what is to become of Ms. Grondseth? Is she retiring or is she to be your associate?"

Mr. Darcy seemed at a loss for how to respond to this question. He finally said, "My position has nothing to do with Ms. Grondseth."

"My mistake."

There was an awkward pause between them. Elizabeth did not want to end the conversation there. She looked around, then pointed to the area where the Round Robin was taking place. "You should participate in the next round," she said. "We need more people with questions."

Mr. Darcy held up his hands. "I'm too new to have any questions for you."

"That's odd," she replied. "I should think at this point you'd have nothing but questions."

Elizabeth returned to her former position feeling some unease about her brief interview with Mr. Darcy. Had she made an enemy? She hadn't meant to, but he certainly had no charm or social graces. It was a good thing he hadn't been hired as the new Marketing Head!

Later, during a break, she was near enough to hear Mr. Bingley approach Mr. Darcy and speak quietly to him.

"Come, Darcy," said he. "Don't sit around moping like that. You're needed here. Make up a question and join us."

"It's all a lot of wasted time as near as I can tell. Bogus answers to bogus questions before the bell rings. It's just a game. I don't think it speaks well for how professionally reinsurance is handled out here."

"You're wrong, I swear it. I can't tell you how impressed I've been with the people I've met here and the answers provided. It's been quite eye-opening for me. Jane from whatever the Pride Team is could - I think - do my job better than I can. I saw you talking to one of her associates earlier. Give her a chance when we restart the Round Robin."

"I cannot speak to your Jane, but I don't believe her associate is the Einstein who's going to solve our industry's trickiest problems. When I told her my title here, she asked if I was taking Ms. Grondseth's position!"

"I'm sure you are being too harsh on her."

"And I'm sure that I am not. You go and enjoy your games. We'll both be up to our necks in real work soon enough."

Mr. Bingley returned to the Round Robin and Elizabeth, no longer troubled by the awkwardness of her discussion with Mr. Darcy, allowed herself to steep in loathing for his smug, unwarranted arrogance and gratuitous unkindness.

When the event was reviewed at the subsequent Pride Team meeting, the primary focus was on Jane's very successful introduction to Mr. Bingley. Ms. Nebbit announced it as a triumph, and was not shy about predicting a bright future for Jane in the Claims Department.

Comic relief at the meeting was provided by Elizabeth's lively recounting of both her interview with Mr. Darcy and his subsequent conversation with Mr. Bingley.

The misunderstanding that had marked her as mentally suspect in Mr. Darcy's eyes had to do with job titles. Ms. Grondseth was the longstanding Executive Assistant to the President - in effect his personal secretary. Mr. Darcy was to be Special Assistant to the President. An Executive Assistant is not an executive but a Special Assistant is. Elizabeth may have missed this obvious distinction due to having begun her studies with an aim towards Elementary Education, where the term Special was generally a reference to students with distinctive needs or challenges.

"You know," said Mr. Bennet. "Special Assistant to the President is a position we haven't had here in the past. It appears to be a kind of lieutenant to the President and may signal that Mr. Darcy is being groomed to be our next president. Does that change your opinion of him at all, Lizzy?"

"No indeed! However, I'm quite happy for him to be the next president, because then I shall never have to interact with him at all. He can send us an email every year urging us all to give to the United Way, and make a speech at the holiday party thanking us for our hard work. After that, he can be as boorish and obnoxious as he is able for the rest of the year for all it will affect me!"

"I'm quite with you Lizzy on this one," added Ms. Nebbit, wagging her finger extravagantly at Mr. Bennet. "That man is insufferable! And you know me. I am always willing to give everyone the benefit of the doubt. But I have had it with this new Mr. Darcy! No Einstein, he says? Not able to solve the tricky questions? Well, if he had said

17

that of Lydia, maybe he could be forgiven - but Elizabeth? He might as well have said it of me!"

CHAPTER 4

Weather and schedules allowing, Elizabeth and Jane would walk outdoors together after lunch. This gave them an opportunity to clear their heads and speak more freely with one another than might be appropriate in the office or the company cafeteria.

"That's a good look today," said Jane as they began their walk. "I like the sweater!"

"And I like your jacket. Of course, you and I are no fashion plates, but we do know how to walk a sensible middle path."

"Is that what we're walking now?"

"Yes, of course. This is where we're walking, so it must be the middle path. Over there is prudery and over there is shamelessness, and here we are as always in the very sensible middle."

"Yes, good for us."

Elizabeth stopped for a moment to look at Jane. "Tell me more about Mr. Bingley."

Jane smiled and they proceeded forward. "Oh, he's the best! He really just gets it. So many people here and probably everywhere give lip service to putting the customer first, but he's committed to transforming the Claims Department. He has a passion for it, and I expect he'll make a real difference."

"And how is he as a person?"

"He couldn't be nicer. He actually listens to what you say and seems to have a great attitude about everything."

Elizabeth smiled and looked at Jane. "And are you in love with him?"

"Don't be stupid! He's at least in his forties – not to mention married and I believe with a couple of kids. I'll admit to having a work-crush on him, but it's purely a Platonic work-crush."

"Meaning?"

"Meaning that I'm his partisan. I intend to contradict anyone who says a word against him, I'd happily be his proxy in any negotiation, and I'd sign up in a minute to work for him, or at least in his department. But no – his wife and my Stefan have nothing to fear beyond that. In fact, that's one of the things that I like best about him. He seems to be able to have a friendly interaction with a young female without getting all weird about it."

"Even one as glamorous as you?"

"Even the smokin' hot glamour girl you see before you! Somehow, he's able to look beyond that and see my reinsurance hotness."

"Well," said Elizabeth, "I generally think you give people too much credit and miss their faults, but I'm very hopeful that you may be correct in the case of Mr. Bingley. I wish you and your Platonic work-crush the happiest of outcomes. I'm not so sure, though, about the Claims Department overall. I believe it still houses some characters who may appear friendly on the outside but are not in fact up to Mr. Bingley's high standards."

"And you, Lizzy, are a suspicious soul. The people I know in Claims all seem quite nice to me." Jane smiled. "And what more do we know about your new nemesis, Mr. Darcy?"

"If I'm his nemesis, I think I shall have good company. He seems so far to have just two friends at the company – three if you include RJT, who must have hired him." This was a reference to Robert J. Turtletaub, President of Juniper Re. "Darcy's great friends with Bingley, which we now know only makes sense because they knew each other at Cornwallis Re and came over here together. But Bingley gets on well with everyone, so I'm not inclined to give Darcy any particular credit for that."

"And who is his other friend?" asked Jane.

"That would be CDB, who turns out to be his aunt." This was a reference to Executive Vice President Catherine de Bourgh, Head of Human Resources. "I think that explains a lot. It explains why she's his friend and supporter, of course. It also suggests that there's a certain arrogant streak that runs in their family, for I find her equally insufferable. I think it also explains how someone so lacking in human grace could be hired to such an apparently important position. It looks to me like nepotism. He had an in."

"So we seem to have added two people who are opposites. Yin and Yang. The immovable object and the irresistible force."

"Yes," said Elizabeth. "In underwriting terms, Mr. Bingley is what we'd call Pig Iron Under Water. That is to say – he's a sure thing, a safe bet."

"And Mr. Darcy?"

"Darcy's the opposite. He's what we'd call Feathers on a Flatbed Truck. A sure thing in the bad direction. A disaster waiting to happen."

"Well then, I will hope for his reformation."

"Oh, Jane. You're so good-hearted! You're the best person I know here. I wonder sometimes why you came here at all. Surely a health clinic or social services agency might seem like a more likely target for your world-improving energies."

"Yes, I thought so myself for a while, but only briefly. The problem is that I'm a chicken. On the one hand, yes, I do want to make the world a better place. Still, on the other hand, if I mess up I don't want anyone to get hurt!"

They walked a little further and then Jane continued.

"When I was in high school, my parents wanted me to apply for a job as a lifeguard, but I couldn't do it. If I'm a lifeguard and I doze off or get distracted, someone could die. It would be too much pressure. So, *No* to being a lifeguard, *No* to being a doctor or a nurse, *No* to being an air traffic controller or a police officer. So, you see, reinsurance is actually perfect for me."

"I do see, Jane, and I think you're very wise about yourself. I'm not so tender-hearted as you, but I end up in a similar place. There's something in me that's eager to build things – not necessarily physical, bricks-and-mortar things, but businesses, ways of doing things. What I like here is the idea that I could build great empires of reinsurance without carving any holes in the ground or chopping down any forests or paving over any wetlands."

Jane stopped. "So I'm a bit confused now. Is it our talents and virtues that have brought us to this place or is it our fears and neuroses?"

"I think," said Elizabeth, "that in our cases it may be a package deal."

"So, we are not Yin and Yang, you and me. We are birds of a feather."

"I'll take that as a high compliment," said Elizabeth. "Although I fear that some might think us Birds of a Feather on a Flatbed Truck."

CHAPTER 5

Situated near the Pride Team was a group of underwriters known as the Surge Team - so named because, unlike other groups within Underwriting, they had no permanent assignment or responsibility, but rather moved from project to project based on the perceived need. Surge Team members, unlike Pride Team members, were under no pressure to find new jobs for themselves, although many were on the lookout nonetheless, fearing that the group's lack of a permanent portfolio might presage a more general lack of permanence. Idea Fairs were desperately important to members of both teams, and their proximity to one another assured that the groups would gather around the walkway that divided their spaces in the days after each one to analyze, relive, and second-guess each element of the event.

The Surge Team included Charlotte, Elizabeth's best friend outside of the Pride Team, and was overseen by Ms. Cullis, a woman who was profoundly dedicated to the career advancement of her mostly young team members. While she had a limited ability to offer them technical underwriting knowledge or training, she was notably able to provide them with minute and up-to-date information on everything happening within the company - what in a different and less constructive context might have been labeled "gossip". Her skills and limitations were, in fact, strikingly parallel to those of Ms. Nebbit, and there was perhaps an occasional bit of friendly rivalry between them.

"Charlotte," said Ms. Nebbit, "I see you had a Round Robin session with our new Mr. Bingley. That must have been pleasing for you."

"Thank you. I thought it went well. But, you know, it was only a single session. I believe you're aware that someone else had a double session with him."

"Kind of you to point that out, Charlotte! Yes, Jane had quite a triumphant double session with Mr. Bingley. Of course, it's impossible to know what he thought of the various sessions. Unless, of course, someone overheard him making a comment about them."

"I thought I'd mentioned that to you," said Charlotte. "Mr. Robinson in Finance told me he heard Mr. Bingley say to that other new officer that he was very impressed with everyone, but he particularly singled out Jane and declared that he believed she could do his job better than he could."

"Did he indeed?" said Ms. Nebbit. "Well that sounds very promising, doesn't it? Of course, it may all come to nothing."

"Yes, but much more pleasant than the other new officer, who was overheard to say that Elizabeth is no Einstein."

"I've told Elizabeth not even to think about it. Good riddance, I say! Mr. Darcy is a snob who wouldn't know Einstein if he bit him!"

Ms. Cullis shook her head. "Mr. Darcy had a bad start, I'll give you that. But I'm not ready to write him off yet. I've seen worse. He may be proud, but at least he seems to have done a few things to give him an excuse to be proud."

"Sure," said Jeremy of the Surge Team. "He was a senior officer at Cornwallis and now he'll be a senior officer here. He was probably rich already, and they probably paid him a bundle to make the switch. If it was me, I'd probably be insufferable."

"I'm sorry to tell you this, Jeremy," said Ms. Nebbit, "but you are insufferable!"

CHAPTER 6

Charlotte looked in at Elizabeth's desk the next day. "Clearly Bingley already thinks very highly of Jane," she said. "She should press her advantage!"

Elizabeth considered this. "Maybe. But Jane, you know, is a gentle soul, not inclined to pressing anything."

"That's why I'm giving this advice to you rather than her. You can build up her courage."

"But what would you have her do?" asked Elizabeth. "Throw herself at Bingley's feet? Beg for a Claims job?"

"Why not? *'Faint heart never won a good job for a fair maiden.'* Or something like that. I've become quite convinced that it's not enough to simply demonstrate your suitability for advancement. You have to ask for what you want."

"Doesn't that seem a little premature to you? They've talked a couple of times and she worked on a project for him. If you're Bingley, is that enough to justify a job offer?"

"In this case, it's plenty! He could wait a year, but how much more will he know? And don't get me started on formal job interviews. Totally worthless. It's like dating."

"I don't follow."

"We're all phonies when we date and when we interview for a job. Big waste of time. We should go back to arranged marriages and arranged job placements. In lieu of that, Jane needs to put Bingley in a headlock and tell him he needs to hire her, period."

"You know, Charlotte - you're one to talk. You practically carry the Surge Team on your back and they're all Underwriting Managers now and you - forgive me for saying this - continue to be just an Underwriter."

"I know! I know! But you're speaking of the Old Charlotte. The Old Charlotte was a pathetic patsy and pushover. In her place very recently now is the New Charlotte, who is quite dramatically different."

"Well! I shall look forward to hearing of the New Charlotte's further adventures!"

Up to this point, it has appeared that Mr. Darcy considered Elizabeth as someone beneath notice. Whether he considered her such because she was relatively young, because she was female, or because she was a non-officer in a non-critical work unit is hardly to the point. Surely there is no good reason for being oblivious to anyone's better qualities.

Personal opinions being as indisposed to change as they are, our expectation is that Mr. Darcy's disregard for Elizabeth would continue indefinitely. In the unlikely event that his opinion of her could change, the turning point might date from a certain Tuesday morning when Mr. Delroy of the Marketing Department was giving a presentation on a new initiative to prioritize the company's pipeline of prospective accounts. The meeting was attended by an august group that included Darcy and several department heads. Mr. Lucas, the Underwriting Head, being unavailable had asked Mr. Bennet to attend in his place, and Mr. Bennet being unavailable had asked Elizabeth.

There was a palpable awkwardness in the room after Mr. Delroy had explained the initiative and asked for questions. Elizabeth raised her hand to speak.

"This is slightly off topic," she said, "but I think there's something that needs to be said here. And let me just start out by saying that I know that off-color humor has a sad history in our business, and I would never want to bring back the bad old days. However, I think we've lost something if we can't find a way to have an innocently naughty laugh about the approach and terminology that has just been described to us. If I understand this correctly, we're going to rate our potential partners on a numeric scale - the classic one to ten, no less - and furthermore the key factors for our rating will be Attractiveness and Penetrability!"

At this point, the room did enjoy exactly the sort of laugh that it had been suppressing until that moment, and the remainder of the meeting proceeded with comfortable goodwill all around. Those present could hardly help observing that Elizabeth had been the one to step into a potentially embarrassing moment and show what - if not for her youth and lack of title - might have been considered leadership.

The following Monday included the Underwriting Department Quarterly Update Meeting – affectionately known as the Udqum. This gathering, which was held in Longbourn, generally provided a good summary of current issues of interest to that department. Accordingly, the meeting usually drew a smattering of guests from other portions of the company, and this particular Udqum drew both Mr. Bingley and Mr. Darcy.

The meeting was introduced by Mr. Lucas - a man who might have risen through the ranks of Underwriting by virtue of his powerful intellect, but more likely rose through the happy state of his being unusually sociable for an underwriter. Mr. Lucas provided a warm greeting for the department members and esteemed visitors. He went on to tell not one but two jokes which - while not particularly amusing to those gathered or strictly relevant to the topics at hand - were nonetheless well appreciated as a friendly effort. As if to make up for such an unserious beginning, he proceeded to read his way through an apparent almanac of company results that was composed almost entirely of numbers - this up two percent, that down seven and a half percent for the quarter but still up one percent year to date. The recitation continued for a sufficient period of time that an entire roomful of people who happily work with numbers every day had become confused and irritable. At that point he introduced the first speaker for the day, who was Charlotte.

"I'm sure we'll all find this very interesting!" said Mr. Lucas. "Charlotte from our Surge Team has been working on a project where we're analyzing the losses from a long-time client, State Line Insurance. This is one way we can add value to our clients. I believe, in this case, that our analysis found that they're having a problem with hospitals. So really, that's half the battle right there. And so - take it away, Charlotte!"

Charlotte made her way to the podium, shook the hand of Mr. Lucas and looked around. She paused longer than she had intended. She was wondering what she might say to prepare her audience for the fact that her conclusions were not at all what Mr. Lucas had just indicated. Would it be rude to contradict him?

While a man as affable and inexact as Mr. Lucas may not seem like an intimidating figure, it must be remembered that he was the boss of the man who was the boss of Ms. Cullis, who was Charlotte's boss. Many people are able to maintain at least the semblance of a calm and casual attitude around someone who is one or even two steps above them in an organizational ladder. However, when faced with someone three or more steps over our head, most of us are liable to succumb to a debilitating hierarchical vertigo. She decided to simply proceed with her presentation.

She explained the background for the project and described the data that had been provided and showed her initial analysis. The accompanying slide did, in fact, appear to indicate that hospital accounts represented the majority of the large losses in question.

"So, at this point," she said, "I was tempted to think this project was over. I had found the answer: State Line has a problem with hospitals. But before reporting back to the account team, I decided to give my conclusion one final test - a test I recommend to anyone. I showed the material to my friend and colleague, Elizabeth Austen of the Pride Team. She looked at my neat charts and obvious conclusion and then reminded me of one important issue. '*You know,*' she said to me, '*State Line has some systems issues. Before you return these results, you might want to look up the names and locations of the hospital accounts generating the biggest losses.*' Now, this wasn't the advice I most wanted to hear. I was getting tired of running reports against this data. But I felt obligated to try what she said, so here is a report showing the twenty hospital accounts with the largest losses."

The next slide was headed "HOSPITAL ACCOUNTS WITH LARGE LOSSES." The first listing was Tri-County Sewage Authority, with an address and a loss amount. The next was Lipscomb Metals.

"Do you notice anything?"

To everyone's surprise, it was Mr. Darcy who answered Charlotte's question. "None of them are hospitals," he said.

"I think there is actually one hospital in there if you look hard enough, but yes - this is not a list of hospitals."

Charlotte went on to explain that the account team reported back to

State Line about a possible data quality issue. Further research found that the class of business field in their claims system was not carried over from their underwriting system but instead was being entered manually for each claim and the code for hospitals was particularly easy to type.

Elizabeth listened to all this with some mixture of emotion. She appreciated Charlotte's generosity in crediting her with solving the mystery behind the data, but she also felt vaguely like a party crasher. This was Charlotte's project and she - not Elizabeth - deserved the credit for it. All Elizabeth had done was toss out a caution based on a lucky guess.

After the meeting, everyone stood and conversed for a few minutes as if they were all suddenly at a cocktail party. The rank and file appreciated the opportunity to hobnob with the senior officers present, and the senior officers appreciated the opportunity to demonstrate to one another that they could mingle comfortably with the rank and file. Mr. Lucas came over to Elizabeth, smiling like a proud paterfamilias, to congratulate her on being so clever, which he said reflected well on the department. Elizabeth had just stated her thanks when he - touching the side of her shoulder lightly to signal she was not to move - turned and beckoned across the room. "Darcy!" he called.

Mr. Darcy made his way over to Elizabeth and Mr. Lucas. "Yes?"

"Have you met Elizabeth? This is the woman our first speaker referred to. The clever one who told her to check the data."

"Yes, thank you," he said. "I believe we met my first day here."

Elizabeth smiled politely and said nothing.

"I have a good feeling about this young woman," said Lucas to Darcy. "I don't know if she's really clever or just lucky, but in my book one's as good as the other. She works on a lot of different projects. You should enlist her to work on a project for you."

Darcy nodded, looked at Elizabeth and looked back at Lucas. "I'd love to have her work on a project for me."

"That's very kind of both of you," said Elizabeth, "but as Mr. Lucas just said, I'm already working on a lot of projects. This wouldn't be a good time for me."

Darcy turned to face Elizabeth. "I see I was addressing myself to the wrong person. Let me say again that I'd love to have you work on a project for me."

"I'm so sorry," she said. "It just wouldn't be possible right now. Please excuse me." Elizabeth, feeling unusually awkward and off her game, nodded to them both and left the meeting room, worried that her visceral reaction to avoid Darcy may have hurt her standing in the eyes of Mr. Lucas.

After she had gone, Darcy nodded and smiled to Lucas. "You win some and you lose some," he said.

Darcy looked in later on Bingley, who was conferring with Ms. Liebling, his deputy in the Claims Department. Caroline Liebling was a longtime member of that department and, as such, was a source of necessary help for him and perhaps also some less necessary counsel regarding the feasibility of any conceivable change to the department's policies and procedures.

Ms. Liebling was not generally fond of change, but she was very pleased with her new boss. When, a few decades earlier, she had started with Juniper Re, it was smaller and more exclusive-seeming and located in the city. She saw Mr. Bingley and his friend, Mr. Darcy – both freshly arrived from the posh Cornwallis Re -- as people who could restore a measure of class and sophistication to her working life. From her excitement at this prospect, one can perhaps infer the degree of class and sophistication that characterized her life outside of work.

"What did you think of that meeting this morning?" asked Darcy.

"I made some notes," said Bingley. "I thought that Charlotte woman made a good presentation."

"Yes! And her friend that she mentioned - Elizabeth, from whatever the Pride Team is. I want to get her on a project."

Ms. Liebling rolled her eyes at this. "Pride Team. I say Be Careful!"

They both looked at her. "Why is that?" asked Darcy.

"I don't mind that they can be a little different and have trouble fitting in. What I mind is that they're spoiled. Entitled. No real-world experience, but they expect to be on the fast track."

"I don't know about any of that," said Darcy. "But I stand by what I said. I would like to get her on a project."

"So," said Ms. Liebling with a shrug. "are you going to hire her? Is she going to be your second-in-command? Your heir apparent?"

"I'll see about getting her on a project."

Ms. Liebling gave him a wide smile. "Maybe you could get a package deal for her with Ms. Nebbit!"

CHAPTER 7

Unfortunately for the Pride Team members, there was no career path within their own unit. Ms. Nebbit's role being ad hoc and unofficial, the only permanent position in the unit was Mr. Bennet's. It was understood that - whenever the time came for Mr. Bennet to retire - the program would be moved to another department, probably Human Resources. The program continued to operate out of Underwriting only in deference to Mr. Bennet's status within that department and trusted relationship with Mr. Lucas. The situation was, in a word, grandfathered - a term partially apt, given Mr. Bennet's age, although his adult children were in no apparent hurry to produce or adopt the next generation.

During this time, the attentions of some of the Pride Team members were distracted by the temporary relocation of the Regional Marketing Office, known as the RMO. Because their normal quarters in the city were being renovated, the RMO staff were posted to open space in the Home Office, specifically the former IT space near Meryton. This meant an influx of new faces, many of them young men - Marketers who were, perhaps unsurprisingly, better than the young men in many other departments at marketing themselves.

This was particularly distracting for Kitty and Lydia, who were apparently quite taken by the dress and grooming of the RMO men. Most men in the home office, having little direct interaction with customers, tended to dress for comfort rather than style. The RMO men, by contrast, were constantly interacting with customers and by long tradition wore well-tailored jackets, snappy ties and - this was particularly important to Lydia - really nice shoes. They walked around looking like they were ready to take someone out to an expensive dinner.

"I for one will shed no tears when the RMO heads back to town," said Mr. Bennet to Ms. Nebbit one morning. "I believe their presence is detracting from the team's focus."

"Of course!" agreed Ms. Nebbit. "Kitty and Lydia find any excuse to get to the third floor these days, but you can't entirely blame them. There is something about a man in a uniform."

"There is if you're an empty-headed young woman. I'm disappointed in them both."

Ms. Nebbit waved him off. "Oh, you're too harsh! You shouldn't be calling your girls empty-headed! I like to see a man in a business uniform myself. When Mr. Lucas appears before us all dressed up in his finery for a big meeting - it gives me a flutter. And I assume you wouldn't call me empty-headed!"

Mr. Bennet decided this was probably intended as a rhetorical question and chose not to reply.

Mr. Bennet and Ms. Nebbit both reported to Mr. Lucas – although Mr. Bennet enjoyed the more respectable position of being one branch of the tree growing down from him whereas Ms. Nebbit as Executive Assistant appeared on the organizational chart as a kind of stop-valve to the side of Mr. Bennet's trunk. In practice, they worked together so continuously that they were routinely referred to as one another's "work spouse". This term is sometimes misunderstood by those outside the organization to suggest a personal attachment of some kind, but the term actually refers to a relationship characterized by an ongoing stream of mundane communications that are typically found to dampen, rather than heighten, the ardor of actual spouses.

"Besides," added Ms. Nebbit, "the men here in Underwriting really don't make any effort at all. Their appearance is a sad sight. We might as well be in the IT Department."

Mr. Bennet hesitated. He was in possession of some inside information and knew that such information was Ms. Nebbit's favorite thing in the world - apparently with the exception of the sight of Mr. Lucas in a business suit. He was discreet by nature and cautious about sharing information with people lacking a clear need for it. At the same time, he had a grudging respect for Ms. Nebbit's ability to use information to the advantage of his team members. He leaned slightly towards her and lowered his voice.

"I think this will be an interesting day for our new Mr. Bingley," he said.

She was instantly at attention. "Oh?"

"Yes. RJT is talking to Lucas now and is going to Bingley next. There's a big fire drill involving The Benevolent. I think maybe a rating issue."

"How long before he gets to Bingley?"

Mr. Bennet shrugged. "I don't know. Half an hour."

Ms. Nebbit bolted from her desk without any further word to Mr. Bennet and was at Jane's desk in less than a minute. "Quick!" she said. "What could you hand-deliver to Mr. Bingley?"

Jane thought. "I've been working on an analysis of some personal lines excess claims data, but it isn't quite finished."

"Do you have a draft that you could print up right now?"

"Sure."

"Excellent!" exclaimed Ms. Nebbit. "Find it and print it and take it straight over to Bingley right now so that you can show it to him as a work in progress and get his input and suggestions. Can you do that?"

Jane spoke while finding the file on her computer. "I can do that. Can I ask why?"

"I have reason to believe that a storm is coming very soon and that Mr. Bingley is going to need some help to weather that storm and when that moment comes it would be advantageous for you to be located as conveniently to him as possible."

"Got it. The file is printing. I'm on my way."

Jane rose. Ms. Nebbit held up her finger.

"You might have to get past Caroline Liebling. Tell her it will just take a minute. He needs to know that you're there."

Jane nodded and hurried off - first to the printer to pick up her draft report and then to the Claims area, which was one floor down and on the opposite end of the building. As she power-walked down the halls, she made some token attempts to improve her appearance - smoothing her hair and straightening her blouse. She wondered what she would find and if she were about to make a laughing stock of herself.

When she arrived in the back corner of the Claims area, she was relieved to find that Ms. Liebling was not at her desk and Mr.

Bingley's door was open. He was sitting quietly, doing something on his computer. Jane kept her feet outside his office but leaned her head in.

"Excuse me, Mr. Bingley? I was hoping I could get just a minute of your time?"

"Jane!" he called out, rising to his feet and waving her in. "Come on in! You're just in time to save me from budget re-forecasts. I don't get it. What's the point of having a budget if you're just going to re-forecast it every quarter?"

"I don't know," she said. "Good question."

He indicated a round table flanked by two chairs and they sat. She set her few sheets of paper on the table, oriented towards him. She took a breath.

"I've been working on a study on a certain kind of claim. This started as an Underwriting project but I think it might have relevance for Claims."

He picked up the papers and started scanning them. "Great! What have you got?"

"It has to do with -"

At this point, they heard Ms. Liebling's voice calling from some distance. "Mr. Bingley? Mr. Bingley?" She was getting closer fast and when she burst into the room they were surprised to see Darcy at her side. "Here he is!" she announced to him, before giving a glance of some annoyance at Jane.

Darcy addressed himself to Bingley. "Special drop-everything request from RJT. He was going to tell you himself but has some related issues to work out with Lucas. Big crisis at The Benevolent. They have a meeting with the rating agencies on Friday and they know they're at risk for a downgrade. Underwriting is trying to work out a new treaty that might help some of their ratios. Meanwhile, he wants you to see if there's anything Claims can do to help. They're one of our oldest client companies and we want to make sure we do everything we appropriately can to help them avoid a downgrade."

Bingley had set down Jane's report and was on his feet. "All right! Let's get on this thing. Let's think about this."

Jane turned to the blank back page of her report, took a pen from a jar on the table and started to write.

"Did he have any specific suggestions?" asked Bingley.

"No," said Darcy. "I'm not sure he knows himself. He just wants to make sure we do everything we possibly can."

There was a pause. Ms. Liebling looked at Jane and whispered, "Maybe you can come back another time."

Bingley looked at Jane. "What are you writing?"

Jane looked at her notes. "Step One. Determine which ratios are the problem and what would help make those ratios better. RJT would presumably be the best source for what's going on at The Benevolent, but if he isn't available I'd try Fred Mudge in Finance, who's our rating agency guru. I'd try to get him in a meeting with a really good accountant, maybe Featherstone. Step Two depends on what you find in Step One. Let's assume it's a cash crunch. In that case, Two A would be to review every claim we've agreed to pay to them for the past month and make sure the money has cleared. Two B is to review every open claim with them to see if there's anything we can close and pay before Friday." She looked up from her paper. "That's as far as I got."

Bingley looked around. "Caroline. Clear the calendar for Netherfield 1. See if Mudge and Featherstone can meet us there in ten minutes."

"Yes, sir."

"And maybe Legal, too. Who do you think?" He looked at Jane and Darcy.

"Might as well start with O'Brien, if she's available," said Darcy.

"Good," said Bingley, turning back to Ms. Liebling. "And ask Sheila Brady to run two reports on The Benevolent. One showing all paid claims over the past thirty days. The other showing all currently open claims. Have her bring them to us as soon as she can."

"Yes, sir."

"Jane," said Bingley, "can you clear your calendar for the day?"

Elizabeth had heard the story of how Jane had been sent speeding towards Mr. Bingley in the hope of being on the spot at a time of need. As the morning passed and then the afternoon wore on and still she hadn't seen Jane or heard from her, Elizabeth was anxious for her friend. Had Ms. Nebbit's plan worked? What if it had backfired? What if Jane had interrupted an important meeting on some tissue-thin excuse of an errand and been fired on the spot? This would be a scenario that had never actually taken place at Juniper Re in her experience, but it was one that she had imagined many times - generally with herself in the role of the suddenly unemployed miscreant.

Jane was still absent the next morning during Mr. Bennet's meeting with the Pride Team, at which Ms. Nebbit recounted her quick action that she was sure had cemented Jane's position within the Claims department. In the absence of any word from Jane herself, Mr. Bennet was more circumspect.

"Maybe, Ms. Nebbit." he said. "Or maybe the bold action you urged her towards had a disastrous result. For all we know at this point, she could have been terminated."

"Oh, pooh!" exclaimed Ms. Nebbit with a puff of her cheeks and a wave of her hand. "People don't get terminated for hurrying down hallways and asking people to look at a piece of paper!"

Elizabeth received a text and, suspecting it might be from Jane, broke team meeting protocol by looking at it:

Will be in Claims again today. Could use some help. Ms. L. can show you where I am. Best, J.

She read the text to the group, whereupon Ms. Nebbit declared herself vindicated and Mr. Bennet agreed to cut the meeting short so that Elizabeth could proceed directly to her.

After taking a moment to pack a few items for her trip into a tote bag, first from her own desk and then from Jane's desk, Elizabeth put the bag over her shoulder and started down the hall. "Lydia and I will walk with you as far as the elevator," announced Kitty to her. And so the three of them walked together for a few minutes. At the elevator, they all wished one another a good day, and then Elizabeth headed down towards Claims and Lydia and Kitty ascended to pursue some other doubtlessly worthwhile errand in the direction of the temporary RMO quarters.

If Ms. Liebling was pleased to see Elizabeth, she managed not to betray the fact by her expression or tone of voice. "Yes?" she asked.

"Excuse me," said Elizabeth. "I'm looking for Jane. She said you could show me where she is."

"Oh, she did? How interesting that she's able to volunteer my time as well as her own." She stood and began walking. It took a moment for Elizabeth to realize that she should follow and had to hurry to catch up. At the end of a row of modest offices was a sort of half-office, with a solid wall on two sides and a cubicle divider on two sides. The space where an employee's name could be mounted was empty. Ms. Liebling stopped and indicated the way in. Elizabeth thanked her and stepped into a workspace filled with reams of paper and found her friend leaning close to a computer monitor.

"Jane!"

"Lizzy!"

Jane rose and they hugged warmly. "Look at you!" said Elizabeth, indicating the space and the papers.

"Don't look at me, please!" said Jane. "I'm in the midst of a crazy fire drill, and crazy fire drills are not conducive to glamour!" She did, in fact, look tired and her general appearance was not up to her usual standards.

"I've brought you a Care Package!" Elizabeth set her tote bag on the desk, reached in and pulled out a bean bag frog wearing a cape. Jane took it from her with excitement.

"Mr. Super Frog! Life can continue!"

Jane positioned Mr. Super Frog at his usual post at the upper left-hand corner of the keyboard she was using and watched happily as Elizabeth pulled from her bag a pair of shoes.

"I wasn't sure if you'd need these, but just in case here's a pair of flats from your shoe drawer." Jane received them happily.

"Much appreciated!"

Elizabeth then drew out a thermos of coffee, two napkins, two satsuma oranges and her own laptop, which she opened up on the desk while asking what she could do to help. Soon they were both immersed in a massive but companionably mindless task.

In free moments over the course of the day, they managed a very slow but agreeable conversation. Jane related the events of the previous morning. Elizabeth was quite struck by Jane's presence of mind in making her list at the critical moment. Jane thought this over for some minutes before replying that she attributed this to their good training. "Really," she said, "it felt exactly like a Round Robin question."

Jane related that she had gone to the conference room with Bingley and Darcy and participated in the meeting with the ratings expert, the accountant and the company's General Counsel. As soon as it was determined that the steps Jane had suggested were appropriate and potentially helpful, she volunteered to take on those tasks herself. Her offer was immediately accepted and Ms. Liebling was directed to find Jane an open office and bring her the reports that had been requested.

At this point, Elizabeth had some misgivings about her friend's ability to look after her own interests. As nearly as she could tell, Jane's eagerness to be helpful had cost her a seat at the table. Bingley and Darcy were in Netherfield 1 the rest of the day, presumably strategizing with a rotating series of company officials, while Jane was by herself in an unused half office poring over reports and looking up transactions on a pathetically dated computer system.

"What's driving you on this?" asked Elizabeth at one point. "Is this about Bingley?"

Jane replied without looking up from her work. "This is about me. This is my sickness. I have a need to be helpful - helpful to anyone but especially to customers. If there's something practical I can do to help a customer, that's energizing for me. So much of what we all do seems unconnected to helping customers that I'm grateful for an exercise like this."

"You are good," said Elizabeth. "We don't deserve you. Your sickness is not always to your own benefit, but it's quite inspiring."

"And what about you?" asked Jane. "You've been here all day working as hard or harder than I have. What drives you?"

"Oh, that's easy. It was Mr. Super Frog. He wouldn't give me a moment's peace until I'd brought him over to you!"

By mid-afternoon, they'd made considerable progress on the remaining pile of reports - but were by no means near the end - when Ms. Liebling looked in on Jane and was surprised to see Elizabeth still there, working across the desk from her. Ms. Liebling stopped, stared at the space between them, and made the following announcement:

"For those who might be working later than usual on this project, Mr. Bingley will be hosting a light supper in Netherfield 1 and 2 starting at five."

CHAPTER 8

When five o'clock arrived, Elizabeth looked at Jane, and Jane leaned back in her chair and looked at the ceiling. "You go to the dinner," she said. "I'm not stopping now. You can bring me back something before you go home."

Elizabeth rose and stretched. "I see your sickness isn't getting any better. Well, I for one need a little sustenance from time to time. I'll see what I can smuggle back to you."

As she walked into Netherfield, Elizabeth found Mr. Bingley, Mr. Darcy and Ms. Liebling. She also found two Claims friends of Ms. Liebling: Mr. Hurst and Ms. Thrush. Chairs lined the walls and a table in the corner was covered in containers of Chinese or Thai take-out food.

"Welcome!" said Mr. Bingley. "Where's Jane?"

"Jane sends her regrets," said Elizabeth with a nod. "She has a bad case of obsessive customer focus and is unable to leave her room."

This evoked a chorus of sympathetic noises from the group.

"It's a very uncomfortable and inconvenient condition," announced Ms. Thrush. "I believe we're especially susceptible to it here in Claims."

"I had to spend a week once in New Orleans auditing Hurricane Katrina losses," added Mr. Hurst, working carefully at his plate of noodles. "We'd be at it every day all day until the restaurants opened."

"Oh," said Elizabeth. She wanted to ask him when the restaurants in New Orleans open. She suspected that she might have a different sense than Mr. Hurst of just what constitutes obsessive customer focus. She was afraid, however, that the question might appear judgmental, so she made no further comment.

Elizabeth spooned some food onto a plate, sat and ate. She felt as if she were intruding on an otherwise-comfortable clique and wasn't inclined to linger. After a few minutes, she cleared her place, spooned some food onto a fresh plate, thanked Mr. Bingley for his generosity in hosting the dinner, and left to carry the food back to Jane.

After Elizabeth left, Ms. Liebling glanced down the hall to make sure she was safely gone and then turned to the group and said, "What's up with her?"

"Maybe it's not her fault," said Ms. Thrush. "Maybe she was raised in a barn. I believe it's difficult to learn to make interesting conversation when your principal role models are livestock."

Ms. Liebling looked around. "I mean, what's she even doing here? Jane, I can understand. Mr. Bingley specifically invited her to help with this project. But that woman," with a wave toward the departed Elizabeth. "She just elected herself to come stick her nose in this project. Probably thinks she's doing us all a huge favor."

"She's here, working hard as near as I can tell, out of loyalty to her friend," said Mr. Bingley calmly. "I see nothing wrong with that."

"Still," said Ms. Thrush. "It is pretty weird."

Ms. Liebling turned and addressed herself to Mr. Darcy. "I imagine that you must be rethinking your stated intention of wanting her to work on a project for you."

"Not at all." said Mr. Darcy. "My sense of her capabilities isn't swayed by whether or not the people in this room find her an engaging conversationalist."

Ms. Liebling gave him a wide smile. "You're very kind, Mr. Darcy, and I'm sure we all appreciate that about you. But you don't know the Pride Team like we do. They think they're God's gift to reinsurance. I exempt Jane from that statement. Somehow – miraculously! – Jane seems very sweet and unaffected. I have no ill-feeling towards Jane. I only pity her."

"You pity her?" said Mr. Bingley. "Why is that?"

"I pity her because she's doomed to be underemployed. Who's going to hire her for any job worth having? She has no connections, no history in the business, no credentials. She has a time-limited spot with that poor step-child of the Underwriting Department, the Pride

Team. And that association – which gets her in the door and raises her hopes – probably in the long run hurts her prospects more than it helps them." She waited a moment and heard no contradiction. "The other one – Elizabeth – I think deserves to be in that situation, but Jane as I said is very sweet and so I pity her."

Elizabeth, meanwhile, delivered the dinner to Jane, urged her to go home before it became too late, and then attempted to set a good example by heading home herself. As she was leaving, Jane asked her to thank Mr. Bingley for the food. So Elizabeth circled back to Netherfield, where she found the group playing a game involving coins held in their fists.

"Sorry to interrupt," she said to Mr. Bingley. "Jane asked me to thank you for the food."

"How is she doing?"

"Still feverish as ever, I'm afraid."

"It's the Claims sickness, I think," offered Mr. Hurst, who continued to hold out his fist. "It's in the water here. I mean, here we all are, aren't we?"

"Yes," said Elizabeth. "Very impressive and inspiring."

"Will you join us?" asked Ms. Liebling with a smile. "We're Hully-Gullying for the cost of the dinner."

She had seen Hully-Gully played before and had a general sense of the rules. Players put zero, one or two coins in one hand and then took turns predicting the total number of coins in everyone's hands. The winner of each round was eliminated until the final person left was the loser of the game.

"Not as high stakes as it might sound," added Ms. Thrush. "Loser puts the cost on their expense account. Whatever the result, the company pays."

Elizabeth looked at Mr. Bingley. "And this passes muster with the company's expense guidelines?"

The rules she was referring to stipulate that any shared expense, such as a business meal, should always be paid by the highest-ranking participant. The purpose of this rule was to avoid the situation where a boss and subordinate might, for example, enjoy an inappropriately lavish meal together and then have the subordinate submit the expense and the boss approve it. Having a separate boss approve the expense may not guarantee that all expenses are reasonable and appropriate – a boss might, for example, have an interest in maintaining a culture of lavish business meals – but does at a minimum provide the appearance of accountability.

Mr. Bingley smiled. "You're as quick as Jane, aren't you? It passes muster because I'll actually put the cost on my expense account if the loser is anyone in Claims. So the only real risk here is to Mr. Darcy. If Darcy loses, I'll happily let his budget cover our dinner. If you were to play - which I don't recommend - then I suppose your budget might be at risk as well."

Elizabeth nodded. "Thank you. I think I'll just watch, if I may."

In the event, the final loser was Ms. Thrush, so the bill stayed with Mr. Bingley.

After the game was concluded, Mr. Darcy turned to Elizabeth. "So, what do you think? Was this a harmless bit of fun or a lapse towards something improper?"

Elizabeth hesitated.

"Please speak freely," he said. "I ask not to put you on the spot. I'm not sure what I think myself."

"I think," said Elizabeth, "that it can be good for co-workers to play games together. You do see different sides of people and possibly come to appreciate their skills in a new way. At the same time, I'm not fond of a game such as this that's designed to crown a loser. I prefer games that enable us to celebrate a winner."

"And what about me? Was it right for me to play the game?"

"Oh yes. It was quite right. You were almost offering to pay for the dinner. It would have been even more appropriate for you to be the loser of the game. That would have been most polite of you."

"Yes," agreed Mr. Darcy. "It was probably rude of me not to lose the game. I have an aversion to fraud of any kind. In my former position, they wouldn't let me play golf with certain clients because when I play a game, I play to win."

He said this with an earnestness that gave Elizabeth some pause. She scanned the room. Quiet conversations were proceeding around them.

"There's something more, isn't there?" he asked her. "Something else about the game?"

"Well, yes. Now that you mention it. I don't like the feeling of it. The original purpose of the game was deciding who would pay the bill. That purpose has all but gone away, but we play the game anyway. I worry that people might start to feel the same way about this company and our business. When we're comfortably profitable and our clients are comfortably profitable - seeing who wins or loses on a treaty in a given year can feel like a meaningless Hully-Gully game. Who cares who wins or loses? Everything's paid for anyway."

Mr. Darcy considered this for a moment. "And what do you tell yourself to remember that what we do is not a meaningless game?"

"It's corny."

"I'm O.K. with corny."

"I have a speech in my head that Mr. Bennet gave us very early on. He said we are the promise behind the promise. The insurance industry is a really huge institution that every person and every business and organization depends on to protect them from all the worst things that can happen. People have lost faith in so many institutions. If they lose faith in the insurance industry, then we might as well all start living under our beds. But people do still trust their insurance to be able to protect them when they need it most. Why do they trust it? They don't know why, but we know why. It's because of us. We keep the industry strong. We are the promise behind the promise."

"Thank you for that. I salute Mr. Bennet and I thank you passing on his good words."

Shortly after this, Elizabeth thanked Mr. Bingley once more and then took her leave. After she had left, Ms. Liebling leaned towards Mr. Darcy and gave him a meaningful eye roll. "Oh, the self-righteous idealism of youth!"

"Yes," he replied. "It may be our only hope."

CHAPTER 9

The next morning featured an Employee Meeting, for which all employees on the premises gathered in the cafeteria, while employees at field offices and those who worked from home tuned in with their computers to watch and listen. The meetings were held on a quarterly basis and rarely featured any dramatic or even interesting news but were always very well attended. Perhaps this was because of the remote possibility that some blockbuster announcement might be made, or perhaps it was simply interesting for the company's employees to see themselves gathered in a body and behold their otherwise abstract community.

Prior to the meeting, Elizabeth made her way to Jane's temporary half-office, where she found her friend still working. She suspected that Jane had not gone home the previous night. Her appearance had slipped from noticeably sub-par to alarmingly sub-par. Her outfit seemed to be a rearranged version of her outfit from the day before. Still, she seemed in good spirits.

"Still at it?" said Elizabeth. "You are sick, sick, sick!"

"But about to be better!" announced Jane with a smile. "The finish line is in sight. Whatever isn't done by noon doesn't matter anymore."

"Are you coming to the Employee Meeting?"

"I think not. I believe I'll finish up here and then nip home."

"Good plan. I'll let you know if anything interesting is announced."

There was still plenty of time before the meeting when Elizabeth went down to the cafeteria, where she saw Ms. Nebbit and Lydia. They sat together in the second row of chairs. The first row of chairs was traditionally reserved for the most senior officers, but there was no hierarchy of seating beyond that. As it happened, Mr. Bingley and Mr. Darcy entered and sat in the first row, immediately in front of them.

"A good day to you all," said Mr. Bingley with a smile to the three of them, before he sat with Mr. Darcy.

"And a good day to you," replied Ms. Nebbit, "although I don't know how good it will be for our poor Jane!"

At this, Mr. Bingley turned in his chair to face Ms. Nebbit. "And what is the latest with Jane?"

"Elizabeth here has just been to see her, and she's been working feverishly all night. We only hope that this ordeal will finally break today." At this, Ms. Nebbit fanned herself with her notepad and rolled her eyes upwards, apparently beseeching the heavens to have mercy on her poor Jane.

Mr. Bingley touched Ms. Nebbit lightly on the shoulder. "Please give her my thanks and best wishes if you see her before I do. We've all been very impressed and inspired by her example."

Leave it at that, thought Elizabeth in the direction of Ms. Nebbit.

"I should think so!" declared Ms. Nebbit. "I should think every last one of you in Claims should be kissing the soles of that girl's feet at this point! I don't know when I've seen such dedication! Oh, if only there was a way you could get her into your department as a real, full-time member! Can you just imagine!"

"Thank you, Ms. Nebbit." And Mr. Bingley turned to face forward.

"And are you going to be staying with us awhile?" she said to his back. "Or will you be flitting off to some other reinsurer?"

Mr. Bingley turned back to her. "I hope to be staying quite a long while - but I'll admit that it was a bit impetuous for me to leave my former position and come here, so I can't guarantee something like that won't happen again."

"We're his rumspringa," said Elizabeth. "His seven-year itch." She leaned towards Mr. Bingley. "How long were you at Cornwallis Re?"

"Eight years."

She held up her hands in a shrug of victory. "Seven-year itch plus one to grow on! I think we can assume that he's safely settled here for at least the next six."

"Oh, he'll want to stay longer than that," said Ms. Nebbit. "Isn't that right, Mr. Bingley? You must be quite happy to be out of the city. Out here with a few trees around and without all the dirt and crime and squalor."

"I'm very happy to be here," he replied, "but it would be unfair to my former employer to suggest that they subjected me to any of those things. I believe Darcy here will back me up on this."

Mr. Darcy half-turned in his chair. "Cornwallis Re may have its faults, but those faults don't include dirt, crime or squalor. In fact, I believe that place may be the polar opposite of squalor."

Elizabeth found herself attempting once again to restrain Ms. Nebbit through telekinesis.

"They may have nice offices. I'm sure they do," said Ms. Nebbit. "But still - it's in the city! Nobody I know ever goes to the city anymore. Why would you, now that we have such nice restaurants and things out here where it's so much more convenient?"

Mr. Darcy appeared to consider several possible answers to this comment. After a few moments, however, he simply sighed and turned to face forward. Ms. Nebbit turned to Elizabeth and Lydia. "He doesn't have an answer for that, does he?"

Mr. Bingley looked back at Ms. Nebbit. "These things, of course, are a matter of taste. I believe, however, that many people feel that the restaurants and the cultural opportunities in the city are more varied and interesting than what you find in the suburbs - even as nice a suburb as we are in right now."

"Yes," said Elizabeth, "and I'm sure Ms. Nebbit didn't mean to suggest that we have anything like the variety of restaurants and - and things - that are in the city. She was speaking to her own preference for the convenience of what is near at hand."

"My own preference and everyone I know!" said Ms. Nebbit.

"Oh, look - there's Charlotte!" said Elizabeth, pointing across the room. "Didn't she give a fine presentation at the Udqum?"

Elizabeth was embarrassed by Ms. Nebbit's prejudice against the city, which she considered narrow-minded provincialism, and was eager to shift her attention. It was perhaps a crude strategy to point and call out the name of a colleague, but a lack of subtlety can sometimes be surprisingly effective.

"Yes!" agreed Ms. Nebbit. "Charlotte is a dear girl and has a good head on her shoulders. I love her to pieces. Of course, she's nothing compared to Jane. But still - a dear, dear girl!" She smiled in Charlotte's direction. "Doesn't have anything like Jane's work ethic. Jane can out-work a horse! Don't take my word for it. Ask anyone! I'll tell you who you can ask - you can ask Willcox from Financial. He had some big project the week after Jane started here and she got it done for him so fast and in such detail that he told me he couldn't believe it. Could Not Believe It. I thought he was going to offer her a job in Financial - right there on the spot, her first week with the company. I'm not sure why he didn't. Maybe because she was so new. In any event, he did invite Jane to the Financial Department Holiday Lunch."

"And so her career in Financial ended before it began," said Elizabeth. "Nothing is so fatal to a potential recruitment as a Holiday Lunch."

At this, Mr. Darcy looked back. "Is that right? I should have thought that a Holiday Lunch might be a good introduction to a new department."

"Oh, yes," Elizabeth replied. "A good introduction if you're actually on board - but a fatally awkward setting if you're not a part of the team."

This statement hung in the air for a moment, until Lydia spoke up. Lydia was the most forward and unfiltered of the Pride Team members and had just looked up from her phone. "I have a question for Mr. Bingley, if I may."

Mr. Bingley turned to her. "Fire away!"

"Did you know that the Claims Department is in line to host the next Idea Fair?"

"Yes," he said. "I did know that."

She smiled and nodded. "And have you set a date for it yet?"

"No, but I thank you for the reminder. Now that this very busy week is ending, hopefully your colleague Jane will be returning to normal and I can catch up on some neglected pieces of business, such as the next Idea Fair."

"Don't wait too long," said Lydia, as if instructing a child. "I'm thinking that we should try to fit an extra one in this year and have the RMO host, since they're in the building. Maybe you or Mr.

Darcy could talk to Mr. Armstrong about that. If you schedule yours before the end of the month, we could have Idea Fairs from both the RMO and Underwriting next month."

"Well," said Mr. Bingley, "we'll see what we can do."

At this point, they were all interrupted by the onset of the Employee Meeting, which contained no news of any large import. Ms. Nebbit and Lydia were each able to settle into the meeting with satisfaction at having scored a point for a cause of interest to themselves. Elizabeth had no such satisfaction, but was happy to set aside worrying about what her colleagues would say to the officers seated before them. As to Mr. Bingley and Mr. Darcy, we can assume that their necks were happy to be at liberty to aim their heads straight forward.

CHAPTER 10

It was with some misgivings that Elizabeth ventured back to Netherfield the next day at lunchtime. The invitation - while emailed to a distribution list - had been cordial and emphatic. Those on the distribution had been of service to the Claims Department during the special labors of the week and were therefore urged to gather at noon and claim their well-deserved Free Pizza. The list included Jane and herself, but Jane - presumably still recovering from her extended bout of workaholism - had taken the day off.

Should Elizabeth go and avail herself of the Free Pizza? Having just recounted the story the day before, she was quite conscious of the possible analogy to Jane's awkward holiday lunch with the Financial Department. Still, it might seem cold and unsociable to snub the invitation. And, of course, there was on offer Free Pizza. In the end, fear of further alienating a department where she saw no future for herself could not compete with the steaming, aromatic prospect of hot and well-oiled mozzarella cheese.

"I've come to claim my loot!" she announced to Mr. Bingley, gamely holding up the small, round paper plate holding a slice of cheese pizza and a plastic cup of diet soda that she'd picked up on her way in.

Mr. Bingley was seated amid the usual group of the week. "Welcome, Elizabeth!" he said. "I'm glad you made it. Where's Jane?"

"Not with us today, I'm afraid."

"Come have a seat. We've just discovered that Mr. Darcy here knows Ms. Liebling's cousin."

"Knows her?" said Ms. Liebling. "Why, until just a few weeks ago she worked for him!"

Mr. Darcy smiled but seemed less than eager to continue this line of discussion. He gave a nod to Ms. Liebling.

"If you see Georgiana, please give her my best regards."

"I certainly will. I just love Georgiana! How could anyone not love Georgiana? I mean, really! She's so smart and clever and gorgeous! Did you know she's a whiz on the piano? Well, you probably know everything about her. You must miss her terribly!" Ms. Liebling seemed to be energized by this connection to Mr. Darcy's former life. She paused and let out a sigh. "Left behind. Oh, the sacrifices we make to advance our careers! Any particular message for her?"

"My best regards will be fine, thank you."

"Best regards! Of course. You always know just exactly what to say." Ms. Liebling looked around the room. "Mr. Darcy writes the most amazing emails. They should be printed up and published in a book!"

Mr. Bingley lifted his finger at this. "Don't encourage him! Darcy's emails are amazing in their length and ponderousness. Who does he think has time to read these things? You think you're going to get a quick update on our combined ratio and the next thing you know you're in the middle of a Russian novel. If we had Mr. Darcy's emails bound and published it would decimate our forests."

"My style of writing is very different from yours."

"Oh!" cried Ms. Liebling. "Mr. Bingley has little patience for anything longer than a tweet, and he prefers abbreviations or initials to actual words."

"True enough. I write in the moment, without any fuss or style. As a result, my communications can look like eye charts and probably convey about as much useful information."

Mr. Darcy was about to respond when Elizabeth spoke up. "Surely, Mr. Darcy, there can be no piling on at this point. Mr. Bingley has just humbly admitted his shortcoming in this area."

"He's done nothing of the sort. He's delivered an object lesson in the humblebrag, the indirect boast. He clearly continues to believe that his electronic grunting – while it may mean nothing to anyone else – is somehow superior to more traditional writing because it's shorter and uncompromised by any trace of human thought. He was also humblebragging yesterday when he told you, Elizabeth, that his decision to come to Juniper Re was sudden and impetuous and therefore his exit might be equally unpremeditated."

"This is too much!" cried Bingley. "I'm sure I said many foolish things yesterday, but I don't see how that qualifies for the list. It was a simple statement of fact. My decision to come to Juniper was, in fact, sudden and impetuous. When I get a notion in my head, I follow through and do it – unlike some others, who think things through over and over again. I sometimes wonder, Darcy, how long it takes you to brush your teeth at night."

"So he says, but is he really so quickly decisive? It's my observation that when he gets a notion he can be prevented from following through on it by a simple request from any of his friends. And this is complicated by the fact that he considers pretty much everyone on the planet to be his friend."

"But surely now," said Elizabeth, "you are bragging on Mr. Bingley's part. For it must be a good thing to have many friends and to be accommodating to them."

"You are kind," said Bingley, "to interpret his words so positively. I believe we can safely assume that they weren't intended as a compliment. He thinks it's a sign of weakness if you change your mind about anything just because a friend asks you to. Which may explain why he has as many friends as he does."

To this point, Elizabeth had been enjoying the dialogue as a kind of genteel insult contest between two friends. Now, however, she became interested to understand Mr. Darcy's position.

"Is that right?" she asked, turning to Mr. Darcy. "Once we decide something we shouldn't let our minds be changed by our friends?"

"It depends," he said, "on what we're talking about. If you decide you're going to have peach cobbler for dessert and I'm your friend and I say, *'No, you should try the cherry cobbler. It's very good!'* - then by all means go ahead and change your mind. On the other hand, let's say you decide to deny a claim on a property catastrophe treaty because the insurer is claiming that hundreds of otherwise unrelated losses should be considered one single catastrophe due to the fact that the accounts were all written by the same underwriter who happened at the time to have an untreated mental disorder and you don't consider that scenario to be a valid application of the intended scope of 'one occurrence' under that treaty. Now I'm your friend and maybe I work for the company making the claim, or maybe I'm a broker or some other interested party, and I say '*Oh, please, Elizabeth. as a personal favor to your old pal, interpret that treaty the way I want you to.*' Then I say - don't let your mind be changed by your friend."

She looked back at Mr. Bingley. "It's a made-up example," he said. "If I'd actually done something like that Darcy here would have killed me."

Darcy continued. "It's my considered opinion that being a professional reinsurer is like being a baseball umpire. Requirement Number One is not letting your judgment be moved by any outside influence. Period. Otherwise, the whole thing collapses like a house of cards."

Mr. Bingley held out his hands as if he were bragging about the size of fish he'd caught. "There's a lot of middle ground between a dessert flavor over here and criminal malfeasance way over here. Darcy protects himself from making the mistake way over here by drawing the line right next to this side. He says he'd change his dessert order at the request of a friend - I've never seen him do such a thing, but he's an honorable man so I'll grant the point - but I doubt that he'd be so accommodating if a friend urged him to change his main course. I agree that it's sometimes right and noble to remain fixed in the face of friends begging you to change your mind, but sometimes it's just stubbornness."

At this, Ms. Liebling stood. "Surely there's something more entertaining we can devise than berating Mr. Darcy for his constancy. I, for one, am pleased that he joined us for this lunch and was very happy to hear about his connection to my dear Georgiana."

"I take your point," said Mr. Bingley, rising. "and declare myself the loser of this debate. Let peace reign across the land. Please be sure to exchange a friendly word with those around you."

The room relaxed and various conversations started up. Elizabeth smiled at Mr. Hurst and Ms. Thrush, then noticed Mr. Darcy staring at her from across the room. She couldn't make out the reason for his fixed attention. Was something wrong? Had she lost a tooth or an earring? As she was not at pains to impress Mr. Darcy, she turned her attention back to her pizza and had just taken a large bite when Mr. Darcy moved across the room and sat in the chair next to her.

"I was wondering," he said, "if it might be possible to pose a question to you as if this were an Idea Fair and we were paired together in the Round Robin."

She smiled, but made no answer. He repeated the question, with some surprise at her silence.

"Oh!" said she, "I heard you before, but I couldn't immediately answer. My mouth was full, but also I didn't know what to say. You wanted me, I know, to say *Yes*, but why? If you had any interest in my thoughts about things, you could have asked me any question you liked at a real Round Robin your first day here. So I assume that you're teasing or making sport of me somehow, and my answer is '*No Thank You, Sir*'."

"I understand."

He sat meekly in his new seat while Elizabeth wondered why he didn't dispute with her as he had with Bingley. In fact, Darcy was experiencing a phenomenon not uncommon in either a business setting or in personal life. Having initially been oblivious to Elizabeth's capabilities, he was determined not to underestimate her again, and so was inclined to believe her infinitely capable.

Ms. Liebling had become increasingly conscious of Darcy's newfound admiration for Elizabeth and saw her as a rival. It was unclear - possibly to Ms. Liebling herself - whether she saw Elizabeth as a rival for his approbation and career help or for his affection. Her strategy was to treat the alarming possibility that he might elevate Elizabeth to a position of importance on his staff as a whimsical notion regarding which she could tease him.

She returned to this theme as they strolled outdoors. He had excused himself from the end of the lunch party saying he needed to pick up some legal documents from Building Three before an afternoon meeting and Ms. Liebling - who explained that she had heard about but not yet seen for herself the new carpeting in Building Three - had very generously volunteered to accompany him.

"Just imagine the scene," she said to him. "You hire Elizabeth Austen to be your chief of staff. You'll need to give her an officer title, of course. And not some dime-a-dozen Assistant Vice President. At least a Second Vice President and maybe a full Vice President. You can't leave her too far to go when you become president and she becomes your Special Assistant. Then, of course, there's the matter of Ms. Nebbit. She's a package deal with

Elizabeth, so you'll have to find a good role for her as well. Maybe Political Liaison. She's so discreet. And you'll want to round out your staff with one or two of those younger Pride Team members everybody's so crazy about. Maybe you could arrange some kind of ambassador role to the Regional Marketing Office. I believe they're very well received there. That could be a different sort of liaison role."

"I have no idea what you're about. Trying, I imagine, to dissuade me from having anything to do with Ms. Austen. If that's the case, you're wasting your time. I remain determined to make as full use of her as possible."

At that moment, they were met at an intersection of walkways by Ms. Thrush and Elizabeth herself.

"I didn't know you intended to walk," said Ms. Liebling, in some confusion, lest they had been overheard.

"Fancy this!" exclaimed Ms. Thrush. "I was just keeping Elizabeth company, since she normally walks after lunch with her friend, Jane. Where are you headed?"

"Building Three," said Ms. Liebling, pointing.

"Lead on."

They had proceeded a few steps with Ms. Thrush and Ms. Liebling flanking Mr. Darcy, when he realized they were just three and stopped. He called back to Elizabeth. "Will you join us?"

"No, thank you. You are charmingly grouped just as you are. Good-bye."

And Elizabeth doubled back, cheerful as a schoolchild released from a long morning of classes.

CHAPTER 11

As Elizabeth was returning to her desk, she saw that Jane was back - back in the building and back at her old spot, typing on her computer under the watchful eye of Mr. Super Frog and looking much better than the last time Elizabeth had seen her. They had a hug and Elizabeth urged Jane to return with her to Netherfield to make a belated appearance at the pizza lunch intended to reward hard workers such as herself.

Jane perhaps lacked the energy or perhaps lacked the inclination to stand against such urging, and so the two of them walked together to the Claims area and into Mr. Bingley's office, where they found Ms. Liebling and Ms. Thrush cleaning up and returning the room to a more businesslike appearance.

To Elizabeth's surprise, the two women seemed delighted to see Jane. They directed her to a seat of honor and brought her food and drink and asked after her health. They teased her about her improved grooming and asked after Mr. Super Frog. Ms. Liebling made a point of texting Bingley, Darcy, and Hurst to let them know of Jane's late and unexpected appearance.

When the men arrived, Ms. Liebling stepped back to wave her arm in Jane's direction. "Here she is!"

Mr. Darcy wished Jane well. Mr. Hurst following him nodded as if to second whatever Darcy had said. Mr. Bingley then took the seat next to Jane. After receiving assurances from her regarding her health and good spirits, he declared that her sudden appearance was as pleasing to him as an unexpected subrogation recovery.

This may warrant an explanation. Subrogation refers to the transfer of certain rights from an insured to an insurer - and by extension a reinsurer - who has paid a loss. They get first claim on any subsequent recovery made to the insured – for example, if a third party makes a payment because they're found liable for the loss.

In comparing Jane's appearance to a subrogation recovery, Mr. Bingley was suggesting unexpected good news, an unbudgeted windfall, analogous to a tax refund or a bank error in one's favor. If he intended the comment as a metaphor, it's unclear to whom Mr. Bingley had paid a loss that now earned him the right to claim the unexpected good fortune of Jane's presence.

Elizabeth meanwhile was struck by the change in Ms. Liebling and Ms. Thrush. She'd been impressed by the warmth and affection they had shown to Jane on her arrival. But after the men arrived, Jane was no longer their first object. Ms. Liebling in particular was keen to make Jane's appearance a topic of conversation between herself and Mr. Darcy.

"I was so surprised when she appeared here - and isn't she looking so much better?" she asked him. He was checking something on his phone and shook his head absently in her direction.

She tried again. "Isn't this nice - being altogether with Jane in this way?"

Her comment elicited no response. Looking around, she heard Bingley mention the Idea Fair the Claims Department would be hosting. She called over to him.

"Is Claims really going to host the next Idea Fair? How does your friend feel about that?"

"If you mean Darcy here, I imagine he's indifferent at best. I expect it to be a great triumph despite his absence."

"I should like Idea Fairs infinitely better," she replied, "if they were carried on in a different manner. They're so boring! It would surely be much more fun if dancing instead of conversation were made the order of the day."

"Much more fun, perhaps - but it wouldn't be near so much like an Idea Fair."

Ms. Liebling made no answer, and soon afterward she got up and walked about the room, stopping at the large window. Darcy remained focused on his phone, Bingley and Jane were reviewing lessons from the recent effort for The Benevolent, and neither Mr. Hurst nor Ms. Thrush appeared to be fully engaged in their surroundings. As Ms. Liebling sighed by the window, the only one giving her any notice was Elizabeth.

Ms. Liebling motioned to her. "Come look with me. It's very refreshing to see the larger perspective."

Elizabeth was surprised but agreed to it immediately. Darcy looked up.

"Mmmmmmm," said Ms. Liebling, pointing vaguely out and down.

"Mmmmmmm," Elizabeth replied, looking in the indicated direction.

Ms. Liebling invited Darcy to join them at the window. He declined, stating that he was better off not seeing whatever it was that they were seeing.

"What could he mean?" she asked Elizabeth.

"Don't ask him," she replied. "It's ju-jitsu. You want him to look out the window and he wants you to ask what he means."

Ms. Liebling was not to be deterred. "What do you mean?" she asked him.

"There are two possibilities here," he replied. "Possibility One is that there is something unusual to be seen out the window. In that case, the more of us who see it the less special it is for you to have seen it and the less interested we will be to hear you describe it to us. Possibility Two is that there is nothing at all unusual to be seen, and the invitation is a sort of prank that will annoy me and damage your credibility."

Ms. Liebling looked back at Elizabeth. "What can I say to that?"

"If you recall, I advised you not to ask him the question in the first place. Still, I'd push back at his premise that there are only two possibilities. Surely, there must be endless possibilities, and it will do him good to receive a bit of teasing for lack of imagination on this point."

"I'm not sure that Mr. Darcy is one to be laughed at."

"I'm sorry to hear that. I dearly love a laugh."

"I think," said he, "that Ms. Liebling is mistaken in her premise. Any of us can be laughed at. In fact, I take some comfort in knowing that absolutely anyone - however wise or good they may be - can be made fun of by someone who's determined to make a joke."

"Yes, and it's not just people. Reinsurance treaties that are sound and profitable can be ridiculed based on scant information or sloppy loss projections. Departments that strengthen the company can be laughed at for no apparent reason. Still, if we hold fast to our correctness, we can rise above the ridicule and avoid receiving any embarrassment or correction from it."

"I hope never to rise above correction. I only hope to rise above distraction."

"We are, I'm sure, all very impressed with the humility of your rising."

"Thank you for your irony. Did I mention that anyone can be made fun of by someone determined to make a joke?"

Ms. Liebling turned to Elizabeth. "Was I correct?" she asked. "Does he allow himself any weak points?"

"No, indeed. I can see that he's a perfectly good and wise person, and if anyone can find a way to make fun of him then it will prove his own point."

"That, I think, is an overstatement," said Darcy. "I am, for example, stubborn. Also, my capacity for forgiveness is very limited."

"We asked for weak points," said Elizabeth, "and you've given them to us. I can't laugh at them. You're safe from me."

"In my defense, I believe that these weak points – and maybe all weak points – grow out of virtues. My stubbornness starts with being conscientious, which is a good thing by itself, and enables me to end up often being right about things. The problem is that I then expect to be right about everything - which, of course, is unrealistic. My lack of forgiveness starts from a strong and clear moral sense, which again I believe is a good thing. But the result is that it's all I can do to ignore or forget small wrongs. At a certain point, my ability to forgive disappears altogether and is replaced by implacable opposition."

Elizabeth turned to Ms. Liebling. "Perhaps I've spoken too soon. It turns out that he hasn't given us weak points after all, but only perfections in disguise."

Darcy also looked at Ms. Liebling. "This is not an easy person to have even the semblance of a serious conversation with."

Ms. Liebling, happy to be looked at but restive at having become peripheral to the conversation, looked around and called out to Mr.

Bingley: "Is there a sound system in here? We should have some music!"

CHAPTER 12

The question of whether or not Netherfield contained a sound system must remain a mystery, because at that moment Ms. Nebbit strode purposefully into the room and looked around. "Begging your pardon for interrupting this very busy and obviously hard-working gathering! People tell me I should IM, but I say this is my own version of IM – it's I-apostrophe M. I'M here and I'M going to give you a message."

Satisfied that she had the room's full attention, she continued. "The message is that Jane is needed back in Underwriting. While she's been busy bailing out the Claims Department this week, demand for her services has been growing from all quarters, and we've been scheduling her time as carefully as we can. I swear, this week I've felt like the maître-d of one of those exclusive restaurants where everyone is begging for a reservation."

At this point, she addressed herself directly to Jane. "Just this afternoon, we've got you meeting with You-Know-Who from Finance and two different vice presidents from the Program Group."

Looking up at the ceiling, she continued. "I don't know how much longer we'll have you in the Pride Team. It will be so interesting to see where you end up!"

Mr. Bingley rose. "If Jane is needed, here she is. Sorry we can't continue to enjoy our pleasant after-party, but duty probably calls for all of us."

"Indeed it does, Mr. Bingley. Duty calls and it doesn't wait as patiently as we'd like to suppose. Can I just mention" – here she moved closer to Mr. Bingley – "that I had a disappointing experience with some real estate a year or two ago. There was the cutest little cottage I had my eye on. I went to multiple open houses and had the whole place decorated in my mind and then I woke up one day and it was sold. My cottage – I thought of it as my cottage – was sold and I wasn't the buyer. I was the dilly-dallyer who took that cottage for granted, and who now feels a stab of regret every time I drive past it."

"I'm sorry to hear that," said Mr. Bingley, although it was unclear if he was sorry for Ms. Nebbit's loss or sorry to have heard about it.

Ms. Nebbit looked around. "Will you join us, Elizabeth?"

"I will indeed. Duty calls for us all."

"Sorry to interrupt and run, but we're off! A good day to you all!" And Ms. Nebbit swept out of Mr. Bingley's office with Jane and Elizabeth in tow.

As they made their way back to Underwriting, Jane asked, "Are there in fact meetings that I'm needed for?"

"Well," said Ms. Nebbit, "possibly. But possibly not exactly as I described them."

"I see. And am I right then in thinking that hauling us off like that was some sort of stratagem on your part? And if so, could you explain it? It seems not long ago that you were rushing me down these same halls in the opposite direction."

"I should have thought it would be obvious to you. In my day, girls learned these skills in their bones for reasons having nothing to do with career advancement. You bait the hook with availability, but you close the deal with unavailability and competition."

Jane and Elizabeth looked at one another.

"Bait the hook?" said Jane.

"Close the deal?" said Elizabeth.

"Don't play the innocent with me!" said Ms. Nebbit. "I don't think any of us here are just off the turnip boat!"

When they arrived in the Underwriting Department, they looked into one of the conference rooms, where Mr. Bennet was seated with Kitty and Lydia.

"Well met! Well met!" he called out to Elizabeth and Jane. "Come join us! We need some ballast here. I'm trying to work out the outlines of a business plan for Workers Comp in states with high assigned risk pools, but somehow the conversation keeps drifting to the question of which member of the Regional Marketing Office has the nicest shoes!"

CHAPTER 13

"Sorry to trouble you with this extra meeting," said Mr. Bennet to the Pride Team the next morning, "but I wanted you to be prepared for a visitor who's decided to sit in on our regular meeting this afternoon."

"A visitor?" asked Ms. Nebbit. "I didn't know people could just decide to sit in on Pride Team meetings!"

Mr. Bennet paused for a moment. He may have been contemplating a comment to the effect that Ms. Nebbit herself had decided to sit in on innumerable Pride Team meetings.

"Someone important I hope?" continued Ms. Nebbit. "Maybe Mr. Bingley - come to see Jane in her natural habitat?"

"It's not Mr. Bingley," said Mr. Bennet.

There was a general buzz at this point. Kitty and Lydia speculated on the possibility that the visitor might be one of their well-shod friends from the Regional Marketing Office. They, like other members of the team, imagined the visitor they would most like to see at their meeting. The exception to this rule was Elizabeth, who envisioned the unhappy prospect of the visitor being Mr. Darcy.

Mr. Bennet held up his hand. "It's someone I've not yet had the pleasure to meet," he said. He then pulled some paper out of his portfolio. "I received an email recently. In fact, I found it somewhat curious to receive this message by email when the writer could easily have called or stopped by. In any event, I ask your indulgence while I take a few minutes to read the text of this message to you all."

He then lifted the paper to his face and read the following:

I don't know that we've been introduced, but my name is

William Collins, and I am Director of Succession Planning. As such, it is my distinct honor to work in the Human Resources Department under the direction and guidance of Executive Vice President Catherine de Bourgh.

As you may be aware, it has been decided that, when you retire, the Human Resources Department will take over responsibility for what is currently known as the Pride Program. As Executive Vice President Catherine de Bourgh has said in my hearing, the Human Resources department is looking forward to transforming that program into a professional recruitment and development program following proven best practices. Not that you should feel in any way rushed to retire before you are fully prepared for that important life step.

The reason for this message is that Executive Vice President Catherine de Bourgh has done me the tremendous honor of personally asking me to take charge of the program when it moves to Human Resources. (Although, when the time comes, it won't be what we call a Substitutionary Succession. I have been asked to remain on in my current position even as I take on this important new responsibility, so this will be a Consolidating Succession - also known as a Redundancy Succession.)

As you may imagine, I am looking forward to enabling the transformation my mentor and guide has envisioned for the unit. Not - I repeat for emphasis - that you should feel in any way rushed to retire before you are fully prepared for that important life step.

The prospect of an upcoming transition of leadership is known to be stressful for the affected employees. I expect it may be especially stressful for employees who are relatively young, inexperienced, and poorly integrated into the larger organization. Fortunately, this sort of transition is my professional specialty. I am, after all, and will be remaining, Director of Succession Planning.

As a first and important step towards a smooth transition, I am planning to join your next Pride Team meeting. I expect the current members of the team may have some questions and concerns about the future direction of the program. I am eager to assure them that the changes to come will be great improvements that will make the program better able to achieve the goals of the organization. They may also be gratified to hear that it is my intention that this transition, even as it boosts my own career, should not come at the detriment of their careers - and may even accrue some career benefit for at least one of the team members. However, I cannot speak in any detail on that particular point at present.

My appearance at your meeting will be followed by a co-location period during which I will be using the unassigned office next to your own to facilitate my first-hand interaction with the team. This is a standard part of the recommended process, and I can assure you that it can be accomplished without any serious disruption to my oversight of Succession Planning within the organization. Please go about your normal routines during this period as if I were not there. The exact length of this co-location period has not yet been determined, but I imagine it will be a matter of a few weeks.

I look forward to seeing you and the current team members at your upcoming meeting.

William Collins

"So - this afternoon we will all get to meet this clearly conscientious executive," said Mr. Bennet, as he folded up the text of the email. "He should be a valuable acquaintance for you all, if only because of his connection to a certain Executive Vice President. I don't know what he means when he says he hopes to further one of your careers, but I'm all in favor of it, whatever it is."

"He seems logical enough," said Mary. "I hadn't thought about the various types of succession before."

"I hope you're clear," said Kitty to Mr. Bennet, "that you should not feel rushed in any of your important life choices."

"He does seem to take an interest in our well being," said Jane.

"Although," said Elizabeth, "I wouldn't expect he'd be very supportive if one of us got on the wrong side of Executive Vice President Catherine de Bourgh."

"Maybe not," replied Jane. "But, in fairness, Lizzy - any of us would throw you under the bus if you got on the wrong side of CDB."

"As well you should!" said Elizabeth. "Still - he sounds quite singular to me. It appears that we have a current leader who's a lame duck and a future leader who's an odd duck!"

That afternoon, Mr. Collins arrived exactly on time for the Pride Team meeting. He was relatively young and extremely polite in the surprisingly formal manner sometimes seen in serious-minded young adults.

Mr. Collins was greeted warmly by the group and contributed many words - if not quite a commensurate number of ideas - to the group's discussions. He was at pains to declare his admiration for the abilities and achievements of the team members, and his absolute confidence that each of them would find excellent permanent positions within the company. This won him considerable favor with Ms. Nebbit.

"You are very kind, I am sure, and I wish with all my heart it may prove so, because there's no long-term future for them here on this team."

"Which, in fairness, I believe is the idea of the Pride Team. Still, I'm sure the prospect of a transition - whenever it might happen - casts a shadow, if only a psychological shadow, on their way forward."

"A shadow indeed, Mr. Collins! Not that I mean to find fault with you. As far as I know, you had no choice in the matter - and for all we know you'll be no worse than any other new manager would have been."

"You're very generous-minded, Ms. Nebbit. I hope to live up to your kind words." Then, with a look over at Mr. Bennet, "When the time comes, of course."

"I couldn't help noticing, in your message to Mr. Bennet-" continued Ms. Nebbit, who then stopped. "It was all right for him to share that message with me, wasn't it?"

"Mr. Bennet may share messages with whomever he pleases, I am sure," replied Mr. Collins. "If the message had been confidential, I should have identified it as such."

"Very good. Anyway, I couldn't help noticing that you made a reference to assisting one member of the team with her career. Could you please enlighten us further on this topic?"

"You are most perceptive, Ms. Nebbit! I can see that the team is fortunate to have your example and influence. However, it would be inappropriate for me to say anything further on that topic at this time - for reasons that I'm sure someone of your perception can easily imagine."

Ms. Nebbit nodded in appreciation and all was cordial between them until, a few minutes later, when they were reviewing a presentation on team goals and accomplishments for the year. Mr. Collins remarked on the artful eye of whichever of the team members had assembled the graphics for the presentation. Ms. Nebbit replied with some asperity that the team worked on the content of its presentations and looked to Corporate Communications for any necessary assistance in making the content "look pretty". He begged pardon for having displeased her. In a softened tone she declared herself not at all offended, but he continued to apologize at considerable length.

CHAPTER 14

As the meeting was winding down, Mr. Bennet turned to Mr. Collins. Eager to hear his guest speak from the heart, he said, "Tell us about the Human Resources Department. What's it like working for Ms. de Bourgh?"

Mr. Bennet couldn't have chosen better. Mr. Collins was eloquent in her praise. The subject elevated him to more than usual solemnity of manner. With the earnestness of an undertaker, he assured the group that he'd never in his life witnessed such magnanimous behavior in a senior officer - such affability and such an openness to see beyond the difference in their stations - as he himself had experienced from the great lady. She had been most helpful and supportive of his efforts when she reviewed his documentation of succession plans, and had personally invited him to be the United Way captain for the Department.

"Some people think she's haughty or standoffish, but she's always been remarkably generous with me. I mean, who am I?" Mr. Collins shrugged with becoming modesty. "But she makes a point of allowing me to help set up before her weekly staff meetings, and will sometimes ask me afterwards what I thought. It's a challenge for me to think of new ways to say '*Best Staff Meeting Ever!*'"

"A challenge that I'm sure you're able rise to," said Mr. Bennet.

"I do my best. Sometimes I'll think of something ahead of time - which I suppose is cheating. I mean, it hasn't been the Best Staff Meeting Ever at that point, right? I just know it will be."

"Quite understandable," said Mr. Bennet. "And what can you tell us about her thinking?"

Mr. Collins rubbed his chin. "Have I told you of her description of the three waves of diversity?" he asked. "I believe it will help you to understand your own current role a little bit better. The first wave" - here he paused and helpfully lifted his index finger to signal the connection of this wave with the number one - "was characterized by the full integration of women into the workforce. We've always had women employees here, of course, but there was a strict separation of jobs. Clerical and secretarial jobs were reserved for women, while the managerial and professional jobs were reserved for men. This was a bad thing for both men and women, because all of us are individuals. If a woman wants to be a manager or a man wants to be a secretary, they should each be able to do so. Provided, of course, that they have the proper skills and attitude. CDB likes to point to her own career as evidence of the transformation that has taken place through the first wave. The second wave" - here he illustrated the concept by lifting a second finger, "brought into our workforce people who had either been absent before or who had been seriously underrepresented. Racial, ethnic and sexual minorities, people with physical challenges, and so on. So the first wave was about integrating the people who were already here, the women, while the second wave was about bringing people into the mix who weren't here before. That's the second wave."

"And what then is the third wave?" asked Elizabeth.

"Ah!" exclaimed Mr. Collins. "This is where CDB demonstrates that she's no ordinary thinker in her role. The third wave is diversity of spirit!"

This interesting announcement caused the group to lapse into an extended thoughtful silence, which was eventually broken by Mr. Bennet.

"And what does that look like?"

"Exactly!" said Mr. Collins. "We don't know what it looks like. In fact, you can't tell by looking. It's not about how things look at all. It's about what's on the inside. So, what you, Mr. Bennet, have been presiding over during your many years with this program has been a mixture of Wave One and Wave Two diversity programs. This has been important work, and you should feel gratified to have established this foundation so that I and the Human Resources

Department can take the next step by moving this program on to Wave Three."

"Oh, that does sound good," said Mr. Bennet. "But I'm a little confused about something. If you can't tell by looking, how do we know that the third wave hasn't started already?"

"Oh, I'm quite certain on that point. I'll admit that I'm a little unclear regarding when exactly Wave One and Wave Two each began, but CDB was very clear that Wave Three is still ahead of us. I believe we expect it will begin quite soon. Although, let me just say once again: not that you should feel rushed regarding any important life choices."

"Most kind of you," said Mr. Bennet with a smile and a nod.

"The three waves of diversity are similar in concept to what CDB has described as the three waves of performance reviews."

He paused, possibly awaiting some prompting to elaborate. Instead, Lydia spoke up.

"I understand that Mr. Denny may be retiring from the RMO. That's what I heard from Ms. Phillips who keeps their schedules and knows everything. It's so nice to have the RMO in the building with us. I'm planning to go there tomorrow and see what I can find out."

There was an awkward silence at this. Elizabeth gave Lydia a meaningful look and said quietly, "I believe Mr. Collins was about to tell us about something quite interesting."

Mr. Collins gave an audible sigh, perhaps hoping it would make him appear weary rather than offended.

"I forget sometimes that people who aren't used to thinking strategically about the organization's human resources may not recognize the value of such a perspective. Personally, I've always felt that the proper and necessary subject of study for people in organizations is people in organizations. It just stands to reason. But I shouldn't expect to change anyone's attitude in a single staff meeting."

"So," said Mr. Bennet, "You've left us hanging. What are the three waves of performance appraisals?"

"Performance reviews," he said, correcting. "But no - I've said enough for today. Please proceed with your meeting."

And Mr. Collins sat quietly as the group members briefly concluded their updates for the day.

CHAPTER 15

Mr. Collins was a person with some limitations. He wasn't comfortable in groups and had no close friends. As a boy, he'd learned a tactical subservience by virtue of having a tyrannically controlling father. Academically, he made his way through college and an MBA program primarily by avoiding subjects with right and wrong answers and focusing his efforts on ingratiating himself to his professors. He was relieved and gratified to find that his social, academic, and various other limitations were largely irrelevant to his prospects at Juniper Re. As a trainee in the Human Resources Department, he attached himself immediately and successfully - somewhat in the manner of a pilot fish - to Ms. de Bourgh, and was able to live quite comfortably and securely as part of her ecosystem. As he gained some measure of success, he didn't abandon the outward humility that had worked for him thus far, but the practiced eye could detect a growing level of self-satisfaction disguised behind it.

Having a secure position and a sense of upward mobility, he was now in the market for a protégée - a direct report, but also someone who would appreciate and absorb his wisdom and be his youthful proxy and female brand extension in the larger organization. In order to smooth out any awkwardness in his accession to the head of the Pride Team, he was determined to bestow this honor on a member of that team.

His first thought was to grant this favor to Jane, as she was the most senior member of the young group and also quite good-looking. We are speaking here of her résumé and accomplishments, although Mr. Collins was not blind to the fact that the physical attractiveness of a protégée is typically understood to be a signifier of the mentor's status. The next morning, after having moved into the open office next to Mr. Bennet's, he took a moment to seek out Ms. Nebbit in order to sound her out. He alluded to the possibility that he might consider recruiting a team member to be his lieutenant. She was very encouraging to him regarding such a notion, with the only proviso being that he shouldn't expect Jane to be available. "I know of no reason why any of the others wouldn't be ready and eager for such an opportunity, but as for Jane - I think I can say with some certainty that she's being actively recruited already and will soon have a new position outside the team."

At this point, Mr. Collins had only to change from Jane to Elizabeth - next in line and, as a potential candidate for the position, equally attractive.

Ms. Nebbit was pleased to hear his intimations and mentally checked off another team member as being as good as hired to a secure permanent position.

Mr. Collins proceeded to Mr. Bennet's office, where he stopped demurely at the entryway.

"Come in, please!"

"Are you sure?" asked Mr. Collins. "I'll try to be invisible, but I'm bound to be a distraction for you."

"Come, make yourself at home."

"You're very kind, I'm sure. Very gracious. Most accommodating. Please don't let me keep you from anything. Just pretend I'm not here. I'll make every effort to be quiet as a mouse."

"Are you sure? I'm happy to answer any questions you have."

"No, no. Just go ahead. Here," he said, taking a binder out of Mr. Bennet's bookcase, "I'll just do a little light reading."

"That binder's pretty old. I'm not sure why I even have it there."

Mr. Collins set the binder on his lap and began flipping slowly through pages. "Just ignore me. I'm not here."

Mr. Bennet shrugged, turned toward his computer screen and started to read his email.

"What's guneppy?" asked Mr. Collins.

"Excuse me?"

"Guneppy. G-N-E-P-I."

"Ah," said Mr. Bennet. "Gross Net Earned Premium Income. Gross

74

Net I know sounds like a contradiction in terms, but it's a pretty standard way of referring to top line reinsurance revenues."

"Just the thing. Very good!"

Mr. Bennet turned his attention back to his email, but looked up later to watch as his guest, who still had the binder in his lap, hold up his smartphone and aim it at various points of the office.

"Excuse me?"

Mr. Collins became flustered and put away the phone. Mr. Bennet was confused.

"Was that a measurement app?"

"Maybe. It might be. A foolish distraction, I know." He stared intently at the binder on his lap.

"If you want to know how big this office is, I can tell you how big it is."

At this point, Lydia looked into the office. "Hey there! The rest of the team is coming with me on my visit over to the RMO. Would either of you like to come along?"

"I'll come!" volunteered Mr. Collins. He returned the binder to the bookcase and smiled at Mr. Bennet. "Good chance to see the team interact with another department. Will you be joining us?"

Mr. Bennet generously agreed to stay behind so as not to overpopulate the outing. If that meant having some undisturbed time in his office, this was a sacrifice he was prepared to make.

Lydia led Mr. Collins, along with Jane, Elizabeth, Mary and Kitty, to the temporary quarters of the RMO. They were scheduled to have a meeting with Ms. Phillips, who was Events Manager for the RMO and also happened to be Ms. Nebbit's sister.

As they were nearing the conference room where they were to meet with Ms. Phillips, they saw Mr. Denny standing in the hallway and speaking with a man who was unknown to any of them, but who appeared to be the personification of the reason Lydia and Kitty made a point of visiting the RMO. He was handsome and beautifully dressed, with possibly the nicest pair of men's dress shoes they had ever seen in person. He appeared to be charmingly at ease as he bantered cheerfully with the soon-to-be-retired Mr. Denny.

Lydia, quickly joined by Kitty, made a point of greeting Mr. Denny, congratulating him warmly on his impending retirement, and then waiting politely to be introduced.

Mr. Denny thanked them and introduced the handsome stranger as Mr. Wickham, a new recruit to the company who would have reported to Mr. Denny but would now be reporting to his successor, Mr. Forster. Mr. Wickham proved every bit as charming and well-spoken as one could have wished, and the group had a cheerful moment of sociability in the hallway.

At this point, attempting to pass through the press of people and introductions, came Mr. Bingley and Mr. Darcy. They stopped on seeing Jane and Elizabeth. Mr. Bingley inquired after Jane's health and she assured him that she was perfectly well. Mr. Darcy nodded to them both and Elizabeth said, "Have you met the new recruit here, Mr. Wickham? Mr. Wickham, this is Mr. Darcy and Mr. Bingley."

Mr. Darcy and Mr. Wickham each changed color and avoided looking directly at the other. They nodded awkwardly in each other's direction. What could be the meaning of it? It was impossible to imagine; it was impossible not to long to know. Mr. Bingley smiled and waved and then he and Mr. Darcy took their leave.

Mr. Denny and Mr. Wickham escorted the group to Meryton 3 where Ms. Phillips was waiting, but declined the many offers to join them for their meeting.

Ms. Phillips was very pleased to see the members of the team, whom she thought of as so many nieces due to their connection to her sister. She was just getting caught up on their news when Jane introduced her to Mr. Collins, who apologized at some length for his uninvited appearance at the meeting. He threw himself metaphorically on her mercy, pleading his admiration for the team members and his great desire to better understand their culture and community. Ms. Phillips was quite impressed with his good breeding, but her contemplation of one stranger was soon put to an end by exclamations and inquiries about the other; of whom, however, she could only tell what they already knew, that he was new to the company.

Ms. Phillips continued: "If you'd like to meet more of the RMO staff, and, I imagine, have the opportunity to get acquainted with the mysterious new Mr. Wickham, I suggest you all come back tomorrow afternoon at three. We're going to open up Meryton and have a reception to honor Mr. Denny on his retirement. You'd all be most welcome to join us."

As they walked back to their desks, Elizabeth related to Jane what she'd seen pass between Mr. Wickham and Mr. Darcy. Jane would have defended either or both, but she had no explanation for their behavior.

Ms. Nebbit was pleased to hear Mr. Collins describe her sister's hospitality and professionalism in the most glowing terms. He was especially impressed that she had included him in the invitation for the reception. After all, who was he that she should show him such gracious regard? Nobody at all, really.

CHAPTER 16

The next day, Mr. Collins accompanied the team members to the reception for Mr. Denny. He expressed some compunction about failing to enact his original plan to shadow Mr. Bennet for the day, but Mr. Bennet assured him that spending the time with the team members was the better course.

Tables of refreshments had been set up in Meryton. On one table was a large sheet cake featuring the company's logo and warm wishes to Mr. Denny neatly executed in icing. As Mr. Collins and the team members arrived, there were twenty or more employees standing around and chatting quietly but not yet touching the cake or any of the other refreshments. The crowd formed a standing semi-circle as Ms. Phillips pointed to her watch and Mr. Armstrong, Head of Marketing, stepped up to a lectern.

"I'm so glad to see you all here today," he said with a smile. "I know that if we weren't having this event you would all be working hard right now. Or perhaps hardly working."

This was a very well-received opening, as the elevated status of the speaker and the inclination of the group to have an enjoyable break from their normal labors both served to magnify the inherent wit of Mr. Armstrong's remark. He went on to explain that he had been doing some reading in Mr. Denny's personnel folder and had found some interesting nuggets he wanted to share.

The truth of the matter was that Ms. Phillips had done this research and prepared the remarks for Mr. Armstrong, who had reached the happy station where his existence at the company amounted to a sort of assisted living. He was routinely cited as the author of ghostwritten articles and regularly delivered speeches that reflected his personal brand more than his personal efforts. Still, Mr. Armstrong played his part with the verve and gameness of an experienced actor or politician and then graciously ceded the floor to the guest of honor.

Mr. Denny surveyed the room as if he were looking out over his hometown before leaving it to seek his fortune. Having fixed the scene in his memory, he thanked his friends and associates for their kind thoughts and best wishes and declared it an honor to have been their colleague.

"If I may bore you with a few serious thoughts after nearly forty years with this fine organization: the challenge for us all in our work lives is to find the right balance. Not just the balance of time between work and personal life - which, by the way, has become increasingly challenging over the years. It's also the balance of who you are. How much of yourself can and should you bring to your work? There are some interpersonal boundaries, of course, that I urge you all to respect. But there are also some departmental boundaries, that I urge you to ignore.

"One goal during my career has been to bring as much of myself as I could without regard to what departmental team I was supposed to be working for. Our role at the RMO is a Marketing role, but I've always believed that Underwriting is too important to leave to the underwriters. And I'd hope that they'd think that Marketing was too important to leave to us. And they'd be right!

"The easy thing is to play the same note all the time, to repeat the same strategy, the same decision, over and over. That doesn't take any thought or effort. What takes thought, what takes effort, is to find the right balance.

"So that's my advice. Find your balance. Find your balance between work and life. At work, find your balance between top line and bottom line, aggressiveness and caution, Underwriting and Marketing. In the rest of your life, find your balance between taking care of yourself and taking care of others.

"This is a great company, I've had a great run here, and I'm very grateful to you all. I haven't sold my company stock, so I'm counting on you all to be very successful in the years ahead. Thank you!"

Soon the speeches were over, Mr. Denny and his career were applauded one last time and the social hour began.

Mr. Collins made his way to the cake that Ms. Phillips was serving and discoursed to her at considerable length on the value of employee social occasions. Ms. Phillips listened with a most polite interest, while those waiting in line for cake may have harbored somewhat less generous thoughts towards him.

Elizabeth put some chips and dip on a paper plate, picked up a cup of ginger ale, and moved on from the refreshment table with both her hands full. She had intended to mingle in the crowd, but she saw that the furniture in the area included two low-slung leather chairs, neither of which was occupied at the moment. She decided to sit down and take her chances regarding who might claim the second chair.

"Mind if I join you here?"

Elizabeth looked up and was surprised and pleased to see the dapper and mysterious Mr. Wickham.

"By all means!"

"I was tempted by some of the snacks, but it's too much to hold things in your hands and socialize while standing - as you figured out before me. You came through yesterday with the Pride Team, right?"

"Yes, that's correct. I'm Elizabeth Austen."

"George Wickham. Very pleased to meet you."

Elizabeth considered what to say. What she chiefly wished to hear she didn't want to ask directly—the history of his acquaintance with Mr. Darcy.

"Can I ask you a question?" he said.

"Of course."

"How long has Darcy been here at Juniper Re?"

"Not long at all. A month maybe. I understand he was formerly at Cornwallis Re."

"Yes he was. I was at Cornwallis before starting here this week, and I knew Mr. Darcy very well there."

Elizabeth waited, but no further information was forthcoming. "This may be nosy of me, but I couldn't help noticing a certain awkwardness between the two of you."

"That's all right. There's an irony to this story that I don't mind sharing with my long-term friends here at Juniper Re - and you qualify as a long-term friend for me here because I met you yesterday. Mr. Darcy was, in fact, a significant factor in my decision to leave Cornwallis. The awkwardness you noticed was the moment of unhappy surprise when I found out that he'd made the same move I had."

"I see. My condolences."

"I've probably said too much. I don't want to poison you against him. Have you had the chance to meet him?"

Elizabeth smiled at this. "I've had a handful of interactions with him. If he drove you away from Cornwallis, then it probably won't surprise you to hear that I found him somewhat unpleasant."

"So you've not been swept up in the Darcy tide?"

"Maybe there was a Darcy tide at Cornwallis, but I don't see one here. He hasn't endeared himself to the locals. He tends to come across as a prematurely grumpy old man, yelling at us all to get off his lawn."

"Well, that's something, anyway. At Cornwallis, his more-serious-than-thou schtick played very well, and nobody would say a word against him."

This was better and juicier than Elizabeth had dared to hope for. Wickham continued.

"It helped, of course, that he was Paternoster's golden boy. Paternoster was the president at Cornwallis until a few years back. He built that company and was universally admired - and deserved every bit of it. So you can see why people would give Darcy the benefit of the doubt."

"Yes. I hope his presence here won't give you second thoughts about joining us here at Juniper Re."

"No! It's not for me to be driven away by Darcy. If he wants to avoid seeing me, he's the one who must go. We aren't on friendly terms, and it always gives me pain to meet him, but I have no reason for avoiding him. What I find sad is that he didn't live up to the trust that was put in him and the example that was provided to him by Mr. Paternoster - who was one of the best men that ever breathed. I think I could forgive Darcy anything and everything other than his disappointing the hopes and disgracing the memory of a man who was a great mentor to us both."

She asked his impressions of Juniper Re. He spoke highly of the company and was particularly complimentary regarding the RMO, whose members had been very hospitable in their welcome to him.

"I think my timing is good. I interviewed with both Denny and Forster, who's taking his place. Denny's a great fellow, but it's my impression that he's been holding the unit back. I think Forster is ready to break some china and make big things happen. Also, I'm very pleased the unit is located here, if only temporarily. I'm a home office underwriter by training and inclination, but was driven to field marketing by that prematurely old man yelling at you to get off his lawn."

"Darcy?"

"Yes. I'd started as an intern in Operations, but Paternoster had promised me a nice step up to an underwriting role in a new unit that was being started up. But after he retired, Darcy took over the unit and didn't even consider me for the position."

"But you said Paternoster was his mentor."

"Right - until he retired. Then he was history. I think maybe Darcy was unhappy that he wasn't chosen to be the new president."

"But still. Why wouldn't he consider you for the position you'd been promised?"

"A very determined and personal dislike of me. I'm not sure where it came from. It's not like I ever did anything to him. My working theory is that he felt some kind of jealous rivalry because I had a close and friendly relationship with Paternoster. Darcy wanted that Paternoster seal of approval all to himself."

"Well, I already had a low opinion of Mr. Darcy, but clearly it wasn't low enough. I'd been thinking of him as stuffy and self-important, but not as mean and unfair."

She stopped for a moment to consider this. "Actually, now that I think of it, I remember him saying once that he has great difficulty forgiving even minor offenses and said that he's prone to 'implacable opposition'."

"No comment."

"You must have known and worked alongside Mr. Darcy for a long time."

"Oh yes. You might say we grew up together in the business. We were in the same executive training class - Charm School. We weren't a bad team in our heyday. I was good at putting deals together, and he was good at getting them approved and taking credit for them."

"You'd think that someone as proud as he is would want to treat people better - if only out of pride."

"I've seen him be very generous at times, and I attribute it to just that. He wanted to be able to think of himself as the heir and continuation of Paternoster. He's just proud enough sometimes to think that he could live up to that heritage. I'd watch out for him, though, if I were you. It's my understanding that beneath that cold exterior he has an eye for the ladies."

"Oh?"

"There were rumors about him and a young woman on his staff."

"I think I heard her spoken of. Georgiana Something?"

"Yes. Georgiana Icard. A very promising young woman. I don't know if there was anything to it, but maybe so. Maybe that's why he's suddenly here now. Boss-subordinate affairs can get you in a lot of trouble at Cornwallis. I assume the same is true here."

"Yes it is."

"I understand the logic of those rules - unequal power and all that. Still, it seems a little simplistic to me. Who's to say that one party has power over the other just because of a title or reporting relationship? There are many factors that affect the balance of power between potential romantic partners. OK, so maybe he's the boss - but maybe she's richer and more popular and better looking than he is. Job title isn't everything."

"Very interesting. So you're either unusually enlightened or an enabler of harassers."

"Thank you. I like to think of myself as walking a fine line between enlightenment and enablement, but just to be clear I'm not looking to justify Darcy. I do think we sometimes do a disservice to women by casting them as powerless victims."

Elizabeth pondered this as she finished her refreshments. "And what of Mr. Charles Bingley? Do you know him, too?"

"Not really to speak of. Happily, I never had much need to interact with Claims."

"He seems very nice. Everybody likes him and speaks well of him. And yet he seems to be great and close friends with Darcy. How is that even possible?"

"Bingley's a senior officer and no direct competitor to Darcy. Why shouldn't Darcy be nice to him and cultivate him as a friend and ally? It's my understanding that Darcy can be a very pleasant companion if you're important enough and not standing in his way."

At this point, Mr. Collins passed by and bowed to Elizabeth. "I didn't mind chipping in a few dollars to the collections for Denny's gifts. Events like these are very conducive to community building! I know CDB is a strong proponent for them."

Elizabeth nodded to Mr. Collins and he continued making his rounds.

"CDB?" asked Mr. Wickham.

"Catherine de Bourgh. Head of Human Resources."

"Did you know that she's Darcy's aunt? Her sister was Darcy's mother."

"I'd heard they were related. I didn't know the details."

"I don't know her at all, but the word at Cornwallis was that his aunt made all his personnel choices for him. If that was true there, I imagine it will only be more true here."

Elizabeth smiled to herself to think of how assiduously Caroline Liebling was angling to get herself recruited by Darcy. Apparently, she would be better off focusing her attentions on CDB.

"Well, I hope you'll be an active presence here in the Home Office as long as the RMO is in the building."

"Oh yes, I plan to take full advantage. I've heard about your Idea Fairs, and I intend to be at every one with bells on. Perhaps you'll do me the honor of solving a problem or two for me!"

"Absolutely!"

"Tell me, Ms. Austen, if it's not too forward of me - what are your career ambitions here?"

This was a question that she thought about constantly but didn't particularly like to be asked. "I don't have it all mapped out, and it remains to be seen what kinds of opportunities will be open to me, but I love Underwriting and Strategic Planning. That's for the medium term. For the long term, I'm thinking: *'Juniper Re - a Wholly Owned Subsidiary of Elizabeth Austen Enterprises'*."

"Sounds good to me! Let me just say for the short to medium term you should think about the RMO. They pay well, and a little field marketing experience would give you more credibility in Underwriting."

"Thank you. I'll bear that in mind."

"And maybe at some point we can share a drink of something more enjoyable than ginger ale."

As she was returning to her desk, Elizabeth pondered what to make of Mr. George Wickham. He was a little different from the standard-issue Juniper Re employee, which she appreciated - and he hated Darcy, so he couldn't be all bad! When Lydia asked her about him, she said, "He's very charming, but I think maybe he's a bit of a hound dog."

"Oh yes, exactly!" she said. "But the really wonderful thing is that he's a hound dog you could take home to meet your parents!"

CHAPTER 17

The next day, Elizabeth made a point of having a good, long after-lunch walk with Jane, during which she provided a thorough account of her conversation with Mr. Wickham. Jane was stumped as to how to make sense of Elizabeth's report - as she was unwilling to see Darcy as mean-spirited or Wickham as untruthful.

"This must be some kind of terrible misunderstanding," she said.

"It's nothing of the sort!" declared Elizabeth. "We have very clear evidence telling us exactly what we should think of Mr. F. William Darcy."

"It's a difficult case, I'll give you that. We have a very credible-seeming George Wickham telling you a story that's quite detailed and based on his own personal experience. All true. And yet the story itself is impossible to believe. Darcy just isn't capable of such things - and Bingley wouldn't be his friend if he were."

"I think you should forget about Claims and aim for a Marketing position. From what I hear, those jobs require a keen ability to overlook all manner of warning signs and bad reports."

"Yes, thank you, Ms. Underwriting!" said Jane, pausing to curtsy. "Well, you can make fun of me as much as you like, but I'm adamant and I expect to be vindicated in the end. However Wickham has been mistreated, he's somehow mistaken in blaming it on Darcy. Call me a Marketer if you must, but I'm true to my team. Darcy is a friend of Bingley, and I'm a partisan for Bingley, so I refuse to believe that Darcy is a bad person."

"I admire your loyalty, but here's the thing. It says nothing against your hero, Mr. Bingley, if his friend happens to be a conniving two-face who manages to be pleasant to him while being horrible to others. Bingley just sees Darcy's stuffy but fair-minded good side. And Bingley is so friendly and pleasant that - like you - he can't imagine that someone can be pathologically mean or petty."

"No, I disagree. Bingley and Darcy are clearly close. If Darcy is a conniving two-face, then Bingley ought to know. It would mean that he's either also a bad person or else an oblivious idiot. And I refuse to go there. Bingley is neither of those things."

"Because Bingley is what?"

Jane tipped her head towards Elizabeth. "Well," she said, "for one thing, Bingley is right there."

Approaching them from the direction indicated by Elizabeth's head tip was Mr. Bingley, accompanied by Ms. Liebling and Ms. Thrush. The three of them were clearly headed for a meeting - probably cutting across the courtyard from the Main Building to Building Three. Elizabeth and Jane could not help noting that the group had sought them out, as they were well beyond a normal beeline between the two buildings.

Going beyond what is expected or required may be celebrated in general, but it's discouraged and only reluctantly accommodated in the insurance and reinsurance world. A company may sometimes make a seemingly unwarranted payment to settle a dispute and keep the peace with a valued client. The term for this is Ex Gratia - that is, payment out of goodness rather than out of the necessity of honoring a commitment. This is not unlike the legal maneuver of paying a settlement without admitting liability. While a little generosity may seem harmless enough or even commendable, a payment that isn't actually warranted means there will be less money to meet legitimate commitments and raises the risks of favoritism or discrimination. As the three Claims colleagues crossed the courtyard, it appeared that Bingley was going out of his way in a spirit of generosity, while Ms. Liebling and Ms. Thrush were following with a reluctance that showed their consciousness of the dangers of Ex Gratia acts.

"Jane! Elizabeth!" called Mr. Bingley. "Beautiful day to get outside, isn't it?"

Jane and Elizabeth both agreed.

Mr. Bingley continued: "I wanted to let you know that we've finally scheduled the Claims-sponsored Idea Fair. It's going to be next Tuesday in Netherfield at 10."

"Wonderful!" said Jane.

Ms. Liebling came forward, gave a slight nod to Elizabeth, and then took Jane's hand. "I wish you were coming with us to this meeting! It's about requirements for the new Claims System. You'd know exactly what's needed, I'm sure you would."

Elizabeth set aside her feeling that she also would be a valuable person to have in such a meeting and instead was pleased to see that Jane had been accepted by the Claims staff.

Mr. Bingley asked Jane and Elizabeth to forward the news of the Idea Fair to the rest of the team, and then he and Ms. Liebling and Ms. Thrush were off.

Jane forwarded the invitation at the next Pride Team staff meeting. Ms. Nebbit announced that the fact Mr. Bingley had crossed the courtyard to deliver the message personally was a sure sign that Jane would soon be employed in the Claims department. "Out of his way to make sure you'll be there. I think he has a Claim on you!"

Each of the team members welcomed the prospect of another Idea Fair. Jane hoped to cement her standing with Bingley. Elizabeth found herself wondering what questions George Wickham would be bringing to the Round Robin. Lydia and Catherine were also thinking about Wickham - or anyone else who might show up to represent the RMO. Mary said, "The thing about the Round Robin is that there's an awkwardness I feel in needing to express myself without having enough time to think things through as thoroughly as I'd like. It feels uncomfortable at the time, but maybe also a bit exhilarating. Somehow it feels almost pleasant to me in retrospect."

"And what of you?" Elizabeth asked Mr. Collins, who was once again sitting in on the team meeting.

"CDB is a huge supporter of Idea Fairs, and I don't believe it's a coincidence that it's been during her tenure as Head of HR that this important innovation has been developed and taken root as part of our culture. I'm gratified that I've now reached a position where I can make a small repayment to the organization by mentoring our next generation. I plan to bring some questions to the Round Robin. In fact, Ms. Austen, would you do me the honor of being my partner for the first round?"

Elizabeth caught her breath. She had no interest in using any part of the Round Robin to achieve face time with Mr. Collins - who seemed to be in her face plenty enough already. She was reminded of competitive situations where brokers will "reserve" reinsurance markets – that is, claim the right to represent them. In such cases, the broker will inevitably use the fact that they picked Juniper Re as pressure - assuming their choice to have put a burden of obligation on the company to give the broker a good quote.

As a rule, the effect on Elizabeth of an unsought partnership was likely to be the opposite of whatever obligation the other party might assume. However, she saw no acceptable way to refuse the offer from Mr. Collins. She agreed and quietly hoped the event would balance out for her, that later in the Round Robin she would have the chance to be paired with partners more interesting to her and more germane to her career ambitions - perhaps even Mr. Wickham.

Elizabeth began to be aware that Mr. Collins was showing distinct interest in her. She began to feel conspicuous as his target for the deputy position he was apparently authorized to fill. If being paired with Mr. Collins for the first Round Robin session was a dreary prospect for her, the thought of working for him was considerably worse. Still, there was nothing to be done. She could hardly refuse him unless and until he asked.

CHAPTER 18

Elizabeth arrived early at Netherfield to review the layout and see if there was a posting of executives who'd be participating in the Round Robin. The list was printed and taped to the wall and Elizabeth was surprised to see that it didn't include Mr. Wickham.

Why not? Was he avoiding Darcy after all? Or did Darcy somehow arrange for him to be excluded?

She looked around and spotted Ms. Phillips. "Your new Mr. Wickham told me he'd be participating in the Round Robin, but his name isn't on the list."

"No," said Ms. Phillips. "Something came up and he's out of town today." She gave her a significant smile. "I think the fact that he needed to be away today may have had something to do with a desire to avoid crossing paths with a certain executive here. Apparently they have a bit of history."

So, she thought, the situation is pretty much what she had guessed. Wickham's absence was Darcy's fault. When Darcy himself appeared and gave her a friendly greeting, she gave him no smile and a tiny, silent nod, then turned immediately to whomever was available to speak with in the other direction. Darcy, she told herself, is not the only person here who can freeze out someone they don't care for.

She was also a bit curt with Mr. Bingley. She was in a boycotting mood and, while Bingley was amiable enough on his own, he was unambiguously a Darcy partisan.

Still, Elizabeth hadn't come to the Idea Fair to be disagreeable to everyone she met. As she saw more people, she was able to recover her general enjoyment of humanity and have a nice chat with her friend, Charlotte, whom she hadn't seen in a week. She pointed out Mr. Collins to her and described his entry into the life of the Pride

Team - with a particular focus on the eccentricities of his that she thought Charlotte might find amusing.

Mr. Bingley stepped to a microphone to open the festivities. He gave everyone an enthusiastic greeting, but then rambled a bit. Elizabeth appreciated his unfiltered humanity, but thought it would come across more effectively with just a bit of added preparation. She could detect the germ of a self-deprecatory joke he'd apparently intended, which was that while this was his first time hosting an Idea Fair he hoped it wasn't his first time hosting an idea. Succinctly stated, it might have served the occasion very well. She remembered Darcy either nagging or teasing Bingley - it was hard to tell with Darcy - about his ad hoc, unstudied emails. She hated even to think it, but maybe Darcy had a point.

When the time came for the first round of the Round Robin, Elizabeth lost much of her regained *joie de vivre* as she sat down across from Mr. Collins - who had apparently decided that the proper way to assert his fitness for the role was to be as grim and haughty as humanly possible.

"Good day to you, Ms. Austen. I'd like you to take a look at these pie charts."

"Thank you. These? You know, they aren't actually pie charts. They're scatter diagrams."

"My dear Ms. Austen," he replied with a patient smile. "The charts have a generally circular pattern. Any circular diagram may be referred to as a pie chart."

Incorrectly by a simpleton, she said silently to herself as she nodded her appreciation to Mr. Collins.

For the next round, Elizabeth was paired with Mr. Armstrong, Head of Marketing. She took the opportunity to ask him about Wickham, and he spoke enthusiastically about him. He declared that they were lucky to get Wickham and that he was already very well liked within the unit.

"Things happen in threes," he told Elizabeth. "We never get anyone from Cornwallis. That place is a lobster trap. People go in and they never come out. But the last few months we got Darcy, Bingley and Wickham."

"That sounds a little superstitious."

"Well, touch wood - we wouldn't want to be superstitious!"

Elizabeth sat out the next round and was chatting with Charlotte when Mr. Darcy interrupted.

"I'm going to take a slot in the next round. Come join me. I'll be at Table Four."

"Sure."

Darcy strode off and Elizabeth looked at Charlotte. "What was I thinking?"

"It'll be fine. He might be president eventually. Let him see how smart you are. You'll probably have a good time."

"I don't want to have a good time! I just want to revel in my dislike of him."

But she had accepted the offer and at the appointed time sat down at Table Four across from Mr. Darcy. She was conscious that many of those in that part of the hall were watching the two of them.

For her part, she was studying him closely. Maybe he knew she was becoming a Wickham partisan and would be mean to her. Maybe he saw her as a potential replacement for Georgiana and would hit on her.

"You have a question?" she asked.

"Yes, of course. I have a certain close associate. Let's call him Mr. X. This Mr. X. is relatively new to the company, but he has a large job - too large to do on his own. He needs to hire some staff to help him. He'd like to hire from within the company, but he doesn't know the available people here very well yet. How does he know who will be best for a given job? How does he know who he can trust?"

Elizabeth considered this. "Do you find us untrustworthy here?"

"Not at all. But when any of us comes to a new organization or community, it's always a kind of an unmarked ship channel. It takes some time and experience to learn where the rocks are."

She felt she was being tested, but she couldn't tell how. Was he dangling a job opening before her nose to test her character? "Let's see," she said. "Here at Juniper Re we have an Open Posting process so that everyone in the company has a fair chance to hear about a new opening. That'd be a good place to start. It might help if Mr. X. had a friend or maybe even a family member in the Human

Resources Department." She looked to see if he would react to this last comment, but he remained poker-faced. "What kind of a reputation does Mr. X. have as a boss?"

"No reputation at all yet - at least not here. As far as I know, Mr. X. was an exemplary boss in his earlier life."

"Based on your objective and unbiased assessment?"

"Based on my assessment that is stubbornly clear-eyed despite my considerable bias in the case."

"So, you think you're able to be a fair and objective judge of character? I have to say, that's not what I hear."

Darcy flinched at this. "Let me guess. You've been speaking with my former colleague, George Wickham."

"My guide to the rocks lurking below the surface at Cornwallis Re."

"Maybe so, but let me first appeal to your Underwriting training. Don't put your pencil down too soon. Before you make a decision - about me or about anything else - get as much information from as many sources as possible."

They were interrupted at this point, by Mr. Lucas, the Underwriting Head. "Darcy! Don't stop - I know you're on the clock! I just wanted to take one second to say how pleased I am to see you participating in this event. I've always thought these Ideas Fairs are wonderful training grounds and one of the best things about Juniper Re - and I take a special pride in knowing that they're a creation of the Underwriting Department. And, of course, you have the perfect partner here in our Ms. Austen. If she can't answer your questions, heaven help us all! And you aren't the only Cornwallis transplant who's noticed the value of our Pride Team members." He pointed to Table One, where Bingley and Jane were engaged in an animated discussion. Lucas leaned towards Darcy. "It's my understanding that she's practically a member of the Claims Department already."

Mr. Darcy glanced at Bingley and did not seem at all pleased. Elizabeth wondered if he disapproved of Jane or simply thought Mr. Lucas was being indiscreet. The timer rang and Mr. Lucas gave a wave.

"Oh, there's the bell! I've spoiled your session. Please forgive me!"

Elizabeth excused herself, leaving the session with a feeling of annoyance at both Darcy and herself that she realized was becoming a familiar experience after any conversation with him. Darcy, on the other hand, left the session primarily with a feeling of annoyance at George Wickham.

Soon afterwards, Elizabeth was approached by Ms. Liebling, who looked even less pleased than usual. "So," she said. "I understand you've been making inquiries about George Wickham. I'm not sure if that means you're taking his side or just flirting with the idea of it. Either way, my friendly advice to you is this: don't! Don't let yourself become associated with him - professionally or personally. The man's a liar and a loser and he brings down everything he's associated with. The story he tells about Darcy being unfair to him is just his way of trying to get attention. You know, he was just a low-level person in Operations at Cornwallis. He probably didn't tell you that."

Elizabeth took a breath. "Thanks for your kind concern, Caroline. I'm not sure what your sources are for being so sure that Wickham is a liar, but I personally like to keep an open mind. Try to get all the facts before making a decision. The only fact I heard in what you just said is that Wickham was in the Operations Department - which is exactly what he told me as well."

"Suit yourself. Just trying to be helpful."

Elizabeth - now upset with Ms. Liebling in addition to Mr. Darcy, Mr. Bingley, Mr. Lucas, herself and possibly Mr. Wickham - sought out Jane, who always helped her to feel better. Jane was in especially good spirits, having enjoyed her session with Bingley.

"It went very well," said Jane. "He was asking about the new Claims system they're planning. Fortunately, it's something I've thought about and we had a good discussion."

"Great! And what about the dirt? Did you get a chance to ask him what he knows about Wickham and his claims against Darcy?"

"Of course I did. He didn't know much. He'd heard there was a dispute, but he doesn't know the details. His theory is that Wickham is exaggerating his claim to the position he didn't get."

Elizabeth pondered this. "He's exaggerating it?"

"Right."

"So the former president only sort-of promised it to him?"

"Something like that."

"So Darcy only sort-of cheated him out it?"

"Now don't be cross!"

Elizabeth laughed. "Thank you! I don't know what's wrong with me today. You were very nice to ask about it, and I need to drop the whole thing and take some vicarious pleasure in your productive session with Bingley."

"And how was your session with Darcy?"

"Not quite so productive, I'm afraid. I've been in a very judgmental mood today. I know that your instinct is always to find a way to exonerate both parties, but my instinct is to assume they're both guilty. Darcy's mean and Wickham exaggerates."

"And Bingley?"

"Bingley's fine. He's the exception that proves the rule. You can say as many nice things about him as you like and I won't contradict you. And, in fact..."

Elizabeth had turned around to see Mr. Bingley moving in their direction. "Good to see you both!" he said and shook hands with them.

Elizabeth excused herself so that Jane could continue to dazzle Bingley with her ideas for the new Claims system. She found herself immediately face to face with Mr. Collins.

"Do you know what I've just found out?" he asked her.

"No idea. Please tell me."

"I feel so stupid for not knowing this before."

"What is it?"

"I just found out that Mr. Darcy, our new Special Assistant to the President, is a near blood relation to my boss and patron, Executive Vice President Catherine de Bourgh. It turns out that CDB's his aunt!"

"Yes. So I've heard."

"Apparently everyone knew this but me. I have to find him and pay my respects!"

At that moment, Elizabeth realized why she was finding this particular Idea Fair such a trial. It wasn't just her disappointment at Wickham's absence. She'd also been harboring a happy daydream of teaching Darcy a lesson. He was so smug that the universe cried out in Elizabeth's ears for him to be humbled and struck dumb - not by Elizabeth alone, but by the collective brilliance of everyone at Juniper Re, and especially everyone associated with the Pride Team. Instead, Elizabeth had been awkward in the Round Robin, and Mr. Lucas had been an embarrassment and singled out Jane and Bingley in a way that clearly didn't make a favorable impression on Darcy, and now Collins was going to make a scene.

"You don't need to pay your respects here and now. Ms. de Bourgh has been his aunt for many years and in all probability will continue to be his aunt for many years yet to come. This is a busy, crowded event. You should leave Mr. Darcy in peace today and pay your respects some time in the future."

"One of the things we all prize about you, Ms. Austen, is your forthrightness - even and perhaps especially with your superiors. Heaven help us if we all become a bunch of unthinking yes-men! That forthrightness is a quality that I support completely and try to model in my own example. While it hasn't been necessary yet for me to disagree with CDB, and it may even seem unlikely given her excellent history to date, I think of it like one of those airplane pep talks: in the unlikely event of a water landing, we must be ready! I look forward to the day when we can perhaps work together more closely, when I can provide you with some coaching on finding the right mix between the negative and the positive as you provide your thoughts to others. The key is balance! Anyway, because I'm such a strong believer in sharing warnings and misgivings up the chain of command, I don't want to ignore your advice as if it had no value. Instead, I want to explain to you why I won't be following your advice - which is that we're dealing here with a matter of personal and organizational protocol, something that clearly falls within my area of expertise. If you were to advise me, say, on the proper limit or deductible for a treaty, I'd be much more likely to heed your advice, but on a matter of Human Resources I believe it only makes sense that you should yield before my superior knowledge and experience. Excuse me!"

Mr. Collins left Elizabeth, crossed the room and presented himself to Mr. Darcy with a bow that wouldn't have been out of place directed to a particularly beloved figure of visiting royalty. Even across the room, she could hear the beginning of his speech: "On behalf of the

Human Resources Department and also - although perhaps not yet officially, yet still very much in spirit - on behalf of the Pride Team..."

At this point, Elizabeth felt she'd heard enough and made her way to the refreshment table, where she downed two plastic cups of cola without bothering to check for either sugar or caffeine. She dropped the cups into a wastebasket and returned to her former spot in time to meet Mr. Collins, who was clearly very pleased with himself.

"What did I tell you?" he asked. "Mission accomplished! Mr. Darcy couldn't have been nicer. He listened to me all the way through without interrupting, nodding several times when I made particularly important points, and capped it all off by thanking me for introducing myself. He thanked me! It's just what I would have expected from CDB's nephew."

Elizabeth chose at this point to retreat to the refreshment table. She was determined to hold onto a happy thought of Jane finding professional advancement, personal growth, and comfortable contentment working in the Claims Department. It seemed reasonable to expect that Mr. Bingley would challenge and empower her, although she had her doubts whether others in that department - say for example Ms. Liebling or Ms. Hurst or Mr. Thrush - would be so welcoming or helpful.

Approaching the table, she was distressed to hear Ms. Nebbit regaling Ms. Cullis at full volume regarding Jane and her certain and bright future in Claims, where she was bound to be an indispensable favorite of Mr. Bingley. And didn't his appreciation for Jane clearly demonstrate how valuable it was from time to time to bring into the organization a clear-eyed outsider or two? And wouldn't Jane's success in Claims create a clamor and quite possibly a bidding war across the organization for the remaining talented young Pride Team members? And yes - she'll be sorry to see them all go, but it's the duty of mentors such as herself to push their charges out into the world with little or no consideration of their own needs or feelings. And she certainly hoped and expected that the Surge Team members would have similarly bright futures, especially once the Pride Team members had all been spoken for.

Darcy was talking with someone else at the time, but wasn't more than four feet away from Ms. Nebbit at the time and could hardly avoid hearing every word. Elizabeth caught Ms. Nebbit's eye. With a meaningful look around the area, she said in a low voice, "I'm not sure this is the best time for this conversation."

"What?"

"Not Sure this is the Best Time for This Conversation."

"Not the best time? This is the Perfect Time to discuss well-earned career advancement of our young colleagues! What's the problem? Do we have some colleagues here whose protégées aren't faring so well? Will it hurt their feelings to see the success of others? What? Who? Mr. Darcy? Elizabeth, my dear, you of all people should know that offending Mr. Darcy would be a feature, not a bug!"

"Excuse me," came Mr. Bingley's voice through a sound system. "Sorry to interrupt the party, but I have one last item before we end this event."

The crowd quieted and people oriented themselves to face in his direction.

"I'm looking for one or two volunteers - brave souls - willing to come up now to the microphone and share with the group one thing that you learned during today's Idea Fair."

Gutsy Move, thought Elizabeth. *This will be embarrassing if nobody speaks up.* There was an awkward pause. She saw a stirring and Mary stepped forward.

"I'm Mary of the Pride Team. This isn't actually something I learned today, but it's something I've been thinking about. It seems to me that when we draw diagrams of reinsurance placements, everything is always a rectangle. If we have an excess layer it's a box this way and if we have a pro-rata layer it's a box that way, but either way it's a box. What if somebody wants to participate for the whole thing from top to bottom but more at the top and less at the bottom or maybe more at the bottom and less at the top? You could draw that with a triangle instead of a rectangle and you could write a formula to describe the area covered."

Elizabeth's eyes were fixed on her with most painful sensations, and she watched her progress through several minutes of what was evidently a presentation she hadn't been asked to make. It became clear that Mary took the quiet attentiveness of the group as signal to continue indefinitely.

Elizabeth saw that Ms. Thrush and Mr. Hurst were finding the scene extremely amusing. She looked around further and caught the eye of Mr. Bennet and gave him her most emphatic Significant Look. Surely there was some way he could intervene for the benefit of everyone - not least for Mary herself. Mr. Bennet returned to Elizabeth a reluctant Significant Look of his own, then moved and stood immediately to Mary's side. When she looked over at him, he took the opportunity to speak.

"One of the things I have learned today is that it's a dangerous thing to give our eager and creative Pride Team members an open mike."

Mr. Bennet winced through the long and loud laughter that ensued, worried that Mary would feel that his little joke had been designed to humiliate her. As things settled down, he said, "We'll see about having a session sometime on Mary's idea, but we'll let others have their say now."

Another awkward silence ensued until Mr. Collins stepped to the microphone.

"I just want to say that I believe these Idea Fairs are an excellent practice. It's too easy for all of us to think of learning as something that we do as children going to school or as young adults when we attend college or in my case when I went on to get a Master's in Business Administration - from quite a prestigious school actually. There are more prestigious schools that I suppose I could have gone to, but it would have been very easy to spend twice what I did on my advanced degree and today be no further ahead in my career than I am anyway. But back to learning. Learning should never end for any of us, however many degrees we may have. And these Idea Fairs are an excellent way to start. I hope you'll all join me in supporting them into the future, and let us now signal our approval of Idea Fairs with a hearty round of applause!"

Mr. Collins took a bow to the ensuing applause. Many stared and many smiled, but no one looked more amused than Mr. Bennet himself, while Ms. Nebbit commended Mr. Collins for having spoken so sensibly, and observed in a half-whisper to Ms. Cullis, that he was a remarkably clever, good kind of young man.

CHAPTER 19

Mr. Collins was not one to overthink things. His young career had been well served by his cheerful readiness to do the obvious. In this case, he had a position to fill and knew he would soon be leading the Pride Team - and who better to take on as his first direct report than the most eligible member of that team?

The morning after the Idea Fair at Netherfield, he began the process by addressing himself to Ms. Nebbit.

"A good morning to you, ma'am! I have a question of some delicacy and would appreciate your input on a discreet, off-the-record basis."

"Why, of course, Mr. Collins. As you well know, I'm as delicate and discreet as a dead judge."

"Indeed! And well put, too, if I may say so. A very striking image. Now then, Ms. Nebbit, as I believe I've alluded to you before, I'm empowered to make an offer of a position, and for that position I've been seriously considering one of the team members - to be specific, Elizabeth Austen. I know that you take a close interest in each of the team members, and I wouldn't want to proceed with any plan that contradicted or complicated yours or anyone else's plans or desires for her."

"Very kind of you to ask, Mr. Collins! I believe my plans and desires for Lizzy are exactly in line with your plans and desires for her. May I ask when she might expect to receive an offer from you?"

"Would now be a good time?"

"Now is always the best time, Mr. Collins! Come with me, please."

She headed down the hall and pulled open the door of Longbourn 2. The room was occupied by Mary, Kitty and Lydia, who all looked up from some contract language they were reviewing.

Ms. Nebbit clapped her hands. "Sorry!" she announced. "The room is needed immediately. Clear out!"

Mary appeared annoyed but neither Kitty nor Lydia betrayed any disappointment at the interruption. As soon as they were out of the room, she waved Mr. Collins in.

"Wait here!" she directed and headed back towards Elizabeth's desk.

"Yes?" said Elizabeth.

"Your future is waiting for you on a silver platter in Longbourn 2. Don't screw it up!"

Elizabeth rose, took a pencil and a pad of paper and walked immediately to Longbourn 2, where she was singularly disappointed to find Mr. Collins - someone she considered to be neither her future nor a silver platter.

"Elizabeth! Come in, please! If you don't mind, shut door the please. I have a private matter I'd like to discuss with you."

Elizabeth sat without closing the door. "My life is an open book, Mr. Collins. I see no need for closed doors."

"Quite admirable, I'm sure," he said, rising and closing the door himself, "but we in Human Resources find that privacy is essential to the very strategic work we're called upon to do for the organization."

Elizabeth took a deep breath and decided her best course of action was to hear him out and have the ordeal over as soon as possible. Mr. Collins returned to his seat and nodded wisely to her.

"I understand your reluctance, and it's quite commendable on your part. You understand that I mean to offer you a position and you - surprisingly smart and sensible for such a young woman - are keenly aware that the proper formalities for such an offer have not been observed. You haven't posted for the position and I haven't interviewed you or anyone else. I can fully understand why this would give you pause. Surely the Human Resources Department of all places should be managed according to the very highest standards! Well, you'll just have to trust me on this score. I do, after all, have just a little bit of experience with HR matters, and I think you'll find everything will be addressed in a satisfactory manner."

He smiled and leaned back.

"But first things first. Why do I need to fill a position at all? Isn't it enough just to keep doing the work that I do on behalf of CDB and the Human Resources Department? I might have thought so myself, but just last month she turned to me during one of her incomparable staff meetings and said, '*Collins!*' - that's how she addresses me, by name - '*Collins! You should have an assistant! You can't get anywhere if you have to do everything yourself!*' Well, of course, I thanked her at the time, but the best way to thank someone is to take her advice, and I immediately thought of the Pride Team. In fact, the Pride Team has never been very far from my thoughts since I found out I'll be taking responsibility for it once Mr. Bennet retires. Not that anyone's necessarily in a hurry for that to happen. And even if some people might possibly be eager for fresh leadership, still it's very important that Mr. Bennet's incumbency should be respected. And finally, I want to assure you that this position will not be some sort of indentured servitude. I'm looking for a full partner in the work that I do. Someone who-"

"Um.." said Elizabeth, holding up a finger.

"Let me finish, please! I'm looking for someone who may need to learn at first but someone who will have a voice and a say and a seat at the table. I'm looking for someone-"

"Um.."

"What is it?"

Elizabeth shrugged apologetically. "I'm sorry to interrupt. You paint a very nice picture. But I'm really not interested, thank you. And I have a project I'm supposed to finish this morning."

"Of course you're interested! No, don't get up! You're going to sit at this table and hear me out! Now then. Oh, I wish you hadn't interrupted me. Where were we?"

"Someone with a voice and a seat at the table?"

"Thank you, yes! I'm looking for someone who - once she learns the ropes and all - will be able to have her say when decisions are made. Someone who is listened to."

"Um.."

"Not now, please! A full partner in the important work of managing human resources here at Juniper Re. Someone who can ride my coattails, yes, but also someone who can make her own mark as a member of my team. Now, I know you have some quite admirable qualms about the circumstances of this offer, but I assure you that all the niceties will be observed in due course and the final arrangement will be signed off on by CDB herself, so there can be no ambiguity that everything will have been done according to all the HR best practices. I'm thinking this will be effective the first of next month."

Elizabeth waited a moment to be sure it was now her turn to speak. "You do me a great honor, Mr. Collins, and I wish I had a different answer I could give you, but as I indicated earlier, I don't believe the position you're describing lines up well with my interests and desires - and I especially don't believe that my skills and temperament line up well with your position. I wish you all the best and mean no disrespect, but believe the best thing for both of us is that you find a different and worthier candidate for the very important and exciting position you've just described to me."

"Still hung up on the niceties, I see. Well, it's understandable. We in HR do need to set a good example, you're right about that. I'll see that everything's taken care of 'according to Hoyle' as CDB likes to say. I think the expression has something to do with card games, but she uses it metaphorically, poetically."

"For someone who claims to be offering me a voice, you don't seem to be listening to me, Mr. Collins! My objection is not to the lack of a posting or an interview. My objection is that I am not a good fit for the position! It would be bad for me and I would be bad for it - no amount of HR procedure can overcome this simple fact!"

Mr. Collins smiled indulgently. "I hear your words well enough, but I feel free to ignore them when they don't line up with common sense. The reality is this: as a Pride Team member, you have, if I may speak bluntly, a limited shelf life. You're like a senior in college. Whether or not you have a plan, you're going to graduate. Coming back for another year isn't an option for you. In fact, the longer you wait, the less leverage you have. With all due respect to Mr. Bennet and Ms. Nebbit, they haven't exactly created an atmosphere where company managers are falling over one another to hire Pride Team members. So here I am with a very solid, reasonable, and professional offer to work at the right hand of a rising young force within the organization, someone who reports directly to and is on a name-basis with the Head of Human Resources herself, and when you say you aren't interested I can hear one of two things. Option One is that I can hear greed. There are some who routinely turn down offers they're interested in because they assume it's a negotiation, like buying a car, and that only a chump would take the first offer. I choose not to hear this from you because I think you have more sense than to take such a risk when the timing would not be favorable for it. Option Two is that you object to the informality of the current process, which might put you on the defensive later on. This would accord with your being a sensible person who takes a long view of things. So, you see, I do hear you better than you think. Now, I'm sorry we haven't been able to reach a conclusion here today, but my attitude about such things is that as long as we're talking then it's just a matter of working things out. I'll do what I can to get the procedural arrangements into a more traditional order and we'll see how things look to you then."

"I'm grateful for your interest and hope you know me well enough that I wouldn't make a fuss about process. This isn't about procedures and it's not about greed. I'm not speaking in code here. Can I speak plainer? This is about me not being able to work effectively for you."

"A perfectly reasonable cover story for the time being. I appreciate your sense of corporate propriety. You'll see the posting before the end of the day today."

To such perseverance in willful self-deception Elizabeth would make no reply, and immediately and in silence withdrew. She was determined, if he persisted in considering her repeated refusals as encouragement, to apply to Mr. Bennet, whose negative might be uttered in such a manner as to be decisive, and whose behavior at least could not be mistaken for punctilious corporate propriety.

CHAPTER 20

The moment Elizabeth left the conference room, Ms. Nebbit, who had thoughtfully remained at a convenient proximity, looked in on Mr. Collins.

"So? Is it all settled? When is Lizzy to start in her new position? Oh, I shall miss having her here as part of our team!"

"Yes, well I'm afraid I can't give you a date. I'd thought it might be the first of the month, but that seems unlikely at this point. Her official position is that she's declining the position."

"Declining the position?"

"As I say, that's her position. My guess is that she's being a stickler for the proper hiring procedures, which have not yet been fully observed. Perfectly reasonable on her part - in fact arguably admirable. I assume I'm reading her correctly, but you would know her better than I."

"Yes, I know her all too well. Not speaking what's really on her mind? Turning down something she really wants? Wanting to make a point about following company rules? I hate to say it, but that doesn't sound like Lizzy at all."

"So you think she might actually be turning down the position? Does she have something else lined up that we don't know about?"

"Oh, I'd know about it if she did. This is just Dizzy Lizzy not having the sense God gave the geese. Give us thirty minutes! Mr. Bennet and I will straighten her out."

"If she's prone to bad judgment, maybe she's not the best candidate."

"No! She has great judgment 99% of the time. This is just one of those one percents when I want to strangle her. She's young! It won't happen again! Thirty minutes!"

Ms. Nebbit hurried up the hall to Mr. Bennet's office. His door was shut but she entered without knocking. "Mr. Bennet! There's a crisis in the Pride Team! We need your help or Lizzy will lose a very valuable offer!"

Mr. Bennet pointed to his speakerphone, which was providing the audio of a conference call he'd been listening to. "Lucky thing this is muted."

"Luck has nothing to do with anything," said Ms. Nebbit, touching the button to disconnect the call.

Mr. Bennet sighed and turned to face her. "What is the position and why is Lizzy in danger of losing it?"

"The position is the chance to work as an assistant to Mr. Collins, and even though Mr. Collins has offered this position to her, Lizzy is in danger of losing it because she's foolishly turned it down."

"I see. So what do you propose? Should we force her to accept the position from Mr. Collins?"

"Exactly! I'm so glad you see what needs to be done here. If we let our girls turn down every good offer that comes their way, where will it all end?"

"A very cogent question, Ms. Nebbit. 'Where will it all end?' I ask myself this question with increasing frequency lately. Where is Lizzy?"

"I'll get her. Wait right there!"

Ms. Nebbit returned shortly with Elizabeth at her side. They entered Mr. Bennet's office and closed the door.

"Elizabeth," said Mr. Bennet, "I understand that Mr. Collins has offered you a position as an assistant reporting to him. Is that right?"

"Yes it is."

"And I further understand that you've refused him. Is that also correct?"

"Yes it is."

"And Ms. Nebbit - do I understand correctly that you insist that Elizabeth must accept this offer from Mr. Collins?"

"She must, yes, or I'll never speak to her again."

Mr. Bennet nodded his head sadly. "Elizabeth, you're faced with a very unhappy choice. Whatever you do, you're going to be estranged from someone who's an important part of your life here. Ms. Nebbit won't speak to you if you don't agree to work for Mr. Collins - and I won't speak to you if you do."

This pronouncement pleased and amused Elizabeth but not Ms. Nebbit. Elizabeth left quietly but Ms. Nebbit stood glaring at Mr. Bennet.

"What are you thinking? If Lizzy wants to jump off a cliff should we celebrate and root her on? Am I the only one left who cares what happens to these girls?"

"I think perhaps Elizabeth is able to care what happens to herself. And please knock next time. I don't always have my conference calls muted."

Ms. Nebbit exited the office, determined still to prevail over Mr. Bennet's late-career retreat to *laissez faire* lack of leadership and Elizabeth's youthful, short-sighted foolishness. Was Mr. Collins not good enough for her? Oh, this would just encourage the Ms. Cullises of the world who like to whisper that the Pride Team members are just so many prima donnas, too spoiled to cope with the rough and tumble of the real world.

Walking past Elizabeth's desk, she leaned behind her. "This isn't over! I'll get you to do the right thing if I have to do it for you!"

Mr. Collins remained seated in Longbourn 2, contemplating the surprising turn of events. Given that Ms. Nebbit didn't believe Elizabeth would decline the position on procedural grounds, and also didn't believe Elizabeth had another position lined up, what could possibly explain her apparent declination?

Eventually, one possible solution to the puzzle occurred to him. Perhaps Elizabeth was smitten with him? It would only be natural. He was still more young than not and not unattractive. No one could deny that he was well-spoken, and he was certainly successful. In fact, as he continued to work his way inexorably up the greasy pole of corporate management, he should probably expect to become the object of an increasing number of fond longings.

The more he thought about it, the more this possibility became a sort of Occam's Razor, explaining all in its path. Elizabeth could not work for him because she couldn't trust herself in such close confinement with him. And, of course, any actual romantic relationship between a boss and subordinate would be out of the question - most especially in the Human Resources Department itself! By declining the position, Elizabeth avoids the risk of a career-ending scandal for them both. She sacrifices her own career prospects, but presumably hopes to keep alive her chances to have a different sort of relationship with him. And it goes without saying that she can't admit why she declines the position. Even for as forthright a young woman as Elizabeth, it would be too much to say she can't take the job because of her smoldering, unrequited love for him. Better just to give no reason at all. Or a reason that's open to interpretation: *'I can't work effectively for you.'*

Ms. Nebbit found a coterie of young employees lingering perhaps a little too casually near the doorway to Longbourn 2. Jane, Lydia and Kitty were there, as was Charlotte. She could see in their eyes that they knew at the least the broad outlines of what was taking place.

"Nothing to see here! Lydia and Catherine - I know you have a project to finish with Mary." Jane and Kitty wandered off, but Lydia and Charlotte stayed to see how the matter would end. Ms. Nebbit entered the conference room and took a seat. "Well, then - Mr. Collins."

"I think," replied he, "that we shouldn't belabor this potentially awkward matter. I, for one, am quite willing to forget the whole thing. If there's any fault on my side - and I believe it's important to be open to the possibility, however remote, that one has made a mistake - the fault would possibly be one of allowing sentiment to cloud what should be a rational and data-driven process. I'd been thinking that some continuity with the current members might be a welcome gesture for the Pride Team, but it seems clearer now that, as is so often the case, the best way to re-energize a working group is to bring in a fresh perspective from the outside."

CHAPTER 21

The next few days passed awkwardly. Ms. Nebbit complained with some regularity that job offers for the remaining team members would be especially difficult to secure given 'the recent situation'. While Elizabeth wished that Mr. Collins would simply return to HR, he persisted in attending Pride Team meetings, where he sat stiffly and avoided looking at or speaking to Elizabeth. Outside of such meetings, he made a point of chatting up the Surge Team members and spent a fair amount of time lecturing Charlotte on the finer points of succession management. Elizabeth was grateful for her friend's patience and politeness with Mr. Collins.

Elizabeth accompanied Kitty and Lydia on their next visit to the RMO, where they saw Mr. Wickham. Elizabeth gave him what she hoped was some friendly chiding.

"We missed you at the Idea Fair! You told me quite specifically that you wouldn't let Darcy's presence scare you off."

"Yes, and I'm afraid now you see exactly how reliable I am. Because I could have been there. I had a client meeting, yes, but I could have rescheduled it. And I'll admit as well that my reason was none other than Darcy. So if you want to say that he scared me off, then perhaps you're justified. I can only say in my own defense that I was less afraid of what Darcy might say or do to me than what a scene of some kind between us might do to the tone of the event. I would have hated for the baggage that Darcy and I bring from our former life to interfere with the training and career advancement of our future leaders - such as yourself."

"Ah! So it is your virtue that kept you away?"

"I'm sure that seems unlikely to you, but it's at least a possibility. I try to keep my virtue on a short leash, but I believe sometimes it does get the better of me."

When Elizabeth returned to her desk later, she was concerned to see Jane looking quite unsettled. She approached and asked her what was up.

Jane undocked her laptop and suggested they see if one of the conference rooms was free. So Elizabeth found herself once again in Longbourn 2.

"I got an email today from Caroline Liebling giving me a heads up. There's going to be an announcement tomorrow. Bingley's making a nationwide tour of Claims Department offices and staff."

"Makes sense to me," said Elizabeth. "He's in charge now and probably hasn't met a lot of the people yet or seen where and how they work."

"He's going to be out of the office for three months. And he's taking a working group with him."

"Seems like overkill to me, but all right. Let me guess. Ms. Liebling? Ms. Thrush? Maybe Mr. Hurst?"

"Yes to all three, plus Anne Burgoyne."

"Who's Anne Burgoyne?"

"Exactly! Anne Burgoyne is a trainee in Human Resources. Word is that CDB takes a special interest in her, maybe has been grooming her for grander things."

"There's no job announcement, right? Anne Burgoyne is going on this trip as a member of HR. It's probably a good training opportunity for her."

"Sure. And it would have been a good training opportunity for me, too, but I'm just reading about it now. Lizzy - everyone's been saying I'm a sure thing for a position in Claims, but I don't see it happening. I see Bingley leaving town for three months, and I see a working group with a built-in Jane replacement."

"Hold on! Hold on! Deep cleansing breath! The headline here isn't *'Bingley to Jane: Drop Dead!'*. The headline is *'Bingley Touring Claims Offices'*. It's not a bad idea. So he didn't get you hired before his trip? That's too bad. It would have been a great training trip for you. But it doesn't mean your opportunity is gone forever. You know he isn't going to be living on the road for three months. He'll be back in town from time to time. He'll be sneaking into the office to get some work done. He'll need someone who can keep him up to date on what's happening in the Home Office."

"Maybe."

"I've seen Bingley with you. He's very comfortable with you. He trusts you. And he could hardly have missed Ms. Nebbit announcing to the world that you're already as good as hired by him. If he had no intention of bringing you on, I'm sure he would have said something."

"Yes, you'd think so. But you have to admit that my position isn't very strong. Even if Bingley wants me in the department, it's not clear how many others do. What company connections do I have? They've been very nice to me, but I expect they'll be even nicer to a CDB protégée. Let me read you a little from this email:

> 'While, of course, we'll be sorry not to see you for so long, one of the things I'm most looking forward to is getting to know Anne Burgoyne better. What an impressive young woman she is! I believe she'd make a wonderful addition to the Claims Department - and I'll be very surprised if our Mr. Bingley doesn't decide the same thing before this trip is over!'"

"It's my observation that Ms. Liebling is obsessed with Mr. Darcy, and so any favorite of CDB is practically a member of the royal family to her. Bingley's the decision-maker. And I'm convinced he's in your camp. You know, Jane, it's possible that Ms. Liebling is the problem here. For all her seeming friendliness, she may not approve of you. Why that would be - don't ask me. Maybe she just looks down on the Pride Team. She's certainly never been very friendly with me. So maybe she's steering things to keep you out of this trip and insert somebody else. I think that's entirely possible. But at the end of the day, I don't think it matters. Bingley's the boss. His opinion is going to carry the day."

"I don't believe Caroline Liebling is deliberately stabbing me in the back. I just don't believe it. Maybe there's some kind of misunderstanding."

"I love how you refuse to think badly of anyone! I hope you're right - by all means, let's call it a misunderstanding!"

"For one thing, if I do end up in Claims, I'd hate to think that all my co-workers were out to get me."

"That would be awkward, yes. But I expect that when you do end up in Claims - and you will end up in Claims - that anyone who wasn't your supporter before will come around. Once you're a member of a team, you're a member of the team."

"Oh, I don't know what to think! If it turns out that I've missed my chance with Claims, then what's my fallback? Nobody's even been looking at me because supposedly I was already spoken for. When word gets out that I'm not going to Claims, it'll look like I've been dumped! People will wonder what's the matter with me. I'll be damaged goods."

"Easy now! Deep breath! You haven't been dumped, you've just been left hanging for a while. It happens. My advice - as if I knew anything about having a career myself - is to start now living into the future that you want. If you had a start date in Claims, what would you be doing now? How much of that could you be doing now anyway? Assume the best and live into it."

"Oh. That sounds like pretty good advice, actually."

"Of course it is! Call me pushy, but it might not be a bad plan with your Stefan, either. I'm just saying."

"Can we focus on one issue at a time, please?"

"Right. The point is that the world doesn't owe us a living. Juniper Re doesn't owe us a living. We have to earn it, and we earn it by adding value."

"That's what we do."

"And if that doesn't work, then we think about kidnapping Bingley's dog."

"That's terrible! I'm sticking with the adding-value plan. I'll spend some time each day thinking about what I can do to be useful to Bingley and Claims. And I'm going to send a reply to Caroline Liebling that's exactly what I'd write to her if I'd just been hired by Bingley. I'll be warm and appreciative, and I'll be excited about the working group's trip and Anne Burgoyne and ready to do whatever I can to be helpful."

"Good! And you should probably let Ms. Nebbit know about the trip. She's bound to worry about it, but she'll worry less if she hears about it from you."

Ms. Nebbit did, in fact, take the news in stride when she heard it from Jane.

"Oh, that's too bad, my dear! It could slow things down a bit for you. And it would have been a nice launch for you if you'd been hired already! But it can't be helped. We'll just have to make sure to keep up a steady flow of contacts. I'm sure Mr. Bingley will be around from time to during over the next three months. I'll make sure we invite him to some of our team meetings. Maybe it's time for me to bake some of my cookies."

CHAPTER 22

Elizabeth found a quiet moment to express her thanks to Charlotte. "You've been so kind and patient with Mr. Collins this week. I'm sure it's used a lot of your time, but I'm very grateful. As you know, this was an awkward week for me with him, and I'm more obliged to you than I can express."

"It's not a problem, believe me."

What Charlotte didn't share was that she was perfectly happy to have the time with Mr. Collins because she had a profound interest in the position that Elizabeth had declined. While Charlotte wasn't blind to the challenges that would be involved in working for Mr. Collins, she saw no future for herself in her current position and was prepared to overlook a great deal for the opportunity to have a fresh start. She was prepared, in a word, to settle.

Charlotte assumed that this would be more than a short-term project, as it seemed unlikely to her that Mr. Collins would be prepared to make a second offer while he was presumably still smarting from the rejection of the first. However, she underestimated his resilience and his bias for action - particularly action suggested to him by Executive Vice President Catherine de Bourgh. She suspected as much when she received an invitation for a one-on-one meeting with him in Meryton 1 with the topic 'Career Planning'. It seemed unlikely to her that all of the Longbourn meeting rooms were booked, but it would be logical for him - if he was prepared to extend a job offer once again - to do so inconspicuously and out of the sight of both the Pride Team and the Surge Team.

Charlotte arrived at the appointed hour and was not disappointed. In as short a time as Mr. Collins's long speeches would allow, everything was settled between them to the satisfaction of both. He asked when she was prepared to start and she replied that, as far as her own wishes were concerned, she could start that moment, but that he should consult with Ms. Cullis. She added that, as a courtesy, it might also be wise to consult with the department head, Mr. Lucas. She further added that she would like him to hold off any public announcement for at least a few days, so that she would have the opportunity to tell her friends and co-workers. She was particularly thinking of Elizabeth, whose friendship she was very eager to hold onto through this awkward matter.

Mr. Collins was delighted with the prospect of discussing Charlotte's future with Ms. Cullis and Mr. Lucas. He was less enthusiastic about holding off on the announcement, but was sufficiently pleased overall that he didn't mind granting Charlotte her wish.

When he spoke with them later, Ms. Cullis and Mr. Lucas were both pleased to hear about Charlotte's new position and willing to release her from her current duties within a matter of a few weeks. Ms. Cullis in particular was moved by the additional satisfaction of a trifecta of triumph over Ms. Nebbit: a plum position was offered to a Surge Team member; the position did not go to a Pride Team member; and the position would ultimately - depending on when Mr. Bennet decided to retire - be helping to oversee the Pride Team itself.

Mr. Collins, having promised to hold off on the announcement, simply let Mr. Bennet and Ms. Nebbit know that he was concluding his co-location with the Pride Team and would be returning to his former office to focus on his HR duties. Mr. Bennet struggled to find the appropriately polite words to express his sadness that the visitation was ending, but Ms. Nebbit supplied what she could.

"Come back any time! You're one of the team around here now, Mr. Collins."

"Thank you, yes. I expect to be back in this area quite a bit in the weeks to come."

"Don't neglect your HR duties on our account," suggested Mr. Bennet, helpfully. "We wouldn't want you to lose favor with Ms. de Bourgh."

"Oh, no indeed! You're most kind to keep that idea fixed in my mind. However, I am fortunate to have a patroness who is herself the dictionary definition of generous fair-mindedness. When the time comes, I think you'll see that I have every reason to believe she'll be supportive of my future visits."

"Well," said Ms. Nebbit, "we're glad to hear it. Maybe you'll get a chance to spend a little more time with Mary! She's remarkably clever, that one!"

"Yes. Quite remarkable indeed, I'm sure. It has been quite an honor and a privilege to become better acquainted with all the Pride Team members - a most impressive and accomplished assembly! Please pass on to each and every one of them my most grateful and heartfelt thanks. And let me be clear that there is no reason on my account to exclude Elizabeth from that statement."

And Mr. Collins was off and things returned to what passed for normal with the Pride Team. The time had now come for Charlotte to muster up the courage to tell everything to Elizabeth. She expected Elizabeth to disapprove. After all, if Elizabeth thought working for Mr. Collins was a good plan, she would have done it herself. Elizabeth had enjoyed sharing amusement with Charlotte regarding Mr. Collins's various quirks and foibles - and Charlotte was well aware of the fact that, for someone seeking mirth in such things, Mr. Collins provided a target-rich environment.

Charlotte didn't doubt or second-guess her decision. She was, however, worried that Elizabeth's reaction to it might cause a rift between them. As she was preparing to leave her team and her department, she was very eager to retain her most valued friendship within the organization.

The next morning, Charlotte looked in on Elizabeth and suggested they take a quick walk together. The weather was too cold to walk outside, so they proceeded to the cafeteria where they secured for themselves two mugs of coffee and a quiet corner.

"There's going to be an announcement pretty soon," said Charlotte, "and I wanted you to hear it from me first. I'm going to have a new position."

"Congratulations! What is it?"

"I'm going to be Senior Manager in Human Resources, reporting to William Collins."

"Ha! No, really. You have a new position?"

"Yes."

Something in the tone of the word 'Yes' gave Elizabeth the sudden realization that Charlotte wasn't kidding and was probably already offended.

Charlotte continued: "Is it so impossible to believe that I might be interested in a position that wasn't right for you?"

"Of course not! I'm so sorry for mistaking you. It wasn't what I was expecting to hear, and I stupidly assumed you were making a joke."

"I can understand why it would be a surprise. It's been very sudden, as you can imagine."

"Let me try again. Congratulations, Charlotte! So this is the New Charlotte you've been telling me about - ready to take charge and make things happen!"

"Exactly, yes. Obviously not the same things that you would choose for yourself."

"That has no significance now. You're quite right to point out that something can be right for one person without being right for somebody else. I'm sure you see that in Underwriting all the time. You decline to participate on a program and some other company you respect takes a big line on it. It doesn't necessarily mean that they're wrong or that you're wrong. It may simply be that their situation is different from yours."

"Thank you, yes! And in this case, I believe my situation was quite different from yours. My career - if you can even call it that - has been frozen in time. I think I've broken the all-time record for length of time in the department without being promoted to manager. I actually had to re-order my business cards. Who in the history of the world has ever had to order a second set of business cards with the same title? I figure if I'm not going to be appreciated for my underwriting skills, then I've got to stop being a one-trick pony. I've got to branch out."

"Yes! A two-trick pony doesn't sound a lot better, actually, but I expect you're right - people do value versatility."

"Anyway, when someone comes along and offers me a way out of this logjam and into a fresh situation with new challenges, I'm not going to be too picky about who's making the offer. Not that I'm saying anything against Mr. Collins. I'm grateful for the chance he's giving me, and I'm determined not to disrespect him. I know you and I have enjoyed sharing some laughs at his expense in the past, but that's going to have to end now. I hope we can find many other things to laugh about."

"I'll drink to that!" said Elizabeth, clinking her coffee mug against Charlotte's.

But afterwards, Elizabeth found herself troubled by the prospect of Charlotte working for Mr. Collins. It was bad enough for a sensible person and a foolish person to be yoked together as partners, but all the worse when the foolish one was the boss. And yet that seemed so often to be the pattern. Sensible bosses don't have to hire foolish assistants but sensible people may be constrained by their circumstances to serve as assistants to foolish bosses. Would Charlotte come to regret her decision? Elizabeth hoped not but suspected that she would.

CHAPTER 23

Elizabeth was sitting in the next Pride Team meeting wondering if she was authorized to mention Charlotte's news when there was a knock on the door and Ms. Cullis entered.

"Sorry to interrupt your staff meeting! I have some news to share. This won't take a minute."

Mr. Bennet welcomed Ms. Cullis in. She took a seat and looked happily around.

"I know how close you all are, the Pride Team with our Surge Team - practically sharing quarters and all. I didn't want you to hear our latest news second-hand. This has to do with Charlotte. She'll be leaving the Surge Team at the end of the month as she takes up her new duties as Assistant Manager of Human Resources, reporting to Mr. Collins."

After a pause, Ms. Nebbit spoke up. "Thanks for sharing this report, Dorothy, but I'm not sure we can give it much credence. We've been quite fortunate to have extremely close connections with Mr. Collins over the past weeks and, while I can confirm that he does, in fact, have a position to fill, it's not at all clear to me that your Charlotte is even a serious candidate to fill it."

"He wants Lizzy!" Lydia added with a smirk.

Ms. Cullis appeared unfazed. "I'm not here to have an argument," she said. "You can believe what you like. I've spoken with Mr. Collins and I've seen the draft announcement and I can tell you that - unless he's playing an elaborate practical joke on us - Charlotte will, in fact, be in her new position in a matter of a few weeks."

"Ms. Cullis is right," said Elizabeth. "I've talked with Charlotte about this. Mr. Collins has offered the job to her and she's accepted. And let me just say that I'm very happy for Charlotte. She's ready for a new challenge. Thank you, Ms. Cullis, for your courtesy in bringing this news to us, and let me say that we here at the Pride Team congratulate Mr. Collins on securing a wonderful addition to his department, and we wish Charlotte every success in her new position."

"Yes!" added Jane. "We'll miss having Charlotte near us, but she's definitely earned whatever success is coming her way."

Ms. Cullis nodded her appreciation of the kind words and excused herself. There was a quiet moment and then Ms. Nebbit began shouting.

"How is this possible? Our only job here - Our Only Job - is to get you girls hired to real, proper positions before your time runs out. And what happens? You get job offers and you turn them down! Not only that - that would be bad enough, but not only that - you conspire to deflect job offers to your friends outside our team! Oh - how sharper than a den of serpents is the ingratitude of you prima donna Pride Team members! Lizzy first and foremost, but not just Lizzy! I've got my eyes on the rest of you as well! Who's next? Maybe Jane's going to turn down that job in Claims and ask Mr. Bingley to offer it to that nice Jeremy on the Surge Team instead! If Lydia ever manages to get a job offer, she'll trade it to some Ken-doll of an RMO marketer for a night on the town! Look folks - if we can't all stand together, we're doomed to sit alone!"

Possibly concerned that she hadn't adequately expressed her feelings on the subject, Ms. Nebbit stood, upsetting her chair, and stormed out of the conference room, shutting the door behind her with as much emphasis as the door would allow. The team members all looked at Mr. Bennet.

"I want to apologize for a comment I made a few months ago, when I said that you were the five most empty-headed employees in the entire organization. In retrospect, that was an unfair statement on my part. Clearly, Charlotte is more empty-headed than at least one of you if she thinks working for Mr. Collins is going to make her life better in any way. Also, while I may not agree with Ms. Nebbit on this or many other things, I never doubt the strength of her support for you all, and I suggest that each of you provide whatever comfort to her that you can during the days to come."

Jane confessed herself a little surprised at the combination of Charlotte with Mr. Collins, but she said less of her astonishment than of her earnest desire for their mutual success - nor could Elizabeth persuade her to consider it as improbable. Kitty and Lydia were far from envying Charlotte, for they had no interest in Human Resources. It affected them only as a piece of news to spread at the RMO.

In the weeks that followed, Ms. Cullis made a point of looking in regularly on Ms. Nebbit and keeping her informed of all the finer points of Charlotte's transition. Yes, she would miss Charlotte terribly, but it was also a great comfort to know that she would be so close, and certainly it was gratifying to watch the flowering career of a worthy young person one has helped to mentor.

Ms. Nebbit fully understood that the purpose of these visits was to gloat over her, but she put her best face on and bore it as with as much patience as she could manage. She saw herself as playing a long game, and continued to hope for the possibility that the tide would turn in her favor. In her calculation, it was necessary to bear the indignity of the moment in order to keep open the possibility of her own future gloating.

Elizabeth and Charlotte weren't in close communication with one another through this time. Neither was sure where she stood with the other, and their interactions were too tentative and formal to allow for sharing of confidences. Elizabeth was focused on Jane's prospects, and was becoming concerned, as Jane had been making a good effort to be helpful and communicative with Bingley and the working group accompanying him on the trip, but she'd heard nothing from any of them. Jane was determined to maintain a positive attitude. She told herself that they were all very busy and that she was bound to hear soon from Mr. Bingley and Ms. Liebling and the others.

Elizabeth's underwriting training led her to assume that the safest assumption to make about the future was that it would be a continuation of the past. No email from Bingley in weeks one and two strongly suggested to her that there would be no email in week three.

Formerly, Elizabeth's thoughts had been caught up with the question of whether or not Bingley was snubbing Jane. Now her thoughts turned to the question of why. Had they misread his interest and intentions? Did he find out some unpleasant secret about her? Had Ms. Liebling or others in the department blackballed her somehow -

and, if so, why didn't Bingley have the will and the means to hire the person he wanted in spite of them? It was an unhappy puzzle.

Mr. Collins was seen from time to time during these weeks visiting with Charlotte. This in itself was annoying to Ms. Nebbit, but what she found particularly insensitive and galling is that both of them seemed quite cheerful. Ms. Nebbit complained about it to Mr. Bennet.

"I saw them just now! Whispering their secrets back and forth. They're talking about the Pride Team, I know they are - they're plotting the total ruination of the Pride Team!"

"Or they might be working out her schedule and new duties. But you're probably right, Ms. Nebbit. You usually are. Chances are they're plotting the total ruination of the Pride Team."

"I wouldn't have minded so much if it was just a question of some brazen nobody stealing a job offer that should have gone to one of our girls. I could have accepted that as calmly as a woolly llama! But the thought that they'll take over the unit the day you retire - I don't know how I'm going to live with it!"

"You need to think more positively. For all you know, you may never have to face this existential crisis. With a little bit of luck, maybe before I retire you'll be downsized to make way for some redundancy succession!"

This was not very consoling to Ms. Nebbit, who chose to ignore it and continue as before.

"Why should this all be settled ahead of time, and why should I be the odd man out? It's like I'm invisible to the organization!"

"Oh, I doubt that very much. I think you are seen very well. In fact, I believe that, within this organization, you're impossible to miss."

"Kind of you to say so, but it leaves a puzzle. If people in power here know me and know my connection to the Pride Team, why would they freeze me out of the plans for its future?"

"That is a puzzle indeed, Ms. Nebbit. A puzzle on which we should all contemplate as seriously as we can."

CHAPTER 24

When Jane did finally hear from Ms. Liebling, she wasn't encouraged or consoled. The working group would, in fact, continue to be absent from the home office for a full three months. Thanks for her kind offers, but none of them needed any assistance from Jane while they were away. Mr. Bingley had asked her to forward his apologies and best wishes.

Jane looked at the message and had to acknowledge that she wasn't going to be hired by Claims. The expectation that had seemed so reasonable and widespread just a month earlier was now, for whatever reason, shown to be unfounded.

The point was further driven home by an extended description of the many excellent qualities of Anne Burgoyne, and what a favorable impression those qualities had made on Mr. Bingley, and Ms. Liebling's expectation that Ms. Burgoyne was likely soon to become a member of their department.

Elizabeth, when Jane forwarded her the email, was torn between concern for Jane and resentment against all others. Mr. Bingley? A jerk for leading Jane on. Ms. Liebling? A two-face who pretended to be Jane's friend while stabbing her in the back. Mr. Hurst and Ms. Thrush? Toadies and losers. Mr. Darcy? A certifiable psychopath who was behind it all somehow. Anne Burgoyne? Probably a horrible person. Ms. Nebbit? Her boorish interfering must have turned the tide against Jane. Mr. Bennet? His passive manner was no help at all. Elizabeth herself? She held out false hope when Jane should have been facing the facts. All guilty!

Elizabeth had a day to cool off before she had the opportunity for a private conversation with Jane. This was shortly after a staff meeting during which Ms. Nebbit had complained about Mr. Bingley's long absence. "How is he ever going to get Jane hired if he's never here?"

she demanded irritably. Jane said nothing, but Elizabeth could see that she was pained by the topic - and by Ms. Nebbit's continuing and oblivious assumption that Jane was already as good as hired by Claims.

"Why does she talk that way?" Jane asked Elizabeth. "That's not what I need now. I need to just forget about Bingley and Claims and figure out what's next for me."

Elizabeth looked at Jane with incredulous solicitude.

"Don't give me that look!" cried Jane. "It's not like I'm in love with Bingley. Remember? He was just my Platonic work-crush. But I'm still his partisan! Even as I forget about ever working for him, I intend to remain loyal to him. I don't blame him at all. He never promised me anything. There's no sense in blaming anyone else. I'm responsible for what happens to me. I got a little carried away and have learned a valuable lesson."

"My dear Jane," exclaimed Elizabeth, "you're too good! You belong in a church or an ashram or a hospital or a charity or anywhere but a big, heartless financial organization full of people who are blind to any human value or emotion that can't be tracked on a spreadsheet! I want to argue with you, you know. I don't believe this situation is your fault at all - and I'm quite prepared to call down merciless divine judgment on a whole laundry list of blameworthy people! But I wouldn't want you to agree with me. I wouldn't want you to become someone as cynical, suspicious, and judgmental as I am. But, at a minimum, you must grant me this: If you're determined to overlook all faults and see only the best in everyone around you, then you must view yourself through that same friendly lens. You have been ill-used, Jane - whether through anyone's deliberate malice or just through unfortunate happenstance - you have been ill-used, and it's never right to blame the victim. *Oh, your house got robbed? Shame on you. You must not have locked it up securely enough.* No! If your house got robbed, shame on the thief!"

"Thank you. I love your fighting spirit, Lizzy."

"If you won't gossip with me about the horrible people who sabotaged your hopes for a career in Claims, maybe you'll at least gossip with me about our friend, Charlotte, and her decision to align herself with that ridiculous Mr. Collins. Surely there's no other way to view this than as a terrible, terrible decision on her part."

"I disagree. There are any number of ways to view her decision. You know Charlotte as well or even better than I do. She's not a stupid person. She needed to make a change, and she decided her best option for the next step of her career was to work with Mr. Collins."

"But surely it's a bad decision either way. If you show up at work with one red shoe and one blue shoe - does it matter if you got dressed in the dark and made a mistake or if you made a conscious decision not to have matching shoes? Either way, it's a mistake and you look ridiculous. In fact, it's probably a bigger and more embarrassing mistake if it was deliberate."

"I think you should give Charlotte the benefit of the doubt. I say hold off drawing any judgment until you see how things work out for her in HR."

"Done. I'll temporarily hold off drawing any definitive judgment on Charlotte. I'm afraid, though, that it's too late for me to promise anything of the sort as respects Mr. Collins. And really - I'm not built to be endlessly tolerant and forgiving. You've got to leave me a few bad apples to ridicule."

"You can ridicule anybody you please - although, of course, I don't want to hear a word against anyone for whom I am a partisan - which would include you and Mr. Bennet and also, as I think I mentioned earlier, continues to include Mr. Bingley."

"You're taking away all my best material! And really, at the risk of crossing one or more of your red lines, I think the most perplexing question of the whole business with you and Bingley is what happened on his side. Because it was crystal clear to me that he was ready to hire you. We can blame Ms. Nebbit for being indiscreet about it and for holding onto the idea after it became less and less plausible, but her original observation was absolutely correct: Bingley wanted to hire you - and had at least one position open and is a senior officer to boot. Why didn't it happen? Was he playing at something or did he have second thoughts or was he steered away from you somehow or was he thwarted? And if he was steered or thwarted, who did it? Who was driving the bus that you got thrown under?"

"So this is your conspiracy theory, right? And in your mind who are the suspects? Ms. Liebling? Mr. Darcy?"

"Yes."

"But they're friends with Bingley. They like Bingley. They want him to be happy and successful. If Bingley wanted to hire me, why wouldn't they just support him?"

"Because there's something weird going on between them. I don't think Ms. Liebling even wants to be in Claims. She wants to work for Darcy. She's so crazy to work for Darcy that she hates me because she sees me as a threat. Hah! I'd rather work with Attila the Hun than F. William Darcy! Anyway, I think the whole Anne Burgoyne business is an around-the-horn attempt to curry favor with Darcy. She's a protégée of CDB, who is Darcy's aunt. Now, I agree that this is all a bit convoluted and maybe even a little paranoid, so maybe I don't have the details all worked out, but I'm not convinced that any of those people are really focused on Bingley's best interests."

"You're very clever, Elizabeth," said Jane, "and your support means more to me than I can say. But I must tell you that your conspiracy theories aren't helpful for me. I'd rather think Bingley simply decided to go in a different direction. Then there's no need to fuss over it or hate anyone. The bottom line is that I need to move on, so that's what I need to focus on right now."

Elizabeth could not oppose such a wish, and from this time Mr. Bingley's name was scarcely mentioned between them.

Ms. Nebbit continued to ask how Mr. Bingley would be able to hire Jane if he was continually absent. Elizabeth finally managed to convince her of what was clear by that time to everyone else, that Mr. Bingley wasn't planning to hire Jane. When Ms. Nebbit asked why not, Elizabeth told her it was because his absence had caused him to lose focus and interest in her, but she apparently wasn't able to deliver the reasoning with sufficient force and conviction as she found herself needing to repeat it to Ms. Nebbit day after day.

Mr. Bennet treated the matter differently. "So Lizzy," he said one day, "Jane has had a setback. Close but no cigar. Bridesmaid and not the bride."

"Yes. So it seems."

"Setbacks aren't all bad, you know. You can't get everything on the first try. What's the challenge in that? You need to pick up a few stories along the way. Someday, when you and Jane are heading your own companies, you'll have to speak to the Rotary Club or

Junior Achievement and you'll need some stories of setbacks and disappointments, just to make the rest of us mortals feel OK about ourselves."

"Yes, of course. Like a juggler dropping a ball every now and then just so people can appreciate how hard it all is."

"So Lizzy - when is your turn to come? We can't have Jane be the only one around being snubbed. I'm thinking that Wickham fellow in the RMO might be just the ticket. He seems very smooth. I'll bet he could dangle a plum position as gracefully as your juggler then disappear into thin air like a magician. Who could be angry at him? We'd all have to applaud."

"It need not be such a performance. I'll content myself with a plain, old-fashioned snubbing from some pedestrian functionary who was just about to bring me on as deputy assistant dogcatcher until he noticed that I write the number seven with a little line across its middle and that's the end of that!"

As it happened, Mr. Wickham did become a regular visitor to the area and patron of the Pride Team's services. His account of Mr. Darcy's character and actions became widely known and confirmed the general dislike of Mr. Darcy among pretty much everyone in the area other than Jane - who continued to believe that there must be a misunderstanding or extenuating circumstances that, when fully known and understood, would ultimately show Darcy to be a fundamentally good human being.

CHAPTER 25

The unassigned office one down from Mr. Bennet's office, which had been used on a temporary basis by Mr. Collins, was normally available to employees of the company who didn't work in the home office but were visiting there. It was known informally to the Pride Team members as Ms. Gardiner's office. Ms. Gardiner was a good friend of the team who regularly visited the home office and always arranged to work out of that office when she was there. At least four times per year she would settle into that office for a week or more, and her presence was appreciated by them all.

Ms. Gardiner's official title was Vice President of Strategic Relationships, but she was more often referred to as Ambassador to DES. Juniper Re, like any reinsurer, expended considerable efforts to track accumulation of property loss potential and model the likely impact of various catastrophic events, such as windstorms, floods, and earthquakes. There are a handful of companies that specialize in helping insurers and reinsurers build and operate such models, and the one that Juniper Re primarily contracted with for such services was known by the initials DES. Ms. Gardiner managed the relationship between Juniper Re and DES. In that role, she worked primarily in Chicago, where DES was headquartered.

Ms. Gardiner had few of the normal markers of status within the organization. She had no staff or direct reports. She wasn't responsible for any revenue. She was all but invisible to most of her fellow employees. But Ms. Gardiner was very well respected by the senior management of both Juniper Re and DES, and this gave her an earned status that can be very powerful in its own way. Some of this may have been due to the importance of DES to Juniper Re, but much of it was doubtless due to Ms. Gardiner herself. She was smart without being pedantic, refined without being stuffy, and managed to be simultaneously briskly efficient and warmly personal. The team members, especially Jane and Elizabeth, were devoted to Ms. Gardiner and grateful for her example as a woman of substance within the organization whom they could imagine wanting to emulate. They were also in awe of her stylish accessories, which seemed each day to include a new and artfully tied scarf.

Ms. Nebbit viewed Ms. Gardiner as a fellow role model - her sister in aspirational femininity - and therefore the perfect person with whom to commiserate over the sorry state of current affairs.

"It's been a very bad spell for the team, I don't mind telling you! It looked like we had two of the girls all set, but it didn't work out for either one of them. Jane maybe lacked the spunk needed to close the deal with Claims, but mostly I don't blame her. I think something fishy was going on there, I do! But Lizzy! It was in her hand! She could be working at a nice, respectable job over in HR right this minute today if she just had the sense to keep her mouth shut for two minutes! So what do we get instead? We get Ms. Cullis lording it over all of us that her little Charlotte not only got the job that should have gone to Lizzy, but also stands to help take over the whole team when the time comes. I tell you, my dear, between our own team members stabbing me in the back and our neighbors in the area circling like vultures, you're a welcome, happy sight today!"

Ms. Gardiner, who already knew as much or more about these matters than Ms. Nebbit, nodded her condolences and did what she could to steer the conversation towards more cheerful subjects. Later, she had a private word with Elizabeth. "It's too bad about Jane," she said. "It seems like it would have been a good fit for her in Claims, and I hear good things about Bingley. Still, these things happen. People change their mind. And who knows if there was ever an intention in the first place? You and I both know that there are some people around here whose minds jump too quickly from a good meeting or round robin session to an assumption that there's going to be a job offer."

"This wasn't just Ms. Nebbit imagining things," said Elizabeth. "It looked very real to me. I believe Mr. Bingley was set upon hiring Jane and someone - maybe one of his staff members, I'm not sure - managed to talk him out of it."

"But how could you tell? You say it looked very real to you. What does that even mean?"

"I never saw a more promising inclination. They were like an old married couple. Any question that came up, he needed to ask her. Any idea he had, he needed to test out on her. He didn't know what to do if she wasn't available. Isn't that usually a pretty good sign that someone should be your subordinate - that you're helpless without them?"

"Yes, I'm afraid that does sound rather serious. No wonder everyone had their hopes up. Poor Jane! She puts her whole heart into things. Forgive me for saying this, but it would have been better if this had happened to you. A little ironic detachment can go a long way toward keeping your sanity in a business environment. But let me ask you this: what if I commission Jane to work on a project for a week or two back in Chicago with me? Do you think a temporary change of scene might be good for her?"

Elizabeth thought this was a very good idea and expected that Jane would jump at the chance.

"I know," said Ms. Gardiner, "that Mr. Bingley and his associates will be passing through Chicago during that time, but it shouldn't be a problem because they'll be at the field office and we'll be across town at DES. There's very little chance they'd bump into one another, unless he made a point to come over and see her. And I'm thinking that, if that were the case, it might not be so bad."

"Yes, well don't get anyone's hopes up, because it seems clear to me that it's not going to happen."

And yet there was something in Elizabeth that did think it likely that Bingley still wanted Jane in Claims - and that whatever was currently thwarting this impulse might eventually yield to his wishes in the matter.

Jane readily accepted Ms. Gardiner's invitation and began planning for the trip. She claimed to have no expectation of seeing Mr. Bingley while she was there, but said she did hope it might be possible to arrange a quick get-together with Ms. Liebling.

Over the week of her residency with them, Ms. Gardiner had the opportunity to watch the team members interact with various friends and colleagues. She paid particular attention when Mr. Wickham looked in on Elizabeth, as she'd heard that he might be a dark horse candidate to provide her with the next step in her career. She could understand why Elizabeth might feel an affinity for him, but she concluded that he had nothing useful to offer her future. She made a note to have a serious talk with Elizabeth about him before her visit to the home office was completed.

One thing that Ms. Gardiner did appreciate about Mr. Wickham was his knowledge of Cornwallis Re and its people. She had begun her career at Cornwallis and enjoyed hearing about former co-workers, most of whom she hadn't thought of in years. She continued to hold Mr. Paternoster - who was president of the company when she was there - in the very highest regard, and Ms. Gardiner and Mr. Wickham were able to entertain one another with their stories about him.

Ms. Gardiner was sorry to hear about Mr. Wickham's poor treatment by Mr. Darcy. She didn't have any clear recollection of Darcy from her time at Cornwallis, but managed to recall the nickname "Frozen Chosen One" being used to refer to a favored young executive who was distinctly lacking in Mr. Pasternoster's charm and charisma.

CHAPTER 26

Ms. Gardiner's caution to Elizabeth was punctually and kindly given on the first favorable opportunity of speaking to her alone. After honestly telling her what she thought, she thus went on:

"You're too sensible, Lizzy, to do the opposite of whatever I tell you to, just out of spite - and therefore I'm not afraid of speaking openly. Watch your step with that Mr. Wickham!"

"Watch my step?"

"An interesting young man. Let him tell you stories every now and again, but don't even think about working for him."

"I see. Anything else?"

"It's a bit academic at this point, but you shouldn't think about hiring him, either."

"And why is it," asked Elizabeth, "that I should avoid any professional association with Mr. Wickham?"

"When we agree to work with someone or have them work for us, we associate ourselves with more than one person. It's like a merger. You might think it's one worker or one boss, but you're really becoming part of someone else's network. In an organization, you want to be connected to as many people as possible, particularly useful people, people who are clever or powerful or well-respected. One of the challenges for you and the other team members is that your connections within the company are very limited. You don't want to get hired by someone who also has limited connections. Together you'll be an island of obscurity."

"I see. Well, I'll take care of myself and of Mr. Wickham, too. He won't hire me if I can do anything to prevent it."

"I don't think you're taking this seriously."

"Oh? I mean to be serious. I understand what you're saying. But it's hard to make blanket statements about the future, isn't it? I mean, what if he gets promoted? What if he offers me a really good job with a fabulous salary? At some point, I imagine, even you would say that I should take the offer."

"I don't want to get caught up in hypotheticals. My point is - as someone who takes a strong personal interest in your career - that your time and attention are a limited and valuable commodity. There are much better candidates for you to focus on than Mr. George Wickham. I don't believe he's Boss Material for you, and yet he seems to be hanging around here quite a lot."

"Maybe, but I'm not sure this a typical week. Among other things, I think he's enjoyed sharing Cornwallis stories with you. But I take your point. I also have a strong personal interest in my career and will endeavor in all things to follow your good advice."

"Well then," said Ms. Gardiner, "my advice is to think of your career as getting across a stream and the different job possibilities are rocks sticking up out of the water. You need to think a couple of steps ahead. You might be tempted to step out onto a nice, flat rock, but does it get you closer to another rock that will get you closer to another rock that will enable you to get to the other side? It's possible to have a career like mine, where you do the same thing for twenty years, but I don't recommend it. My peers who switch positions every five years or so have done better than I have. So plan ahead. Your next step in the company is very important, but it's only one step."

The day came when Charlotte was to leave their floor and take up her new post in Human Resources. Before leaving, she came around to say her goodbyes to the Pride Team members.

By this time, Ms. Nebbit had become resigned to the fact that Charlotte was indeed taking the position that should rightly have been Elizabeth's. She didn't raise her voice at Charlotte or even make a point of reminding them all how Charlotte was callously betraying her friends and colleagues. Ms. Nebbit even managed to say that she hoped Charlotte might be happy in her new situation, although a keen-eared listener could possibly have detected in the statement an undercurrent of reproach – for surely, if Charlotte had any remaining shred of human decency, she would be as miserable as possible in the job she had stolen.

Elizabeth, wishing to provide a friendlier send-off for her friend, offered to accompany Charlotte on her short walk back to her soon-to-be-vacated desk. As they headed off, Charlotte said:

"I shall depend on hearing from you very often, Lizzy."

"That you certainly shall."

"And I have another favor to ask you. We must work on a project together."

"I'd be delighted. But will you be able to spare the time from your new duties?"

"No, I want you to come work on an HR project with me. Here's my thought: give me a month or two to get my bearings and then I'll arrange to have you work with me on a spring-cleaning kind of organizational project. I've been making lists already. There's a lot we could do. The systems we use to keep track of the accounts the company writes are much better than the systems we use to keep track of the people. Say that you're in and it will give me something very happy to look forward to."

Elizabeth couldn't refuse, although she anticipated little pleasure from the exercise.

As Charlotte settled into her new position, she communicated regularly with Elizabeth, but never to complain about her situation or to poke fun at Mr. Collins. Her texts and emails were friendly and informative and could have been published verbatim on the front page of the New York Times without causing the least embarrassment to Charlotte or her new colleagues. Elizabeth, as she had promised, communicated just as regularly back to Charlotte with her own news of the day and the latest happenings within the Pride Team. She did this faithfully but without the easy companionability of their earlier friendship. She felt the need to be somewhat guarded regarding her views of certain individuals, and she wasn't convinced that Charlotte was being entirely forthcoming regarding the challenges and disappointments that she was almost certainly having to deal with in her new environment. This left Elizabeth to conclude that she would have to judge the situation for herself when she joined Charlotte for her project in HR.

Elizabeth was also feeling the need to read between the lines as she heard news from Jane, who was now on assignment with Ms. Gardiner in Chicago. Jane, like Charlotte, was apt to put the best possible face on whatever information she had to share.

In this case, her news was that she'd tried to contact Ms. Liebling to arrange a get-together, since the Claims group was also in Chicago. She heard nothing back and finally concluded that some issue of travel logistics was preventing Ms. Liebling from receiving her messages.

This was followed by a message in which Jane recounted being in the neighborhood of the Juniper Chicago office and stopping in unannounced. She found Ms. Liebling in a conference room. "I didn't think she was in spirits," were Jane's words, "but she was very glad to see me, and reproached me for giving her no notice of my coming to Chicago. I was right, therefore, that she hadn't gotten my earlier messages. I asked about Mr. Bingley, of course. He was well, but so constantly on the phone with Mr. Darcy that he was scarcely a participant in the meetings with the field office staff. I'd also been hoping to meet Anne Burgoyne, but she wasn't available, either. I did get to see Ms. Thrush. My visit wasn't long, as Ms. Liebling and Ms. Thrush were going out. Now that they know I'm in town, I expect to see them again soon."

Elizabeth read this message as a general confirmation of her suspicion that Ms. Liebling had taken on the role of human firewall, preventing any contact between Jane and Mr. Bingley.

At the end of the week, she received another message from Jane.

"Lizzy - I'm sure you'll be much too nice to say You Told Me So more than five or six times. I finally have to admit that you were right about Ms. Liebling. I'm still convinced that at some previous point she was genuinely my friend and supporter, but clearly for whatever reason she is no longer either one. After our brief meeting at the field office, I waited for her promised visit day after day, hearing nothing from her, until finally on my last day out here she stopped by. She made no apology or explanation for her silence or delay, she sat with me for a few minutes as glumly as if she were visiting the dentist, then took her leave without saying anything about wanting ever to get together again. She is so changed in her attitude towards me that I'll be happiest if I never have to see her again. I have no idea what brought this change. I assume she thinks she's protecting Bingley from something, and I suppose I should give her credit for that. I do believe she tries to act out of duty and loyalty to him and to the Claims Department. What threat I possibly pose to him or the department is an interesting mystery, but one that I should probably stop trying to work out. At the end of the day, the reason hardly matters. If Bingley was going to hire me, he would have done it by now. If he wanted to meet with me, he could easily have done it himself. So that business about me being destined for Claims is all over as far as I'm concerned. I thought I was being pretty clear about that, although Ms. Liebling kept making a point about how Anne Burgoyne is sure to be hired into the department. I wasn't looking for a job in Claims at this point. I just wanted to stay in touch with the people I've come to know there - partly as a way to maintain contacts across the organization, but also because I've enjoyed those people and thought of them as friends as well as colleagues. You saw it coming before I did. I should have listened better to your good advice. I just assumed that when someone is friendly and welcoming to me that it's genuine. I just assumed that they're on my side somehow. You'd think that working in Underwriting at a reinsurance company I'd be more careful about what I assume."

A quick note here to explain that last comment: when an insurer passes risk to a reinsurer, they are said to "cede" the risk and reinsurer is said to "assume" the risk.

"I'll be back in the office on Monday. Ms. Liebling said she didn't know when they'd all be back in the Home Office, and I'm not sure I care at this point. I hope your project for HR provides you with a much happier outing than I've just had. My advice is to tune out Mr. Collins and have a good time with Charlotte."

This message gave Elizabeth some pain, but her spirits returned as she considered that Jane would no longer be duped, at least by Ms. Liebling. Jane and everyone around her could stop focusing on Claims as her next step. Mr. Bingley, meanwhile, had sunk in her estimation from a figure of hope and inspiration to one she simply preferred not to think of. There were various ways to explain his warm and then cold and finally non-existent interactions with Jane, but none of the possible explanations reflected well on him. Elizabeth decided her hope was that he would hire Anne Burgoyne and then find out that she was a disaster and end up wondering how he ever let Jane get away.

Soon after this, Ms. Gardiner followed up to ask Elizabeth about Mr. Wickham. She was able to report to Ms. Gardiner that he seemed to have a new favorite - a Ms. King - who might not have Elizabeth's business savvy or quick wit, but who did have better connections in the company by virtue of being recently engaged to a rising young vice president. Elizabeth also reported that she wasn't put out by this, and even thought it showed good judgment on the part of Mr. Wickham. Her conclusion from this was that she must never have had a genuine passion for working in the RMO and that everything had worked out for the best.

For surely if she had really wanted to work in the field for Mr. Wickham, she would have pushed herself forward shamelessly and seen Ms. King as a rival to be outshined and a foe to be bested. She could tell that Kitty and Lydia wished to take exactly this view on Elizabeth's behalf, and would have been fully prepared to further her cause by skewering a Ms. King voodoo doll.

Elizabeth herself, however, bore no animus towards anyone in the matter. However interesting a companion he might be, Mr. Wickham, didn't owe her a job, and she didn't actually want one from him anyway.

CHAPTER 27

The Human Resources Department was located in Building One, a venerable structure known as the Old Building - just as Building Two was known as the Main Building. For her project with Charlotte, Elizabeth would be relocating for a few weeks to a temporary office in the Old Building, near Charlotte's new quarters and not far from the Rosings conference room.

It wasn't a long walk from the Main Building to the Old Building, but quartering there meant being out of daily contact with her colleagues on the Pride Team, and Mr. Bennet was sorry to see Elizabeth go. "Stay in touch!" he ordered her. "Send me an email every day with an update. If I have any questions, I'll reply."

Mr. Wickham came by to wish her well. "I'll be very interested to hear your opinion of HR in general and Ms. de Bourgh in particular," he said. "I don't know why, but it's very important to me that you and I have the same opinion about everything, so when you come back please try to have the right opinions, if you can."

"Consider it done! I'll have exactly the right opinions on everything - and if there's any discrepancy between your opinion and mine, you shall have no one but yourself to blame."

Elizabeth enjoyed the playfulness of Mr. Wickham and felt a small pang of envy for Ms. King, whom she anticipated would soon be working in a Wickham-suffused atmosphere.

Ms. Gardiner had arrived in town for a brief Home Office visit. The day before Elizabeth was scheduled to move herself over to the Old Building, she looked in on Ms. Gardiner in her usual temporary office near Longbourn.

They spoke first of Jane, and Ms. Gardiner confirmed what Elizabeth had thought - that Jane had clearly harbored hopes of maintaining her friendships in Claims and possibly reviving her chances of a career in the employ of Bingley, but repeated snubs and disappointments had finally convinced her to set aside all such hope and focus elsewhere. It wasn't a conclusion she'd come to quickly or easily, but she was certainly now convinced. Ms. Gardiner said that she didn't think Jane had yet figured out where her next step should be, but she had no remaining doubt that it was necessary for her to move on.

"Speaking of moving on, I must compliment you on your ability to take the long view regarding Mr. Wickham. But my dear Elizabeth, what sort of person is this Ms. King? I should be sorry to think your Mr. Wickham is simply a favor-currying mercenary."

"We're all mercenaries when it comes to hiring or getting hired. What was your advice to me? Don't pursue Wickham as a boss because neither one of us had sufficient connections in the company. We wouldn't be a winning combination. Fine. So now he's interested in someone who's become well connected in the company and you want to say that's not right, either. He's being mercenary."

"I repeat my question. What sort of person is Ms. King? What's her background? Does she bring anything to the table other than a well-placed fiancé?"

"She's fine. I don't really know her, but she seems to have a good head on her shoulders."

"It just seems too sudden. I presume he never noticed her when she was just another assistant in Quality Assurance - but, as soon as it gets out that she's going to marry a vice president in Legal, he's chatting her up to be his inside sales support."

"There was no good reason for him to notice her before. If he wanted a support person with no useful company connections, he could have just asked me."

"And I hope you would have turned him down - but that's not the point here. The point is that it seems uncomfortably transactional. If he could at least pretend to be interested in more than just her connections, it would show a little human consideration."

"If he offers her a job, it's a business proposition. It's a contract. When you're talking about consideration in the context of a business contract, you're talking about payment."

"So in business there's no room for human consideration?"

"I hope there's plenty of room for us all to get together as pleasantly as possible. But not everyone has the time or the leeway to pursue their goals with polite indirectness. I don't think Ms. King took any offense at Wickham's sudden interest."

"But maybe she should have. She wouldn't be the first woman who decided not to take offense at something that was, in fact, offensive."

"Well," cried Elizabeth, "have it as you choose. She shall be foolish and he shall be mercenary."

"No, Lizzy, that is what I do not choose. I'd be sorry to think ill of them – especially Mr. Wickham as he's your friend and my former colleague at Cornwallis."

"Not me! I've had it with all the men of Cornwallis! The mercenary is the best of the lot. We also have the self-righteous snob and the disappearing two-face. From a distance, you'd think they were model executives, endlessly clever and with all kinds of fine qualities. But look closer and it's all disappointment. Lucky for me, I'm going tomorrow where I'll find a man who hasn't one agreeable quality. The best way to avoid disappointment is to hang out with people for whom you have no regard."

"Take care, Lizzy. You need a few more years and a lot more setbacks for you to earn such bitterness."

Before they separated, Elizabeth had the unexpected happiness of an invitation to accompany Ms. Gardiner to a conference in the city a few months out.

"The conference itself shouldn't be very demanding," said Ms. Gardiner, "so there should be good opportunities to see the sights and take in some cultural events."

No scheme could have been more agreeable to Elizabeth, and her acceptance of the invitation was most ready and grateful. "This will be wonderful!" she cried. "Something civilized to look forward to! You've given me fresh life and hope. *Adieu* to disappointment and resentment. Who cares about company politics when there's art and urban sophistication to be enjoyed? I'll start making a list of everything I want to see and do. And when the time comes, I'll keep notes on every point. If I can take detailed minutes for meetings of the Commercial Lines Limits Stacking Task Group, I can certainly keep good records of the fun and worthwhile things of life."

CHAPTER 28

It was perhaps a ten minute walk for Elizabeth from her desk on the front side of the Main Building second floor to the back corner of the Old Building first floor, where she was to find Charlotte's new quarters. She could have taken the elevator down, but preferred the aerobic virtues of the stairwell, despite the fact that she was toting a purse and two bags - one with her computer and the other full of personal and office supplies. She exited through the lobby and past the main reception desk.

Well, she thought, *if I run out of time to find a high-powered position guiding the company's strategy into the future, maybe this can be my fallback position. I could sit behind the counter and welcome visitors to Juniper Re.* On further reflection, however, she doubted she'd be able to muster a sufficiently welcoming attitude prior to noon.

She passed through inner doors then outer doors then out into the early spring sunshine that promised more than it was able to deliver. The property was referred to as a campus and it did have a collegiate look - well-kept buildings surrounded by lawns that featured a simple web of walkways and the occasional tree. She took the pavered walkway to her right, which followed a long arc around the Main Building before bending back to the left and terminating at Building One, the stately Old Building.

Building One was the original Juniper Re Home Office, and over the years its interior had been remodeled with an eye to preserving the colonial-style architectural details that were included when the building was erected in the 1920s. Elizabeth wondered if she would need a new wardrobe to fit the setting. Maybe a bonnet.

She followed the signs to the Rosings conference room and, circling the hallway around it, easily found the office of Mr. William Collins - which appeared to be protected by an entranceway that featured a desk at which sat Charlotte, who saw her immediately and rose to give her a hug and take one of her bags.

On hearing their greetings to one another, Mr. Collins emerged from his office, shook Elizabeth's hand with a deferential bow and said, "Welcome to the Patronage!"

He explained that "the Patronage" was his expression for the suite consisting of his office and her antechamber – named in recognition of the patron who had granted them such an attractive workplace. In general, CDB was known to be a strong proponent of collaboration-encouraging open office environments, but clearly she was willing to make an exception for members of her own staff.

Mr. Collins offered to provide a tour. Elizabeth set down her remaining load and followed him down the hallway, thinking he was going to show her Rosings. Instead, he led her back outside and around the perimeter of the Old Building, pointing out details both subtle and obvious. He was eager to provide her with a close look at the genuinely old stone wall along the back perimeter of the property, but Elizabeth had to plead that her shoes weren't up to the task of carrying her comfortably across the intervening expanse of wet grass.

Back inside, he explained the history, design and construction of the Old Building, through all of which narration the figure of Ms. de Bourgh loomed nearly as large as the building itself. Her vision, leadership, and patronage were apparently responsible for every aspect of the building in its current remodeled form, from its divided-pane windows to its colonial waste-paper baskets. Mr. Collins led Elizabeth through most of the interior space - not including Rosings, which was in use, and the CDB office, which clearly wasn't a place to be entered into uninvited.

The tour ended back at the Patronage - first with a careful appreciation of the outer office where Charlotte presided, and then of the inner office, where Mr. Collins had the benefit of just the sort of pleasant view and ornamental ceiling details that would enable him to think the deepest possible thoughts. The suite had clearly been designed in an era when the outer office would be staffed by a secretary to the person in the inner office, but Charlotte didn't appear bothered by the arrangement.

Elizabeth wondered if the point of the tour had been to impress upon her the extremely valuable nature of the opportunity that she'd rejected, or if Mr. Collins was simply so office-proud that he would have given the tour with the same enthusiasm to a group of schoolchildren on a field trip. If he meant to cause Elizabeth regret at her decision, he didn't succeed. She was as much put off as ever by his showy formality and his tendency to expound on one consistent theme.

"This is excellent timing on your part, as CDB is in residence all this week and possibly longer. She travels extensively, of course, so her being here is not something one can take for granted. I have some hope that she may favor us with an invitation during your stay and that you'll be able to see for yourself what a truly remarkable woman and executive she is. I expect you'll find it quite inspiring."

Charlotte added, "She does a very credible job of looking after all of us on the HR staff."

"Very true, Charlotte - that's exactly what I say. She's the sort of woman whom one cannot regard with too much deference. Now then, Elizabeth, I'm sorry to leave so soon, but I have a task group meeting on travel expense guidelines that starts on the hour in the Main Building."

"He's on quite a lot of task groups," added Charlotte. "Very much in demand."

"It's of some consolation to me knowing that I leave you in Charlotte's very capable hands." With that, Mr. Collins bowed, gathered up his folders and departed.

Almost immediately, an air of peaceful calm settled over the area. Elizabeth didn't doubt that Charlotte encouraged Mr. Collins to serve on as many task groups as possible. Still, as she had the opportunity to focus on her without distraction, she saw that her friend and colleague wasn't someone to be pitied or worried over. She seemed reasonably happy. While Elizabeth was certain that Charlotte's new situation didn't meet her every hope and expectation, it apparently met enough of them to constitute a satisfying improvement.

Elizabeth resolved to stop worrying about Charlotte, who clearly could take care of herself. She also resolved to be less judgmental of her friends and colleagues who - unable to find the perfect boss, job, home or life partner - adjust their standards and settle for the attainable. Previously, she'd seen this as a lack of will and a betrayal of principle. Now she found herself able to better appreciate the value of a strategic retreat, the occasional necessity to settle a borderline case or negotiate a dubious claim - particularly if it could be accomplished with Charlotte's grace and good nature.

The two friends and colleagues spent the next hours in companionable teamwork, working out a detailed plan for their project. Charlotte's original plan had been to update and standardize the census data on the company's staff. Elizabeth, she knew, had a gift for sifting through piles of information to find anomalies, trends and storylines. However, it was quickly made clear to her that Elizabeth, not being a member of the HR Department, couldn't be allowed to see such sensitive information as the names, birthdays, and home addresses of her fellow employees. Her fallback plan was to do a review of the company's mandatory ethics training materials. HR administered these materials, but several departments had been involved in developing them and there had been mixed feedback about them.

Elizabeth had been offered a cubicle desk not far away, but she found it easier and more pleasant to set up her laptop on the far side of Charlotte's desk - which was where she was sitting the next day - watching a video drama about "Dan" who inadvertently abets a reinsurance fraud scheme - when Mr. Collins bolted out of his office with a quick, "Look sharp! Three o'clock!" to Charlotte. She followed him to the edge of the hallway and they both looked to the right. Elizabeth was confused, as Charlotte quite reliably looked sharper than Mr. Collins and the time was nowhere near three o'clock.

Soon they were engaged in a serious conversation with two women, one middle-aged and the other young but lacking the energy and cheerfulness generally associated with youth. At one point in the conversation, Elizabeth was pointed towards, but no one called her over, so she stayed working where she was. She had expected from the stir that one of the passers-by would have been Ms. de Bourgh, but she didn't recognize either one of them.

Eventually, good-byes were said, the two women continued down the corridor and Charlotte and Mr. Collins walked back to Elizabeth.

"That was Ms. Jenkinson and Anne Burgoyne," said Charlotte. "Ms. Jenkinson is a sort of lieutenant to Ms. de Bourgh, and Ms.

Burgoyne, who reports to Ms. Jenkinson, is a great favorite of Ms. de Bourgh."

"Yes, I've heard of her," said Elizabeth. She paused to take some satisfaction in observing that the young woman in line to take what should have been Jane's place in Claims appeared to be humorless, low-energy, and self-involved - just the sort of protégée one would choose at this point for the fickle and feckless Mr. Bingley. Although the fact that she was apparently now back in residence in the Home Office, while Bingley and Ms. Liebling and the others continued their national Claims tour, made Elizabeth wonder if Ms. Burgoyne was, in fact, going to be hired into the Claims Department.

"Good news," added Mr. Collins. "They've let us know that we're all invited to join them at noon in Rosings for *Lunch With A Purpose* with CDB herself."

CHAPTER 29

It was Ms. de Bourgh's regular practice to gather an eclectic group of company employees - usually about half HR and half non-HR - for a light lunch and a similarly light discussion on topics of interest to herself. This was known as *Lunch With A Purpose*. Invitations to such lunches were thoughtfully extended with very little advance notice so that the informality of the event would be clearly understood and no one need feel in any way awkward if they had a previous commitment that was more important than lunch with head of Human Resources. For today's lunch, they were given to understand that the other guests would include Mr. Lucas, Head of Underwriting, and Maria, an underwriter from the Surge Team. It was possible that Maria was chosen because she worked not far from Elizabeth and was a former co-worker of Charlotte, but it could also have been that she was simply someone who was available on short notice.

Mr. Collins's triumph, in consequence of this invitation, was complete. It validated his standing in the department, and it provided the opportunity for Elizabeth and others to see first-hand just how impressive CDB was and how kind she could be to him.

"I'm so pleased you'll have this opportunity," he said to Elizabeth. "Don't worry about the way you're dressed today. These lunches are really very informal - and there's no helping it now, anyway."

Elizabeth hadn't been at all concerned about her outfit, which she considered significantly above average for business purposes. She was, however, determined not to let him put her in a bad mood. She had wanted to see Rosings and speak with Ms. de Bourgh, so she was happy for the opportunity. She wasn't going to lose sight of her good fortune due to a few patronizing comments - nor would she be put off by her dislike of the event's name. It was her considered opinion that a good, ordinary lunch already had quite a sufficient purpose.

Mr. Collins insisted that they leave the Patronage no later than 11:45, figuring that fifteen minutes was a safe amount of time to allow for the thirty second walk to Rosings. Not wanting to arrive too early, they then stood in the hallway outside the door to Rosings for a full ten minutes, at the end of which they saw Mr. Lucas and Maria approaching. Maria looked like she was being marched to her death, and Mr. Lucas seemed a bit uneasy himself. Elizabeth attributed this to Ms. de Bourgh's reputation as an intimidating presence, but she wasn't yet convinced that the reputation was rationally justified. She was determined to remain calm and shield her eyes only if truly dazzled.

Mr. Collins led the way in, followed by Charlotte and Mr. Lucas, with Elizabeth and Maria behind. They passed through an entrance alcove featuring an oil portrait of Mr. Rosings. Mr. Collins described in rapturous terms both the painting and Mr. Rosings, who was president of the company in the 1930s.

Beyond the alcove was a large room with a high ceiling, white wooden paneling, and polished brass lighting sconces. The room contained a large, square table of dark wood, surrounded by leather chairs, with enough space left to allow room for credenzas and upholstered side chairs along two walls. Elizabeth decided it looked to her like a high-stakes gaming room in a low-key, colonial-themed casino. Ms. Burgoyne, Ms. Jenkinson, and Ms. de Bourgh were seated at the table as the line of guests entered, and Ms. de Bourgh with great condescension rose to greet them.

Mr. Collins had arranged that Charlotte should make the introductions, which she did with a polite crispness that saved a good deal of time compared with the oration that Mr. Collins would likely have provided.

Mr. Lucas presumably needed no introduction to CDB, and yet seemed uneasy in the setting and silently nodded his greeting. Maria was apparently terrified of destroying her career by saying or doing the wrong thing in such powerful company, and so she said and did nothing at all. Elizabeth was quite equal to the scene and calmly observed her hosts.

Ms. de Bourgh was a large woman with strongly-marked features - the fact that she was striking to look at was somehow a matter of her

147

own will rather than any inherent virtue of her appearance. Elizabeth wanted to like her. After all, here before her was a woman to be reckoned with - probably, in an earlier time, one of the first in the company's history - and even now still very much in the minority as a female senior officer. Still, she didn't warm to her. Elizabeth's ideal of female empowerment was more along the lines of a firecracker, a feisty upsetter of apple carts. Ms. de Bourgh was something entirely different. Forceful and powerful, yes, but not a change agent. Wickham had described her as a throwback, a respectable pillar of convention, and Elizabeth decided immediately that his description had been quite apt. She thought she might even detect a little family resemblance between Ms. de Bourgh and that other throwback pillar of humbug rectitude, Mr. Darcy.

Next to Ms. de Bourgh sat Anne Burgoyne. Elizabeth had expected she would be a younger version of her mentor and patron, but instead Ms. Burgoyne was a study in quiet self-effacement, like a pet content simply to be in her master's presence. Meanwhile, Ms. Jenkinson was absorbed in attempting to discern and attend to Ms. Burgoyne's unspoken needs and desires. Was she warm enough? Was the light in her eyes? How about a glass of water?

The lunch was attractive to look at and unobtrusively delivered by two adjunct members of the cafeteria staff who seemed to have learned exactly how the great woman wanted her lunches served. As each course was presented, Mr. Collins provided a running commentary of appreciation for the incomparable excellence of the food and the amazing taste and refinement of their host and the honor - to himself and to his fellow guests - of being included in such a fine assembly. Mr. Lucas quietly seconded many of these sentiments. Elizabeth wondered if Ms. de Bourgh would be put off by the flattery, but it quickly became clear to her that her hostess was perfectly content to receive as much admiration as people were willing to offer up to her.

Elizabeth was ready and even eager to have a share in the conversation, but found no opening. She was seated between Charlotte and Anne Burgoyne - and Charlotte was silently focused on Ms. de Bourgh, while Anne Burgoyne appeared absorbed in her own thoughts. Ms. Jenkinson was chiefly employed in watching how little Ms. Burgoyne ate, pressing her to try some other dish, and fearing she was indisposed. Maria thought speaking out of the question, and the men did nothing but eat and admire.

So there was little to be done but to hear Ms. de Bourgh talk, which she did without any intermission until coffee came in - delivering her opinion on every subject in so decisive a manner as proved that she was not used to have her judgment controverted. She inquired into Charlotte's daily schedule and gave her a great deal of advice as to time management, told her how everything ought to be regulated in her areas of responsibility, and instructed her as to the file names best used for documents and spreadsheets. Elizabeth found that nothing was beneath this great woman's attention so long as it could furnish her with an occasion of dictating to others.

In the intervals of her discourse with Charlotte, she addressed a variety of questions to Maria and Elizabeth, but especially to the latter, of whose connections she knew the least. She asked her, at different times, how many others were on the Pride Team, whether the others had been with the company for a longer or shorter time than she had, whether any of them were likely to be hired to permanent jobs soon, whether they were smart, where they had been educated, and whether Mr. Bennet did their performance appraisals individually or together in a group. Elizabeth felt all the impertinence of her questions, but answered them very composedly. Ms. de Bourgh then observed,

"Mr. Bennet is a lame duck, is he not? It has been established that on his retirement the oversight of the team will fall to Mr. Collins here." She turned to Charlotte with a smile. "I'm glad of it for your sake, but in general I think it's poor policy to decide such things ahead of time. Best to keep one's options open! Do you ever do any training presentations, Ms. Austen?"

"I worked on the requirements for the facultative account reservation system and did some training demonstrations for the rollout."

"The AV equipment in this room is truly superior. Next time you come to one of these lunches bring your laptop and we'll have you run your demonstration for us. What professional designations have you earned?"

"None so far."

"No professional designations at all? You're not a CPCU or a CRM or a CFA?"

"No, I'm not."

"Perhaps you have a graduate degree. An MBA maybe or a PHD?"

"No."

"Have you completed any actuarial exams?"

"No."

"A license maybe? Do you have a broker's license? A claims adjuster license? Perhaps a National Board license to inspect pressure vessels?"

"No."

"How singular! And what of the other Pride Team members? Are they similarly uncredentialed?"

"For the most part. One has a broker's license and two have passed the first CPCU exam."

"Well, I expect Collins will be taking a look at the unit's recruiting standards when he takes the reins. In the meanwhile, it's not clear to me how you expect to get hired beyond the Pride Team. That is the point, is it not?"

"Yes it is. I believe the plan was to try to make up for our lack of credentials with an abundance of skill and hard work."

"Yes, well I suppose something like that will have to be your story. The problem is that everyone can claim skill and hard work, but a credential is a fact. You either have it or you don't. That's very reassuring for the person doing the hiring. Those of us in HR learn what goes on in people's minds when they're hiring. Do you know what they're thinking about? They're thinking about the risk to their reputation. What if they hire you and you turn out to be a bust? What then? If you have good credentials, that will help shield them from second-guessing."

"But isn't that the wrong way to be thinking when you hire someone? Wouldn't it be better to be focused on success rather than failure?"

"Yes, well I don't think you're in a position to tell people what they should be thinking about when they hire anyone. When you're in a position to make a hire of your own, you can be as high-minded as you please. Have you used MENTOR?"

Her reference here was to a program created by HR, an online career planning resource - the rarely-used full name of which was *Making*

150

an Excellent New Tomorrow Of Reinsurance. 'Best to just call it MENTOR,' Elizabeth had thought when she saw the full name in an announcement. In particular, she was bothered by the "Of" - which shouldn't have been capitalized and, in the absence of the need for catchy abbreviations, would probably have been "for". Elizabeth had spent ten minutes with the tool before renaming it *Checklists of the Obvious* and returning to her work.

"Yes," she said. "Yes, I have."

"We've been getting many, many compliments on it. I got the nicest email recently from McAllister in Actuarial. Called it the best tool of its kind he'd ever seen. Wasn't sure how his staff had lived without it. You know, historically, we just assumed people could do career planning on their own. But how can they do it without a tool?"

"Incorrectly?"

"*Ineffectually* is the word I'd use. It's less moralistic. People don't like it if they think you're judging them, so you should try to stop it right now. What were we discussing?"

"MENTOR."

"Yes, of course. So now I'm curious. How did you answer the question about where you see yourself in five years?"

Elizabeth paused - partly because she found the question intrusive and partly because she hadn't actually filled out any of the answers and didn't want to risk perjuring herself any further than she already had.

"I'm afraid I'd rather not share my answer to that question."

Ms. de Bourgh seemed quite astonished at not receiving a direct answer. Elizabeth wondered if she were the first person who'd ever dared to challenge the great woman's dignified nosiness.

"There's no need to be coy about these things. The first step towards achieving your goals is to say them out loud."

"Yes, but it's egotistical to aim too high and pathetic to aim too low. Let's just say that my five-year plan culminates somewhere in the range between being unemployed and having the organization renamed in my honor."

At this point, they were served a colorful dessert of cherries in a sauce, and Ms. de Bourgh allowed the searchlight of her attention to sweep back to the others in the room. Elizabeth was unsure if she'd followed the best path, but wasn't inclined to second-guess herself, as sometimes the first step towards abandoning one's goals is to say them out loud to an unreceptive audience.

Soon they were all standing and Ms. de Bourgh - after giving the HR staff in the group detailed instructions for their upcoming departmental meeting - wished everyone a good afternoon. Mr. Lucas and Maria nodded their thanks while Mr. Collins supplied sufficient verbal expressions of gratitude for all the guests.

Elizabeth and Charlotte returned to the Patronage with Mr. Collins. Charlotte asked what Elizabeth had thought of the lunch and of Ms. de Bourgh. Elizabeth did her best to compliment both the event and the woman, but her commendation, though costing her some trouble, could by no means satisfy Mr. Collins, and he was very soon obliged to take CDB's praise into his own hands.

CHAPTER 30

Elizabeth liked the Old Building and enjoyed strolling around it after lunch. She settled into a comfortable work pattern alongside Charlotte, and they made good progress on their project. Elizabeth was sorry not to be writing business or analyzing losses or doing some other task that connected directly to financial results, but found some lurid interest in exploring the various legal and moral pitfalls that company employees needed to be trained to avoid. Clearly, a brazen deceiver, possibly with the help of an obtuse dupe, could cause some serious damage in the reinsurance business.

Their efforts were assisted by the general absence of Mr. Collins - who spent most of his time away at task group meetings or quietly in his office. Still, they were interrupted from time to time with the helpful suggestion from Mr. Collins that they should Look Sharp as someone important was approaching. It appeared to Elizabeth that Mr. Collins spent most of his office time watching the walkways for any sign of important people. Clearly, he could monitor the outdoor walkway through his window, but it took Elizabeth longer to discern the fact that he could monitor the nearby indoor hallway through his computer. He had managed somehow to get a CCTV feed, and it was inspiring to see how diligent he could be in focusing his attention on his computer.

Elizabeth and Charlotte would Look Sharp for Anne Burgoyne once or twice a day, and she would speak a greeting to them but never stepped in from the hallway to join them. On one memorable occasion, they Looked Sharp for CDB, and she performed a brisk inspection of the Patronage that addressed such matters as the contents of drawers and the evenness of the blinds. Her visit wasn't ten minutes long, but she managed to leave behind a prodigious wake of improvements.

It seemed, in fact, that Ms. de Bourgh had generously decided to take on the supervision of all HR staff, and not just those who reported directly to her. Presumably, this freed up the supervisors in her department to focus on issues more strategic to the HR mission than the needs of the people who worked there.

Luminaries beyond the bounds of the HR Department would make their way to the Old Building from time to time. Mr. Collins reported that CDB was keenly anticipating a multi-day consultation with her nephew, Mr. Darcy. One of his responsibilities now was helping to prepare the president for the quarterly board meetings, and this required him to do a thorough review with each of the senior officers. His arrival was widely anticipated in the department, as Ms. de Bourgh was known to speak in very high terms of her regard for Mr. Darcy and her expectations for his future.

Elizabeth, though she had no particular interest in seeing Mr. Darcy, thought it might be interesting to see him with Ms. de Bourgh - partly to see family resemblance side by side and partly to see whether two such egos could fit into the same room.

It was, of course, Mr. Collins who first detected Mr. Darcy approaching the Old Building, walking with another man not yet known to him. Elizabeth and Charlotte dutifully Looked Sharp, but the men passed without appearing to notice them.

The next morning, when Mr. Collins returned from an early staff meeting, he was accompanied by Mr. Darcy and the other man, whom he introduced as Brian Fitzwilliam, a management consultant. Mr. Fitzwilliam was impeccably dressed and very well spoken, but was sufficiently ordinary in his appearance that one could believe he might actually be a first-rate management consultant. Mr. Darcy, aside from being also well dressed, was the opposite. His implausible handsomeness made him seem like someone hired to play an executive on television - or perhaps, given his awkward manner of speaking, a haberdashery model.

Mr. Fitzwilliam engaged first Charlotte and then Elizabeth with a few short, well-chosen questions and comments. Mr. Darcy then congratulated Charlotte on her new position, nodded his greeting to Elizabeth, and sat in a side chair. Elizabeth hadn't formerly seen anyone sit in that chair and had come to think of it as purely decorative. There seemed something fitting to her in seeing Mr. Darcy uneasily perched on a decorative representation of a chair.

Eventually, he ventured to say, "So, Elizabeth - how are your colleagues on the Pride Team?"

"Everybody's well and working hard, thank you." Then, after a pause, she added, "Jane was working on a project in Chicago. I understand you were also in Chicago. Did you happen to see her?"

She was perfectly sensible that he never had, but she wished to see whether he would betray any consciousness of what had passed between Jane and Bingley and Ms. Liebling. She thought he looked a little confused as he answered that he had not been so fortunate as to meet Jane in Chicago. The subject was pursued no farther, and the two men soon afterwards went away.

"What was that about?" Elizabeth asked Charlotte.

"I think it was about you. I think Darcy wants to keep tabs on you. See how you're doing, what you're up to."

"That seems pretty unlikely to me - but even if you're right I probably just cured him of the habit!"

CHAPTER 31

Two days later, they were Looking Sharp as Ms. de Bourgh was hurrying past in the hallway when she stopped and turned towards Mr. Collins.

"What's the deadline for the picnic announcement?"

"It's coming up!" he said with a smile. Charlotte spoke something quietly into his ear. "Tuesday of next week!" he added.

"Oh, good - that gives us plenty of time. I was afraid it might be this week. It's disconcerting, is it not, to have things thrown at one at the last minute?"

"It is indeed. Happy to be of service. Good of you to be so ever-vigilant about these things. But you're right - we still have plenty of time."

She was about to continue on, but then stopped and turned back to him. "We're a few short for *Lunch with a Purpose* today. The three of you should join us. And remember: one of our core values in HR is punctuality."

"Excellent! We'll be honored to be there. Thank you for your very kind consideration and a good day to you until we meet again, which of course will be very soon."

Mr. Collins delivered this last speech primarily to the memory of CDB's presence, as she herself had disappeared. This did nothing to dampen his excitement regarding the invitation, an excitement that he knew Charlotte and Elizabeth must also be experiencing.

Elizabeth, meanwhile, was wondering whether she should bring her laptop. Ms. de Bourgh had asked her to bring it next time she came to a lunch, but still it seemed somewhat presumptuous - as if she were asking to perform for the group. She decided to carry it as inconspicuously as she could in a large bag.

At the proper hour, they joined the gathering in Rosings. Ms. de Bourgh provided them with just enough greeting to meet her social obligation without losing her focus on Mr. Darcy and Mr. Fitzwilliam. The latter, possibly needing a break from HR strategic planning, seemed genuinely glad to see them. He made room at his side of the table for Elizabeth to sit down, and they were soon engaged in a very animated discussion of passwords. Why do they need to change so often? Is it a terrible security breach to write them on sticky notes attached to one's computer? How else can anyone keep them all straight?

Elizabeth enjoyed Mr. Fitzwilliam's playful banter, and they conversed with enough spirit and flow to draw the attention of both Mr. Darcy and Ms. de Bourgh. She eventually called out:

"What is that you are saying, Fitzwilliam? What is it you are talking of? What are you telling Ms. Austen? Let me hear what it is."

"We are speaking of passwords," he replied. "Logging into systems."

"Do you find it difficult? I'm told that many people do, although I myself have a gift for systems. I understand them intuitively somehow. I don't work on systems, of course, but that's for a reason. It's very important for those of us in HR to step back and let the people in each of the other departments function in their assigned roles. It's good for their self-esteem. But I believe systems work would have come very naturally to me. People tell me I should have gone into IT rather than HR - even Litchgate says so. But, of course, the one thing deeper to understand than systems is people. Are you afraid of systems, Will?"

"No," said Mr. Darcy.

"I'm glad to hear it. Too many people are afraid of things for no reason. Ms. Austen, I recommend that you practice working on systems night and day. These are the tools of our trade nowadays. One can't spend too much time working at them."

Mr. Darcy looked a bit ashamed of his aunt's surfeit of opinions and directed the conversation to the upcoming employee picnic.

After lunch, Ms. de Bourgh turned her attention back to Elizabeth. "Did you bring your laptop as I requested?"

"I did, yes."

Elizabeth pulled it out from under her seat.

"Rodrigo is here to operate the projection system. He'll show you how to connect."

A wall of paneling was folded back to reveal a large screen, Rodrigo handed Elizabeth a dongle to connect with and soon her login screen appeared larger than life before them all.

Elizabeth began with a brief acknowledgement of the fine work accomplished by the IT team that had created the system and the Operations officer who'd been the project's sponsor. She felt odd presenting herself as someone entitled to express an opinion on the quality of systems design, but she was determined to avoid the mistake she saw many of her colleagues make, which was to express a compliment and then immediately undercut it by adding a disparaging word about one's own competence to judge.

"I'll be using a test version of the system, so we can enter some made-up accounts without compromising the actual system."

At this point, Ms. de Bourgh asked Mr. Darcy his opinion of the lunch, but rather than answering he stood and moved to a point where he had a good view of the large screen and also over Elizabeth's shoulder to her keyboard and smaller screen.

"What are you doing back there?" Elizabeth looked back at Mr. Darcy.

"I'm getting properly situated. When you go to a piano concert, you want to sit to the left of the center aisle so that you can have a view of the musician's hands."

"Are you looking to intimidate me?" Elizabeth asked Mr. Darcy. "It won't work. If I can make this presentation to the field underwriters of the Northeast Region, which is a very tough crowd, I can make it to *Lunch with a Purpose*."

"I won't say you're mistaken," he replied, "because you couldn't really believe me to entertain any design of alarming you. I've had the pleasure of your acquaintance long enough to know that you find great enjoyment in occasionally professing opinions which, in fact, are not your own."

Elizabeth laughed and said to Mr. Fitzwilliam, "He'll teach you not to believe a word I say. I'm particularly unlucky that he's here, because otherwise I might have passed myself off with some degree of credit. But he'll need to watch out or I might retaliate with stories about him."

"I'm not afraid of you," said Mr. Darcy with a smile.

"Please retaliate!" cried Mr. Fitzwilliam.

"His first day here at Juniper Re, we had what we call an Idea Fair - which is a big chance for ordinary workers such as myself to interact with executives such as himself. And how many Round Robin sessions did he participate in? Zero. Waiting lists of workers looking for a turn with an executive and he didn't speak to a single one of them."

"I was new. I didn't know anyone."

"True. And nobody can ever be introduced in a Round Robin. Now, Mr. Fitzwilliam, give me a name for the account we should enter in the system. My fingers wait your orders."

"I think," said Darcy, "I'd have made a better show of it if I had my bearings. I don't do well when I'm in a room full of strangers."

"Should we ask him the reason for this?" said Elizabeth, still addressing Mr. Fitzwilliam. "Should we ask him why a man of sense and education, and who has lived in the world, is ill qualified to recommend himself to strangers?"

"I'll answer for him," said Fitzwilliam. "He won't bother to learn how."

"Different people have different skills," said Darcy. "Some people fit in anywhere and converse easily with anyone and, when they see someone they met a month ago, they not only remember that person's name, they also remember the names and ages of all that person's children. Such skill is a wonderful thing, but it's not my gift."

"Very few of the things we all do here come naturally to most of us," said Elizabeth. "I believe that's why we call this 'work'."

Darcy smiled and said, "You're perfectly right. And I give you insufficient credit when I think that your skills seem to come so easily to you."

Here they were interrupted by Ms. de Bourgh, who called out to know what they were talking of. Elizabeth resumed her demonstration. Ms. de Bourgh rose to stand next to Darcy and, after listening for a few minutes, said to him: "Ms. Austen could make a reasonably good presenter with proper training and experience. She has a good, clear voice and is decently well-spoken. Better than you might expect given her lack of background, although not, of course, in Anne's league."

Darcy shrugged but said nothing. Elizabeth, who was continuing her presentation, wondered if Darcy was, in fact, a supporter of Anne Burgoyne. She'd seen no evidence that he had any regard for her, and it seemed unlikely that he'd be urging his friend Bingley to hire her.

Ms. de Bourgh began providing her helpful suggestions directly to Elizabeth, which she accepted with patient appreciation - feeling that it represented an improvement over hearing Ms. de Bourgh's comments about her directed to others.

CHAPTER 32

The next morning, Elizabeth was working at the Patronage while Charlotte and Mr. Collins were off at a departmental meeting when she heard a knock on the wall by the hallway. Looking up, she was surprised to see Mr. Darcy - and for the first time in her memory was sorry Mr. Collins wasn't there to provide advanced warning.

He seemed surprised as well and asked where the others were, which she explained. She expected that would be the end of it, but he looked around and sat on the decorative chair. They exchanged a few pleasantries and then seemed in danger of sinking into total silence. Elizabeth wondered if he might be attempting to be more personable - possibly in response to her teasing on the subject at the lunch the prior day - but, if so, he didn't appear to be making any progress. It would apparently be up to her to find them a suitably discussable topic, so she decided to pursue her own curiosity.

"I understand you spent some time with Mr. Bingley when he was in Chicago. I hope all is well with him and Ms. Liebling and the others."

"Yes. Perfectly well."

She found that she was to receive no other answer and, after a short pause, added: "It seems a shame for Bingley's nice office near Netherfield to go empty all this time. Do you think maybe he should sub-let it?"

"Even when the trip is officially over, I don't expect he'll spend much time in his office. His presence is in demand many places."

"Yes. We might say he has many claims on his time."

Another pause followed, and Elizabeth was determined to let Darcy find the next subject.

"This is a nice working area," he said, looking around. "I believe

Ms. de Bourgh had a hand in the furnishings and arrangement."

"I'm sure you're right about that, and I'm sure that Mr. Collins in particular has been duly appreciative of all her generosity and good taste."

"He seems to have found an excellent assistant."

"He's very lucky to have her. I have my doubts at times whether it was a good decision for her, but she seems perfectly happy."

"It's not like she's lost her old life. Her previous colleagues are just down the path in the Main Building."

"Maybe it seems that way to you, but I don't believe that's her experience. For those of us trying to get our careers established, a ten minute walk to another building might as well be a five hundred mile drive through the country. She never gets back there, and I haven't seen any of her old colleagues look in over here. The Old Building is her world now."

"I see."

"Think about your move here. It's not like Cornwallis Re is an impossible distance away, but I don't imagine you get back there very often. When we take a job, we accept the place and the people who go with it."

"And what about you? Are you going to be ready to leave the nest of your Pride Team?"

"Not to come here, thank you - although I appreciate Charlotte's hospitality during this project. This visit has reminded me of the importance of personal chemistry in job satisfaction. I could never be happy working somewhere unless I was comfortable with my boss. When you go to work for someone, you might as well be joining their family. If you don't respect them, if you don't get along with them, if you can't talk with them in a comfortable, relaxed and open manner - well, you might as well be throwing your life away, as far as I'm concerned."

"Yes, I can see that's very important to you," he said. "As it should be." He pondered this for a moment. "We all want to be comfortable," he said, and then added, "With our colleagues, that is." He pondered some more. "So we must pick them carefully. That is, as we are able."

He sat thinking on this quietly for several minutes until Charlotte returned. He explained that he had looked in thinking they would all be there and had now used up enough of Elizabeth's time and excused himself.

"What can be the meaning of this?" asked Charlotte as soon as he was gone. "Lizzy, my dear, he must have his eye on you, probably for a position on his own staff. Why else would he just stop by like that?"

But when Elizabeth told of his long silences, it didn't seem very likely, even to Charlotte, that he was there on a recruiting mission. After various conjectures, they could at last only suppose that his visit proceeded from boredom with his project working with CDB. This might be due to the nature of the project itself or to some familial awkwardness or to his impatience with her apparent need for continual affirmation or possibly to his preference for dealing with accounts and deals and strategy rather than people - with people being, of necessity, the focus of Human Resources.

In the days that followed, Darcy and Fitzwilliam visited regularly, sometimes together and sometimes separately. It was plain to them all that Mr. Fitzwilliam came by because he enjoyed being with them. He and Elizabeth would alternate between light banter and serious discussions of reinsurance and the world. She was reminded of her enjoyment of Mr. Wickham's company and thought that Mr. Fitzwilliam might not be as amusing in his banter but was clearly more substantive when the talk turned serious.

Why Mr. Darcy came by so often was more difficult to understand. It could not be for information, as he rarely asked any questions. Nor was it likely to be for conversation, as he rarely participated in anything beyond the most minimal of small talk. If the visits gave him any pleasure, he gave no sign of it.

Mr. Fitzwilliam would sometimes chide Darcy for being such poor company on their visits together, which suggested to Charlotte that he wasn't always so withdrawn. Why the odd behavior when he visited them at the Patronage? She continued to consider the possibility that he was scouting Elizabeth for a position on his staff. She watched him carefully, but without much success. He was certainly aware of Elizabeth and paid close attention to anything she said, but his face betrayed no admiration for her or even enjoyment in her company.

She suggested once or twice to Elizabeth that he might be looking to recruit her, but she laughed at the idea. Charlotte didn't pursue the idea, partly because she was unsure herself and partly because she didn't want to raise Elizabeth's hopes - for Charlotte was convinced that, while her friend claimed to have no regard for Darcy, she would feel differently if the opportunity to work with him actually presented itself.

It was clear to Charlotte that Mr. Fitzwilliam visited the Patronage because he had a very high regard for Elizabeth, but it seemed unlikely that he would ever offer her a position. As a rule, management consultants aren't at liberty to hire away their clients' employees. Given the choice for her friend, Charlotte would pick Darcy - while Elizabeth might have better chemistry with Fitzwilliam, Darcy had the more promising career potential.

CHAPTER 33

The next day, as Elizabeth was taking what had become her daily post-lunch walk around the Old Building, she saw Darcy also out walking. The intended purpose of her mid-day walks was to clear her head and remember the larger world before submerging herself once again in her project on reinsurance ethics training, and she found that the sight of Darcy approaching on the walk path did nothing to further either of those goals. Her annoyance was multiplied when, rather than passing by with a wave or a nod, he said Hello and then changed direction to walk with her. Had she asked him to walk with her? Had she ever suggested to him that he would be welcome to join her for such a walk? Was it not readily apparent from the mere act of walking by oneself on a little-used outdoor path that one was not looking for company? And if you aren't seeking the company of your own friends, shouldn't it be very clear that you have no interest in the company of an intermittent acquaintance whose conversation is stilted but who's too high-ranking to tell to buzz off?

He asked her random questions. How is she enjoying her time in the Old Building? Why does she take walks? Did Charlotte make the right choice coming to work for Mr. Collins? What does she think of *Lunch with a Purpose*?

Under better circumstances, she'd have been happy to expound at length on any of these topics - the question about her reason for taking walks fairly begged for a snappy rejoinder pointing out that one key aim was to avoid just such questions. Not being in a playful mood, however, she gave brief and straightforward answers and didn't choose to probe or parry with any questions of her own.

When they reached the door to the Old Building, Darcy said, "I hope the rest of your project goes well. I'm sure you're looking forward to being back with your Pride Team, maybe for one last time." He then turned and headed down the path toward the Main Building.

What was that supposed to mean? Was he implying that the team was being closed down? Or maybe he meant that she was about to be offered a position - but, if so, by whom?

The following day, Elizabeth tried once again to clear her head with an after-lunch walk. This time, she was surprised to see Mr. Fitzwilliam out for a stroll. The thought crossed her mind that Darcy might have had Fitzwilliam in mind when he alluded to the impending end of her time with the Pride Team, and also that Darcy might have told him that the walkway after lunch was a good opportunity to have a word with her.

He greeted her and asked if it would be all right for him to join her for a portion of her walk. She appreciated being asked and agreed.

"When do you move on to the next department?" she asked him.

"Last Thursday was the original plan, but Darcy decided to push it back. Now the plan is to start at Financial on Monday. When you're the consultant, you have to resign yourself to the fact that you aren't the one with the power, you aren't the one driving the bus."

"Hold on. I'm trying to remember your business card. As I recall, it doesn't say 'Brian Fitzwilliam, Powerless Nobody' - it says something like 'Brian Fitzwilliam, Managing Director.'"

"Yes, I'm sorry if I sound like I'm complaining. It's not a bad gig. I get to be in the room when big decisions are made, and best of all I'm not held responsible for any of them. Although I have to admit that Managing Director isn't as impressive as it sounds. In the consulting business, we have title inflation that's maybe even worse than brokerage houses. Our summer interns start as Assistant Vice Presidents."

"I see. So if a consulting company offers me a job as a Vice President?"

"Fetching coffee, probably. The problem, of course, is that it won't happen. Where I really am powerless is in the area of hiring. We can't even consider anyone from one of our clients. It's actually in the contracts. If we were to post a position online and you were to send in a résumé - once we see that you're at Juniper Re we toss it out. It wouldn't matter how wonderful we thought you were, how highly we thought of your abilities, how great a fit we thought you'd be for our organization - by definition you'd be ineligible."

Elizabeth took all this as his way of saying that he'd hire her if he could. She wondered if Darcy didn't understand the situation - if, perhaps, Darcy considered everyone as unconstrained as himself - and this is what caused him to suggest that Elizabeth's time on the Pride Team might be nearing an end.

"Did you know Darcy when he was at Cornwallis?"

"I did indeed. I've had the pleasure of having Mr. Darcy as a client for several years, first at Cornwallis and now here. As a consultant, I'm duty-bound to claim a personal friendship with a long-term client, but in the case of Darcy it's absolutely true. He and I and his assistant, Georgiana Icard, were known at Cornwallis as the Three Musketeers. We worked on several successful projects together and had a wonderful time doing so."

"I've heard Georgiana spoken of by Ms. Liebling."

"She's a wonderful person and very good at what she does. You and she would make good Musketeers together. I don't think I know Ms. Liebling."

"She's in our Claims Department, reporting to Mr. Bingley."

"Bingley I know. He's a great friend of Darcy's."

"Oh yes!" said Elizabeth drily. "Darcy is uncommonly kind to Bingley and takes a prodigious deal of care of him."

"I'm not sure how you mean that, but I believe it's quite true. Darcy looks out for Bingley as a friend as well as a fellow officer. I'm pretty sure it was Bingley he was talking about when he told me he'd made some fairly elaborate arrangement to help one of his colleagues avoid something. It's a delicate matter - not something to be widely spoken of."

"I won't share it any further."

"And remember, it may not be Bingley, but there was some friend of his here at Juniper Re who was on the brink of making a recklessly inappropriate hire for an assistant, and Darcy was able to intervene."

"And did Darcy give you reasons for this interference?"

"I understood that there were some very strong objections against the candidate."

"And what arts did he use to prevent the hire?"

"I don't know the details. I believe he created some kind of delaying tactic that enabled cooler heads to win out."

Elizabeth made no answer and walked on, her heart swelling with indignation. After watching her a little, Fitzwilliam asked her why she was so thoughtful.

"I'm thinking of what you've been telling me," she said. "Your client's conduct doesn't suit my feelings. Why was he to be the judge?"

"I see. You think he should have stayed out of it?"

"I don't see what right Darcy had to decide who his friend should hire. That should be the friend's decision. If having Darcy as your friend means that he gets to make every decision in your life, then we're all better off not having him as our friend. But," she continued, recollecting herself, "as we know none of the particulars, it's not fair to condemn him. It might be nothing at all."

"Yes, but if it was nothing then it isn't a good example of the point I wanted to make, which is that Darcy cares about and tries to be helpful for his friends."

Elizabeth didn't trust herself to have a civil response to this, so she changed the subject. When she returned to the Patronage, she went into full Stew Mode. She tried to find other possible explanations for the information she'd received, but nothing else made sense. What other friends did Darcy have at Juniper Re besides Bingley? Who else was Bingley on the brink of hiring other than Jane? Apparently the Claim Tour had been a diversionary tactic to get Bingley out of town and talk him out of hiring Jane. Elizabeth had suspected something of the sort, but had assumed it was Ms. Liebling or others in Claims who'd conspired against Jane out of jealousy or the simple provincialism that she wasn't from Claims. No, as it turned out, it was Elizabeth's personal nemesis, Mr. Darcy, who engineered Jane's unhappiness - motivated apparently by some kind of snobbery. What made her unacceptable in Darcy's eyes? Not enough credentials? Not enough letters after her name?

This was baffling. How could anyone disapprove of Jane? This is Jane we're talking about - the nicest and best person in the world and smart as a whip and harder working than a clown car full of senior executives.

So, maybe it wasn't Jane herself. Maybe those 'very strong objections' related to something else. But what? Could it be the

Pride Team? Is there something a little déclassé in the name? Something embarrassing, perhaps, in the boosterism of Ms.Nebbit? Something suspect, perhaps, in being explicitly recruited to enhance the firm's diversity?

Maybe. Then again, maybe Darcy simply disapproves of Juniper Re in general and thinks all future hires should be recruited in from Cornwallis!

CHAPTER 34

The next day, Elizabeth stayed in after eating her lunch. Clearly her walks were neither clearing her head nor helping her to remember the larger world. The Patronage was unoccupied for the time being and her corner of Charlotte's desk could be used as well as any other place to contemplate issues unrelated to her project. As if intending to exasperate herself as much as possible against Darcy, she sorted through her past emails and texts with Jane, retracing the entire episode with Bingley and Claims: the initial excitement, then the calm hope, then the doubts and uncertainty, and finally the brave-faced abandonment of all her original ambitions.

Through it all, Jane had been remarkably steady, yet Elizabeth was also struck by a change. The later messages lacked the sparkle that characterized the earlier ones and that she'd always loved about Jane. As might have been expected, this revived her anger at Darcy, who was apparently pig-headed enough to boast to Fitzwilliam that he'd done Bingley a wonderful favor by sticking his nose into the situation and preventing what would have been a first-rate hire and - to boot - robbing Jane of her sparkle. And now what? If Darcy won't let Bingley hire Jane, will he let anyone else? Is he bent on making her *persona non grata* across the entire organization?

She looked up and there stood Darcy before her. Was this a bad dream, conjured from her agitation? No, he was really there.

"You aren't walking today?" he asked.

"No."

"Not feeling the need to clear your head?"

"It hasn't been working very well for me, lately."

"I see. But you're OK? You aren't ill or anything?"

"I was feeling fine a minute ago." She tried to deliver this with some cutting irony, but either she was too unhappy to make it work or he was too oblivious to notice.

"Good. And the others?"

"They're fine, too, as far as I know. I believe they're having lunch with the training staff."

Darcy nodded, looked around and sat on the decorative chair. After a moment, he stood and paced.

"I'm about to do something quite stupid," he announced.

"Oh?"

"I'm about to do something so stupid that, if it were not me doing it but a friend or a colleague, I'd intervene and prevent it from happening." He stopped pacing and stood in front of her. "You're aware, perhaps, that I'm currently a department of one. I have no assistant, no lieutenant, no aide-de-camp - while at the same time I report directly to RJT and am told I'm on the short list to succeed him when that time comes. So one of the most important decisions I'll make all year will be who I choose to work with me. It's like being a candidate for president of the country. Once you get the nomination, then everyone wants to know who you pick as your running mate. The running mate is supposed to check all kinds of boxes, but the most important box is that he or she is supposed to be a smart pick that will confirm the candidate's good judgment. So the very stupid thing I'm doing is to pick you. You of all people - with no credentials worth mentioning, with no connections in the company that'll be of any use to me - and some that, frankly, are likely to embarrass me - and zero connections outside the company. A young woman, no less - and won't that set the tongues to wagging about what's really going on here! But - stupid though I know it is - that's my decision. I like the way you handle yourself. Always thinking. I like the way you feel free to challenge me. Not some simpering toady. So I'm just going to have to man up, swallow my pride, hold my nose, and tell the world that my chosen assistant, unlikely as it seems, is you."

He smiled and indicated that a response was now called for. He seemed relieved to have gotten his announcement out of the way. Elizabeth took a breath to compose herself.

"I believe what's traditional when you receive an offer for a position that you didn't seek and don't want is to try to make up for your refusal with lavish thanks and a show of sorrow that you're unable to accept. But since my refusal to be a toady is apparently one of the few things you can stand about me, I'll give it to you straight. I'm not grateful for your offer and not sorry to be turning it down. I don't mean to be rude. I wish you and your career all the best. In fact, I hope I've contributed to your future success by helping you to avoid the mortifying blunder of having any formal connection to me, the embarrassing nobody."

Darcy stood staring at her, visibly upset. Elizabeth waited nervously, wondering if she had just ended her own career.

At length, in a voice of forced calmness, he said, "That isn't the response I was expecting or even thought possible. I was thinking this would be a very pleasant surprise for you. Do you want to give me a reason?"

"A reason?" she replied. "I think maybe you need to give me some reasons. Like, what's the reason for making such a big deal out of what a horrible job candidate I am? I didn't ask you to hire me - why are you moaning about how unqualified I am? Maybe you could tell me the reason you think I could bear to work for you when I know that you sabotaged the job prospects of my best friend in the company."

At this, Darcy changed color, but the emotion was short and he listened without attempting to interrupt while she continued.

"You want reasons? I have every reason in the world to think ill of you. It's one thing for you to make a sneering comment about me to your friend, Bingley, because that's not going to do me any long-term damage. But it's something else completely for you poison him against Jane. She was going to be an absolutely first-rate assistant to him, and you did them both wrong by preventing him from hiring her. Your friend Bingley will land on his feet, I don't doubt - but it remains to be seen how well my friend Jane will come out that mess you made."

She paused, and saw with no slight indignation that he was listening with an air which proved him wholly unmoved by any feeling of remorse. He even looked at her with a smile of affected incredulity.

"Can you deny it?" she asked.

With assumed tranquillity he replied, "I have no wish to deny that I did everything I could to prevent my friend from hiring your friend, and I'm glad that I succeeded. I believe I did right by him."

Hearing no mitigating circumstances and seeing no remorse, Elizabeth warmed to her subject.

"Since you asked for reasons, I could also point to your treatment of George Wickham. He gave me quite an earful regarding your poor treatment of him back when you were both at Cornwallis."

"You seem to take quite an interest in Mr. Wickham."

"I think anyone who hears his ordeal would find it pretty interesting."

"His ordeal!" repeated Darcy contemptuously. "Yes, let's all feel the pain of his terrible ordeal."

"How can you be so dismissive?" asked Elizabeth with energy. "Maybe you don't feel any pain but your own, but I can assure you that the rest of us do feel pain. When Wickham was shut out of a job that had been promised to him, that hurt him. And when he had his career blackballed and options narrowed, he felt that. And then, when he escaped to Juniper Re only to find you here as well and ready to continue making his life miserable - anyone would feel that as an ordeal."

"And this," cried Darcy, as he walked with quick steps across the room, "is your opinion of me? This is the estimation in which you hold me? Well, thank you for explaining it so fully. My faults, according to this calculation, are heavy indeed! I wonder, though," he added, stopping and turning towards her, "if you might have seen past my horrible offenses if I'd sugar-coated my offer a bit - that is, if I'd kept my mouth shut regarding the difficult politics of hiring you. I happen to think that was an important piece of background and would have been germane for you as well if you'd seen clear to accept the offer. I happen to think it's important to be entirely frank and open with anyone I'd consider having on my staff, whether the information flatters them or not."

Elizabeth felt herself growing more angry every moment. She tried to the utmost to speak with composure.

"You're mistaken, Mr. Darcy, if you think that your bluntness affected my decision - except that it freed me up to communicate that decision back to you with some rude bluntness of my own. If you'd asked nicely I probably would have responded with a softer tone, but the answer would have been the same however you might have asked me."

Again his astonishment was obvious, and he looked at her with an expression of mingled incredulity and mortification. She went on:

"From the first moments we met, you've demonstrated your arrogance, your aloofness from ordinary human interactions, your disregard for the feelings of anyone other than yourself and maybe the one or two friends you've somehow managed to make. I don't think I'd known you a month before I came to the conclusion that you are the last person in the world I'd ever want to work for."

"You've said quite enough, thank you. I believe I understand your position with complete clarity. I won't ask you again, and I won't trouble you any further. Sorry for taking so much of your time, and please accept my best wishes for your success and happiness."

With that he turned and walked away without looking back. Elizabeth was in a turmoil. Darcy had wanted to hire her? A surge of regret washed over her. What had he seen in her? What would her title have been? What would her salary have been? But as she replayed the scene in her mind, she was confirmed in her angry refusal. He was proud of ruining Jane's opportunity in Claims! He was contemptuous of Wickham! He was so full of himself that he thought he could walk in and admit the terrible things he'd done and insult her training and connections and she'd still accept any offer he might make!

She heard Charlotte and Mr. Collins approaching and decided it was time to take her walk.

CHAPTER 35

The next morning, Elizabeth was still consumed by the same thoughts and feelings. She couldn't recover from the surprise of what had happened and found it impossible to think of anything else. Useless for her work and unready to discuss the situation with Charlotte, she considered where she could go to be alone with her thoughts. She put her laptop and a few papers in a bag and headed off without knowing where she was going.

She walked down the hallway. Should she go outside? Maybe walk back to the Main Building? No - she knew too many people in the Main Building, and there was no telling who she might run into on the walkway. She took the stairs to the second floor, then walked down the hallway and found a few small conference rooms. The first was occupied, but the second was dark and empty. She turned on the light and sat on the far side of the table, where she could watch the hallway. She opened her laptop, thinking it unlikely that she'd get any work done but feeling that she'd look less conspicuous if she appeared to be working.

Without thinking, she logged on and checked her email. She had a new message from Darcy. The message was dated early that morning and the subject line was Apologia.

She wanted to think it was a fancy word for apology, but the more she looked at it, the more she recollected that it meant something more like justification. With no expectation of pleasure but with the greatest curiosity, Elizabeth opened the message.

Personal and Confidential

Please rest assured that the point of this message is not to reopen the misguided offer I presented you with yesterday. I have no interest in causing any more pain to you or any more embarrassment to myself, and I would undo the entire episode if I could. Rather, the point of this message is to provide you with some additional information regarding certain actions of mine that became a part of our discussion. The additional information may or may not cause you to change your judgment of me, but since you clearly have a strong interest in these actions I want you to have as much information about them as reasonably possible.

The first action of mine under discussion was in regard to your friend and fellow Pride Team member and her potential candidacy to work for Bingley. In that case, I stand accused of ignoring the wishes and the best interests of both of them by contriving to sabotage the potential job offer and whisk Bingley out of town to avoid any further contact with Jane, all apparently motivated by my snobbish disapproval of her credentials and connections.

The second action of mine related to George Wickham. In his case, I prevented him from being able to assume a position that had been promised to him and took additional measures to harm his reputation and hinder his career - and I did all this for no discernable reason, although I believe the suspicion may be that I was jealous of his close relationship with my mentor at Cornwallis.

Either one of these offenses taken alone would be sufficient to mark me as morally stunted, but considered together they present a stunning picture of inhumanity. I make no claim to be a paragon, but I believe a full accounting of the facts will demonstrate that neither am I quite the monster I may have appeared. In order to provide such an accounting, I will of necessity need to relate some unflattering information about others that I would not normally choose to share, but feel that the present circumstances leave me no choice.

In the case of Bingley and Jane, I could see that they had a very friendly working relationship and that a job offer was appearing increasingly likely. Lucas, you may remember, as much as told me I should expect it. So I began watching them closely, and the conclusion I came to was that Bingley was looking for an able assistant but Jane was looking for a life partner. That is to say that she had lost whatever professional detachment she may have started with and had fallen in love with him. I could see it in her eagerness to be with him, in the energy she brought to their meetings together, and in her unwillingness to hear anyone say the slightest word against him. I made some inquiries and found more than one report of her being heard to admit having "a crush" on Bingley.

An infatuation of this kind may seem a small thing, something we would expect to dissipate quickly once it becomes clear that the feeling is not reciprocated. However, I have seen first-hand how much damage can be done to both parties when a close working relationship involves one person who is in love with the other. There is virtually no good outcome for this situation and several possible bad outcomes.

Bingley is the last person to be aware of this sort of danger. He assumes that the eagerness of a co-worker reflects the same disinterested love of the work that generates his own eagerness. That is why I believed it was necessary and appropriate to intervene. My first step was to prevent a precipitous hire on his part by encouraging him to speed up his plan for a national tour. I was aided in this by Bingley's openness to impulsive decisions. With the immediate danger passed, I visited him in Chicago and spoke to him quite directly regarding my belief that Jane was harboring a personal, romantic attachment to him. He was surprised to hear this and took some convincing, but once he was convinced of the matter he could see that it was necessary for him to drop the idea of hiring her and minimize all further contact with her. This caused him no small discomfort and unhappiness, but he rightly concluded that this was the kindest thing he could do for Jane as well as the safest for his own career and family.

Was I predisposed to doubt Jane because of the shortcomings in her background? Probably so. Was I inclined to doubt her because of her connection to the Pride Team? Yes to that as well. The team seems like a perfectly good idea in theory, but in practice it seems to bring out something less than the best in both its patrons and its members - as evidenced, for example, at the Netherfield Idea Fair. Despite all my doubts, however, I would not have intervened to prevent her being hired by Bingley if I thought she was interested only in being an effective assistant for him. Nor would I have hesitated to intervene in exactly the same way regarding a candidate who was better connected and better credentialed if I believed that candidate was in love with Bingley.

This may not be germane to these explanations, but I would like to add that, as a general rule, I believe it is a good thing for people to fall in love with other people. You and others might be surprised to know how much sentimentality lurks beneath my business-obsessed formality. I am not normally one to interfere in such matters. The issue here that required my intervention was the prospect of having Jane report directly to someone with whom she was in love. This would have been entirely inappropriate and dangerous for them both. A manager should never hire someone, nor should a candidate ever allow himself or herself to be hired, if either party harbors even the hope of a romantic relationship with the other. It may sometimes happen that someone who is already in a close business relationship develops personal feelings for the other person. The necessary action in such case is to end the business relationship before seeking to establish a romantic relationship. The temptation would be to test out the feelings of the other person first, in order to avoid disrupting the business relationship for no purpose, but that would be wrong. Any romantic relationship begun while one party is under the power of the other party has been tainted at its foundation.

Regarding Wickham, it may be helpful to provide a more complete overview of his history with me than you are likely to have received from him. He and I came up through the ranks together at Cornwallis Re. We had complementary strengths and weaknesses. His analysis and judgment were sometimes suspect, and my people skills were no better then than they are now. Each of us was mentored by the company's then-president, Mr. Paternoster. He very generously and inspiringly prepared me for senior management responsibility. At the same time, he tried to encourage Wickham to become a thought leader. Wickham had and probably still has wonderful communication skills, but would use them mostly to amuse himself or his co-workers. Paternoster wanted him to harness those skills to higher aims, to bring positive change and innovative thinking to the company. He told Wickham that he wanted him to consider joining a new unit he was planning to create focused on non-traditional risk management solutions. That unit was created after Paternoster retired. It fell within the portion of the company that I was responsible for, so I approached Wickham and invited him to join it. However, that particular year was one of strong top-line growth for the company and Wickham figured that he would be better off financially to join a field marketing unit with the hope of participating in what promised to be a very large bonus pool for the year. This was a good decision for him in the short term, as he was able to collect quite a substantial bonus for results that he had little to do with achieving. The following year, however, the market was much less favorable, and it became clear that a similar bonus would not be repeated. He then contacted me and told me that he had reconsidered his decision and would like to join the new unit. At that point, the new unit had already been staffed and had developed a good working environment and was beginning to find some success. I felt it would be disruptive to add Wickham to the mix at that point, and I also felt that he had been given a chance to be part of the group and had chosen instead to take some ready cash. I declined to hire him into the group, and he became angry at me for not giving him the position he felt had been promised to him and began telling people that my decision in this matter was somehow dishonoring Paternoster's wishes and legacy. Let me say that I know Mr. Paternoster's ways of thinking as well as anyone, and I believe that he would have offered Wickham the job once but would not have treated it as a perpetually open invitation to join the team whenever it suited Wickham's convenience.

I must now mention a circumstance which I would wish to forget myself, and which no obligation less than the present should induce me to unfold to anyone. I ask that this information not be forwarded or repeated to anyone else.

When I was at Cornwallis, I had an assistant named Georgiana Icard. She was extremely valuable to me professionally and also a dear friend. Wickham worked long and patiently and creatively to ingratiate himself with Ms. Icard. I suspected that his motive had something to do with his animus towards me, but I saw no benefit in trying to prevent his being charming towards her. As he gained her confidence, he enlisted her in a scheme to create a legal entity, authorized to sell reinsurance, separate from Cornwallis. Georgiana was critical to this plan, as she had a broker's license. She was unaware of the significance of the plan. Wickham had presented it to her as a special purpose entity that would allow added service convenience for some of the customers that Wickham was handling. She was happy to help with the project and allow her broker's license to be used in the registration of the new entity. Fortunately, being unaware of the conflict of interest and potential fraud that could arise from the scheme, she made no attempt to hide it and mentioned it to me one day as a project to which she had lent some support. I asked some questions and then some more questions and then asked to see the supporting documents. Then I had a dilemma.

It was clear to me that this scheme was undertaken with bad intentions. Customers would assume that any program offered by Wickham was supported by the full faith and credit of Cornwallis Re - which would not be true for any program written through such a separate entity. At worst, Wickham could use the lack of oversight to offer programs with no backing at all, trading worthless paper for payment that he might have planned to pocket for himself, hoping that there would be no losses. My first inclination was to sound a general alarm and subject Wickham and his scheme to the full scrutiny of the Legal Department and possibly regulators and law enforcement. Two considerations held me back from this. First, the scheme had not been finalized, and I had only my own speculation regarding what the entity might have been used for. Secondly, any punishment would inevitably fall on Ms. Icard as well as Wickham.

These are the decisions that drive management but also drive law, politics and public policy. Is it more important to punish the guilty or to avoid punishing the innocent? Is it more important to prevent the ineligible from collecting a benefit or to make sure that all the eligible are able to collect it? Is it more important to avoid paying an uncovered claim or to avoid denying a covered claim? My decision in this case was to handle it quietly. The scheme was abandoned, Wickham was put on notice and Georgiana learned a valuable lesson in the value of caution and skepticism.

If I had better anticipated your position yesterday, I might have been able to give you an orderly accounting of all this information then. As I then lacked the necessary calmness and presence of mind, I have tried my best to lay out for you the facts of these cases in this admittedly over-long message, which I forward with my best regards,

180

F. WILLIAM DARCY

CHAPTER 36

Elizabeth hadn't known what to expect from Darcy's email. She'd been concerned when she saw how long it was and had begun by skimming it. She was pleased to see that he wasn't dwelling on his offer, either to reiterate it or to complain about her response to it, but she was unhappy to see that, rather than apologizing for his interference with Jane and Bingley, he offered an implausible and poorly-supported argument for why his actions were reasonable and necessary. Jane was in love with Bingley? Were they all in middle school where the boys and the girls need nosy interlopers to say who likes whom? And does anyone think it's fair to deny someone a position based on a hearsay theory? When he mentioned in passing what Elizabeth knew to be the real reason for his opposition to Jane - the shortcomings in her credentials and connections and in particular the weaknesses of the Pride Team - she felt it as a gratuitous insult to both Jane and herself, and she felt her resentment of his cool arrogance being reignited.

But when this subject was succeeded by his account of Wickham - when she read with somewhat clearer attention a relation of events which, if true, must overthrow every cherished opinion of his worth, and which bore so alarming an affinity to his own history of himself - her feelings were yet more acutely painful and more difficult to define. Alone in the second floor conference room, she found herself talking back to the email. *"No! That can't be right! He's making this up!"* She skimmed her way to the end, closed the lid of her laptop, and promised herself that she wouldn't look at the message again.

She raised her eyes and looked around. No one was in the hallway. She sat alone in a small, unfamiliar conference room seated in front of a closed laptop computer. She could get up, she could take a walk, she could go back to the Patronage, or she could open her laptop and take a closer look at Darcy's email.

For her second time through, she decided to skip the introduction and the business about Jane and go straight to the discussion of Wickham. Once she'd found the spot, she forced herself to read every word of every sentence and to consider each statement as a new data point. A good underwriter should always be open to revising her judgment based on additional information. The account of Wickham's early years at Cornwallis was entirely consistent with the information he'd offered about himself. The generosity of Mr. Paternoster and the promise to Wickham also lined up neatly with the story she'd heard before. But then the stories diverged. Did Darcy deny him the promised position from the beginning or did he deny it only when Wickham asked a second time, after having refused it once for a more attractive offer? If Darcy's version was accurate, then Wickham's version was - if not an outright lie - at least selectively edited to be misleading. If, on the other hand, Wickham's version was the whole truth, then Darcy's version must be an outright lie.

She stopped for a moment to consider the competing versions. Which was more likely? Would there be a way to verify one or the other? Lacking an objective third party eyewitness, she was left to consider the relative reliability of each party. Is Darcy someone who would conjure a story to justify his actions? This notion had some appeal to her. Surely Darcy was someone who cared about his reputation. But would he fabricate a story, particularly one that could potentially be disproven? She stopped to consider the alternative: Is Wickham someone who would omit important facts to gain sympathy for himself? She had to admit that this seemed the more likely possibility. Omitting inconvenient facts comes more easily to most of us than generating useful fictions. She had a sense that Darcy, whatever his considerable faults, was at heart a punctilious old-school boy scout. But what was her sense of Wickham? She realized that she'd attributed a certain character to him, working back from his wit and ironic detachment to assume a disappointed but not defeated idealist. But what evidence did she have that this was his real character? What corroboration did she have for any of his accounts of his own history? Whose trustworthy judgment could she cite to ratify her regard for him? Wasn't it possible that his ironic detachment was merely narcissism?

Here Elizabeth began to berate herself. She'd prided herself on her underwriter's caution - check the facts, find additional data points, keep an open mind, consider other possible explanations. In the case of Wickham, however, she'd set aside all these rules and consequently had been oblivious to what she could see now were warning signals. Why had he been talking so indiscreetly to her about his own personal history in the first place? Why had he skipped the Idea Fair at Netherfield after he claimed he wouldn't be cowed by Darcy? Why did he find it so easy to complain about his treatment at Cornwallis only when there was no one present who could contradict his story?

She also began to wonder about his interest in Ms. King when she was newly married to an officer in the Legal Department. At the time, Elizabeth had seen it as a refreshingly frank acknowledgement of the value of office politics, but now she wondered if, taken together with his attempt to use Ms. Icard at Cornwallis, it represented a pattern. Maybe he likes to find credulous enablers with powerful connections. They'd be helpful to get a plan off the ground and, provided they were sufficiently implicated, their connections could provide protection if the plan went sideways.

How to compare Wickham with Darcy? She considered again Wickham's eagerness to complain about Darcy when she first spoke with him at the party for Mr. Denny. Darcy, on the other hand, while making it clear that he had a different view of Wickham than she did, was reluctant to provide any details and only told his own side of the story under duress and with a demand that the information be held in the strictest confidence. Some of this reluctance must relate to his desire to protect his former colleague, Ms. Icard, but Elizabeth sensed that there was more to it than that. He clearly cared about the atmosphere within the company, which is harmed when people speak badly of a co-worker who isn't present.

Elizabeth kicked herself mentally. She was ready to kick herself physically if she could figure out how to do it. She'd been so busy being mad at Darcy that she hadn't stopped to notice how he acted or what he said. In the course of her project with Charlotte, she'd had several opportunities to see him at close range. Had she seen anything to indicate that he couldn't be trusted? Had she seen any evidence of his being unkind or unfair, apt to cut corners, or prone to focus on his own benefit to the detriment of the company or anyone else? No, no, no, and no. Even Wickham grudgingly admitted that Darcy was good to his staff and colleagues. Meanwhile, if Darcy was really the way Wickham had described him, how could he be such good friends with and so clearly esteemed by that paragon of niceness, Charles Bingley?

She grew absolutely ashamed of herself. She couldn't think of either Darcy or Wickham without feeling that she'd been blind, partial, prejudiced, and absurd.

"I'm a complete idiot!" she said aloud, and then continued at high volume within her own head. "Little Miss Know-It-All! When Jane tries to give people the benefit of the doubt, I turn up my nose and say, *'Don't be so gullible! Be doubting and skeptical like me!'* As if I had any discernment at all! A love-sick teenager couldn't have been more blind than I've been! I was pleased to be - so I thought - confided in by the one and annoyed to be - so I thought - neglected by the other. Now I see that I was totally wrong about Wickham, totally wrong about Darcy and totally wrong about myself!"

At this point, she realized that she would need to take a closer look at the first portion of the letter. If Darcy was right about Wickham, maybe she'd need to reconsider his views on Jane and Bingley. On first reading, she'd found his explanation forced and insufficient. Widely different was the effect of a second perusal. With her newly discovered respect for Darcy and trust in his sincerity, she found his account compelling and reasonable. She still disagreed with his conclusion that Jane was in love with Bingley, but she could see that it had been a logical conclusion for him to reach. It was unfortunate that Jane, in her innocent enthusiasm, had used such easily misconstrued language - herself as Bingley's partisan and Bingley as her work crush. If Jane had really been in love with Bingley, Darcy would have been right to intervene.

Still, it pained her to think of anyone losing an opportunity because they're suspected of harboring fond thoughts. It's the sort of charge that one usually isn't given the chance to refute and, even if you were given the chance, how could you prove the negative? She had a fleeting memory of an elementary school rumor that she liked a boy named Bradley. What could she do about it? Nothing. You can't just go over to Bradley and say, *'I don't like you!'*

She wondered if something along these lines was the root cause of gender disparities in so many businesses. Not so much the intervention from a friend as the person himself suspecting that a candidate is in love with him. How many men are convinced that all the women love them? If you think you're God's gift to women and you can't hire anyone in love with you, what do you do? You have to limit your hires to men - and, just to be safe, maybe only straight men.

Was there anything to be done for Jane? It would be nice to snap her fingers, explain the misunderstanding and restore the status quo ante. Some reinsurance contracts provide for a reinstatement. Having collected the limit once, you can pay the premium again and get access to the same amount of limit again. Could Jane pay some premium and have her Claims career prospects restored? Elizabeth felt it was somehow impossible. Pick your metaphor: you can't reset an odometer, unring a bell, put the toothpaste back in the tube. Hard enough to go tell Bradley that you don't really like him, but harder still to then start working closely with Bradley every day. No, she would probably have to content herself with coaching Jane on how to express her future enthusiasms in ways that wouldn't be misunderstood.

She pondered her own future. If a connection to the Pride Team was a negative in Darcy's opinion, it was probably viewed the same way by many others. While she'd suspected that the team's reputation was not great, it pained her to see Darcy's explicit judgment on the matter - which was apparently so clear to him that he believed it required little in the way of explanation.

At this point she roused herself. How long had she been sitting in that conference room? Almost certainly longer than was good for either her physical or her mental health. She packed her things and returned to the Patronage.

"You missed two visitors this morning," said Charlotte. "Mr. Darcy came by to say he was finished with the HR portion of his project and was taking his leave from the Old Building. It was a message to all three of us, but I believe it was really a message to you. Mr. Fitzwilliam came by later with an identical message. He stayed quite a long time waiting to tell you himself, so I'm sure he was sorry to miss you. He has his eye on you, that one."

"He can't hire me. It's in his contract."

"Maybe he has his eye on you for something else."

CHAPTER 37

Mr. Collins made an excuse to look in on his patroness early the next morning. He was thinking she might be in need of some cheer now that Darcy and Fitzwilliam were no longer around, and in this he had guessed correctly.

"I'm bereft, just bereft!" she announced to him. "All my favorite people are gone or unavailable! There's nothing for it. I'm down to the bottom of the barrel. You and those two young women will have to join us today for *Lunch with a Purpose.*"

He was, of course, delighted by the honor of this most generous and considerate invitation, and he hurried back to inform the two young women. Elizabeth, when she heard of the invitation, paused for a moment to consider what lunch with CDB would have been like if she were being introduced as Darcy's new assistant. She suspected that the great woman would have been torn between her doting on Darcy and her horror at the imprudence of his choice. Would she have fussed and fumed? Elizabeth, who was already second-guessing her emphatic refusal, now faced another reason to doubt her choice. It would have been worth accepting his offer just to see how Ms. de Bourgh would have coped with the news.

In the absence of any such shocking news, lunch was a quiet affair. CDB looked around, sighed and said, "It just isn't the same without Darcy and Fitzwilliam around, is it?"

"Of course not," agreed Mr. Collins.

"I'm a tender soul. I feel it when my dear colleagues are no longer with me."

"They're reviewing IT now, right?" said Elizabeth. "So I assume they've only moved on as far as Building Three."

"Yes, well to you that may seem like a small difference, but to me it's enormous. It's been such a delight this year to have my Will, whom I've known his whole life, finally with us here at Juniper Re. And then to have him and that nice Mr. Fitzwilliam actually in residence with us in HR has been, I think, one of the real highlights of my career. So now, it pains me more than I can say to be giving that up, to have them off on the other side of the campus, busy with a different department. They might as well be a hundred miles away!

"I know it may seem sentimental to make a fuss about such a thing, but I believe sentiment is underrated. There is, you know, a pernicious stereotype of the successful business person as some sort of automaton, coolly analyzing numbers with no human feeling. In my experience, nothing could be further from the truth. Reinsurance, in particular, is a people business. It has to be. What do our customers buy? They buy a piece of paper that says if certain complicated conditions are met we'll pay them a hundred million dollars. Who's going to buy something like that over the internet? Nobody. Everything's based on relationships. It's a community, held together by traditions and bond of mutual dependency and trust and no small of amount of human feeling."

Mr. Collins turned to Elizabeth. "What Ms. de Bourgh is saying…"

"I'm perfectly capable of speaking for myself, Collins! What I'm saying is that, in this business, we're tied together in bonds of genuine friendship and mutual respect. Please don't interrupt me like that again."

"Of course."

"You see, I'm not the only one feeling sad about this departure. When Darcy and Fitzwilliam came to say good-bye to me this morning, it was obvious that they too were in very low spirits. I could tell that each of them in his own way was as sad about leaving me as I was sad to see them go. Maybe sadder.

"Clearly, they've come to value our relationship as much as I have and are feeling a similarly deep sense of loss as they need to move on and away from the Old Building and, of course, me.

"There's a tremendous burden that comes with senior management. There is, of course, the pressure to lead the company. *'Heavy is the head'* and so forth. But there's something more. There's an obligation to empathize with every employee on the team, from the president down to the most lowly assistant nobody. We need to see the world through their eyes, feel what they feel, connect at the level of our common humanity. Darcy and Fitzwilliam understand that burden and share it with me in a way that a middle manager or non-manager couldn't even begin to imagine."

She sighed and looked around. "We take what consolations we can. None of you is leaving us, are you?"

"Actually," said Elizabeth, "My project here is also ending. I'll be back in the Main Building on Monday."

"But you've only just gotten here! We can't have you rushing through things or cutting corners."

"I agree, but we've done what we can and I need to start in on my next project."

"Well, if you must go, call Regina in Location Services. She's such a dear! They provide these yellow, plastic containers with lids and wheels - as many as you like! You just load all your things into them and tell Regina where you're going and she'll take care of the rest."

"Thank you for the kind suggestion, but there's no need. I hardly brought anything with me at all."

"So you say, and I don't doubt it. Let me just give you one final piece of advice before you leave us. When you go anywhere - not just here to HR but anywhere - bring everything. If you're going to be part of an organization or a department, bring your full self and everything that goes with it. Nobody wants to see the travelling version of a Broadway show; they want to see the real version. Nobody wants to play the travel version of a game; they want to play the real game. Yes?"

"Yes. Thank you."

The conversation then swerved to new guidelines requiring all documents to be coded for degree of confidentiality. Elizabeth was happy to be out of the spotlight, and glad that the final piece of advice she would receive from CDB during this visit was something that she could respect and consider.

Her thoughts returned to Darcy's offer and Darcy's email. She bounced between them like a shuttlecock. The offer had struck her as impudent and maddening. Its only redeeming quality at the time had been the opportunity to speak her mind to him freely. The email opened up to her his thinking in a way that she appreciated and learned from, but it gave her no voice to respond. So, if she had misjudged him, does that mean she should have agreed to work for him? Not necessarily. How do you work for someone who makes you so mad? You can't ask your boss to communicate with you only in writing!

And what can be done to shore up the Pride Team? How can Mr. Bennet be so wise and kind, and at the same time be unwilling or unable to take the reins and exert some leadership? He rolls his eyes at the meddling of Ms. Nebbit, but he doesn't do anything to change the situation. He expresses his concerns about Lydia and Kitty privately to her, but what does he say to them?

And what about Jane? Elizabeth was relieved to be able to stop hating Bingley. She saw him now as a good and honorable manager doing what he thought he had to do under the circumstances. But this also took away the cold comfort of being able to say Good Riddance. No, Jane would have thrived and been great as an assistant to Bingley.

"Good bye."

Elizabeth realized that lunch was now over and Ms. de Bourgh, perhaps still under the sway of her own sentimental reverie, had actually stood and shaken her hand.

CHAPTER 38

That afternoon, as Charlotte was away at a meeting and Elizabeth was packing her tote bags for the walk back to the Main Building, Mr. Collins came out of his office, looking to pay her the parting civilities he deemed indispensable.

"I can't, of course, speak for Charlotte, but I'm sure she'd agree that it's been wonderful to have you here with us for these weeks. I know that we're a bit off the beaten path over here, and I also know that HR work isn't part of everyone's blueprint for their own ideal career, so we appreciate the fact that you very kindly agreed with Charlotte to take on the project that the two of you have just concluded so successfully. I haven't seen the final materials yet, but Charlotte assures me that you both rose the challenge very effectively, which of course is what we like to see around here."

Elizabeth was eager with her thanks in return. It had been a pleasure working with Charlotte, and she appreciated the many kind attentions she'd received during her visit. Hearing this, Collins relaxed a bit and smiled.

"I'm very pleased to hear that you've passed your time not disagreeably. We've done our best, and of course we're most fortunately situated to enable a visitor such as yourself to interact with a very elevated strata of the organization. I think we may flatter ourselves that your visit to HR can't have been entirely irksome. Our situation here with regard to CDB is really quite an extraordinary advantage for us, as you've now had the chance to see for yourself. I don't know how often you might have dined with senior officers prior to your visit, but I expect many people would find this a uniquely stimulating environment."

Words were insufficient for the elevation of his feeling, and he was obliged to walk around the desk, while Elizabeth tried to unite civility with truth in a few short sentences.

"You know," he said, "I sometimes hear reports that there are people who question Charlotte's move here, who hold her up as an object of pity or derision."

Elizabeth wondered if he meant her. She began to speak but he held up his hand.

"My hope is that - having been with us and seen first-hand what her situation is here - you can communicate back to the doubters in the Main Building that her situation is not a bad one at all. That she is perhaps someone to be envied rather than pitied, someone to be looked up to and not down on. And I also hope that you'll be inspired by her example and find a situation for yourself that will be equally satisfactory in its own way."

Elizabeth smiled and pondered her response. There was much that she could happily agree with, but in the middle of it all was the prospect of a situation equally satisfactory to Charlotte's. And how satisfactory is that? Being a Main Building Doubter at heart, she continued to suspect that it wasn't very satisfactory at all.

She was spared from committing either rudeness or perjury by the appearance of Charlotte herself. As usual, she radiated a clear-eyed sense of purpose that blunted Elizabeth's tendency to assume she must be miserable in such company. This was her choice, made freely, and she was going to make the best of it that she could. This department, this desk, this boss. They came as a package, and she was committed to them all.

Elizabeth stood, gave Charlotte a hug, gave Mr. Collins a wave, shouldered her computer bag and tote bag, and started off down the hallway, followed shortly by Mr. Collins.

"Is there some message I can communicate back to CDB on your behalf?"

Elizabeth stopped. "Some message?"

"Perhaps your humble respects with grateful thanks for all her kindness to you during your time in HR."

"Yes. Thank you."

Walking back to the Main Building, she wondered what she should say to Jane. She was prepared to tell her everything about Darcy's offer and her refusal - everything, that is, except for the matters touching on Bingley and Jane herself. How could she look Jane in the eyes and tell her such things? On the other hand, how could she look Jane in the eyes and not tell her such things? Also, it would be difficult to give Jane an accurate account of her back and forth with Darcy if she left out the matter of Bingley and Jane. It was a key part of her refusal and half of Darcy's email.

As she walked in past the security desk, she was thinking that she should try to lie low for a few days until she worked out what she ought to say to Jane.

Her phone buzzed and she pulled it out. There was a text from Jane: *Meet us at George 1.*

CHAPTER 39

George was a set of conference rooms on the third floor of the Main Building, sufficiently distant from Longbourne that the Pride Team members could feel they were out of view and just close enough to Meryton to provide a whiff of interest to Lydia and Kitty, who'd organized the gathering in honor of the return of Jane from Chicago and Elizabeth from the Old Building. Mary, who generally preferred work to parties, had opted not to attend.

Elizabeth had come straight to George 1 without stopping by her desk to drop off her bags, but she was still the last to arrive. She found her teammates in high spirits, hugged them all, and cheerfully accepted a glass of ginger ale, while quietly declining Lydia's offer to spike it with something from her thermos.

"Isn't this nice?" asked Kitty.

"Check out the sideboard!" added Lydia. "This is the Deluxe Cold Cut spread! It was supposed to be our treat, but it turns out we can't sign for it. Can one of you put it on the department account?"

"I can," said Jane. "I have the code. I'm not sure, though, about the business purpose."

"The business purpose is to welcome you both back!" shouted Kitty.

"We can't have you both creeping back into the department like thieves in the night!" said Lydia. "And we can't have you going hungry or thirsty, either. And it would be rude for you to eat and drink in front of us without offering us any, so we ordered enough for us all!"

"Jane and I thank you for your hospitality," said Elizabeth. "We can talk to Mr. Bennet about the niceties of the bill, and whatever isn't covered by the department we'll split as our Thank You to both of you. Agreed?"

"Agreed!" said Jane.

They set to making their sandwiches and pouring and doctoring their soft drinks and soon they were seated around the table, with the door shut, enjoying a private meal together.

Lydia and Kitty were quick to report that the RMO's remodeled quarters in the city were nearly ready and consequently the RMO staff would be vacating the home office within two weeks.

"Are they indeed!" cried Elizabeth with the greatest satisfaction.

Lydia, who was not always a careful listener, said, "I know, it's terrible, isn't it? We're starting a campaign to lobby Mr. Bennet to assign a few of us to an extended project with the RMO after they relocate. I've talked to Ms. Phillips about it, and she was very encouraging."

Elizabeth shook her head. "Bad idea. I can't tell sometimes if you and Kitty are looking for a boss or a boyfriend. I don't know if you've gotten the memo on this, but it can't be the same person."

"There's the buzzkill we've been missing!" shouted Kitty with a laugh.

"I think sometimes she's Bennet dressed up in drag," added Lydia. "But here's something that might catch your attention: your friend and ours, Mr. Charles Wickham, is in the market again! That's right - no more Ms. King in the picture. She and - we assume - Mr. King are having a baby, and she's decided to take an indefinite leave of absence."

"Good for them!" said Jane. "I don't know her, but Mr. King in Legal is very nice."

"She's a pig!" opined Kitty. "I say good riddance! And it clears the field for our Lizzy - if she's still available?"

"Thank you," said Elizabeth. "I'm eminently available, but somehow, and against all odds, I still have some standards. And by my standards, I'm perfectly happy to see the whole RMO - most especially Wickham - ride off into the sunset."

"Sounds like sour grapes to me," said Lydia. She turned to Jane. "Any current prospects for you?" Jane shook her head. "You know," Lydia continued, "Kitty and I were hoping you'd both be taken by now. We wish you well, of course, but also it would help our own market value. We wonder sometimes if you're making enough of an effort. We love you to pieces, but you can both seem a little cold and stand-offish at times. We think you need to do more job flirting."

Elizabeth and Jane looked at each other and rolled their eyes.

"Not Level Two job flirting. Just enough Level One job flirting to get yourselves back in the game."

"I'm not sure I want to know," said Elizabeth.

"It's like regular flirting. Level One means you signal interest and availability. We don't think that's too much to ask. Nobody's going to hire you if they don't think you're interested."

"I don't like this whole concept," said Elizabeth. "I don't even like it for regular flirting. It's no way to start a relationship with any mutuality."

"What's Level Two?" asked Jane.

"We're not asking you to go there. Level Two means signaling your willingness to do anything."

This elicited much laughter and hooting. Jane was embarrassed and Elizabeth was appalled.

"Oh, don't give us that look, Lizzy!" urged Kitty. "The field people in the RMO are looking for inside sales support, not more rules and oversight - especially now that Denny's gone and Forster is running things. You know they call Underwriting the 'Sales Prevention Department'. They need to know that we'll be on their side."

"We're not talking about embezzling or anything," said Lydia. "Maybe polish up a file so it passes muster for an audit. Maybe backdate a transaction that everyone meant to happen earlier. None of that's going to hurt Juniper Re one bit, and might actually make it stronger. The big-wigs need to make a lot of rules in order to protect their own deniability. But they also know that business has to be written, and so they leave a little slack in the system. The company's success ultimately depends on the willingness of us non-big-wigs to fill that gap and do what's actually necessary."

"I don't know," said Elizabeth. "Is that you talking or Wickham? Call me crazy, but I believe the key to this business is to do as many good deals and as few bad deals as possible - and it's not always easy to tell the difference between them. If we're going to add any value at all, we have to be thinking critically about every piece of business we touch. I don't know Forster, but I have to think that the vast majority of the RMO staff understands and appreciates this as well or better than I do. And as long as I have the floor and am being a crank, let me point out for the record that what you call Level Two flirting is bad in business and worse in romance. The words 'foolish' and 'dangerous' come to mind."

By this point, Lydia's attention had passed to the screen of her phone. She spoke without looking up. "Whatever. We can maybe just agree to disagree. I'd point out, though, that your approach doesn't seem to be working very well. Maybe we should make a bet on which one of us will be hired first."

The rest of the meal passed with more general company gossip, Elizabeth and Jane sorted out the bill, and they all passed as an entourage back to their work area, where Mary was working quietly on a spreadsheet.

"You should have come, Mary!" announced Lydia loudly. "We had such fun! And we were able to arrange quite a nice welcome-back meal for Jane and Lizzy! It was the Deluxe Cold Cut Platter, and there would have been plenty for you, too! And then we gossiped and argued and had more fun and made more noise than has probably ever been contained in the history of George 1!"

To this, Mary very gravely replied, "Far be it from me to tell other people how they should spend their time or what they ought to enjoy. As for me, however, I made some really meaningful progress over the last few hours on an analysis I've been working through recently, and I wouldn't trade that for all the cold cuts in the world."

But of this answer Lydia heard not a word. She seldom listened to anybody for more than half a minute, and never attended to Mary at all.

Elizabeth looked in on Mr. Bennet in his office. He rose and smiled at her. "I'm glad you're back, Lizzy."

"What's this talk I hear of sending Lydia and Kitty chasing after the RMO after they return to their normal quarters?"

"A terrible idea. I agree completely."

"They're drawn to them like moths to light, but it doesn't seem to me to be a healthy combination. Also, I'm worried about where that unit is headed now that Denny's gone."

"I agree completely."

"Well, don't let it happen!"

"Thank you, Lizzy. It's certainly not my plan."

CHAPTER 40

The next morning, Elizabeth saw that Longbourn 2 was unoccupied, so she signaled to Jane and they went in and shut the door.

"I have so much to tell you," she said, "but I need some kind of disclaimer first. I'm sworn to secrecy on some elements that I'd otherwise want to share with you, so this will be the truth and nothing but the truth, but it won't be the whole truth."

"Got it, and good on you. Don't break any confidences."

"I need to tell you some things about you, and I need to tell you some things about me. The things about you are going to be hardest for me to talk about, so I'm thinking I should probably start there."

"Let's do this! I'm sitting down."

Elizabeth considered how to begin. "So this is about you, but maybe it's also about Bingley. Do you remember a gathering in Claims to celebrate the end of the project for the Benevolent? You were indisposed but I went - I'm not sure why, but I was there. Bingley and Darcy got into an odd argument over whether or not it's a good thing to be susceptible to having your mind changed by your friends. Did I ever tell you about this? Darcy thought it was best to stick to your guns, whatever your friends might say, but Bingley thought it was a good thing to listen to your friends and give them a fair chance to change your mind."

"I don't know. Sounds to me like you're stalling."

"I'm getting there. I think of that argument now because, in fact, what seems to have happened with Bingley is that he made up his mind to hire you, but then he allowed his mind to be changed by his friends. And the argument they used against you? This is hard to talk about but I'm going to keep going. Some of it was your low connections and the somewhat sketchy reputation of the Pride Team

- but most of it was more personal to you. Specifically, it was the charge that you were in love with Bingley, and therefore both a professional and a personal danger to him."

Jane was stunned and began to tear up. "But that's so stupid!"

"Yes! It's stupid and it's horrible! It's the sort of thing that people will whisper and no one will say to your face. You had no way to answer it or defend yourself or set the record straight. In fact, even now that you know what was said, I don't know how you make it go away."

"What can I do?"

"I'm sorry. I don't know. Try to keep a professional door open to Bingley and the others in Claims, but that's about it. If you chase after him, it's just going to look like his friends were right - and if you go punch him in the nose, it's still going to look like his friends were right. I'll do what I can to let people around Bingley know they had you all wrong. My advice to you would be to focus on being more careful with your next opportunity. I don't mean to suggest that any of this was your fault, but the lesson is to be more careful - a little more guarded maybe in how you show your enthusiasm, a little more paranoid about using phrases like 'work crush' that can be too easily misunderstood."

"Oh, man! This is horrible!" said Jane. "I feel cheated and wronged, but I also feel really stupid! I feel like I'm the only person in this whole company, maybe in this whole world, who doesn't understand the rules, who didn't get the memo. I'll need to stew on it for a while." They sat quietly for a moment. "Let's talk about something else. What's your news? What's the Lizzy Update?"

And so Elizabeth related to her, in considerable detail, the scene between Darcy and herself. Every minute or two, Jane would say "No!" - each time a little louder - but when Elizabeth had completed her recitation of the scene, Jane shrugged and said, "Yes, of course he offered you the position. You're the smartest person in this whole place. You're going to be president of the company someday. He would have been lucky to get you. Of course, he should have asked more nicely. His being so sure of succeeding was wrong, but consider how much his certainty must have increased his disappointment!"

"Yes," replied Elizabeth, "I gave him a bit of a verbal beating, and I don't think he was expecting it. It's probably good for someone in his sheltered existence to get dumped on every now and again, but I do feel badly about it nonetheless. Do you blame me for refusing him?"

"Blame you! Oh, no."

"But you blame me for giving him such a hard time about Wickham?"

"No. I don't see why there's anything wrong in that."

"But you will see what's wrong in that when I tell you what happened the very next day."

She then described receiving Darcy's email and recounted as much of its contents as she felt was appropriate to share. Jane was glad to have Darcy vindicated, but wounded to think of Wickham as a person of anything less than total integrity. She exerted her creativity to find some misunderstanding or alternate explanation that would allow Darcy to be honest and Wickham to be honorable.

"This won't do," said Elizabeth. "They can't both be in the right. Take your choice, but you'll have to be satisfied with only one. At most, there's one good person between the two of them. I'm currently inclined to think the good one is Darcy, but you can decide for yourself."

"Oh, have your way! Wickham is a bad person. I can say it, but I still find it hard to believe. And poor Darcy! He thinks he's going to recruit you and instead you not only turn him down, you beat him over the head - unfairly as it turns out - with his meanness to Wickham! So then he felt he had to sit down and write you that long message about lots of things he'd probably wish he could just forget. You must feel horrible about it all!"

"Not really. I decided long ago to outsource all my regret and compassion to you. You do such a wonderful job feeling bad for all the people I mistreat that it eases my mind completely."

"It's a shame about Wickham. He has such a nice face and manner."

"Yes, he and Darcy make an odd couple. Apparently, one has all the goodness and the other has all the appearance of it."

"I never thought Darcy was as bad as you used to think."

"No, you didn't. I thought you were being blind and I was being realistic. I think maybe I held onto the idea that Darcy was bad because I enjoyed the freedom to make jokes about him. And some of them seemed like pretty good jokes, too, at the time."

"So how did you feel when you read his long message?"

"Very uncomfortable - uncomfortable and unhappy and sorry you weren't around. I wanted to talk about it with someone. I wanted you to help me feel better by saying something unwarranted but nice."

"It was bad luck on your part. You didn't get things wrong on purpose. You wanted to take a stand against people treating other people badly."

"That's what I'm talking about! Unwarranted but nice. But let me ask you a question about now. What should we do with this information? Should we let all our friends and colleagues know about Wickham's dark side?"

Jane pondered this. "I'm not keen on the idea. What do you think?"

"I'm thinking not. Darcy was very clear that his information was shared in confidence - and there are some details I haven't shared that might be at higher risk of becoming public if the general story becomes more widely known. Wickham will be gone from the home office in another week. My plan is to hold my tongue and wait for him to disappear. Besides - we can hope that he's learned a lesson or two in the intervening years."

"There," said Jane. "You're beginning to sound like me!"

As Elizabeth settled back into her life with the Pride Team, she was able to see for herself how Jane was faring. What she saw convinced her that Jane had not yet turned the corner in her efforts to move past Claims and restart her job search through the rest of the organization. Her heart clearly wasn't in it.

"Well, Lizzy," said Ms. Nebbit one day, "what's your opinion of this sad business of Jane's? For my part, I'm determined never to speak of it again to anybody. That's just what I told Ms. Phillips yesterday. Did Mr. Bingley even so much as say Hello to Jane when they were both in Chicago? I don't think so. He's a horrible person as far as I'm concerned, and what's worse is he's never here. He's always off somewhere. It's like he's afraid to face us all. They should rent out his office over by Netherfield. Jane's confidence has been completely shot by this experience. What's to become of her? If she ends up out on the street, panhandling with a cardboard sign, my

202

only consolation is that it'll teach Bingley to trifle with the feelings of a Pride Team member!"

Elizabeth was unable to see the consolation in this, but chose not to press the point.

"So, Lizzy, tell me about Collins and Charlotte. How are things running over there in the Old Building? Are they keeping busy? Does Charlotte seem to be fitting in over there?"

"They seem to have plenty to do, and Charlotte's making the most of her opportunities."

"Yes, I can believe that. If she has a talent for anything, it's making the most of her opportunities. Soon enough they'll both be running the Pride Team. I expect they can't wait. I assume they were too polite to rub your nose in it, but make no mistake. When it's just the two of them, they're rubbing their hands together at the prospect of being King and Queen of the Pride Team!"

CHAPTER 41

The last week of the RMO's residence in the home office felt, to Kitty and Lydia, like the final days before a very unpleasant and unpromising surgery. Their usual cheery demeanor was replaced by a brave but grim fortitude. Ms. Nebbit, who wanted her charges to be happy and who had enjoyed having her sister in the building, was nearly as morose. The others felt the pain less sharply, if at all, but attempted to maintain a sober and serious tone out of respect for their suffering colleagues.

"Things are going to be so dead around here!" moaned Kitty.

"Oh, don't even talk about it," said Lydia. "It just makes it worse!"

"It's not like the RMO will cease to exist," said Elizabeth. "They'll just be in the city."

She'd intended this as an encouraging word, but it seemed not to have the desired effect. Lydia gave Kitty a meaningful look and said, "She's probably happy about it. She's never liked the RMO."

"Maybe we can arrange a project for one or two of you at their new offices," suggested Ms. Nebbit. "I know Mr. Bennet has spoken against it, but he can sometimes be made to see reason, and he isn't the only management fish in the sea!"

Elizabeth tried to wait out the week with patience, but in her own way she was as unhappy as Kitty or Lydia. She'd seen how the lack of seriousness and credibility of the Pride Team had become an obstacle to Jane's and her own advancement.

Then Lydia received an invitation from her friend, Ms. Candice Estroff, formerly of the Surge Team and now personal assistant to the new RMO Head, Mr. Forster. Ms. Estroff requested Lydia's assistance setting up their new offices. This was to be a one-month assignment beginning the day the RMO started work in their new quarters.

Lydia was instantly revived, brimming with energy and loud with enthusiasm. Kitty, not being the recipient of such a happy invitation, was left worse than before. Rather than rejoicing in the good fortune of her fellow team member, she took it as a snub.

"Candy was my friend before she was Lydia's friend," Kitty explained to Jane and Elizabeth. "I introduced them. I was the one who told Lydia that Candy was going to work for Mr. Forster. How can she treat me like this?"

"I'm sure that if she could have brought in two people, she would have included you as well," said Jane.

"I'm not talking about Candy - I'm talking about Lydia! How can she go along with this? She should have put her foot down. *'No!'* she should have said. *'Kitty and I are a team. If you want me, you'll have to include her as well!'* I could understand her throwing the rest of you under the bus. No offense, but Jane, you're naively goody-goody, and Elizabeth, you're a preachy bossypants, and Mary is deathly boring. But Lydia and I are a team, and she should never have thrown me under the bus!"

Elizabeth was also unhappy about the invitation, although for different reasons. She sought a private word with Mr. Bennet in his office, where she reiterated her concerns: on the one hand, Lydia's lack of judgment; and on the other hand, the RMO with Denny gone and Wickham in, out from under the watchful eye of the Home Office, and under the untested leadership of a young man looking to make a name for himself. This was a potentially combustible combination, and she urged him to prevent it. He heard her attentively, and then said:

"We can't control everything, Lizzy. We can't do everyone's job for them. At some point, we have to stand back and let them succeed or fail on their own. Sometimes they surprise us."

"I worry that the foolishness of some, if allowed room to grow and become increasingly conspicuous, will harm the prospects of the rest of us. Has, in fact, probably harmed them already."

"You speak of yourself? You speak of Jane?"

"Yes, both of us."

"Are there any details you wish to share with me?"

"No. I think not."

"Well, I'll simply say that anyone who decides to ignore Jane's value or yours because you have one or two unserious members in your team - a team that you didn't pick - such a person doesn't deserve either one of you and isn't likely to go far in any event."

"Jane and I picked the team by deciding to be part of it. We want to see it succeed and continue. This team is your legacy here. How many times have you told us that we need to be active and not passive? Active not passive in underwriting, active not passive in pushing the company forward, active not passive in managing our careers. What about active not passive in managing the team?"

Mr. Bennet sighed and shook his head. "I brought Lydia into this world. She impressed me with her energy and enthusiasm and won me over with her charm. If I lock her up, maybe she'll be safer, but we'll lose the reason she was hired in the first place. I don't think even Lydia can go too far off the rails in just one month in the city. I continue to believe that she can bring a lot of value to Juniper Re, but it looks like she's going to have to make a few mistakes and learn a few lessons along the way."

With this answer Elizabeth was forced to be content, but her own opinion continued the same, and she left him disappointed and sorry. It wasn't in her nature, however, to increase her vexations by dwelling on them. 'Know when to put your pencil down' is an expression used by underwriters to convey the idea that one shouldn't keep analyzing a question forever. Elizabeth's thinking rarely involved the assistance of a pencil, but she took the expression to heart and tried to avoid ruminating on issues for which she already had enough information to make a decision or for which the decision was out of her hands. In this case, having given her opinion to the responsible person, she turned her attention to other matters, one of which was a going-away reception that was to be held for the RMO staff.

Should she attend? It would be hard for her to avoid it. Her teammates would all be there, and the event was being held in Longbourn, just around the corner from her desk. Still, she would have preferred to avoid exchanging parting words with Wickham.

On her return from HR, she'd tried to create some distance between herself and Mr. Wickham without having an explicit falling out with him. She didn't want to precipitate a scene that might hurt her relations with the RMO, and she didn't want to get into an argument in which she might betray information given to her by Darcy in confidence. She just wanted to be sufficiently cool and standoffish so that Wickham would understand that she no longer enjoyed his company or saw him as a kindred spirit or had any interest in working with or for him. It was unclear to her, however, that Wickham had received and understood this message. Possibly Wickham was self-absorbed; those who fit this description tend to notice and misinterpret warmth and be oblivious to coolness and distance.

The reception was held on the Thursday afternoon of the RMO's last week in the Home Office. Elizabeth made the short walk to the now-undivided Longbourn and was soon face-to-face with Wickham.

"Elizabeth! So nice of you to come say Good Riddance to us all! Here - let me offer you a cup of this very posh ginger ale. I've hardly gotten to see you recently. How was your time at HR?"

"It was very nice, thank you. Lots of interesting people in and out. Darcy was there much of the time, and a consultant named Fitzwilliam who'd worked with Darcy back at Cornwallis. Do you know him?"

He winced briefly, but reasserted his smile and maintained his composure. "I remember him. Very personable fellow. What did you think of him?"

"I was very impressed and taken by him. He seems quite genuine."

"Yes, well, you know he can't hire you."

"Who says I want him to hire me?"

There was a pause while Wickham pondered what she meant by this, but chose not to ask. Instead, he said, "They make an odd pair, Fitzwilliam and Darcy. The personable and the not-so-personable."

"Yes, they're very different. But I think Mr. Darcy improves upon acquaintance."

"Indeed!" cried Wickham with a questioning look. "I always like to hear reports of improvement. Tell me about it. Where do you think the improvement is located? Is he learning to show the world a friendlier face, or do you think he's improving in his essential character?"

Elizabeth smiled and looked straight into his eyes. "Oh, no! In his essential character, I believe he's exactly what he's always been."

Wickham appeared unsure whether to rejoice over her words or to distrust their meaning. He listened with an apprehensive and anxious attention while she added:

"When I said that he improved on acquaintance, I didn't mean that his mind or his manners were in a state of improvement, but that, from knowing him better, his disposition is better understood."

Wickham appeared agitated but was silent for a few minutes. He turned to her again, and said in the gentlest of accents, "Let's hope you're right. Wouldn't it be wonderful if Darcy is actually becoming the pillar of virtue he's always claimed to be? Wouldn't it be great if no one else ever has to experience the kind of mistreatment I've known? Still, I'd recommend keeping your eyes open. It's possible, you know, that he was on his best behavior visiting CDB - a powerful woman and his aunt. It's my understanding as well that he's looking to hire that protégée of hers, Anne Burgoyne."

Elizabeth could not repress a smile at this, but she answered only by a slight inclination of the head. She saw that he wanted to engage her on the old subject of his grievances, and she was in no mood to indulge him. The rest of the evening passed with the appearance, on his side, of usual cheerfulness, but with no further attempt to engage Elizabeth in private conversation. They parted at last with mutual civility, and possibly a mutual desire to never meet again.

After the party, Lydia went to pack up her things, surrounded by the noise of her colleagues. Kitty sighed sadly and complained loudly. Ms. Nebbit declaimed advice that Lydia should make every effort to enjoy herself during her project - advice which there was every reason to believe would be well attended to. Jane, Elizabeth, and Mary all expressed their best wishes without being heard.

CHAPTER 42

Elizabeth had boundless affection and appreciation for Mr. Bennet, who was a sort of business-world father to her. At the same time, and not unlike many people with respect to their actual fathers, she didn't approve of him. She considered him good with theory but weak on execution, retreating when he should advance. In poker terms, he might hold reasonably good and potentially winning cards but, frustratingly, he would choose to fold.

She blamed this on Ms. Nebbit - or, more precisely, she blamed it on the combination of Mr. Bennet and Ms. Nebbit. She was his Achilles Heel; something about her simply defeated him. That is not to say that his shortcomings were her fault, but rather that she made evident a flaw inherent in him that, in her absence, might have gone undetected.

Mr. Bennet was used to steering situations and asserting his interests through wit, suggestion, and implication. These techniques worked very well for him in the polite circles that were normal at Juniper Re, but were essentially useless in dealing with Ms. Nebbit. When she first inserted herself into the oversight of the Pride Team, he had dropped numerous polite but pointed hints that her direct involvement with the group wasn't needed or appreciated. Such an approach would have been more than sufficient to ward off an incursion from any of his other colleagues, but they had no apparent effect on Ms. Nebbit, who was increasingly able to establish herself as a fixture in the group's management and operations.

Once it was clear that Mr. Bennet lacked control over the working group that reported to him - a group he had created and made up of people he had hired - he lost credibility, and he lost the confidence necessary to assert influence across the organization. He began to suppress his reforming tendencies - so that, rather than driving change, he was likely to settle for the considerably less helpful option of making ironic observations.

While Mr. Bennet remained charming and sensible, the Pride Team suffered from his lack of control, at least as respects the members' attractiveness to other departments. Organizations, like nations, regions, and peoples, have cultural values, and the culture of Juniper Re distrusted drama and intrigue, while it prized order, decorum, and transparent processes.

While Elizabeth had been eagerly looking forward to the departure of the RMO, she found her daily life in their absence little improved. Things were quieter with Lydia gone and sadder with Kitty moping, but not appreciably more interesting or entertaining. Eventually, the team members started to receive regular reports from Lydia in the form of shared selfies - Lydia with Ms. Estroff; Lydia with Mr. Forster; Lydia with Mr. Wickham; Lydia with a surprised-looking but apparently game visiting broker; and so on. The pictures bore testimony to Lydia's skills of sociability and persistence, even as they documented her shortcomings in business focus and gravitas. Still, the photos were sometimes fairly amusing, and they seemed to cheer Kitty and Ms. Nebbit.

Feeling the need for something to look forward to, Elizabeth turned her attention to her upcoming conference trip with Ms. Gardiner. This promised to be a very pleasant change for her - in the big city with the sophisticated and impeccably-dressed Ms. Gardiner, participating in just enough conference to learn a bit, meet some interesting people, and justify being there, while keeping enough time free to take in culture and maybe be a bit of a tourist. The only shortcoming of the plan is that it didn't include Jane - but she was philosophical about this, telling herself that, if the plan had been perfect in every regard, there would be nothing but downside potential, while, given at least one flaw, the plan had upside as well as downside.

Ms. Gardiner wrote to confirm Elizabeth's understanding. "This isn't one of those general insurance conferences that exist primarily as sales opportunities. Those are lots of work - with a booth to be manned and dinners to be hosted and private meetings with our largest clients and looking over our shoulders at who else is meeting with them. Those conferences mean planning and meeting ahead of time and writing up reports afterwards and, even though they're often held in fairly nice places, you never get a chance to enjoy where you are. You should go to some of those conferences for the experience, but you should go with the understanding that you'll be hard at it all week.

"The conference we'll be going to is a technical conference on risk and catastrophe modeling. There won't be anyone at the conference that we'll need to sell to. There will be people who'll want to sell to us, but being sold to is much less work than selling. Some of the presentations will be on topics that are important to my work, but all of them will be available electronically. So my general approach to these gatherings is to network up a storm at the beginning, follow up with a few trusted colleagues at the end, and play hooky in the middle. Wednesday should be the prime time for a field trip. I'm thinking during the day we could look in at Cornwallis Re. You won't believe the executive offices there. We can firm up our plans during the conference.

"I'll meet you at the conference registration counter on Monday afternoon. My flight arrives around noon, so let's plan to meet around two."

Not wanting to risk being tardy, Elizabeth arrived at the conference hotel around twelve-thirty. The Juniper Re Home Office was only an hour or two outside the city, depending on traffic, so she'd been able to spend some time in the office that morning with the happy thought that she had a packed bag and a hotel reservation waiting for her. She checked into the hotel, had a light lunch, and then found the conference registration table and was wearing a large name tag on a lanyard when Ms. Gardiner arrived.

Wearing the name tag and holding her conference-logo binder gave Elizabeth a reassuring sense of belonging that helped carry her through the following day, which largely felt to her like the first day as a clueless transfer student at a new school. She did what she could to be helpful, and as the conference had many simultaneous sessions, this mostly meant attending whatever session was Ms. Gardiner's second choice for each time slot. She tried to take notes, but struggled to know what was meaningful.

The thought occurred to her that Mary might have been a better choice for Ms. Gardiner to bring to the conference. She probably would have known what "stochastic" means and would have had questions for the presenters and possibly even have been inspired to offer an impromptu presentation of her own. So why didn't Ms.

Gardiner ask her? Elizabeth suspected it might be because Mary wouldn't have been as fun a companion. She would have had no interest in playing hooky, but would have wanted to spend all day Wednesday attending every possible presentation. If so, was that fair? Did ability get recognized and rewarded, or were careers a popularity contest?

She stewed on this question for a bit and then decided that careers are mysteriously random and probably no more or less fair than life itself. She had to admit that she had a certain obsession with trying to decode the mystery, and was prone to seeing ordinary life events as metaphors for career competition. Say, for example, she needed to pick a lane on a crowded highway or a check-out line at the grocery store. Why does one move faster than another? Should she move from one to another, or will the new one just slow down once she's in it? Still, as annoying as a slow lane can be, the reasonable lesson appeared to be that these aren't particularly important decisions. Whether one picks the fast or the slow lane, everyone reaches their destination eventually, and most of us soon forget the delays along the way. Maybe it would take Mary a little longer to advance due to her personality, and maybe Elizabeth would be slowed down by her inability to use "stochastic" in a sentence, but over time they and their colleagues would figure out what works for each of them - and she hoped that some day they would all look back and find that they'd had a career.

"What do you think about tomorrow?" asked Ms. Gardiner at the end of the day. "Would you like to see Cornwallis Re? You've heard so much about it, and it's a place with which so many of your acquaintances are connected."

"Maybe."

"Oh? Do you have an objection or maybe have something else in mind?"

Elizabeth wanted to be enthusiastic for any plan of Ms. Gardiner's, but she wasn't entirely comfortable with the prospect of nosing around the former workplace of Bingley, Wickham and Darcy - any more than she'd want to visit their homes, look through their closets, or chat up their high school teachers. Perhaps it was her own guilty conscience for wanting to know everything about everybody, because what she really objected to wasn't the nosiness or voyeurism, but rather the possibility that Bingley, Wickham or especially Darcy might find out about it.

"I do spend most of my days at the offices of a reinsurance company," said Elizabeth. "If I were a coal miner and had a midweek day of liberty, I'm not sure I'd want to spend it going down into a different mine."

"If this were a matter of cubicles and offices, I'd agree completely. But what you and I are going to peek into are the executive offices at Cornwallis, which are in a very posh separate floor of what is already a very posh downtown building known as Pemberley. So this won't be a maze of cubicles; this will be more like the Winter Palace of the Tsar. And you needn't have any concern that we'll be in anyone's way, as the president and senior officers who normally work there are away all week at an off-site conference."

This entirely satisfied Elizabeth's objections and the question was resolved. They would proceed the next day to see Pemberley.

CHAPTER 43

The Cornwallis Reinsurance Company was headquartered in the upper floors of the Pemberley Building, a fine Art Deco structure in the downtown financial district. The lobby had generously high ceilings, featuring representations of the signs of the zodiac intricately crafted in chrome. It was built to convey wealth and solidity, and that message remained strong and clear - perhaps stronger than ever compared with newer buildings designed to communicate efficiency and caution.

They were met in the lobby by a young man named Jonas, who saw them through the security process - 'This is my big week for nametags!' thought Elizabeth - and onto a wood-paneled high-rise elevator.

"This will take us to the lower level of the executive offices," he explained. "If you can manage a few stairs, it's best to start there and then walk up to the upper level."

When the elevator stopped, he led them along a hallway to a wide set of glass doors labeled:

Pemberley Executive Offices
Cornwallis Reinsurance Company

A monitor screen showed the day's date and:

Welcome:
Juniper Reinsurance
Gardiner and Austen

A woman behind a counter checked their credentials and then made a brief call to say the visitors had arrived. After a moment, they were joined by Ms. Reynolds, executive assistant to the president, a friendly and welcoming woman who appeared to relish the opportunity to put people at ease in such a formal setting. She introduced herself, apologized for the security, welcomed them, and explained that Mr. Lanier - Ms. Gardiner's counterpart at Cornwallis Re, whom Elizabeth had met the previous day - had given her strict instructions to give them the Deluxe Tour. "Unfortunately, Mr. Lanier himself isn't here today. He's off at a conference."

"Yes," said Ms. Gardiner. "We're at the same conference. We're just taking a break this morning."

"Very good!" She then explained that the senior officers were all away at an off-site meeting, so this would be a bad day to meet people but a good day to see the offices. Were they ready? They were indeed, and so they proceeded through a sunny atrium decorated with mammoth urns planted with vines and flowers as Ms. Reynolds described the history of this portion of the building and the architects and designers who'd been involved in its original creation and then in its more recent refurbishment. At the end of the atrium, they came to a wide, seemingly-unsupported stairway that curved gracefully up, looking like the entrance to a posh, corporate heaven.

They ascended the stairs at a respectful pace, Ms. Reynolds narrating details of the colorful, hand-blown chandelier, the bas-relief bronzes on the wall, and the Fibonacci arc of the stairway. On reaching the upper floor, they faced a central court set up as a sleekly modern, open working area, with long desks and glassed-in meeting rooms, populated by a handful of quietly busy-looking workers. It took Elizabeth a moment to get her bearings, but eventually she was able to see that the three other sides of the court were bounded by glass walls that gave a view through to large offices attractively furnished in a mid-century modern style. Most surprisingly, beyond the offices, visible through large windows, there were outdoor gardens.

Elizabeth was dazzled. She'd been expecting something mildly impressive, but also stodgy and not to her taste. This was a perfect balance of old and new, audacious and beautiful, grand and inviting. Her thoughts turned to Darcy. He'd worked here, had probably had a hand in guiding the refurbishment, and by all accounts had been well-positioned to be the next lord of this manor. Why had he left? What more than this could any executive be looking for?

Elizabeth had never been in the Juniper Re executive offices, but she assumed they weren't as stunningly impressive. Still, she wondered how nice they were, and whether she should be feeling something like regret for having refused a position reporting to Darcy. She thought to herself that it might have been nice to be able to host her

Pride Team colleagues in anything approaching this regal splendor - but remembering the low view that Darcy and others had of the team, she further thought that her colleagues might not have been particularly welcome in the Juniper Re executive offices.

Ms. Reynolds led them to the president's office, which extended the full width of the far end of the central court and was made up of three distinct areas - a central space dominated by a large, wooden desk; a conversation area with couches to one side; and a meeting area with chairs around a table to the other side. There was a view back to the central court through glass panels and a view out to the roof garden through large windows.

Along one side wall, behind the conversation area, there was a series of large photographs of gathered groups of employees at various company meetings and special events. Elizabeth walked over to take a closer look. She could make out Darcy's serious face in some of them, usually in the back row among a venerable-looking group that she assumed to be the senior management team.

"Anyone you know in there?" asked Ms. Reynolds.

"Mr. F. William Darcy. He's with us at Juniper Re now."

"Oh, don't I know it! How did you get so lucky? It gives me a pang every day to know that he's not here anymore. Have you gotten to know him at all?"

"A little."

"Well, he's a prince. As good as they come! They don't make 'em like that anymore. We all miss him - and not just because he looks like a movie star!"

"How long did you know him?" asked Ms. Gardiner.

"I knew him from the time he was a college student summer intern. He was a stand-up guy even then. And later, when he started working closely with Mr. Paternoster, I got to see up close that I was right to be impressed. A good head for business, of course, but always so fair-minded and conscientious. It wasn't just me. We all loved him! I think he could have taken half the company with him if he'd wanted, but he left very quietly and tried not disrupt anything at all. Mr. Bingley insisted on following him to Juniper, but I don't think anyone else did."

"No," said Elizabeth. "There was a Mr. Wickham who joined us from Cornwallis recently, but I don't believe he was drawn to us by Mr. Darcy."

"I'm sure you're right about that. Mr. Paternoster was always very friendly with Wickham, but there was something awkward between Wickham and Darcy. I don't know any of the details, but in my mind it's no contest as to who must be in the right." She walked over to one of the pictures. "Here's a good one. There's Wickham. Over here is Bingley. Back here is Darcy. That's Georgiana Icard next to him. Many of us kept hoping that they'd become an item. She's smart as a whip, and look at her! They were always so friendly together, you could tell they really liked each other, and they look like the perfect couple. But I guess it wasn't to be. You know, it's funny. In this business we're always backing up other people's commitments, but sometimes we neglect to make any of our own."

"But," said Elizabeth, "didn't she work for him?"

"Well, yes - there is that. And of course Darcy's a straight arrow who'd never cross that line. But I'm a hopeless, old romantic, and it seems to me that, if there's love, it should find a way."

Ms. Gardiner had only a passing acquaintance with Mr. Darcy, and wasn't sure what to make of Ms. Reynold's high regard for him. Based on the reports she'd heard, he was snooty and mean-spirited - and she'd have expected that, if he were remembered at Cornwallis at all, it would be with relief from his having absented himself. Why was Ms. Reynolds so resolute in her praise of him? Was she smitten with him? Was she partial to him because of his connection to the former president?

Elizabeth had learned enough about Darcy to understand that he wasn't the monster described by Wickham, but even she was surprised at the level of respect and admiration expressed by Ms. Reynolds. Having revised her opinion of him once already, she considered the possibility that she might need to do so again. She knew enough of executive assistants to see them as the most reliable judges of the personal character of highly-placed officers - whom they see at close quarters in all manner of situations.

The day being sunny and mild, Ms. Reynolds led them out onto the roof garden, which was charming and immaculately maintained. A meandering water feature was fed by a small waterfall, the burbling noise from which masked the sounds of the city, while tall hedges at the perimeter maintained the sense of being in a private garden. In keeping with the Deluxe Tour, a service of tea and scones was waiting for them at a table under an umbrella, and they happily ate and drank while Ms. Reynolds related more stories about Pemberley, Cornwallis Re, and the exemplary Mr. Darcy.

They eventually insisted that they could stay no longer, and after many cordial expressions on both sides Ms. Reynolds led them to an express elevator adjacent to the president's office.

"And did you find this trip interesting and worthwhile?" asked Ms. Gardiner with a satisfied smile as they were riding back down to the lobby.

"Remind me never to doubt you again!"

As they debarked, Elizabeth was regretting that she hadn't taken any photos during their tour. She announced that she'd belatedly make up for this by taking a picture of the private elevator, and asked Ms. Gardiner to pose in the lobby in front of the elevator door, which she gamely did. They made their way back out through security and stopped to get their bearings in the main lobby.

Elizabeth felt a wave of disorientation as she saw Darcy walking across the lobby towards them. Was this a hallucination? He didn't belong here anymore. Had he been conjured somehow by the steady mentioning of his name? He seemed equally surprised to see them, but approached them without reluctance.

"Ms. Austen and Ms. Gardiner - you've caught me out! Once a month I come back to my old building to get my hair cut. I try to sneak in when my old colleagues are out of town, because it feels vaguely embarrassing somehow - like hanging around the house you sold or spying on your ex. What I hadn't figured on was that I might run into my Juniper Re colleagues. What brings you here?"

"Nice to see you, Mr. Darcy, in your original habitat," said Ms. Gardiner with a nod and a handshake. "We're supposed to be at a conference, but I wanted Elizabeth to see Pemberley. A Ms. Reynolds just gave us a lovely tour."

"Oh, I miss Ms. Reynolds! She's the heart and soul of this place. You could shoot Ms. Reynolds to Mars and join her there five years later and find that she's created a Martian version of Cornwallis Re."

"She speaks very highly of you, as well."

Elizabeth listened to this friendly exchange but couldn't bring herself to say a word. She was feeling like the one who'd been caught out. What was she doing there? She didn't want to work for Darcy, but was happy to nose around his former offices and chat up his former colleagues.

"I'll accept whatever nice things she'll say about me, but I don't think you can give them much credence. She's known me too long, and is therefore biased."

"But surely, Mr. Darcy, such long acquaintance makes her testimony on your behalf all the more credible."

"Not necessarily. I've always thought that people meeting you for the first time are the most clear-eyed judges of who you really are. This is one of the reasons I don't like to meet new people. I'd rather stay close to those who've become habituated to my quirks and shortcomings."

"LIFO," said Elizabeth.

Ms. Gardiner turned to look at Elizabeth. "What was that?"

"I believe," said Darcy, "she's referring to Last In First Out accounting, as opposed to FIFO, which is First In First Out. LIFO accounting prioritizes the most recent transaction, which makes it - I think this was her meaning - a compelling analogy to someone like myself who overvalues the opinion of the most recent person he's met."

"Yes," said Elizabeth.

Darcy shook her hand. "Very apt and economically expressed. And how is Mr. Bennet, and how are your fellow team members?"

"Everyone is very well, thank you."

After a pause, Darcy pointed to the top of his head. "Well, as you can see, I've not yet had my haircut, and I'm sorry to say that my appointment time is almost upon us. This is late notice, but I wonder if you'd be available to join me for lunch afterwards. There are several very good options within a block."

They agreed on a time and place, and with a strong expression of his happiness of having met them and his anticipation of seeing them again shortly, Darcy excused himself and headed down a stairwell. Ms. Gardiner and Elizabeth proceeded out to the sidewalk to enjoy a walk during the interval before lunch.

Ms. Gardiner was full of questions about Darcy. Wasn't this the man she'd heard was so pompous and cold-hearted? He seemed to her quite the opposite. How well did Elizabeth know him? Was it, perhaps, more than she'd let on? This supposition, she noted, was based on his surprising ability to interpret her thoughts from a single, cryptic acronym. Elizabeth listened but said little, still trying to sort through her thoughts. She'd been so emphatically negative and self-righteously accusatory towards Darcy, surely he must wince at the sight of her and want to avoid her at any cost. Why was he being so nice? Didn't he once describe himself as unable to forgive and driven by implacable opposition? Also - surely it should have been possible for her to offer him a more gracious and congenial greeting than 'LIFO'!

They circled the surrounding blocks a few times, enjoying the architecture and people-watching, and then arrived at the agreed restaurant, *Bord de Roe*, a few minutes before the appointed time. There was a woman at a station just inside the door.

"We're meeting a friend here," said Ms. Gardiner. "Mr. Darcy."

"Welcome!" said the woman. "You'll be in the River Room. Follow me!" She led them through a dining room, down a hall, and into a private room that featured leather chairs around a large, wooden table and, across two walls, a mural of a stream winding through a forest. Ms. Gardiner declared it *Very Nice Indeed* and they sat and began to review their menus.

In a few minutes, they heard Darcy having an earnest conversation with someone in the hallway.

"I know this was last minute. I really appreciate it. Well, you're very kind. I'm sure this place would do a great business with any name. That's right. I'm not working in the city anymore. Yes, it's wonderful to see you as well. I need to join my friends."

He then appeared and, as before in the lobby, was all friendly charm. He wanted to know about their day, about the conference they'd been attending and their impressions of the Cornwallis offices. He had suggestions for what to order and what to see in the afternoon. He asked Ms. Gardiner for her opinions on trends in various catastrophe exposures that demonstrated his knowledge of the issues and his respect for Ms. Gardiner's perspective. Elizabeth found it refreshing to be seen by Darcy with a colleague she could be proud of. It was consoling that he should know she had some contacts within the company for whom there was no need to apologize. She listened most attentively to all that passed between them, and gloried in every expression, every sentence from the mouth of Ms. Gardiner, which marked her intelligence, her taste, or her good manners.

They were served their lunches, and shortly after they began eating Ms. Gardiner excused herself, as she'd received an urgent inquiry that she believed herself obligated to respond to. Darcy then turned to Elizabeth and said, "I have a personal, non-business matter on which I'd very much appreciate your advice - if that's all right with you. I know that in the past I've sometimes inappropriately assumed your readiness to follow a plan I had for you."

"I'd be happy to give you my thoughts. What is it?"

"Back where you were just visiting, there's a former co-worker of mine. I haven't said this to anyone, but she's the reason I left Cornwallis. She's a wonderful, beautiful, and talented young woman, and I was - *I am* - smitten with her. But I was her boss, so I couldn't say anything. And I was in line to be president of the company, so there really wasn't any way to solve that problem by having one of us switch departments. Unless I wanted to just forget about her, the only reasonable and honorable option was for me to change companies. So now that I've done that, I'm circling back to see if I have a chance with her. We're having dinner together tonight. I got my hair cut for the occasion."

"Does she know all of this?"

"I don't think so. I haven't told her any of this. I haven't told her that I left the company because of her. I haven't told her I love her. Of course, it would have been nice from my standpoint to sound her out and gauge my chances before going to this trouble, but it wouldn't have been right. If I'm her boss and I'm asking her what my chances are with her, that's harassment."

"That's right. Also, some people will lie if they get a question like that from their boss. Still, my hat is off to you. That's a big step to take with no guarantee of success. So what's your question?"

"What do I say to her tonight? Should I go slowly and drop a few hints that I'd like something beyond our professional relationship? Should I throw myself at her feet? I want to be open with her, but I also really want to avoid something analogous to the scene I'd like to forget with you - where I thought I was doing you a big favor by making you a job offer, and meanwhile I was just causing you pain."

"Yes, I have my own reasons for wanting to forget about that scene, so let's think about tonight. I'm really glad you asked me about this, because I love this stuff! I'm a world-class expert in matters of the heart for other people. Here's what you want to do. Number One: don't lead with the fact that you left Cornwallis because of her. That's a heavy thing, and it could cause her to feel guilt or a burden of obligation. Don't lie about it if she asks you, but you shouldn't volunteer that particular point of information. Number Two: be clear, but take baby, baby steps and watch for her reaction. Is she interested? Is she not interested? Keep your eyes and ears open and you'll know the answer without having to throw yourself at her feet - which could be painful for her as well as for you. Number Three: don't overthink this or rehearse speeches. This isn't some kind of sale you can make with the right presentation. You're hoping for a relationship. Relationships start with genuine, two-way communications, where neither one is the boss of the other."

Elizabeth leaned back and stared at her plate, grateful to have completed her response as Ms. Gardiner re-entered the room. "Sorry about that! One of the perennial issues I have to deal with is that most people, even knowledgeable reinsurance executives who claim to be 'data driven', trust their intuition more than they trust models. And I understand. When you get two five-hundred-year floods in three years, people are going to panic and want to throw out the model."

Elizabeth could only think about Darcy and the object of his affections. Apparently, Darcy was human after all. Once again, she'd have to recalibrate her estimation of him. How could she think badly of an honorable romantic who got his hair cut before dinner with his crush? Also, she was beginning to suspect that what had initially made him seem so stiff and unpleasant to her was his awkwardness in a new environment. Maybe he deserved to be cut some slack for that. Nobody likes to be the new kid in school. And what were his chances with his inamorata? There was no way to tell, but she found that she was rooting for him and eager to find out.

And what a pleasant surprise to find that Darcy had the trust in her to share such a confidence and ask for her opinion! How was that even possible after the terrible things she'd said to him? She felt that he must either put a very high value on rude bluntness or else have very few friends at Juniper Re.

Elizabeth was, in fact, elated. Much as she enjoyed and appreciated her employment at Juniper Re, the work environment was a romance desert. It was also distressingly short on babies and animals. A new parent could draw mobs by bringing his or her infant for a look-in at work. Similarly, a happy or even prospective couple could buoy the spirits of an entire department for months.

After they had all finished their lunch, Darcy saw Elizabeth and Ms. Gardiner into a taxi and sent them off with a wave to their next destination, an art gallery.

"Well, that lunch certainly confirmed my feeling that he's not what I was led to expect," said Ms. Gardiner. "Everything I'd heard before today was that he's a grumpy snob who's not to be trusted. When Ms. Reynolds at Cornwallis went on about how wonderful he is, I thought she was deluded somehow. But now I wonder!"

"Yes."

"Didn't you give me a bad report about him?"

"I'm afraid I did," said Elizabeth. "I think I may have jumped to some unfair conclusions when I was first acquainted with him. I did like him better when we crossed paths while I was over in Human Resources, but I've never seen him so pleasant as today."

"But didn't he cheat your friend, Wickham, somehow? Maybe he's one of those people who can put on a good front."

Elizabeth here felt herself called on to say something in vindication of his behavior to Wickham, and therefore gave her to understand, in as guarded a manner as she could, that by what she had heard when she was at HR, his actions were capable of a very different construction, and that his character was by no means so faulty, nor Wickham's so amiable, as they had been considered within the Pride Team. In confirmation of this, she related some particulars of job commitments and bonus payments, without actually naming her authority.

At this point, Ms. Gardiner began to describe the art they'd be seeing, while Elizabeth continued to ponder Mr. Darcy and his would-be lady love.

CHAPTER 44

The next morning, Elizabeth sat in on various sessions of the conference, but continued to think about Darcy's date and regularly checked her phone for messages. Halfway through *"Is Inland Flood the New Cal Quake?"* she saw that she had an email from Darcy. It was titled "Introduction" and included a copy to Georgiana Icard, using what looked like a personal rather than a Cornwallis Re email address for her.

> Ms. Austen, I was very pleased to see you and Ms. Gardiner yesterday, and I very much appreciated and benefited from your sound counsel. I am copying in my most particular friend, Georgiana Icard, so that you might be able to communicate with one another if you wish. I do this partly because Georgiana was eager to meet you and partly because I believe you have much to offer one another.
> Will

She found the 'Will' an interesting touch. Perhaps, having copied in Georgiana, he thought 'Darcy' would be too formal. The message was soon followed by another from Georgiana to Elizabeth alone.

> I can sometimes be fairly persuasive when necessary, so please don't hold it against Will that he agreed to make that introduction and share your email address. It is true that I'm wanting to make your acquaintance. I'm really hoping you'll find this friendly and not creepy. Will tells me you're in town for one more day. I assume your schedule is full with your conference, but if by any chance you happened to be uncommitted for lunchtime, please let me know, as I could very easily meet you at the conference hotel and would be

grateful for the chance to do so.

Yours in unsolicited outreach,

Georgiana

Having no specific lunch plan, and knowing no one at the conference other than Ms. Gardiner, Elizabeth was pleased to send a positive reply, suggesting a time for them to meet outside the hotel bistro. She herself arrived at the spot early, and occupied herself by watching passers-by for any signs that they might be early-arriving Georgianas. At the appointed hour, the actual Georgiana appeared. Elizabeth recognized her immediately from the picture she'd seen at Pemberley, and was happy and relieved to find that she liked her immediately. The picture had given her a sense of Georgiana's attractive appearance, but, being a picture, had been unable to convey her friendly energy.

Elizabeth had the distinct and exhilarating feeling that she was meeting someone who'd be a good friend for a long time. She'd had this feeling only a few times in her life, so far as she could remember, with the most recent being her first day at Juniper Re, when she'd met Jane. She knew enough about psychology, and her working life kept her sufficiently steeped in statistics, that she could imagine killjoy social scientists telling her that she'd actually had this feeling many times, but only remembered the few times when her premonition proved to be accurate. Still, she enjoyed the feeling, and was not about to distrust her own instincts in the interest of scientific objectivity. They hugged like sisters and took turns affirming how pleased they each were to meet the other. Over lunch, Georgiana made a confession.

"Please forgive me, but I've come this far with pushiness and now I'm going to take this one step further. I want to ask about the nature of your relationship with Will - what it is now and what you want it to be."

"I appreciate your directness," said Elizabeth, "and I can assure you there's no complication on my side. First of all, the person I know is Darcy, not Will, and we have a somewhat awkward business relationship, but it's only a business relationship. The only non-work, social interaction I've ever had with him was a conversation yesterday when he asked me for advice regarding his desire to have a personal relationship with a former co-worker whom I assume to be you - so if he blew it last night, you can blame me. As to my own wishes in the matter, I can tell you that I was briefly nervous when he started bringing up his personal life, and was very happy to find that his inquiry didn't have anything to do with me personally."

"Thank you, and I'm happy to hear it. I asked because he mentioned you in a way that made it seem to me that his work relationship with you was somehow parallel to the work relationship I had with him not so long ago, and so I naturally wondered just how parallel it might be."

"Of course. So, now, you've had your question. My very nosy question is that I'd like to know about the status of things between you and Darcy - not, as I've said, because I have any personal interest in him other than as a business associate, but rather because I have a ravenous vicarious interest in all matters of the heart, and also because he asked my advice. Reinsurance is all right, but someday I may want to become a professional romance coach, and I want to know what my record is."

"Fair enough! The exact nature of our current status is under review, but as of now we at least have a status - which in my book means that you should declare your coaching job an unqualified success. Although, I have to tell you that this wasn't a long-shot. His timetable on all this is running about three years behind mine."

"He was a little slow out of the gate, was he?"

"He couldn't do anything while I was working for him. I get that. But he's been over at Juniper for months now. He took a chance delaying like that. It was getting to the point where I was ready to forget all about him and run off with any of two or three particularly eligible movie stars, if they'd thought to ask me."

"Well - lucky for him they didn't. And you didn't feel you could make the first move?"

"Aside from my email to you this morning, I'm not usually a very forward person. When Will was leaving Cornwallis, I made it clear that I was hoping we could continue to stay in touch - but everyone says something like that, so I went just a little bit further and said that there might be a silver lining regarding the extent to which we could be in one another's lives, since we wouldn't have a business relationship any longer. For me, that was a pretty brazen statement.

226

Anyway, I'm not sure being forward or being retiring makes any difference with him, one way or the other. Will doesn't seem to decide things based on chance of success. He decides things based on what he thinks is right. This can be exasperating sometimes, but it's something I really love about him."

As they continued to converse, Elizabeth ventured to ask Georgiana a variety of questions that were on her mind. When did she first have feelings for Darcy? (At a company holiday party. She looked at him and realized that she wished he was her date rather than her boss.) What was she willing to say about Wickham? (Almost nothing, with a reference to the dictum that begins *"If you can't say something nice about someone..."*) What about the consultant, Brian Fitzwilliam? (A prince. They should all double date.) How did she like working at Cornwallis? (Fantastic space at Pemberley, mostly good people, but a few very annoying self-promoters.)

"And how do you find life at Juniper Re?" Georgiana asked her.

"This is a little embarrassing, but I actually love it. I know it's work, and work is supposed to be horrible, but I'm irrationally happy there. My position is uncertain and some people are very petty and there's politics that I don't understand, but none of that phases me because it's a community. Outside of work, I don't have a lot of community in my life, but when I'm at Juniper Re I feel like I'm living in Mayberry. I exist in a manageable universe, a small town where everybody knows one another, we know each other's histories, we know each other's quirks - and there are plenty of them - where each of us has our role, and we all find a way to work together."

"That is so sweet! And I think I know exactly what you're talking about. Even if it's not perfect, any reasonably functioning organization is somehow humanizing to be a part of. So, I have one, final question to ask you. Saturday is my birthday, and I'm hosting an afternoon party in my own honor. This is late notice, but is there any chance you could come?"

"Well, of course, my social calendar is such that I'm normally booked six months out, minimum, but I believe there may have been a last-minute cancellation that could make that possible."

Georgiana gave her the details, they split the lunch bill, and parted looking forward to seeing one another in two day's time.

Elizabeth wandered through the hotel ballroom, which was set up as a high-tech bazaar, filled with booths of companies hawking various products, mostly computer systems and consulting services, and she pondered the inescapable fact that looks can be deceiving. Who could tell, looking at a booth, whether the product was good or bad? First impressions aren't always accurate; she'd learned that with Darcy. The day she'd met him, at the Idea Fair in Meryton, she'd been convinced that he was proud, shallow, and self-centered. Once she'd gotten such an image into her head, it remained stubbornly and solidly there - with countervailing evidence serving only to chip away at it slowly, bit by bit, over the months. Even now, she was continuing to find that her mental image of him was inferior to the actual article. Clearly he had good taste, falling in love with Georgiana, and remarkable self-control, not speaking of it while he was her boss, and a willingness to make a sacrifice, leaving the company he loved, and at least some measure of humility, being unsure of whether his love was returned. And she could have been working for him - but instead had rudely refused him, telling him off in the bargain, and making quite sure such an offer would never be repeated.

"Ah, well," she thought, looking at the booth in front of her, *"I wonder if Georgiana would like an electrical power outage modeling program for her birthday?"*

CHAPTER 45

The coasters had seemed to Elizabeth like a good idea at the time. Lacking inspiration for a suitable birthday present to bring to Georgiana, she had wandered the aisles of various shops specializing in attractively unnecessary items, where she saw nothing remotely appropriate until a set of coasters caught her eye. Something in their sleek style and jaunty colors made her think of Georgiana, so she decided not to over-think the issue and purchased them on the spot. Now, walking up to the door of a stylish townhouse, she was filled with doubt. She'd never seen Georgiana's home; how could she know what would go with it? And what kind of a gift is coasters, anyway? She was glad the present was wrapped and hoped the presents wouldn't be opened in a public ceremony. She rang the bell and was surprised when the door was opened by Caroline Liebling.

"Elizabeth Austen?"

She distrusted Ms. Liebling and suspected her of working against Jane's interests and her own, but it was a weekend and she was at a party and determined to be as pleasant as humanly possible.

"Yes, that's right. What a nice surprise to see you. It all comes back to me now - Georgiana is your cousin."

"That's right," said Ms. Liebling, stepping aside to let her enter. "And what's your connection?"

"Hardly any. Nothing to compare with being a cousin. I'm tempted to say I heard there was a party, but she did invite me."

"Well, come on in. Everyone is this way."

Ms. Liebling led the way to a living room - Elizabeth was gratified to see that the coasters would fit in perfectly with Georgiana's attractive décor - and waved one arm indicating Georgiana, Ms. Thrush, and two women Elizabeth didn't recognize. "Everyone - this is Elizabeth Austen. Elizabeth, this is everyone."

Georgiana was up instantly and gave her an enthusiastic hug. "I'm so glad you came!" She quickly confirmed that Elizabeth already knew Ms. Thrush, and then introduced her two other guests, one a neighbor and one a colleague from Cornwallis. Elizabeth asked what she did there.

"My boyfriend likes to say that I do modeling, because it sounds like I get my picture taken wearing fancy clothes - but, of course, it actually means very glamorous work staring at a monitor all day playing with numbers and constructing rules for simulations. And what do you do at Juniper Re?"

"She works in the Pride Team," volunteered Ms. Liebling. "I'm not sure if there's any equivalent at Pemberley. It's sort of an in-house temp agency." She looked at Elizabeth and smiled. "Is that fair?"

"It's quite generous, actually. I'm not sure any of us has the office skills to be a proper temporary worker."

The bell rang and Ms. Liebling - who had apparently claimed for herself the role of doorkeeper - left to answer it. Soon, Elizabeth could hear Darcy's voice in the hallway, and she wondered if she were looking forward to seeing him or dreading it. She'd become accustomed to wanting to avoid him, but the pleasant lunch in town, the glimpse into his personal life, and her new friendship with Georgiana all conspired to make her think that he might actually be a welcome - even a friendly - sight.

Darcy entered the living room, led by Ms. Liebling, who was guiding him with a hand on his shoulder blade and laughing eagerly at some private joke that had apparently passed between them in the course of the ten-foot hallway. She stopped to announce, "I think most of you know Will Darcy. Will, you know Georgiana, of course. And Penny Thrush. This is Bridget Connelly, a neighbor. You may already know Kimberly Harano, who works in the modeling group at Pemberley. Oh, and I'm sure you remember Elizabeth Austen, who works in the Pride Team at Juniper. You're still there, aren't you Elizabeth?"

"Yes, I am."

"Of course. And why wouldn't you be?"

"A fine group, all assembled for a very special day!" announced Darcy, and he smiled and nodded to all assembled, gave Georgiana a kiss on the cheek, and set a package on the coffee table.

Elizabeth found herself wondering whether Ms. Liebling's odd remarks were deliberately intended as a dig at her and whether Darcy's statement had been his attempt to change the focus for her benefit. At the same time, she was suspicious of any interpretation of events that assumed her own centrality. These questions returned to her later when she entered the dining room, approaching a table well-provisioned with dips and hors d'oeuvres, and found herself joining a conversation circle with Georgiana, Darcy and Ms. Liebling, who exclaimed, "Here she is! We haven't seen much of her lately, have we Will? I think maybe she was spending as much time with the RMO as she could while they were in the Home Office. You're a great friend of that Wickham fellow aren't you? I understand he used to be at Cornwallis, so maybe Will or Georgiana can give you the inside scoop on him."

Ms. Liebling looked at each of them cheerfully, happy for whatever insinuations she intended to force a pause in the conversation. She was unaware that the mention of Wickham was at least as painful to Georgiana and Darcy as it was to Elizabeth, who smiled back at her and said, "I don't think we need to talk about anyone who isn't here. There are so many people who are here and more interesting to talk about."

"Yes," added Darcy with a nod. "And by all means let's not talk business. First of all, talking business between two different companies risks antitrust violations - but second, and more important, it's a weekend, so we should be at least pretending to have lives and interests outside of reinsurance."

"This is going to be a big challenge for us," said Georgiana. "For years, Will and I have talked about business, and now we can't. So what do we talk about? We tried to talk about pets the other night and before long he was talking about cat exposures."

"Yes," added Darcy, "and loss collars! And the difference between short-tail and long-tail business!"

Elizabeth was grateful for Darcy and Georgiana's good humor, but was still disquieted by Ms. Liebling's apparent enmity. Determined not to overstay her welcome, she was the first guest to excuse herself. Darcy walked her to the door and thanked her for coming. "I know Georgiana very much appreciates your being here today."

At the same time, Ms. Liebling was telling Georgiana that Elizabeth wasn't a very good fit at Juniper Re - in fact, was part of a failed social experiment that was being shut down. In her view, the program had been unfair to Elizabeth as well as to the company, and that she'd be better off once she'd found a position in a setting where she really belonged. Georgiana heard her out, but maintained that she found her extremely pleasant, judicious, and knowledgeable - and liked her shoes.

As Darcy returned, Ms. Liebling looked to him for confirmation. "We were just discussing Ms. Austen. Georgiana seems quite taken with her. It's my memory that at one point you thought highly of her yourself. I could never see it myself. I mean, what skills does she have? Is she an actuary? A lawyer? A contract specialist? No. How much real-world experience does she have? Close to zero. Can she bring in business? Not that I've seen. Is she a leader who can get people to rally around a project? Seems like more the opposite. I suppose she has some skill in ingratiating herself to certain people - generally friendless misfits, who are probably grateful that anyone's trying to seek their favor. And yet, she carries herself like she's God's gift to the world, and that she can look down on us all from the towering heights of her moral high ground." Feeling perhaps some momentum in her favor, she turned to Darcy. "Maybe even you have felt it. Her judgment from on high?"

This drew a wince from Darcy. "Yes. Yes, I have. And, at least sometimes, it was well deserved."

"Sometimes well deserved. Very generous of you, but hardly a ringing endorsement of her judgment. I suppose the tyrants and abusers of this world comfort themselves at the end of the day by saying it was all sometimes well deserved. I remember there was talk at one time that you might hire her to work for you. I used to kid you about hiring her whole motley team. But I notice that months have passed and she seems not to be working for you. Apparently cooler heads have prevailed."

"Yes," said Darcy. "One much cooler head than my own did prevail, and consequently she is not, and probably will never be, part of my team."

This was the conclusion that Ms. Liebling had been hoping for. She considered herself the logical candidate to be Darcy's lieutenant, and had grown impatient waiting for him to choose her - or at least choose someone and settle the matter. She attributed his inaction, not inaccurately, to his interest in Elizabeth, and had spoken as rashly as she had with the intention of forcing the issue. Surely, it was impossible that he could choose Elizabeth, and the sooner he faced that fact the sooner he could move forward and start building his staff. She realized that forcing issues wouldn't add to her popularity, and might hurt her chances to be his choice, but she'd grown rash with frustration. She told herself there was always a chance that, when he was ready to make a hiring decision, he might value a bit of brashness, and even if he ended up considering her a bit of a pit bull, might prefer to have such a creature working with him rather than against him.

CHAPTER 46

Elizabeth normally tried to avoid looking at her work email over the weekend, but she took at peek on Sunday and saw a message from Jane with the subject line: Lydia Leaving the Company? She opened it immediately and read.

> Dearest Lizzy, I have no hard facts at this time, but the rumors flying around are that our own Lydia - together with George Wickham - has left the company to work for a new start-up reinsurer that nobody's heard of before. The name is Utmost Re, and apparently they're headquartered in the Cayman Islands. I'm not sure if that means Lydia will be working there, but if so we'll have to make a trip and visit her! There's nothing but confusion here about the details. Why did they leave together? What's the appeal of the new company? What will their new positions be? Will the accounts that Wickham was handling move their business? I assume this is a desired and exciting outcome for Lydia but, as I say, I don't really know enough at this time to comment. To tell the truth, I'm not really surprised that Wickham would jump to another company, but I am surprised that he would take Lydia with him - as I assume it must have been his initiative in the matter since it seems unlikely that a rival reinsurer would bother to recruit someone as junior as Lydia. But maybe I underestimate her. I apologize for the unhelpful lack of information, but this has been the sole topic of conversation within the Pride Team since the first rumors broke on Friday. I am going into the office today to see if I can find out anything more. I thought you should at least know what little I know at this point. Are you back on Monday? I certainly hope so!

Elizabeth replied, thanking Jane for the information, and assuring her that she'd be in the office on Monday. Later in the day she saw there was a new message: Could Be Bad.

Lizzy, I'm sorry to trouble you again with incomplete information, but I need to tell you that this business with Lydia doesn't seem to be adding up, and I'm getting really worried that she may be involved in something fishy or worse. Personally, I wouldn't have recommended that she sign up with a start-up company - particularly one that's also hiring George Wickham - but I wouldn't have seen it as a big deal. A bit imprudent or sub-optimal maybe, but not dangerous or bad. However, I have to tell you that we've all been researching as best we can, and it appears that Utmost Re might not be a genuine company. I'm very afraid that it's some kind of phony shell company, and that our Lydia may be caught up in a terrible fraud. Everybody's been trying to reach her or Wickham, but they aren't answering their phones and seem to have left the country. Has she been kidnapped? Is she a criminal? I don't know what to think and what to worry about, but I do seem to be able to imagine a lot of terrible things. Mr. Bennet has been in touch with Mr. Forster, the RMO head. Whatever took place must have happened right under his nose, but he doesn't seem to know anything. He can't find either one of them and doesn't know where they've gone. They left their company laptops and Wickham's company phone in the office, but everything had been wiped clean off of them. Meanwhile, he's been hearing from some of Wickham's companies that they'd placed excess treaties with Utmost Re thinking it was a Juniper Re subsidiary. That looks bad for the company already, but it will be much worse if it turns out that Utmost Re isn't really a company at all. Despite it all, and I suspect you will tease me for thinking this way, but I cannot help but hope that there's a reasonable and innocent explanation for everything, and that it will all become apparent once we have more information. As unlikely as that now seems, it doesn't strike me as any less likely than Lydia or even Wickham being an outright criminal. Most of the team is here today. It's sort of surreal to be here together on a Sunday. The building is otherwise empty, but we stay, holding a sort of vigil, thinking that one of us may get news. As you might imagine, Ms. Nebbit is not doing well. She mostly sits in the corner of Mr. Bennet's office talking to herself. He isn't much better. The whole situation appears to have simply defeated him. And Kitty is perhaps saddest of all. She looks absolutely terrible. Mary and I do what we can to keep spirits up, but we don't have much to work with. Sorry this is such a grim message. I really don't know what to think. What I'm most worried about is that something horrible might have happened to her. Nobody's heard from her or knows where she is. My second fear is that she's all right but mixed up in something illegal. I'll admit that I've sometimes thought that Lydia showed poor judgment, but I don't believe she'd do anything really bad. I'm hoping we'll hear from her soon and find out what's really going on.

Elizabeth looked up. What should she do? Who could she turn to? She looked back down and saw that she had a message from Darcy.

Thanks!

It was nice to see you at Georgiana's party today. She and I are worried that at least one of the guests may have caused you to feel less than completely welcome. If so, we both regret that very much and want you to know that your presence was very much appreciated by both of us. I'm eager to make this up to you. Please let me know how I can be of service to you in any way.

She told herself she wouldn't respond to this message and then immediately did.

Thank you for your very kind offer, and although I see no reason to believe that you owe me anything at all, still with all my heart I must ask for your help for the sake of my fellow team member, Lydia - as I'm extremely distressed with worry for her, and don't know where else to turn. I blame myself for whatever danger or difficulty she may be in now, because I didn't think it necessary to let her know what I had discovered from you - namely the scope of deceit in George Wickham. I'm attaching below a pair of emails I received from Jane. This is all I currently know of the matter. I suppose it's possible that this situation has already come to your attention as a matter of risk to the company, and I know that your position requires you to view it from that perspective and do everything in your power to protect the interests of the organization. But I ask - as a terrible colleague and a worse friend, and now as a representative of what I expect is about to be an infamous and soon-to-be-extinguished work team - I ask as a personal favor if you could please, please, please also do everything in your power to protect Lydia. Is she perfect? No, certainly not. Might she have made some bad choices? Probably so. But she is good at heart. Her faults are those of excess enthusiasm, not of greed or malice. I have to think that she's been used by Wickham, and I don't ask you to do anything to protect him. If her life is ruined by this, I will feel it as my own fault forever. There may well be nothing you can do, and your offer of help was probably intended to encompass something more along the lines of a Juniper Re refrigerator magnet, but I ask your help because I want and need to do something and asking your help is the only rational step I've been able to come up with so far.

She sent the message before she could second-guess herself, then pondered who else she might contact. She thought she should check her voice mail, and dialing in heard the following message:

This is Brian Fitzwilliam. I apologize for the very late notice, but I've just come into possession of two very good tickets to the opera Sunday night, and I can think of no one with whom I'd rather watch Tosca meet her cruel fate. I certainly understand if you already have plans or if the offer has no appeal to you - although, if so, please do me the courtesy of saying that the problem is the opera rather than myself. I hope this message finds you well.

She looked at the clock. In a happier universe, there would have just been time to call, accept, get dressed, and arrive before the overture. Instead she dashed out a quick text:

Sorry! Sorry! Just got your message and unfortunately am in

the middle of a crisis regarding a co-worker. Would not only prefer to be watching Tosca tonight, would prefer to be Tosca. Please enjoy with one of your other glamorous clients, because once the crisis becomes common knowledge I may be entering the Witness Protection Program.

She then packed a bag full of fruit and snacks to bring as a Care Package and was heading out to her car when she received a call.

"Darcy here. I got your message, I share your concern, and I'm ready to do whatever I can - but I need more to go on."

"Thank you so much for getting in touch! What do you need?"

"I need some guidance first of all. You know Lydia. Who should we be talking to? What should we be looking for? How do you break this thing down?"

Elizabeth stopped for a moment to put her thoughts in order.

"Lydia is high energy and extroverted. If she's in hiding, she won't be able to stay quiet and unconnected to the world for long. She's close to Kitty on the Pride Team, and also to Candy Estroff, who works for Forster at the RMO office. She's bound to contact one or both of them before long. I don't know who else. She lives alone as far as I know. I don't think I've ever heard her talk about a boyfriend or any of her family members. I assume HR must have something in their files - somebody's name to call in case of emergency."

"Got it."

Elizabeth sat in her car but didn't start the engine. She was starting to feel less bad, less clenched-up inside, less powerless.

"She plays at being a kind of goofball, but she's actually very conscientious. I can believe Wickham would want to set up a shell company as a scam, but that's not what he'd tell Lydia. He'd tell her the new company was needed to streamline operations, serve customers better, write more business - and then she'd do everything, but she'd do everything by the book. Whatever licenses are needed, whatever organizations should be joined, she'd make it all happen. We should be looking for new listings everywhere a legitimate company would be registered. Chauncey in Legal is good with regulatory issues and has a lot of contacts. He might be able to track down some useful information."

"Good. What else?"

"This is going to sound crazy, but I think we need an underwriter who can figure out what the excess treaties on Utmost Re paper are really worth. Forster should be able to get the details. If they're excess property treaties, you want Drummond. If they're excess liability, you want Lee. I'm assuming that one possible endgame to all this is that Juniper Re buys out the treaties - either buys those accounts as a book of business or simply buys Utmost Re. That way, we could honor the treaties that were sold and decide what to do with Lydia and Wickham. But you'll have to know what they're worth. The company could decide to take a loss for business reasons, but you'd have to be able to quantify how big a loss to expect."

"Don't get your hopes up for a buyout, but I agree that we'll need to know what the contracts are worth."

"I understand, but when you finalize that buyout that I'm not allowing myself to hope for, I want you to do what you can for Lydia."

"What would that mean?"

"Bring her back. Let her return to work at Juniper Re. Maybe not in her old job. You know what would be good? Events Planning. Ms. Machado could use an energetic young apprentice."

"Anything else?"

"I assume we're going to have to talk to the police, and I think that's OK. We need to talk to the police, and I want their help to find Lydia. What I don't want is for her to get arrested. Can we make this a missing person case and not a fraud case - at least initially?"

"I think the police get to decide how they're going to treat any case, but you're right that we need to talk to them. At a minimum, we've got to report that Lydia and Wickham are missing, and I'm sure we'll all feel better once we at least know where they are. Thanks for your time. I'll be in touch if I learn anything or if I need to pick your brain some more. Good night."

"Good night."

Elizabeth, after all the misery of the day, found herself shortly on the road to the office, wondering what she would find at Longbourn.

CHAPTER 47

Behind the wheel, Elizabeth pondered what she knew of Lydia's actions. Even assuming that Lydia was innocent of any intent to trick customers into paying for fraudulent coverage, she had clearly made some bad judgments.

First off, it seemed clear that she'd been an accessory to fraud. An unwitting accomplice is still an accomplice. Maybe she'd been used, but she should have known better. She's plenty smart - smarter than she sometimes pretends to be - and it shouldn't have been particularly hard for her to put the pieces together and deduce the fact that Wickham's scheme wasn't about anything other than getting money for Wickham.

Also, it isn't possible to incorporate a company overnight. This was a plan that had been in the works for months - time during which Lydia continued to be an employee of Juniper Re. This was bad. She would have been accepting a salary and benefits from one company while effectively being committed to and working for the advancement of another company that, if it was legitimate at all, would have been a direct competitor.

The normal expectation is that, if you accept a position with another company - especially a competitor - you inform your boss. If you work at Juniper Re and you accept a position teaching high school math, your boss will probably ask you to stay through a reasonable notice period. If you accept a position at a rival reinsurer, your boss will ask you to leave immediately, and someone will chaperone you while you clean out your desk.

Elizabeth wondered how often people fudge this kind of admission. It's probably tempting sometimes to lie low, particularly if one is on the brink of being vested or being eligible for a bonus. But how can anyone continue to accept payment from a company when they've

240

committed themselves to its opponent? Elizabeth couldn't imagine doing that. She wouldn't be able to look at herself in the mirror each morning, and she was sure that someone like Darcy would see such duplicity as unforgivable.

There was something else as well. When a high-spirited young woman and a smoothly manipulative man execute a plan together and then disappear at the same time, one cannot help but suspect that there is something more between than simply a business relationship. And if they had in fact become intimate, this would represent an additional dimension of bad behavior on Wickham's part and poor judgment from Lydia. Wickham, who had effectively been acting as her supervisor at the time, would be guilty of sexual harassment, and Lydia - once again, as with every other element of this unhappy business - should have known better.

Could she have fallen in love with him? The heart goes where it will. Here Elizabeth once again blamed herself and bitterly regretted not giving Lydia more information and a stronger warning about Wickham. If Lydia was in love, did that make her willing to do bad things on Wickham's behalf or did it simply blind her to his shabby goals? And, if she did fall in love with him, should it be considered a mitigating factor? Do we feel less badly about the robbed banks if we think that Bonnie wasn't in it for the money, but rather was in it for Clyde?

Elizabeth wondered how they would each be judged, particularly within the company. In her view, it was obvious that Wickham deserved most or all of the blame. He was, after all, in a more senior and certainly more highly-compensated position. Still, she wondered. As a client-facing marketer, he'd be expected to test boundaries and challenge authority. Lydia, on the other hand, serving in an inside support role, had the responsibility to keep everything kosher and compliant. This, thought Elizabeth, was the root of many problems in business and in relationships - when the ids have more power than the superegos.

It may be easily believed that, however little could be added to her hopes and fears on these interesting subjects by continuous internal debate and speculation, Elizabeth was unable to turn her mind to any other topic during the whole of her drive. Her thoughts spun in a circular path from excoriating Wickham to judging Lydia to blaming herself and then back around to Wickham again. With light Sunday traffic, she made good time to the office and was soon signing in at the front desk and making her way up to Longbourn, where she found Kitty and Mary sitting at a conference table covered with snack food. They rose and hugged her.

"Sorry I wasn't here earlier! Is anyone else around?" asked Elizabeth.

"Jane's in Bennet's office with Ms. Nebbit," said Mary. "We take turns listening to her in there. Jane has the most patience, so she gets the longest turns. Mr. Bennet's at the RMO, seeing what he can find out there."

"Any news?"

"Nothing yet. We'll probably give up and go home pretty soon. Maybe there'll be some news tomorrow. I collected and printed up the most recent messages we had from Lydia. There's a copy on my desk. Here, I'll show you."

Elizabeth nodded to Kitty, then followed Mary to her desk.

"Kitty's as bad as Ms. Nebbit," said Mary in a low voice as she handed Elizabeth a few sheets of paper stapled together. "I mean, I get it that this looks really bad for Lydia and is going to hurt all of us by association. But Kitty's taking it really hard."

"Thanks. You could probably use a break. Stretch your legs a little and I'll have a word with Kitty."

Elizabeth glanced at the papers in her hand and returned to the conference room, where Kitty was absently ironing a candy bar wrapper with her thumbs.

"I'm guessing this must be very hard for you," said Elizabeth. "You're so close to Lydia. You two have been like sisters. Maybe closer than sisters."

Kitty looked up. "When the RMO was in the building and we'd go up there to socialize, I always assumed that it was a game, and that it wasn't really about flirting with the guys. The real fun of it, the real point of it, was her and me doing it together."

Elizabeth sat down. She thought about saying something, but decided it was better to wait. After a moment, Kitty continued.

"The real point of it to me, that is. It turns out that it wasn't just a game to Lydia, and it certainly wasn't about doing something with me. That was my delusion. For her, it really was about flirting with the guys."

"Oh, Kitty! I'd no idea! She's broken your heart. Does she even know?"

Elizabeth came around the table and put her arms around her. "I assumed that she knew. But maybe not. So please, let's just keep this between us."

"Of course."

"And if we find out anything bad has happened to her in all this, then I am a horrible, horrible person - sitting here feeling sorry for myself that she doesn't love me and ran off with that tool, Wickham."

"Yes, well - Wickham is very certainly, as you say, a tool, but we shall all hope that Lydia will turn up soon, and will be found to be just fine. Now, I need to check in on Jane and Ms. Nebbit."

Elizabeth, still holding the papers she'd received from Mary, gave Kitty one last hug and walked up the hall to Mr. Bennet's office. She knocked quietly on the door and then let herself in. Jane, who was standing inside the door, shouted "Lizzy!" and embraced her. Ms. Nebbit, reclining on a loveseat surrounded by wads of tissue, appeared not to notice. She rocked from side to side and spoke quietly and earnestly, as if narrating a documentary.

"And what did I say? I said we should take the whole team for an extended visit to the new RMO. The whole team, I said. An extended visit, I said. And why did I say that? Did I want to go there for my health? No, indeed, I did not! I was thinking about Lydia, that poor, dear child. Helpless as a babe in the woods. I was thinking that poor, dear child needed a friendly eye or two to look over her. That's what I was thinking. And did anyone listen? No, they did not! Did we all go down there and have that extended visit and keep one or two friendly eyes on that poor, dear child? No, we did not! Oh, I am doomed like Casanova! I always know the future and no one will listen to me! And what about Mr. Forster? That rising meteor, Mr. Forster, was supposed to be in charge down there at the new RMO. What about him? Did he do his duty? Did he keep an eye or two on her? Not so much! He was in loco parentis, was he not? And was he a parent to her? Not at all! I think maybe he was just loco! Too busy being a rising meteor to keep an eye on any poor, dear child who wasn't his own poor, dear child!"

Jane sat next to her and put a hand on her shoulder. "Look," she said,

"Lizzy is here."

Elizabeth smiled and waved. Ms. Nebbit looked at her and said, "And what about that Candy Whoever-she-is? Did she keep an eye or two on that poor, dear child? No, indeed, she did not! Lured her down there and left her to fend for herself!"

Elizabeth took her hand and leaned close to her. "We're all very concerned," she said, "but we're hoping for the best."

"Do you even hear me? That's what I said to Mr. Bennet. Did he listen to me when I said we should all make an extended visit to the new RMO. No, he did not, but he's there now. And what about him? He's there, and it will probably end badly for him, too. He'll get fired, forced out, thrown under the bus. What's left of the Pride Team will become a wholly-owned subsidiary of Collins and that sneaky Charlotte. This is probably the best thing that ever happened in the world to that sneaky Charlotte! It's probably a bright scarlet letter day for her and her friends! Ms. Cullis and the Surge Team are rubbing their hands together and getting ready to dance the Zombie Jamboree on our graves, so to speak! And what about me? What did I say? I'll tell you what I said! I said we should all go down for an extended visit to the new RMO to keep an eye or two on that poor, dear girl!"

How difficult it is to handle loss! thought Elizabeth. Just the threat, the rumor, the shadow of loss had crushed Kitty, incapacitated Ms. Nebbit, and depressed the rest of them. She was humbled at how little she or even Juniper Re could do about it. What was their business, after all, but making up for loss? What is reinsurance but a floodwall protecting the world from loss? But when loss hits close to home, one realizes that insurers and reinsurers can't actually make anyone whole. They can't give people back the house and belongings that were destroyed, the limb that was injured, the loved one who has died. In return for loss, all they can offer is money. This isn't nothing, but it's hardly compensation. It's a bit of help against the financial damage that can follow on the heels of actual loss. You're still bereft, but you have the weak-tea consolation of not also being destitute.

Later, with Kitty stretching her legs and Mary taking her turn listening to Ms. Nebbit, Elizabeth and Jane were able to be by themselves for a while. They began by acknowledging the dreadful scenario before them - their friend and colleague an accessory in a large-scale financial fraud - which Elizabeth considered all but certain and Jane couldn't assert to be wholly impossible. Elizabeth continued the subject by saying, "But tell me all and everything about which I haven't already heard. Give me further particulars. What did Mr. Forster say? Had they no warning of anything before Wickham and Lydia disappeared? The two of them must have been working quite closely together."

"Mr. Forster did confirm that Lydia had become quite consumed with working on projects for Wickham, but he didn't see any harm in it. I'm so sorry for him! This is certainly a black eye for him as well, but he's been very attentive and kind to us. He'd alerted Mr. Bennet that she'd gone missing before any of this other business came to light."

"And how did he put together what was going on?"

"He brought Mr. Denny in from his recent retirement. Wickham was working with all of Denny's old clients, so Denny was able to make a few phone calls, sit down with a few of his old contacts, and piece things together - to the extent that anything's pieced together at this point. He was able to identify that Wickham had been selling contracts that used Utmost Re as the reinsurer."

"And what's Denny's opinion on Utmost Re? Does he think it's legitimate or a scam?"

"I haven't heard that he's offered an opinion on that subject. From the perspective of a loyal, old field hand, it may not make a lot of difference. Being on the Juniper Re payroll and selling somebody else's coverage - that's bad enough, whether or not it's outright fraud."

"And when you heard that Lydia and Wickham had joined up with Utmost Re - did any of you suspect that it might be a fraud?"

"Why should such an idea should enter our brains? I felt a little uneasy, a little fearful that she was making a risky career choice, especially since it seemed to be coordinated with Wickham, and you've made me aware that he's not someone who can be wholly trusted. Ms. Nebbit was quite pleased at the prospect of Lydia being recruited away. Of us all, Kitty seemed most alarmed. I took it as her simply being sorry to lose her good friend, but maybe she knew or could guess something more than the rest of us."

"Did Mr. Forster appear to think well of Wickham himself? Does he know his real character?”

‘I must confess that he didn’t speak so well of Wickham as he formerly did. He found him unreliable and overprotective of his client relationships. Not a team player.”

“Oh, Jane! Had we been less secret, had we told what we knew of him, this wouldn’t have happened!”

“Maybe so. But we meant well. It would have seemed mean-spirited simply to expose his former faults. People can change, right? What if he had reformed?”

“Did I understand that Lydia’s last communication was an email to Candy Estroff?”

“Yes. I got it forwarded from Mr. Forster. Here.”

Jane found the document on her phone and handed it to Elizabeth.

My Dear Candy,

You will laugh when you know where I am gone, and I cannot help laughing myself at your surprise tomorrow morning, as soon as I’m missed. I’ll just say it’s an international flight to a new opportunity for me and a very special mentor, whose identity will become obvious, if you haven’t guessed already! Thank you so much for bringing me to the RMO! It’s been a turning point in my life - professionally and personally. Even though I’m leaving now, I’m forever in your debt for bringing me here! Don’t feel obligated to pass this message on to all my other (soon-to-be-former!) colleagues at the RMO and the Home Office. I’ll be in touch with them shortly - on a letterhead and with a title that they may think at first is some kind of April Fools prank! Best wishes for the blockchain conference - I’m sure it will be a huge success!

Your affectionate friend,

Lydia

“Oh thoughtless, thoughtless Lydia!” cried Elizabeth when she had finished it. “What sort of message is this to be written at such a moment? But at least it shows that she believed herself to be heading for an exciting new position and not a life of criminal exile. I assume that this got forwarded to Mr. Bennet as well?”

"Yes. I never saw anyone so shocked. He couldn't speak a word for a full ten minutes. And that was when Ms. Nebbit became so distressed - and here we all still are, trapped in sadness and confusion!"

"So does the whole company know the situation at this point?"

"Not yet. There hasn't been any official announcement, but the word is starting to leak out. Unless Ms. Nebbit decides to take a sick day, I imagine the whole building will know by the end of the day tomorrow."

"Not to add to your troubles, but you don't look well. I believe babysitting Ms. Nebbit has been too much for you. I'm sorry I wasn't around earlier to help."

"Mary takes turns, but she's been busy with Kitty. Ms. Cullis made a brief visit earlier and offered the services of the Surge Team to help in any way they could."

"She had better stayed at home. Perhaps she meant well, but under such a misfortune as this, one can't see too little of one's neighbors. Assistance is impossible; condolence insufferable. Let them triumph over us at a distance and be satisfied."

"And what is Mr. Bennet hoping to find out at the RMO?"

"It's purely a fishing expedition, as far as I know. He's just looking for any clue to where they went or how to reach them. Ms. Nebbit, as you may have heard, is convinced that it's all hopeless, and he's just going to get himself - and, by extension, all of us - into even more trouble."

"She may be right," said Elizabeth, "but it looks like fishing expeditions are all we have at this point." And she began reading through the sheaf of papers she'd received from Mary.

CHAPTER 48

The next morning, Elizabeth and the other remaining Pride Team members found the office looking surprisingly normal - setting aside the fact that Mr. Bennet was still absent and Ms. Nebbit was once again holed up in his office. They had been hoping for some communication from Mr. Bennet, but had heard nothing from that quarter. This wouldn't normally have been surprising, as he'd never been prone to generous streams of language - unwilling to text, reluctant to email, slow to phone, and, in person, not particularly chatty. Still, his words, when they appeared, were always well-chosen and would have been much appreciated under the circumstances, even if they'd contained no particularly helpful insights or revelations.

Elizabeth made the rounds of the various individuals she'd recommended to Darcy. Ms. Estroff in the RMO had heard nothing from Lydia since the message that she'd shared. Drummond and Lee in Underwriting had both been contacted by Darcy. The treaties in question were property rather than liability treaties, and so Mr. Drummond had calculated an approximate technical cost for each of them that seemed to indicate the treaties had been underpriced by about 20%, which was actually closer to a reasonable market rate than Elizabeth would have guessed. Chauncey in Legal had a record of an inquiry from Lydia about the legal requirements for a captive insurance company. Could Utmost Re be a captive?

A captive insurance company, incidentally, is not quite so melodramatic as its name might suggest. It's simply an insurance company created to manage the risks of the company that owns it - typically a large company that requires a lot of insurance.

Still no word from Mr. Bennet, but they did hear from Ms. Gardiner, who was solicitous but unable to be of any practical help. They also received the following message:

My Dear Sir and Various Madams,

I feel myself called upon by our relationship, and by my situation in the organization, to condole with you on the grievous affliction you are now suffering under, which has recently come to our attention. Here in Human Resources, it is our business to know what is happening in the lives of company employees, whether the news be pleasing or horrifying. We are here to celebrate with our employees at their moments of triumph, and similarly we are here to express our sympathies for those employees who see an associate exposed as an untrustworthy fraud - knowing that, rightly or wrongly, their close association with such an individual is likely to strike a decisively negative blow to the prospects for their remaining careers. Speaking on behalf of the Human Resources Special Projects Team, that is to say Charlotte and myself, I want you to be in no doubt that we sincerely sympathize with your entire team in your present ordeal of shame and ignominy. I'm sure that I speak for the entire Special Projects Team when I say that we want you all to know that we stand with you at this difficult time - figuratively speaking, of course, as it will be some time before it is prudent for either of us to pay you a personal visit or to be seen anywhere in the general vicinity of Longbourn. More importantly, I can assure you on my own first-hand knowledge that our Head of Human Resources, Executive Vice President Catherine de Bourgh, sympathizes with you as well. Indeed, she told me herself that she hardly knew whom to pity more: the remaining young women of the Pride Team, whose moderately promising careers will be stunted beyond recognition by their association with this scandal; or Mr. Bennet, whose formerly respectable legacy with the company will be forever overshadowed by this sad but indelible chapter. I also want to assure you that we play no favorites in these matters - unlike the great bulk of our employees who appear to be inclined to judge the Pride Team more harshly than the RMO simply because the RMO is an essential component of the company's operations, while the Pride Team in its current incarnation is, by contrast, an insubstantial hobby unit. However many people feel that way, we will continue to hold quietly in our hearts to the principle of holding all business units to the same high standards. And finally, in these difficult times, it is always best to remain thankful. I, for instance, am now very thankful that I have had the good fortune, aided by a natural caution, to have never been an employee of either the Pride Team or the RMO, and to have never hired anyone out of either of those units. I am sure you will not begrudge me my relief and satisfaction at having dodged the bullet that is currently so fatal to you all. With best personal regards,

William Collins

Elizabeth heard from Darcy from time to time, and while she appreciated hearing from him she was troubled by the tone of his communications, which were consistently curt and impersonal.

"We found some rating sheets in Lydia's files," he said to her on the phone that afternoon without any greeting or lead-in. "They're for excess property coverage on individual large companies. The accounts don't seem to correlate to anything on our books. Looks to me like they must have been quoting some fac business as Utmost Re."

'Fac' is short for 'facultative' - in this case meaning that he suspected Lydia and Wickham were offering reinsurance on individual accounts rather than 'treaty' business which would have been portfolios of similar policies written by a given insurer.

"Yes, maybe," she said. "Send me the names of the companies, though. I have an alternate theory that I'd like to explore."

"Which is?"

"Maybe those big companies have insurance captives. It's possible that Utmost Re was focused on selling coverage to captives. We've been thinking they might be operating out of the Cayman Islands, but maybe we should be looking at the captive capital, Vermont. Lydia's comment about an international flight might have been deliberately misleading. One way to get to Vermont is to fly to Toronto and drive down."

"Do you have any evidence for this?"

"No, it's just a thought."

"I'm sending you the list right now. Do you have anything else for me?"

"No."

And the call was over without a goodbye.

He must be mad at me, she thought. Why wouldn't he be? It's my colleague who's causing this fire drill, and it was my pleading that dragged him into the middle of it. What have I ever done for him? Mostly, I've criticized him - helpfully explaining to him all of his shortcomings, real and imagined. Who wouldn't be mad at someone like that? Yes, we had a few days of truce. I gave him some advice on what to say to Georgiana, as if I knew anything about her at that point. Of course, she already loved him, so it didn't matter what I told him. Really, it was nice of him to let me kibitz on his personal life, just as it was nice for him to treat for lunch and to have Georgiana invite me to her birthday party and to email afterwards to apologize for Ms. Liebling being rude. And how do I repay all that? I impose on his cordiality and demand that he drop everything and try to save my fellow team member from what are probably the inevitable consequences of her own bad behavior. He has a million other things to do, and yet clearly he's spending a lot of time on this thankless and probably unpopular fool's errand - and the worst of it from his perspective is that, if it turns out that anything can be done to help Lydia, it will probably mean also helping Wickham. How galling would that be for him? So, we had our brief truce, but clearly he hates me now. After the lunch and the birthday party, I'd been thinking that we might be able to revisit the job offer he once made me that I so adroitly turned down. Well, I can forget about that now. I took whatever goodwill I managed to build up with him and spent it all on Lydia. And probably that was the right thing to do, because I didn't warn her about Wickham, but still the goodwill is spent and gone. He'll never hire me, and I'll be lucky to get a Hello from him in the hallway.

Oh, and I can also thank my devotion to Lydia for killing whatever personal relationship I might have had with Brian Fitzwilliam. Since I turned down his offer of Tosca, I've only gotten a few messages; friendly, I suppose, but hardly romantic. I gave it a shot and asked him to join me at a wine festival – five days out and on a Saturday, but he couldn't make it, or so he said. Shouldn't he have a little extra free time with Darcy out chasing around creation for Lydia and Wickham? So now it's his turn if he wants to keep trying, but I haven't heard anything. Of course, now that I've missed my chance I realize how good he and I could have been together. Because apparently it wasn't going to be sufficient for me just to throw away

251

my professional prospects - I needed to throw away my personal prospects as well!

CHAPTER 49

Two days later, as Jane and Elizabeth were talking together by the copy machine, Jeremy from the Surge Team walked past them, then turned and came back to stand next to them. "You may know this already," he said quietly, "but your Mr. Bennet got a big overnight envelope this morning from Mr. Darcy. I only know because it was delivered by mistake to Ms. Cullis, and she had me take it over to him."

Without elaborating on whether or not this was news to them, they thanked him and made their way directly to Mr. Bennet's office. The door was closed and Jane hesitated, but Elizabeth gave a perfunctory knock and let them both in. Mr. Bennet looked up at them and nodded.

"We understand you've had a letter from Darcy," said Elizabeth.

"Yes, I have a whole package. Here it is."

"And what does it say?"

"To tell the truth, I haven't been in a hurry to open it. I don't expect it's going to be good news. When you're applying to college and you're waiting to hear, you want to receive a fat envelope. That's when more paper means good news. In contrast, when you have a member of your team who's in serious legal danger, you don't want an envelope, much less a fat envelope. What are the documents likely to be? Accusations, evidence, depositions, extraditions, you name it - none of it good. But I suppose you'll want to read it."

He held it out to her and said, "Read it aloud."

Elizabeth took the package, opened it, and pulled out a sheaf of papers. The top sheet was a letter.

MR. BENNET,

At last I am able to send you some tidings of your direct report, Lydia Sigourney, and as such, upon the whole, I hope it will give you satisfaction. With the help of a crucial tip from a wiser head than my own, I was able to find that she and George Wickham were in Montpelier, Vermont. I have seen them both.

"Then it's as I always hoped," cried Jane. "Utmost Re is a legitimate company!"

Elizabeth read on:

I have seen them both. Utmost Re is not a legitimate company, nor does it appear to me that Wickham ever intended for it to be anything other than the deceptive semblance of a legitimate company. However, the appearance is surprisingly close to reality. With access to some capital and with reasonable corporate oversight, Utmost Re could easily be made into a legitimate company. If you are willing to agree to certain terms detailed in the attached documents, I believe it will not be long before it is. As you will see in the draft Memorandum of Understanding, here are the proposed terms I have tentatively negotiated with Wickham, who currently has the controlling interest in Utmost Re:

- Juniper Re will buy Utmost Re for a fee of $1,000. Upon execution of the buyout, Juniper Re will assume all assets and obligations of Utmost Re. The principal obligations are bound quotes for excess property reinsurance that has not yet become effective.
- Juniper Re agrees to hold both Wickham and Lydia harmless for their actions in establishing the new company, and will not pursue any civil suit or make any criminal complaint in connection with this matter.
- Juniper Re agrees to reinstate both Wickham and Lydia as employees in good standing, and agrees to keep them both employed for at least one month following the execution of the agreement.

I am submitting the agreement for your approval, as one element of its execution is Lydia's ongoing employment. My request is that her initial assignment be documenting the complete history of Utmost Re to date and facilitating its transfer to new management. I would like her to do this under your supervision but no longer as a member of the Pride Team. I will plan to be involved in arranging her subsequent assignment. (I have already made a provision for Wickham's employment, which will not be back at the RMO.)

Please review the agreement carefully and let me know if you approve, or if you have any questions or concerns.

The buyout terms are frankly more favorable than I had feared. There is some loss likely to accrue from the underpriced business on their books, but it's not dramatically worse that other business we're writing already, and it gets us into the captive reinsurance market, where we haven't had much of a presence. I believe that Wickham must be motivated to find a quick and legal resolution to this matter. I await your reply.

Best regards,

F. WILLIAM DARCY

P.S. You may be interested to know that their disappearance was also an elopement. Wickham and Lydia are now married.

"Married?" cried Elizabeth, when she had finished reading. "Is it possible?"

"Wickham is not so undeserving, then, as we thought him," said Jane.

Elizabeth stared at the letter. "*P.S. They're married.* Talk about burying the lede!" She then stepped closer to Mr. Bennet. "You must respond right now! This is wonderful! We'll get our Lydia back, and we'll get our own lives back. We'll be able to put this whole episode behind us."

"Yes," he said. "It must be done."

"You're uncomfortable with the terms?"

"I'm too comfortable with the terms! They seem suspiciously light to me - which means there's some element of this that I don't understand. I'm grateful to have a path forward - for Lydia as well as for the Pride Team, but I wonder who's made this possible, and if we may find ourselves subject to a debt that we don't currently comprehend or appreciate."

"Ever the underwriter - finding bad news in the best possible news."

"Maybe. I don't see any alternative, but I don't like that Lydia comes back to work for me while Wickham doesn't go back to the RMO. Doesn't that look like I have low standards? If you've been tainted by a dodgy deal, we can't let you go back to the RMO, but anyone can go back to Bennet!"

"Lydia isn't anyone. As far as we can tell, it was her good work that made this buyout possible."

"She's also Mrs. Wickham now. How do you feel about that?"

"I'm still processing that."

"She's still Lydia," put in Jane. "And whatever each of us may have previously thought about Mr. Wickham, we must now revise and soften those judgments in the light of his connection to our Lydia. I'm sure he wouldn't marry Lydia unless he had a real regard for her, and his regard shows better judgment than I, for one, would have expected from him. And Lydia clearly must have a regard for him, which tells me that he deserves a fresh chance from us all."

"Well," said Elizabeth, "whether or not he deserves a fresh chance, we'll endeavor to give him one. I think we should leave Mr. Bennet to make his very prompt and positive reply to Mr. Darcy, and you and I should pass this news on to Mary and Kitty and, of course, Ms. Nebbit."

"Very well," said Mr. Bennet.

"May we take Darcy's letter to show?"

"Yes, take whatever you like."

With the precious letter clutched firmly in her hand, Elizabeth led the way down the hall, where they found Mary, Kitty and Ms. Nebbit sitting in Longbourn Two sharing a comforting carton of doughnuts. One communication would therefore do for all. After a slight preparation for good news, the letter was read aloud. Ms. Nebbit could hardly contain herself. As soon as Jane had read Mr. Darcy's intention to arrange Lydia's next assignment, her joy burst forth, and every following sentence added to its exuberance. She was now convulsed with happiness in a manner that was difficult to distinguish from her previous state of being wracked by misery. To know that her protégée was going to make a step forward in the company was enough. She was disturbed by no fear for her felicity, nor humbled by any remembrance of her misconduct.

"My dear, dear Lydia!" she cried. "This is delightful indeed! She has become quite the success, if I do say so myself - now graduated from the Pride Team and ready for an exciting new chapter in her career, under the personal direction of Mr. Darcy himself! And married to boot! So many of these attractive young inside sales girls, they let themselves have a little dipsy-doodle with an officer and that's it - he never so much as sends flowers! But my Lydia, she knows what's what, she knows how to use her leverage to get where she's going!"

Jane coughed and ventured: "Mr. Bennet seemed to think that the terms were suspiciously light. He fears we may find ourselves under some obligation we don't fully understand."

"Mr. Bennet wouldn't know good news if it bit him on the caboose! Of course the terms are favorable! This is our clever Lydia's doing! Oh, but maybe it's time to stop calling her our little Lydia? She's moving forward in her career and in her personal life - she should be Ms. Wickham!"

"I don't believe we've heard if she's taking his name," said Jane.

"She's Ms. Wickham to me! How well it sounds! Yes, she's much too important now for first names, as if she were a child. Oh, my dear Jane, this is such a proud moment for me! I'm in such a flutter that I need your help. Make a list - now, now now! We must arrange a welcome-back party for her!"

She was then proceeding to all the particulars of room reservations, food plates and speeches, and would shortly have dictated some very specific plans, had not Jane, though with some difficulty, persuaded her to wait until Mr. Bennet was at leisure to be consulted. One day's delay, she observed, would be of small importance; and Ms. Nebbit was too happy to be quite so obstinate as usual. Other schemes, too, came into her head.

"I need to get out and about again! Ms. Cullis was so nice to look in on us last week - I should return the favor! And really, once I've crossed the hall, I might as well look in on my friends all over the building! Is that Jeremy over by the copy machine? Jeremy! Yes, you, come over here! Have you heard about our Lydia? She's Ms. Wickham now and will be working on a special project with Mr.

Bennet for a few months before Mr. Darcy takes her away for something even more important. She's quite the rising star it turns out. We're having a big party for her return. We'll be sure to send you an invitation. I'm sure she'll want all her former friends from the Surge Team to be there!"

As Ms. Nebbit made her way towards Jeremy, Elizabeth stayed behind with Kitty. She turned to her and said, "I imagine you must have mixed feelings about all this."

"I'll be happy for her if she is happy."

"My sense," said Elizabeth, "is that Lydia is someone who could have gone in many directions. She's made some choices, and we'll hope they work out for her."

CHAPTER 50

Mr. Bennet had very often wished before this period of his career that, instead of focusing on building the skills and contacts of his young charges, he had invested more of his time and effort in developing their values. He now wished it more than ever. Had he done his duty in that respect, Lydia might still have a very promising career in the business side of their business. She now had no remaining place in that world, and was very lucky to have a chance to rejoin the company in any capacity at all. She would now have to serve in some support function, well insulated from customers and accounts and deals.

He had meant well, and had made a reasonable start of it, grounding his team members in the purpose and value of the enterprise - the Big Picture, the Promise Behind the Promise. But his time and attention had quickly and thoroughly turned to underwriting skills, which in practice, if not in principle, focused on the question of how to maximize the organization's profitability - a consideration that, while necessary, is not sufficient. Having neglected to return to ethical considerations, he feared that he may have signaled that his initial focus was a pious formality, the recitation of a creed for the sake of tradition rather than conviction or urgency.

He was aware that the efficacy of teaching ethics was a matter of debate, with some believing that ethics can be effectively taught to everyone, and others believing they can be taught to no one. In his own mind, he had come to a middle ground, believing that ethics, like sound underwriting, can effectively be taught to most people, but not to everyone. Someone who is innumerate is never going to understand sound underwriting principles. Someone whose universe is encompassed within his or her own self-interest is never going to experience ethics training as anything other than a requirement to be met, a box to be checked off, a hoop to be jumped through. In the case at hand, he was doubtful that any training would have a lasting effect on Wickham, but was convinced that he could have made real progress with Lydia. Maybe she was never going to become the Mother Teresa of reinsurance, but at a minimum he could have brought her to a soldier's code of giving primary consideration to her comrades in arms, the other members of her group. As it was, she seemed quite unconcerned about, and possibly oblivious to, the problems she had caused for the organization, and especially for her fellow Pride Team members. He felt this as his own failing, and saw his upcoming month of working with Lydia as a kind of penance, during which he would belatedly attempt to complete her training, a prospect not likely to be made easier by the fact that her recent behavior would apparently be rewarded with congratulations and welcome back parties.

News of the arrangement spread quickly through the organization. The general perception was that the buyout of Utmost Re was probably a kind of shotgun wedding, undertaken to avoid embarrassment to Juniper Re, but the fact that Lydia and Wickham would be returning muted the complaints against them. As reinstated employees, they were accorded some degree of forbearance based on company loyalty.

For the first time in weeks, Mr. Bennet convened a Pride Team staff meeting, and Ms. Nebbit attended in spirits oppressively high. No sentiment of shame gave a damp to her triumph. Her attractive, young protégée had graduated from the Pride Team and was on the cusp of a glorious new career chapter, and her thoughts and and her words ran back and forth between how best to celebrate their mutual success and speculation regarding what organizational honors lay ahead. She'd been sizing up the offices on their floor to see which might provide Lydia with comfort and gravitas equal to her emerging new station.

"There are some nice offices on the other side of Longbourn, particularly the one on the end, if we can persuade Mr. Gouldings to relocate. Quite a nice view to the west and very convenient to all of us! I know the first floor offices have those high ceilings, which I suppose are pleasant for tall people, but really - who with any choice in the matter would agree to sit on the first floor?"

Mr. Bennet rose and shut the conference room door. "Ms. Nebbit, before you start requisitioning offices, we all need to come to a right understanding on a few key points. First of all, Lydia, for her month in my employ, will be located in her same, old cubicle - and will be lucky, if not grateful, to be there. Next, Mr. Wickham, wherever he may be located and whomever he may be reporting to, is not welcome anywhere in this area. I'm expecting him to steer clear of us all, and, if any of you want to say a word to him, you are not to invite him here, but rather you should seek him out wherever he ends up being located. Finally, there will not be any celebration for either of them sponsored by myself or by the Pride Team or hosted here at Longbourn. We don't approve of what they did, and we aren't going to reward their actions."

A long dispute followed this declaration, but Mr. Bennet was firm. Ms. Nebbit was amazed and horrified to find that he wouldn't agree to fund so much as a fruit plate in honor of their returning team member. She could hardly comprehend it. That his anger could be carried to such a point of resentment as to refuse his direct report an acknowledgement - without which her reinstatement as an employee in good standing would scarcely seem valid - exceeded all she could believe possible. She was more alive to the disgrace which her want of a proper event with refreshments must reflect on the return of their protégée, than to any sense of shame at her having used company time and resources to create a competing and probably fraudulent reinsurer.

Elizabeth was depressed by the contentious meeting, and her thoughts turned to Fitzwilliam and Darcy. Because of Lydia, she'd turned down Brian Fitzwilliam's invitation and begged Darcy to intervene, but now that the situation was on the brink of being resolved, she felt the sting of her decisions. It would have been much better for her if she'd gone to the opera and never involved Darcy in the matter. First off, who knows what sort of relationship she might have had with Brian? At a bare minimum, it would have included one more night out together than had actually been the case to date.

Meanwhile, as far as her career was concerned, she'd already had her second chance with Darcy. After her disastrous rudeness and personal attack on him when he'd made her the job offer, she'd somehow - through his generosity, she felt, more than through any cleverness on her own part - managed to get onto friendly terms with him. She might possibly have had a shot to receive a second job offer; one that she would have accepted as emphatically as she'd rejected the first. Instead, she'd spent whatever capital she had with him, and more besides, to have him save Lydia - a task for which he could justly resent her forever. It clearly had been a difficult and time-consuming project, requiring extensive travel and most of his attention over a period of weeks. If he didn't already have a sufficiently low view of the Pride Team, the project would have brought him into detailed contact with the most unsavory and embarrassing information about her team member. Worst of all, it must have been torture for him to have to negotiate with Wickham, and use company resources to save such an ungrateful and undeserving person from the natural consequences of his own schemes. *No,* thought Elizabeth, *there won't be a third chance for me with Darcy.*

She regretted once again that she had so belatedly realized what a congenial and career-changing mentor he could have been for her. He was exactly the sort of person who, in disposition and talents, would best help and complement her; and she, likewise, was exactly the person to help and complement him. They could have made a wonderfully effective team, and it would have been an enjoyable experience for them both.

But no such ideal pairing could now teach the admiring multitude what perfect organizational teamwork really was. The pairing that would shortly be on display would be a failed partnership converted into an unpromising wedlock. Much as Elizabeth rooted instinctively for all marriages to succeed, she saw little reason to expect a long and happy outcome for Lydia and Wickham. Their age difference, Lydia's obliviousness, and Wickham's absence of character presented a formidable triumvirate of potentially fatal obstacles for their hasty and presumably shallow marriage.

Still, the marriage forced Elizabeth to reconsider her assessment of Wickham. She was unsurprised that he would engage in an inappropriate romantic relationship with a young colleague who, while not technically his subordinate, might as well have been. She was certainly his junior in the same business unit, and during her time there her sole job responsibility was supporting the business he wrote at his direction. But Elizabeth would have expected Wickham's wooing of Lydia to be the hollow motions of a player, not a search for a long-term relationship, and certainly not a prelude to marriage. Was there something in Lydia that brought his baser habits to heel, or was the marriage just some kind of con game? Or a defense - he wouldn't be likely to be accused of sexual harassment by his newlywed spouse. Or perhaps, she thought, the marriage was like Utmost Re - intended by him as a scam, but built so solidly and sincerely by Lydia that, with a bit of outside pressure and help, it could become real.

Over the ensuing week, documents were signed, announcements were made, and one additional detail came to light. Wickham would, at least for a month, be working in a newly-created position reporting to Mr. Tyler in Operations. In discussing this with Elizabeth, Jane asked if Wickham would have anything helpful to bring to that unit, and Elizabeth, while not directly offering an opinion on her question, reminded her that Wickham had begun his career working in the Operations Department of Cornwallis Re.

When the Pride Team met for its next staff meeting, there was a coordinated counter-offensive directed against Mr. Bennet's unwillingness to offer any official ceremony to welcome Lydia back. Ms. Nebbit, inspired by a sermon she'd heard over the weekend, accused Mr. Bennet of being the personification of the jealous older brother in the parable of the Prodigal Son, preferring to nurse a grudge rather than experience the joy of welcoming home someone who was thought to be lost forever. Unlike most of Ms. Nebbit's arguments, this one struck Mr. Bennet's heart, although from long habit he would not admit that this was the case.

Elizabeth then took the opportunity to make a distinction between various types of potential events. Yes, she could see that a celebration for Lydia or Wickham based on their employment or position within the company might be problematic, but surely it would be right and proper to host a belated wedding shower for the recently married couple. In fact, refusing to host a shower because of hard feelings about their recent business behavior would seem to be exactly the sort of short-sighted overreaction that Ms. Nebbit was warning against with her very pertinent allusion to the New Testament parable.

This had the desired effect. Mr. Bennet agreed that a belated wedding shower would be entirely appropriate, and even agreed that such an event should be sponsored by the department, held in Longbourn, and feature a generous assortment of refreshments.

Notwithstanding Mr. Bennet's trials with his work spouse, he remained very fond of his actual spouse, and firmly committed to marriage as an institution. For her part, Elizabeth was happy to have found an amicable resolution to the issue, but she was herself not looking forward to a shower that would feature Wickham as an honoree.

CHAPTER 51

The day arrived for Lydia and Wickham to return to Juniper Re. After spending the morning in the Old Building seeing to Human Resources forms and procedures, they were to start their afternoon together as guests at a special Pride Team staff meeting, after which Lydia would stay to begin work with Mr. Bennet, while Wickham would descend one floor to report to Mr. Tyler in Operations.

As the time crept past one o'clock, the group in Longbourn waited in awkward silence. Ms. Nebbit was eager and excited, but the others were anxious. Jane, in particular, was bothered by a distress that might have been diagnosed as Sympathetic Mortification. She imagined what her own feelings would be if she were facing her colleagues after such a public debacle - not merely a mistake or poor performance, but a moral failure that had threatened to cause damage to her friends, her company, and their industry, damage that in the end had largely been mitigated through expense to the organization and considerable effort and inconvenience to its management team. Jane felt that she would rather drink paint than look her co-workers in the eye after causing so much trouble, and she naturally assumed that Lydia must be feeling some version of the same painful emotions.

However, when the couple came into view, they appeared happy and relaxed. Ms. Nebbit jumped to her feet and began clapping and waving. Jane, Elizabeth, Mary, and Kitty stood and smiled without clapping or waving. Kitty appeared to be on the brink of tears. Mr. Bennet remained seated with the bravely stoic look of one waiting his turn for oral surgery.

Wickham stepped aside and Lydia entered the conference room with easy assurance, circled the room with a breezy hug for everyone, and took a place at the head of the table. She then addressed each of her former team members, demanding their congratulations, and when at length they all sat down, looked eagerly around the room, took notice of some little alteration in it, and observed, with a laugh, that it was a great while since she'd been there.

"You will excuse us if we are not so light-hearted," said Mr. Bennet. "This has not been an easy time for us all."

"You make an excellent point! There's been so much excitement and activity in my life these past weeks and months that I suppose it's hard for me to see past that and look at things from other perspectives. I imagine it must have been horrid for you all, my former team members, to be left behind here, while I was out having adventures in the world, founding a company, and making a name for myself."

Wickham spoke up gently at this. "I'm sure, my dear, that your colleagues here are much too good at heart to be troubled by any jealousy. The Pride Team is like a Girl Scout convention. It's lousy with niceness."

Wickham's manners - his smiles, his easy address, his roguish flippancy - were generally so pleasing that in any other context they all would have found him delightful. Lydia lacked his style, but matched him in brazen self-assurance. Elizabeth sat down, resolving within herself to draw no limits in future to the impudence of an impudent man or woman.

"I'm wondering, Lydia," said Jane, with clear reluctance, "if you see or are aware of any harm or downside that these events with Utmost Re may have caused to others, or to the organization - or, for that matter, to yourself or Mr. Wickham."

"An excellent question," said Lydia, "and one worth considering, I'm sure, but nothing comes to mind. I do know that I and many others see a great deal of good coming out of this venture."

Elizabeth ventured a turn. "Some people have raised the question of whether it was appropriate for the two of you to be working, in effect, for a different entity while you were still with the company."

"Right up to the very last minute, we assumed that Utmost Re would be a subsidiary of Juniper Re. And, as you can see, it has eventually turned out that we were right all along!"

"Why," asked Kitty, "didn't you return any of our messages?"

"Oh, it's just a game! It's called 'Ghosting'. It's like Hide and Go

Seek, and I can tell you it's hard to stay quiet that long! But there was so much going on, and we wanted to announce everything at the same time. Now then, if the Inquisition is quite over, I need to ask about more important things, like office gossip. I'm hopelessly behind on everything!"

There was no want of further discourse. Lydia and Ms. Nebbit could neither of them talk fast enough, and Wickham, who happened to sit near Elizabeth, began inquiring after members of the Surge Team and other co-workers in the vicinity, with a good-humored ease which she felt very unable to equal in her replies. He and Lydia each seemed to have the happiest memories in the world. Nothing of the past was recollected with pain, and Lydia led voluntarily to subjects which the remaining Pride Team members wouldn't have alluded to for the world.

"Only think of its being three months," she cried, "since I went away! It seems like just a week or two, and yet so much has happened in that time. Good gracious! When I went away, I'm sure I had no idea of founding a company or securing a position beyond the Pride Team or getting myself married before coming back again! Although, of course, in my heart I may have been rooting for all those things."

Elizabeth looked expressively at Lydia, but she, who never heard or saw anything of which she chose to be insensible, happily continued, "Oh! Ms. Nebbit, you will know and tell me. Do the people hereabouts know that I'm returned and am, for the time being, working for Mr. Bennet, but not as a member of the Pride Team? I was afraid they might not. We passed Jeremy over by the copy machine, and I made a point of letting him know I was going to the Pride Team meeting as an invited visitor, but I couldn't tell if he understood the significance of what I was saying or not. I think maybe I intimidate him now. He wasn't making eye contact with me. And, oh! Ms. Nebbit, tell me. What do you think of my husband? Isn't he a charming man? I'm sure my former team members must all envy me. I only hope they may have half my good luck, in business and pleasure. They must all go to the RMO! That place is full of eligible men, and full of opportunities to push the boundaries of the company. You should have all come down when I was there."

"Very true," agreed Ms. Nebbit. "And if I had my will, we should have. But my dear Lydia, we have a party planned for later in the day, but it would have been better if you'd let us have a shower for you before the wedding."

"Yes, I know. It was all very sudden for me, too. The two of us were just friends, and then partners in a new business, and then setting up an office up north, and then one day Wicky says to me, *'Let's you and me get married!'* Out of the blue, just like that. Isn't that romantic? So we did. When is our party?"

The remainder of the meeting passed in a discussion between Lydia and Ms. Nebbit concerning the party, covering such important details as the planned refreshments, the invitation list, where the gifts should be placed, and whether there would be any games. Wickham sat smiling indulgently, while the team members and Mr. Bennet looked at the table.

Later, Elizabeth looked in on Lydia as she was getting herself settled into her old workspace.

"Hello again, Lizzy! I sort of feel like when I visit my parents and sleep in my old bedroom. Oh, well. It's just temporary!"

"Do you need anything?"

"I need to tell you about the buyout closing. You wouldn't know, because you've never sold a company before, but it was quite a dramatic moment!"

"Actually, I think I'm happier not knowing any more about it."

"La! You're so strange! But I must tell you how it went off. The closing was set for a lawyer's office in Montpelier - darling little town! Everyone needed to be there by eleven o'clock. So at ten o'clock we're having breakfast with Mr. Darcy at some ancient inn around the corner from the lawyer's office. You always told me that Darcy was a sanctimonious humbug, but I'm not sure I fully believed you until that breakfast. *Blah, blah, blah!* He rattled on the whole time with a lecture about honor and trust and fiduciary something-or-other. Give it a rest, already! It's ten o'clock in the morning! Meanwhile, I'm trying to think about whether I'm wearing the right shoes for the closing. The pumps are pretty and the extra height gives some power, but there's something very serious and no-nonsense about black flats. Right? That's my one regret in this whole thing. Later on, I took one look at the lawyer's office and knew that I should have worn the flats. Anyway, halfway through the breakfast, Darcy gets some kind of urgent call and heads out the door and just disappears. We finish our breakfast and no Darcy. Wicky pays the bill - on us, you're welcome, Juniper Re - and no Darcy. And I'm thinking, is this going to happen? How can we do the closing with no Darcy? Luckily, he came back again ten minutes later, and we all set out. However, it occured to me later that we could probably have gone ahead with the closing without Darcy, since Mr. Fitzwilliam might have done as well."

"Mr. Fitzwilliam!" repeated Elizabeth, in utter amazement.

"Oh, yes! He was there with us as well. But gracious me! I quite forgot! I ought not to have said a word about it. I promised them so faithfully! What will Wickham say? It was to be such a secret!"

Rather than press Lydia further on this point, Elizabeth excused herself and composed a message to Darcy, requesting an explanation of what Lydia had let drop, assuming such knowledge could be shared without breaching any necessary confidentiality.

"You may readily comprehend," she added, "what my curiosity must be to know how a person unconnected with either side of this transaction should have been among you at such a time. Please respond instantly, and let me understand it - unless it is, for very cogent reasons, to remain in the secrecy which Lydia seems to think necessary. If that is the case, then I must endeavor to be satisfied with ignorance."

"Not that I shall, though," she added to herself as she sent the message, "and, my dear sir, if you don't tell me in an honorable manner, I shall certainly be reduced to finding out by tricks and stratagems."

CHAPTER 52

Elizabeth had the satisfaction of receiving a prompt but lengthy answer to her message. She turned her attention to it and prepared to be happy, assuming that a long message meant she was onto something interesting.

Personal and Confidential

I have just received your message and shall devote as much time as needed to answering it, as I foresee that a short bit of writing will not comprise what I have to tell you. I must confess myself surprised by your question, which I did not expect. That is, I did not imagine such inquiries to be necessary on your side. If you do not understand me, forgive my impertinence. If necessary, I must be more explicit.

On the night you first alerted me to the situation with Lydia and Wickham, Fitzwilliam contacted me and volunteered to be my partner in resolving the situation. In fact, he simply informed me that he'd be doing so, leaving me no room to disagree. I was under the impression that there was some degree of a personal relationship between yourself and him, and so I assumed that he'd gotten his own plea from you, which I imagined to be every bit as emphatic as the one you directed to me.

In the days and weeks that followed, Fitzwilliam was extremely diligent and helpful to our efforts. He told me he felt a personal responsibility for the matter, which he attributed to his failure to sufficiently alert me to Wickham's scheming when he was providing consulting for me at Cornwallis. I, frankly, had difficulty seeing how he could find any blame in his own actions during that time, and I assumed that his personal interest in you, rather than a guilty conscience, was his more pertinent motivation.

Please excuse me for making assumptions about your personal life. I can assure you, however, that Fitzwilliam was entirely blameless in this regard. He never attributed his actions to anything other than his own guilty conscience.

He succeeded in locating Lydia and Wickham in Vermont soon after you'd mentioned the possibility to me and before I'd communicated it to him. I assumed you'd given him the tip yourself. I was impressed anyway, and am now in retrospect even more impressed, as it appears that he had no help from you.

I initially approached Lydia with an offer to separate herself from the matter and return to Juniper Re on her own. Whether out of loyalty to Wickham or truly believing Utmost Re to be legitimate and worthwhile, she refused to be so separated, and from that point on our dealings were all through Wickham. I cannot speak to her understanding of what was at stake. It was my impression that she simply trusted Wickham and left the decisions to him. However, as has been noted earlier in this communication, my assumptions cannot always be trusted.

The documentation showed Wickham as having the controlling interest, and he had no reservation in speaking for both of them and their purported company. I began the process believing that I, on my own, could negotiate a settlement with him. He was in an impossible situation - facing very serious legal jeopardy - and I was prepared to cash him out and give him legal amnesty. Time was not on his side. At this point, Utmost Re had orders but had not yet issued any contracts or invoices. That was the only reason we still had the opportunity to offer a path to a legal solution. Wickham, however, seemed to take the attitude that he was in the stronger position, and made impractical and unreasonable demands. It was Fitzwilliam who convinced me that I was not the one who should be negotiating with Wickham, as our mutual disdain made it impossible for us to work constructively together on a delicate negotiation. We needed an intermediary, and so Fitzwilliam stepped in and was able to achieve a most reasonable settlement. In fact, while I have, of course, seen the contracts, I believe there is more that I have not seen - some additional threat or promise that Fitzwilliam was able to bring to bear to achieve the current conclusion.

Through the entire process, he was determined to keep the lowest possible profile. He wanted no one - aside from the handful of us working on them directly - to know that he had anything to do with the negotiations. I cannot say why this was so important to him. Some of the answer may be tied up in his role as a consultant. His ideal is that a good consultant should be invisible. If there is a good result, all the credit should go to the client. This goes against my instincts as a manager. I have had team members who were reluctant to put themselves forward, and it has always been my aim to make sure that each received the recognition that was due him or her. However, I am not Fitzwilliam's boss; I am his client, and somehow that has put him beyond the modest reach of my good intentions.

I believe I have now told you everything. It is a relation which may give you some surprise. I hope at least it will not afford you any displeasure. I saw both Wickham and Lydia regularly over these weeks. Wickham was exactly what he had been when I knew him at Cornwallis. I know that Lydia has been your colleague, and that you have taken a keen interest in her welfare, but I can only report that I have been unsatisfied with our interactions. I talked to her repeatedly in the most serious manner, representing to her the damage she had risked to herself and the company, and the unhappiness she had caused her team members and other colleagues. If she heard me, it was by good luck, for I am sure she did not listen. I was sometimes quite provoked, but out of my regard for your team I had patience with her.

As Lydia indicated to you, Fitzwilliam was present at the closing. His tact and easy nature enabled a moment that could easily have been awkward or contentious to be much closer to pleasant and relaxing than I would have thought possible.

This is not my area to have an opinion, but please do not be very angry with me if I venture to suggest that - assuming my prior assumptions about you and Fitzwilliam are entirely off base - it might not be a bad idea to consider making them a reality.

F. WILLIAM DARCY

The contents of this letter threw Elizabeth into a confusion of spirits, in which it was difficult to determine whether pleasure or pain bore the greater share. She'd been assuming that she'd lost whatever goodwill she'd briefly had with Darcy, but the friendly and even playful tone of his message forced her to consider the possibility that they might continue to be on good terms. Similarly, she'd been assuming that she'd missed her chance to establish a personal relationship with Fitzwilliam, but Darcy seemed to think that his surprising exertions in negotiating a settlement with Wickham and Lydia were somehow motivated by his continuing personal interest in her. If she had clearer and stronger evidence for either of these propositions - that Darcy liked her as a potential assistant or that Fitzwilliam liked her as a potential girlfriend - she would have been happy, for she had come to view Darcy as an ideal boss and Fitzwilliam as excellent candidate for a romantic partner. As it was, however, the signs were ambiguous and circumstantial, and the two possibilities each seemed sufficiently unlikely that, faced with them as a matched pair, she was inclined to suspect that they represented some kind of a delusional episode. However, if she was indulging in foolish and wishful thinking, she felt that she hadn't gone nearly far enough. In a good and satisfying daydream, her future happiness wouldn't depend on the favor of two men, especially when the men in question had apparently found opportunity to use her as a topic of their discussions. Although, in fairness, she did have to allow that she saw nothing inappropriate in Darcy sharing with her his positive opinions regarding Fitzwilliam. She found validation in them for her own feelings, as she knew that, however much he and Fitzwilliam might be friends, Darcy was not one to shade the truth.

She was roused from her reflections by someone's approach, and, before she could make any alternate plan, she was facing Wickham.

"Hello, my fellow Juniper Re employee! I'm afraid I interrupt your deep thoughts. Perhaps I could offer you a penny for them."

"You could try, but I may hold out for more. Word on the street is that, after the buyout, you're now a thousandaire."

"Oh, and I suppose you've had a more lucrative time of it with all the companies you've founded and sold?"

"Point taken. At least you got something. Usually in this business you have to pay to get a reinstatement." This was an allusion to certain treaties, for which limits can be reinstated by paying an additional premium. "Not that it isn't wonderful to see you still hanging around here, but I thought you were heading off to Operations."

"Yes, I'm duly checked in, but they wisely expect very little of me on my first day. Meanwhile, I hear you had the chance to visit Pemberley."

She nodded.

"I almost envy you the pleasure, People expect me to be impressed by the style and grandeur of the Old Building, but for someone who's seen and even worked at Pemberley, the Old Building looks like a colonial-themed motor inn. Did Reynolds give you the tour? She was always very fond of me, but she probably didn't mention my name to you."

"Actually, yes, she did."

"And what did she say?"

"She said there was something awkward between you and Darcy. She didn't know the details, but she assumed that Darcy must be in the right. Of course, you've mentioned in the past that Darcy was always the fair-haired boy at Cornwallis."

"Certainly," he replied, biting his lip. Elizabeth hoped she had silenced him, but he soon afterwards said:

"Do you happen to know a Brian Fitzwilliam? I heard a rumor that he might be interested in you."

"Then I can set your mind at rest. Mr. Fitzwilliam is a consultant, and part of his contract is that he's forbidden to hire any company employees. So however interested in me he might be, I'm strictly off-limits to him. It would be as inappropriate for him to make a job offer to me as it would be for a boss to make a romantic overture to a subordinate - or, you know, someone who might not officially be his subordinate but who worked at his direction."

"Thank you for reminding me of the rules that Lydia and I have managed to rise above. As you may someday discover, the heart goes where it will."

"I hope it was your heart. I've heard a rumor that you got married so that Lydia couldn't be forced to provide evidence against you. I'd find such a notion unbelievable regarding anyone else I know, but in your case I'm reserving judgment."

"Tough crowd! I was hoping you might be glad to see me."

For the sake of Lydia, she was reluctant to pursue a fight with him. Instead, she gave him a good-humored smile.

"Come, Mr. Wickham, we are practically team members now, you know. Let's not quarrel about the past. I'll be in the crowd this afternoon toasting your marriage, and, in the future, I hope we shall always be of one mind."

He smiled, bowed, and wandered off in the general direction of the Operations Department.

CHAPTER 53

George Wickham was so perfectly satisfied with this last conversation that he no longer felt the need to seek out Elizabeth and, when their paths crossed in a hallway or a meeting, his chosen topics of conversation were consistently weather-related.

As it happened, Lydia and Wickham were only in residence as Juniper Re employees for the single month required by their contract. Shortly after their return, the news circulated that they would both be relocating to Chicago, where they'd be taking positions within a large reinsurance broker. Interestingly, they would become the principal members of a new anti-fraud unit the broker was forming. As it was to be a two-person unit, the company had no objection to staffing it with a husband and wife team.

"Set a thief to catch a thief," said Mr. Bennet privately to Elizabeth. "I think there's actually some logic in it, and I hope they'll both do well and do good. I wonder who they knew."

"What's that?" she asked.

"In order to get an opportunity like this, one or both of them must have had a contact with somebody high up in that organization."

Elizabeth shrugged, but she assumed the key intermediary was either Darcy or, more likely, Fitzwilliam. She further speculated that the arrangement had been part of the negotiation, and that this would explain why Lydia and Wickham were willing to settle for a single month of guaranteed employment. But why come back at all for one month? She decided that Lydia must have had a desire for a victory lap, one last chance to get affirmation from her old friends and associates before moving on to her new life. This idea suggested some glimmer of good regarding Wickham, since he had no old friends at Juniper Re, and presumably went along with the interim month for Lydia's sake.

Elizabeth looked at Mr. Bennet and smiled. The official agreement for the sale of Utmost Re said nothing about the positions in Chicago. There had apparently been an agreement behind the agreement, a promise behind the promise.

Ms. Nebbit was depressed when Lydia and Wickham left. From her perspective, it was a triple blow: they were leaving the company; they were leaving the region; and they were gone before they'd had time to make any lasting impression. Yes, she could try to continue to brag about Lydia's fabulous accomplishments, but she wouldn't be able to get much traction out of it without any tangible evidence at hand.

"It's a cruel thing to have our Lydia taken from us so soon after we finally got her back," she announced to a team meeting shortly after Lydia and Wickham had departed. "Ms. Cullis said as much when she looked in on me yesterday. Of course, that just made things worse, which I suppose was the point."

Elizabeth looked to comfort her. "Oh, but you still have us. And we're doing our best to make sure you never lose another one of your charges. We might all still be in the Pride Team thirty years from now."

"Don't be absurd. The problem with Lydia wasn't that she found a new position for herself. The problem was that the position is in Chicago. If any of you could take the slightest bit of initiative, you'd all have good, permanent positions by now, and none of them would be in Chicago!"

But her spirits were revived, and her mind opened again to the agitation of hope, by an article of news which then began to be in circulation. A reliable source in Physical Services assured Doris McMaster, who often sat at lunchtime with Ms. Nebbit, that preparations were being made to relocate Mr. Bingley back to his original office in Netherfield. After his extended national Claims tour, Bingley had set up shop in a shared space with a Juniper sales office in the city. At that point, his office in the Main Building had been converted to a conference room. Now it was being refitted with his desk and other furniture appropriate to an executive office.

"Well, well, and so Mr. Bingley is coming down," she said when Ms. McMaster first brought her the news. "Well, so much the better. Not that I care about it, though. He's nothing to us, you know, and

I'm sure I never want to see him again. But, however, he is very welcome to come back to Netherfield, if he likes it. And who knows what may happen? But that's nothing to us. You know, we agreed long ago never to mention a word about it. And so, is it quite certain he's coming?"

"Absolutely," replied Ms. McMaster. "This isn't just lunch-table gossip. Bingley will be back in residence on Thursday at the latest, very likely on Wednesday. I went to high school with Albert in Physical Services, and he says the work order on the credenza specified that it has to be in place by the end of the day Tuesday at the latest."

Ms. Nebbit immediately forwarded this information to Jane and Elizabeth, who exchanged a look, but said nothing. Later, when they took a walk together, Jane said, "I saw you look at me today, Lizzy, and I know I appeared distressed. But don't imagine that I'm still holding onto the idea that Bingley's going to hire me. I was only confused for the moment, because I remember how awkward it was when everybody thought I was going to go to Claims and it didn't happen. Of course, it made matters even worse when I found out that he didn't hire me because people told him I was in love with him, which was mortifying, but there was nothing I could do about it. Aside from that, I can assure you that the news doesn't affect me with either pleasure or pain. I've been coping with not working for Bingley while he's been away, and I'll cope just fine when he's here. It's his office. He ought to be able to use it! I'll just have to calibrate how friendly I can appear when I see him. Much as I'd hate to be unfriendly, I can't give any fuel to the idea that I'm carrying some kind of romantic torch for him."

In spite of what Jane declared and believed to be her feelings, Elizabeth could see that her spirits were affected. The prospect of Bingley's arrival had put her on edge. It also pulled Mr. Bennet and Ms. Nebbit into a reprise of the argument they'd had when Mr. Bingley first joined the company.

"As soon as Bingley is back," said Ms. Nebbit, "you should look in on him. Put in a good word for the girls."

"Thank you, as always, for your good advice. Although, I seem to remember that, when I took that exact course of action the first time Mr. Bingley moved into the building, the end result was an embarrassing debacle from which, I'm sorry to say, Jane has not yet entirely recovered."

"A quitter, are we? If at first you don't succeed, give up? I'm sure the other business units will all be making an effort to welcome him back."

"Let them!" said Mr. Bennet, more loudly than he'd intended. "My chasing days are over. Mr. Bingley knows who we are and where we're located. If he wants a greeting, he can come and I'll happily give him one. If he's looking to hire an assistant, he knows who we have available."

"Well, you can be rude as you like. That won't prevent me from inviting him to the next team lunch."

Consoled by this resolution, she was better able to bear Mr. Bennet's incivility. Jane, meanwhile, was increasingly anxious.

"I'm sorry he's coming back at all," she said to Elizabeth. "Not because of him, but because of everyone else. Ms. Nebbit means well, but she's causing me more pain than I can tell you. The only thing she talks about is Bingley. Maybe she's the one who's in love with him!"

Mr. Bingley returned to his office at Netherfield. Through her various sources, Ms. Nebbit was able to follow the milestones of his return, and thereby heighten her own anxiety and fretfulness. She thought she'd allow him a week to settle in before sending her invitation. One morning, a few days after his return, she was sitting in Longbourn 2 in the midst of an important meeting with Jane, Elizabeth and Kitty on the subject of preparations for the team lunch, when she looked up to see Mr. Bingley hurrying down the hallway towards them. She announced as much to the assembled team members. Jane declined to look around, but Elizabeth turned toward the glass outer wall of the room and was herself surprised to see, not just Bingley, but also Darcy alongside him, seemingly headed straight for their meeting.

"Who's that with him?" asked Kitty.

"Some acquaintance or other. I'm sure I don't know."

"La!" replied Kitty. "It's the man who used to be with him before. Mr. what's-his-name. The tall, proud one."

Ms. Nebbit rose from her chair. "Good gracious! It's Mr. Darcy! Old Mr. Elizabeth-is-no-Einstein himself! Well, he can walk side by side with the nice Mr. Bingley if he wants, but we know better. I still hate the sight of him!"

Jane looked with concern at Elizabeth, wondering if the impending scene would also be awkward for her. Both of them were uncomfortable enough. Each felt for the other, and of course for themselves. Ms. Nebbit sat recounting her grievances against Darcy, but neither one of them was listening. They were each delivering a silent, internal pep talk, encouraging themselves not to get their hopes up.

"Excuse us," said Bingley, opening the door. "Mr. Darcy and I were just talking about how important we believe the Pride Team is to this organization, and we thought it would be fitting to stop by and encourage you to keep up the good work."

"Wonderful, wonderful - so kind of you, Mr. Bingley!" said Ms. Nebbit motioning him in. "And welcome back to the home office! Mr. Bennet is off at a meeting somewhere right this moment. I know he'll be sorry to miss you. He has, of course, been planning to look in on you and give you his own personal welcome back greeting, because we all know it would be unpardonably rude to let you sneak back into town without getting a personal greeting from us. We certainly appreciate how important Claims is to the organization, and would want to do whatever we can to encourage you and your staff members to keep up your own good work. Yes, and Mr. Darcy you needn't stand there looking like that! Just pick a place and sit down. You're here with Mr. Bingley, so, of course, you're welcome to take a seat, whatever you may have said about some of us in the past. I'm sure that's all forgotten now - and why wouldn't it be?"

Darcy nodded and gave a stiff smile. "Delighted to be here."

"And you know we're pleased to have you with us today, Mr. Bingley! It's a long time since you went away. I began to be afraid that you'd never come back. People did say that you meant to quit the place entirely, but I hope that's not true. A great many changes have taken place around here since you went away - people's careers moving ever forward. Charlotte you might remember from the Surge Team is now an assistant in Human Resources - a nice position that might have gone to one of our team, if a certain someone had half a clue regarding what was in her own best interest. Then there's our own Lydia, who's made quite a name for herself. I hate to mention her now, though, as I'm sure you can imagine. We're so sad to lose her so soon after she was restored to us. I have to say - and I don't mean this to sound like complaining - but I was very disappointed in how the whole affair of Lydia and Wickham was handled. First we allow them to be abused by scandal-mongers in the most horrible way, and then, after we're lucky enough to get them back, we immediately let them slip through our fingers, and they're gone! It seems awfully careless to me. Can no one in this industry hold onto talent? I know there are some who have had longstanding vendettas against George Wickham..." Here she cast a scolding look in Darcy's general direction. "But I would have thought that cooler heads might have prevailed. And the final indignity was that, here they were, heading off to someplace where they'll be appreciated, a very nice set of positions at a very respectable, if somewhat distant, entity, and there wasn't a word about it in the home office newsletter. I don't know what news they think is more important than that?"

Ms. Nebbit continued in this vein for some time. Kitty appeared amused, but Jane and Elizabeth were each mortified. Bingley nodded patiently and Darcy remained stoically poker-faced. Elizabeth couldn't decide which she thought was worse: the flattery of Bingley or the rudeness to Darcy. When Ms. Nebbit made a point of inviting Bingley to the team lunch the following Tuesday, Kitty interrupted to say, "And shouldn't we also invite Mr. Darcy?"

"Oh, well then." She paused and looked around. "What do you think, Mr. Bingley?"

"I think it would be most gracious of you to invite my friend and colleague Darcy to the team lunch as well."

"Well, it's decided, then. Thank you, Kitty, for your well-intentioned suggestion."

As the men excused themselves, Elizabeth was unsure what to think. For herself, she could imagine no career advancement that could possibly repay the agony she felt from such embarrassing scenes. She would have thought Jane would feel the same way, but she could see in her eyes that Jane had found the whole awkward interaction intriguing, and was clearly ready to suffer any amount of Ms. Nebbit in order to have another try to secure a position with Bingley.

CHAPTER 54

As soon as they were gone, Elizabeth walked out and down the hall to recover her spirits - or perhaps to dwell without distraction on subjects likely to deaden them more. What was she to make of Darcy's appearance at their meeting? Why should he bother to look in on her and her team members if only to be silent, grave, and indifferent? She could settle it in no way that gave her pleasure. If he wanted to revive their once-friendly working relationship, why sit so glumly? If he wanted to send a message that the era of breezy informality between them had now ended, why show up at all? If he was there to signal a change of heart regarding Bingley and Jane, why did he look so disapproving? But how could he continue to disapprove of Jane after she'd explained the whole unfortunate misunderstanding to him?

Jane, looking cheerful and relaxed, joined her in the hallway. They headed down the stairwell together. Once they were outside and could talk freely, Jane spoke first.

"Now that I've had this first meeting with Bingley, I feel perfectly easy. I'm over the embarrassment. I'm over the whole thing! I hope he comes to the team lunch."

"I do, too, but watch your expectations. You can fool yourself, but you can't fool me. You aren't over anything."

The following Tuesday, Longbourn 1 and 2 were combined to make a reception room, with one table serving as a buffet, featuring boxes of pizza and bottles of carbonated drinks, and the other table providing seating. By the appointed hour of noon, the Pride Team were all in attendance, along with their overseers and various colleagues eager to honor the team or enjoy a free lunch.

Bingley and Darcy arrived just a few respectful minutes later to find a lively scene - that is, lively within the scope of what might be considered reasonable for a daytime workplace setting. They commented politely on the spread, filled their plates and cups, and came to join the others. Elizabeth was curious in particular to see where Bingley would place himself. Having spent the past several months - it seemed to her - avoiding Jane, would he continue to maintain whatever distance he could within the room, or would he take the available seat next to her? Career options have been known to open or close on such seemingly trivial choices. When faced with the question, he appeared to hesitate, but Jane at that moment happened to look in his direction, and it was decided. He placed himself by her.

A look passed between Bingley and Darcy that she couldn't read. Was Darcy signaling approval or warning? He certainly didn't seem happy, but that could possibly have been related to the fact that the other remaining seat was next to Ms. Nebbit, who appeared to be giving him an unfriendly scowl even before he was able to set down his lunch and be seated. Elizabeth wasn't near enough to hear any of their discourse, but she could see how seldom they spoke to each other, and how formal and cold was their manner whenever they did. She assumed Ms. Nebbit must be oblivious to the critical role Mr. Darcy had played in bringing Lydia back from what had appeared to be her own certain and lasting career death.

Elizabeth looked back towards Bingley and Jane and was struck by a very different scene. Bingley was explaining some issue regarding the new Claims system with emphatic detail, and Jane was asking pointed questions while drawing a diagram for his benefit on a paper napkin. After having counseled Jane not to allow herself to revive her former hopes, Elizabeth felt a pang of guilt that the sight of Jane and Bingley together had rekindled her own hopes for Jane's future in Claims.

And what of Elizabeth's future? She shifted her attention back in the other direction and watched Ms. Nebbit taking a casual hatchet to her slim hopes of getting a renewed chance to work for Darcy. She attempted to view the situation with philosophical detachment. Maybe she and Darcy wouldn't have been the best possible combination. Jane and Bingley were a different case. Bingley was rich in goodwill and enthusiasm but poor in discipline to articulate his vision and achieve his goals - poor, that is, not in relation to an average person you might pass on the sidewalk, but compared to a typical senior officer of a large reinsurer. Jane was a perfect complement to him in that she shared and appreciated his enthusiasms, was wonderfully gifted in the hard work of ordering thoughts, words, and deeds, and had no needy ego to distract her from focusing on what would be best for a department and the organization. This, in fact, is the typical role for the protégée: taking an executive's raw material and copy-editing it into coherence and feasibility. However, this familiar story didn't fit Darcy. He was perhaps too disciplined. He needed humanizing. Was that her gift? Elizabeth wasn't sure. She thought of herself as being somewhere midway on the scale between Darcy and a normal human being - not so much a counterbalance to him as a milder version of him. Still, she thought, it could have worked. She could have been a very effective lieutenant for him. Unfortunately, when she'd had her chance, she'd turned him down.

Before leaving, Bingley and Darcy circled the table - thinking, and not incorrectly, that as the highest-ranking employees present it would be appropriate for them to give an individual greeting to each person. When Bingley made his way to Elizabeth, he was warm and enthusiastic to the point that it appeared to require a pause on his part to recollect the company's personal boundaries training in order for him to refrain from giving her a hug. Darcy followed with a somber nod and "Good day, Ms. Austen."

"Nice of you to join us, Mr. Darcy. Did you get enough to eat?"

"Quite enough, thank you. Which doesn't sound right, I know. It was actually quite tasty. Where was it from?"

"A-One Pizza in the village. They do a good business delivering to the building here."

"I'll make a note of it."

Darcy moved on to her neighbor, and Elizabeth was left to ponder whether this exchange would be representative of the importance of the topics she should expect to be encompassed in her future interactions with him.

"Well, girls," said Ms. Nebbit to Jane, Elizabeth, Kitty, and Mary as they were cleaning up afterwards, "What say you to the day? I think everything has passed off uncommonly well. We had a very nice turnout, the pizza was nicely warm and very tasty, and even that snobbish Mr. Darcy acknowledged that the tomato and pesto pizza was very pleasant indeed! Oh, and Jane - whatever clever story you were telling Bingley about his new system clearly captivated him completely. Miriam from Finance was across from me, and as she was leaving she leaned over to me - she's in Accounts Receivable, which is right up next to Claims - she leaned over and said, 'We'll have her at Netherfield at last!' She did indeed. A most excellent woman, Miriam. And, you know, she wasn't talking about Jane joining Accounts Receivable. Was she Jane? You aren't posting for anything in Accounts Receivable are you? I'm sure not. She meant Jane and Bingley. Word to the wise, girls: Miriam's an excellent woman, but it wouldn't be to your advantage to be too closely associated with her."

Ms. Nebbit, in short, was in high spirits. She'd seen enough of Bingley's behavior around Jane to be convinced that her position with him was once again inevitable, and her expectations of this sort were so far beyond reason that she was quite disappointed at not seeing him back in the department the next day making her a firm offer.

"It did go well, didn't it?" said Jane to Elizabeth. "It seems to me that all the crazy expectations about me and Bingley ended up driving a wedge between us. Now that those expectations are in the past, we can just interact as two relatively normal people who happen to care about claims service."

Elizabeth smiled.

"What's that supposed to mean? You think my expectations aren't in the past? You think I was auditioning - making a pitch for myself?"

"I didn't say anything."

"It's possible to think highly of someone and enjoy their company without expecting or even hoping to be hired by them."

"I'm with you on expecting, but not so sure about the hoping part."

CHAPTER 55

The following week, as Mary was reporting to the Pride Team staff meeting about an algorithm she'd devised to calculate a loss corridor based on a target limit and expected annual loss amount, she was interrupted by Ms. Nebbit.

"Oh goodness heavens, it's him!" She bounded around the table, out the door and down the hall, and the group could easily hear her sturdy voice calling, "Mr. Bingley! Mr. Bingley! Many apologies, I know you're a busy man, but we're in the middle of a Pride Team staff meeting - and, if you could join us for just one minute, it would be a most tremendous help to us. Thank you, thank you! You really are too kind. This will just take the merest second. We're right here in Longbourn 2."

Bingley was duly ushered in, looking surprised but game for whatever the issue might be. The others were curious to hear themselves.

"Now then," Ms. Nebbit continued, taking her seat again, "it's very important for us to understand the Claims business plan for the coming year, including new initiatives and expected staffing levels, particularly here in the Home Office. Not that we all need to hear it directly from you. If, for example, any of us need to leave, those of us who remain can catch them up later. I make a point of this because Mary here was just explaining a most impressive bit of fancy figuring, which I know is of particular interest to Mr. Bennet, and it would be a shame to step on that important moment, so I'm going to suggest that Mary continue her explanation with Mr. Bennet over in Longbourn 1, which - I happened to notice when I bumped into you in the hallway just now - is not currently occupied."

She smiled confidently at Mary and Mr. Bennet, who looked at one another and - because they either found her suggestion reasonable or were unwilling to create more of a scene than Ms. Nebbit had already kicked up - excused themselves quietly and left.

Bingley started with a disclaimer regarding the unfinished state of the Claims business plan, but had not yet progressed to any actual description of it when Ms. Nebbit spoke up once again.

"I'm sure this will be just what we need, but I must apologize for the fact that Kitty and I need to get ready for a very important teleconference with an extremely large client, so please excuse us, and we'll look forward to getting the full report from Jane and Lizzy."

Bingley expressed his understanding and Kitty and Ms. Nebbit departed.

Elizabeth concluded at this point that Ms. Nebbit was attempting to advance Jane's job prospects with Bingley by getting the two of them alone, talking about the Claims Department. So she wasn't surprised when, a few minutes later, Kitty appeared at the door with a message that they needed Elizabeth to come join them.

"I'll be right there," she said, but when Kitty left Elizabeth remained firmly in her seat. She didn't consider Ms. Nebbit's plan - if it was a plan - to be at all helpful. She believed she could make a better contribution to Jane's career options by surrounding her with as much normality as she could muster under the circumstances. So she and Jane listened to Bingley together, with Jane adding some commentary along the way, until he concluded his report and excused himself.

The next day, Elizabeth was looking for a quiet place to read a report on solvency requirements. She knew that she'd only be able to absorb its arcane contents in the business equivalent of a sensory deprivation tank, and so brought a hardcopy of the report and nothing else to the relatively spartan Longbourn 1. On opening the door, she perceived Jane and Bingley seated at the table and engaged in earnest conversation. If this hadn't caused her to suspect that they were up to something, the faces of both, as they hastily turned round and Jane folded up a piece of paper they'd been reviewing, would have told it all. Not a syllable was uttered by either, and Elizabeth was on the point of going away again, when Bingley suddenly rose, whispered a few words to Jane, and left the room.

Jane rushed up to Elizabeth, threw her arms around her, and

whispered in her ear, "Manager of Special Projects, reporting directly to Bingley."

"You did it!"

"I'm the happiest creature in the world! It's too much. I wish everyone could be this happy!"

Elizabeth's congratulations were given with a sincerity, a warmth, a delight, which words could but poorly express. Every sentence of kindness was a fresh source of happiness to Jane. But she would not allow herself to stay or say half that remained to be said for the present.

"I must go instantly to Ms. Nebbit!" she cried. "She ought to hear this directly from me. Bingley's gone to touch base with Mr. Bennet. They'll both be so pleased!"

She then hastened away, leaving Elizabeth alone with a sheaf of papers and no attention to give them. She smiled at the rapidity and ease with which the position had been finally settled, having previously given them so many months of suspense and vexation.

"And this," she said to herself, "is the end of all Darcy's anxious fears and Ms. Liebling's jealous connivings - the happiest, wisest, most reasonable end!"

In a few minutes she was joined by Bingley, whose conference with Mr. Bennet had been short and to the purpose.

"Where's Jane?" he asked.

"She went to find Ms. Nebbit. She'll be back soon, I dare say."

"Well, let me just say that I'm really looking forward to working with Jane and having her on our team. And I know that I owe special thanks to you for helping us to get past some snags that have delayed this moment."

They shook hands with great cordiality, and then, until Jane returned, she listened to all he had to say of Jane's perfections. In spite of his being her new manager and champion, Elizabeth really believed all of his expectations to be rationally founded because they were based on an excellent working chemistry, Jane's unfailingly positive disposition, and a general similarity of goals and approaches between herself and him.

It was a day of no common delight for the team. Jane glowed with satisfaction. Kitty and Mary, feeling a bit better about their association with the Pride Team, each held their heads a bit higher than usual. Ms. Nebbit couldn't give her approval or speak her approbation in terms warm enough to satisfy her feelings, though she talked to Bingley of nothing else for half an hour. Mr. Bennet attempted to maintain his usual poker face, but his voice and manner plainly showed how really happy he was.

Towards the end of the day, he looked in on her and said: "Jane, I congratulate you. You'll be very happy." She thanked him for his goodness, and he continued. "I have great pleasure in thinking you will be so happily settled. I have no doubt that you'll do very well with Bingley. The two of you have similar temperaments. Of course, you're each so complying that Finance is bound to load you up with every expense they don't know what to do with. It's a good thing for you that Claims isn't a profit center."

"I expect you're teasing, but anyway I think you're wrong. While I believe too much effort goes into allocating both income and expenses - as if either one will grow or shrink based on which column it's placed under - I think you'll find that Mr. Bingley and I both know how to look after the interests of a department, and are perfectly capable of disagreeing with someone, even if we don't choose to be disagreeable about it."

"Don't tease the poor girl!" called out Ms. Nebbit, who had been fortunate enough to be nearby at the time, owing primarily to the fact that she had spent the entire afternoon visiting Jane at ten-minute intervals, each time to share an additional thought, suggestion, or observation that had occurred to her since her prior visit. "Claims has budget to spare! She won't be having to count paper clips like some departments I could mention!" Then addressing Jane, "Oh! My dear, dear one! I am so happy! I'm sure I won't get a wink of sleep tonight. I knew how it would be. I always said it must be so, at last. I was sure you weren't so clever for nothing! I remember, as soon as ever I saw him, when he first came to the company last year, I thought how likely it was that you should come together. Oh! He is the nicest and best-looking young senior officer since I don't know who!"

Lydia and Wickham were forgotten. Jane was now beyond competition her favorite. Her impending ascension to report directly to a senior officer was decisively more impressive than Charlotte's position reporting to Mr. Collins. Accordingly, now and for the foreseeable future Ms. Nebbit would have the upper hand in her longstanding rivalry with Ms. Cullis.

In the days that followed, Elizabeth saw less than usual of Jane, who was busy getting herself up to speed on all things Claims, even though she hadn't yet officially assumed her new position. It was, therefore, a treat for them both when they were able to have a long lunch together.

Jane said, "I asked Bingley about that time he wasn't available to see me in Chicago. He said that he was totally ignorant of my being there."

"I suspected as much," replied Elizabeth. "But how did he account for it?"

"It must have been Ms. Liebling and probably others, all lying to me. Maybe she thought she was doing him a favor, I don't know. Maybe she was just being petty. There's an old guard in the department that will just have to get used to me. Now that I'll be part of the team, I expect we'll be on good terms again, though I'll never really be able to trust her the way I once did."

"That's the most unforgiving speech," said Elizabeth, "that I ever heard you utter. Good girl! It would annoy me no end to see you ever again be the dupe of Ms. Liebling's pretended regard."

"He confirmed what you'd heard, Lizzy, that when he was heading off on the field office tour he was ready to hire me, but he was persuaded that I had an unhealthy emotional attachment to him - which is crazy! I'm eager to work for him, but it's all business-business - there's no funny business. I'd be more likely to have a fling with Mr. Super Frog."

"And what happened after that?"

"Well, eventually he was convinced that the stories were wrong, but he held off because he thought it might be awkward for me to work for him after all those stories had circulated. I'm pretty sure it was Darcy who convinced him that he should just hire whoever he wants."

"Could be. As you know, I've repented of my original disapproval of Darcy."

"I think I'm the most fortunate creature that ever existed!" cried Jane. "Oh! Lizzy, I hope things work out just as well for you!"

"Thanks, but I'm not holding my breath. I don't think I can ever be as happy as you are until I'm as good as you are."

In the days that followed, word started to spread about Jane's new position. The result was a positive shift in how the Pride Team was viewed. Perhaps its members had some real value to add to the company. Perhaps, after all, the Pride Team was not simply where promising futures went to die.

CHAPTER 56

The next Pride Team weekly meeting was likely to be the last including Jane. In the midst of a report from Mary on how Residual Value Insurance can affect the pricing of leases, Elizabeth noticed an odd look on the faces across the table from her. She could tell that something was about to happen, but couldn't determine if she should expect it to be pleasant or unpleasant. She heard the door open and a distinctive voice say, "If this is supposed to be a staff meeting, you're doing it all wrong, but there's no time for that now. We're looking for Elizabeth Austen."

Ms. de Bourgh, CDB herself, stood at the door, clearly reluctant to immerse herself in the stale air and modest furnishings of Longbourn 2. The "we" was possibly an overstatement, as she appeared to be alone. Elizabeth stood and spoke.

"Ms. de Bourgh - it's always a pleasure. Would you like to come in?"

Rather than answering her, Ms. de Bourgh looked across to Mr. Bennet and Ms. Nebbit. "Am I correct to assume that you can manage for ten or fifteen minutes without this young woman?"

Ms. Nebbit rose immediately. "Of course we can! Take her for as long as you like!"

Elizabeth left her things on the table and exited the room, shutting the door behind her.

Without turning to face her, Ms. de Bourgh said, "I believe this would be a good morning for a walk out of doors," and set a brisk pace towards the elevator.

Elizabeth followed and they proceeded wordlessly to the elevator, down to the ground floor, out through the main entrance, and along the walkway towards the Old Building. They then veered onto a walkway leading to the far end of the grounds. Elizabeth was determined to make no effort for conversation with a woman who had been more than usually disagreeable.

As they neared the end of the walkway, Ms. de Bourgh stopped and turned to face her.

"You can be at no loss, Ms. Austen, to understand the reason we're having this walk. Your own heart, your own conscience, must tell you why we're here."

Elizabeth looked with unaffected astonishment.

"Indeed, you are mistaken, ma'am. I haven't been able to account for the honor of being asked to join you on this walk."

"Ms. Austen," replied the Human Resources Head in an angry tone, "you ought to know that I'm not to be trifled with. However insincere you may choose to be, you won't find me so. I'm well known for my sincerity and frankness, and I certainly won't depart from that now. A report of the most alarming nature has reached me. Just as your fellow team member is about to make an unexpected and clearly premature career leap to report to one senior officer, the Head of Claims, so I understand that you've attempted to engineer a similarly preposterous leap for yourself, a position in which you'd be reporting to a different senior officer, the Special Assistant to the President. This, of course, is one of those ridiculous rumors where one bizarre but real event spawns tales of other events that are similar but imaginary. So I instantly resolved to make contact with you and confirm that this impossibility won't happen."

"If it's impossible," said Elizabeth, "then that would seem to be your answer right there. I'm not sure why you needed to consult with me."

"The thing about rumors is that the person being spoken of is always in the best position to set the record straight. Also, on the off-chance that such an unthinkable offer did happen to be made to you, I wanted you to be ready with the correct response."

"Which would be?"

"No. A simple *No* would suffice - although, if that seems inadequate to you, it could be something like: *No, thank you, Mr. Darcy, sir. I think perhaps you're forgetting yourself. I'm sure there must be someone who'd be a much more suitable fit for the position you're describing.*"

"I see. And why is it that you believe I should decline this theoretical job offer?"

"There's been a tacit understanding for some time now that Ms. Burgoyne would become Darcy's assistant. She has the prior claim, and she also has the much stronger claim. It's a simple matter of underwriting, my dear. Always there is the need to make the hard choices, to separate the sheep from the goats, to crown the winners and congratulate the losers on making a good effort. So, congratulations, my dear, on your good effort, but don't for one minute think that you'll be declared the winner."

"And what is it, exactly, that makes me in your eyes - what? A goat?"

"Since you ask, I'll tell you plainly. How do we judge someone early in their career? There's no body of work to look at. There's no independent reputation to consider. All we have to go on is credentials and associations. You have no credentials to speak of, so that leaves associations. Who have you worked with and learned from? So, let's consider you in those terms. You're part of the optimistically-named Pride Team, a sort of charity ticket into the company. You've been nominally working for Mr. Bennet, who has some knowledge in his head, I suppose, but lacks any practical ability. And so, filling that vacuum, is the person you've actually been working for, Ms. Nebbit, someone of little knowledge, sense, or decorum. Your fellow team members are a collection of unpromising misfits, one of whom is very lucky to be out of the company without being in jail. I could go on, but I think you see the point. It's a simple matter of underwriting."

"You vastly underestimate the value of my colleagues, Ms. de Bourgh, but since you speak of it in terms of underwriting, I need to point out that there's more to underwriting than avoiding risk. Sometimes, particularly in reinsurance underwriting, there's an important element of loyalty. Sometimes you accept risk on purpose for the sake of a long-term relationship."

"Thank you. Loyalty to a long-term relationship is exactly why this offer shouldn't be made to you. Look, my dear, I don't think you understand what's going on here. I'm the Head of HR. When the conductor says to the piccolo player: *'Don't come in yet; this is not your cue'* that isn't an invitation to a discussion. You nod and come in when the conductor tells you to. Do I make myself clear?"

"No! Shouldn't it be Mr. Darcy's choice? What I hear you saying is that, if he should ask to hire me, I should turn him down - not because I'm uninterested, but rather because I know what's best for the company better than he does."

Ms. de Bourgh hesitated for a moment and then replied:

"Here's the problem with Darcy. He's very strong-minded and capable, but unfortunately he cares what people think about him. And this makes him vulnerable to someone who's obstinate and headstrong, such as yourself. So, yes - thanks to me, you do know better than he does what's good for the company! And that is for you to wait your turn, serve the appropriate apprenticeship, and let the stronger candidate have the turn she's waited for and deserves."

"What is this to me? I certainly wouldn't turn Darcy down if the only objection to accepting a position with him is that you'd rather he hired somebody else. If he himself doesn't feel obligated to hire your favorite, why shouldn't he make another choice? And if I'm that choice, why shouldn't I accept him?"

"Because honor, decorum, prudence, and interest forbid it. Yes, Ms. Austen, interest. It would be a mistake as regards your own personal future here for you to accept any such offer. It would put you in a precarious place where you'd be likely to fail, and the damage to your career at that point would probably be fatal. There's a sort of Zero Lower Bound in career moves that says you can't go backwards. You're allowed to go sideways, of course, but the higher you go the fewer sideways opportunities there are and, if you get there too soon, the more ineligible you're likely to be for anything sideways. And a critical consideration is that, in this scenario, you'd have no friends in Human Resources looking out for you. That is to say, you'd be on a very shaky high wire without a net. Surely we've taught you enough about risk management that you can see how untenable such a situation would be."

"Is that a threat?"

"It's nothing of the sort! Do I look like some kind of gangster? I'm taking time out of my very busy day to give you valuable personal advice. I'm the highest-ranking woman in this organization, and I have a personal stake in the proper and timely advancement of women within the organization, and it pains me when I see women stealing positions from one another. It just isn't right. When an unwritten understanding has been in place, when someone's been carefully groomed for a position, for you to come in at the last minute and make a play for it yourself - why, it's simply unseemly. It would be like flirting with a man at his own engagement party. It's too late! And if the oaf warms to you - maybe feeling some customary cold feet on the cusp of a commitment - you show your virtue by saying *No*." She gave Elizabeth a brief, appraising stare. "I don't know if you have much experience in your life turning down propositions, business or personal, but I can assure you that it can be done."

"And I can assure you that, as an underwriter and as a professional woman, I'm well acquainted with both the value and the occasional danger of emphatic refusals."

"Tell me now. Has he made you an offer?"

Though Elizabeth would have preferred not to answer the question, after a moment's deliberation she could only say:

"He has not."

Ms. de Bourgh seemed pleased.

"And will you promise me, never to accept such an offer if it is made?"

"I'll make no such promise."

"Take a moment. Don't get carried away in the heat of the moment. Consider the percentages. First: what are the chances that Darcy will make you such an offer? Then make a further adjustment for the possibility that you won't like the offer or will have a better offer from somewhere else. What does that net out to? That's what you need to weigh against the one-hundred percent certainty that I'll be angry and disappointed in you if you refuse to make me this promise. Surely even someone with your questionable training and second-rate associates can calculate the prudent course here."

"I believe we've reached the end of our little talk. I don't think you can have anything more to say beyond that. I'll excuse myself now and return to my meeting."

She turned to leave. Ms. de Bourgh was highly incensed.

"You have no regard, then, for what harm you may do to Mr. Darcy?"

"If offering me a position causes Mr. Darcy any harm, I'd say it was self-inflicted."

"You are then resolved to work for him?"

"I've said no such thing. I'm only resolved to act in that manner which will, in my own opinion, be best for both the company and myself."

"And this is your real opinion! This is your final resolve! Very well. I shall now know how to act. Don't imagine, Ms. Austen, that your ambition will ever be gratified. I came to try you. I hoped to find you reasonable - but, depend upon it, I will carry my point."

They walked silently back to where the walkway rejoined the way from the Main Building to the Old Building. Ms. de Bourgh made a turn and spoke to the air.

"I take no leave of you, Ms. Austen. I send no compliments to your work group or your manager. You deserve no such attention. I am seriously displeased."

She walked briskly towards the Old Building as Elizabeth returned to the Main Building and found Ms. Nebbit waiting by her desk.

"Ms. de Bourgh didn't return with you?"

"No."

"Very thoughtful of her to stop by. I suppose she had some business over here somewhere and wanted to let us know how Collins and Charlotte are doing. I don't suppose she had anything particular to say to you, Lizzy?"

Elizabeth wasn't prepared to acknowledge the substance of their conversation, and so felt compelled here to give into a little falsehood.

CHAPTER 57

The discomfort which this extraordinary visit caused Elizabeth could not be easily overcome - nor could she, for many hours, learn to think of it less than incessantly.

Ms. de Bourgh, it appeared, had actually taken the trouble of making her way over from Rosings for the sole purpose of breaking the supposed agreement between Elizabeth and Mr. Darcy. What had made her think there was such an agreement? Elizabeth was at a loss to imagine. Maybe it had to do with the fact that she was a close friend of Jane, and Darcy was a close friend of Bingley. Now that it was becoming known that Jane would be working for Bingley, a parallel arrangement involving their friends might suggest itself into some people's minds.

In reconsidering Ms. de Bourgh's words, however, she couldn't help feeling some uneasiness as to the possible consequences of her persisting in this interference. From what she'd said of her resolution to prevent him from hiring her, it occurred to Elizabeth that CDB must be planning to speak with him directly. And where would Elizabeth stand with Darcy then? She was already resigned to the fact that her chances were slim that, having turned him down once, she'd ever have a second opportunity to work for him. Still, whatever hope she still harbored was sorely tested by the image of the passionate and unstinting opposition of the estimable CDB - not just a senior officer of the company, but also Darcy's close relation. And how would he respond to her arguments about Elizabeth's questionable training and connections? He was, in his way, an old-school executive. Those arguments might seem to him very cogent and reasonable.

And what then? Maybe he wouldn't take an extended national tour like Bingley, but he'd find ways to avoid her. She therefore made a promise to herself that she'd take the hint. Two strikes and she's out.

No sense holding a torch for a job that will never happen.

In the meanwhile, Elizabeth was spared from much teasing on the subject. Her teammates had been surprised that Ms. de Bourgh had appeared and summoned her, but they all assumed it was a matter of passing on some inconsequential news from Mr. Collins or Charlotte.

The next morning, Mr Bennet looked in on her. "Things have been weighing on you," he said.

"Maybe."

"You need a good laugh."

"Definitely!"

"Let it never be said that I refused to be of service when a Pride Team member needed a good laugh. Do you have a minute to come with me?"

She followed him to his office. He shut the door and lowered his voice. "I'm in possession of a very amusing email from our friend, Mr. Collins - who is, of course, the Shakespeare of amusing emails. Scholars debate whether or not he himself really wrote all the amusing emails commonly attributed to him, but I believe he did. Now, I was tempted to forward this on to you with some light-hearted commentary, but email is like plastic; it doesn't biodegrade but lives forever, and funny comments don't necessarily stay funny and appropriate forever. So, I'm going to take the safer approach and open up this message and read it to you myself. Please make yourself comfortable."

Elizabeth took a seat and smiled. "Ready whenever you are."

Mr. Bennet, facing sideways to stare at his monitor, read aloud:

> I write to you today on a professional, Director of Succession Planning to Vice President of Underwriting Operations, basis - but first, on a more personal basis, let me say that I hope this message finds you in good health. Not, let me hasten to say, that I have any reason to be concerned about your health. I send greetings as well to the members of what is still currently known as the Pride Team. That is, I send greetings from myself on behalf of the Human Resources Department, and therefore, of course, indirect greetings from Executive Vice President Catherine de Bourgh.

Mr. Bennet looked over. "No surprises yet, I know, but be patient!"
He continued:

> I know there has been no official announcement yet, but we in HR are generally aware of all important career moves within the company, and therefore I am in a position to congratulate you and the team on Jane's impending promotion into the Claims Department, reporting directly to Mr. Charles Bingley himself. This is quite a coup for someone of a young age and limited experience, particularly someone coming from a business unit that has been, perhaps more than was completely warranted, but still unmistakably, tainted by scandal in recent months. It is a tribute to Mr. Bingley's generous and risk-embracing character that he was willing to make such an unorthodox and potentially controversial choice. Executive Vice President de Bourgh said in my hearing that she believes it is possible that Jane will prove an adequate addition to the Claims Department, and that the hire should in the long run do little to harm Mr. Bingley's career.

"High praise there! We're getting closer!"

> I come now to the principal point of this message. It concerns Elizabeth Austen, who, as you know, is also a Pride Team member.

"Generous of him to grant that I would know such a thing!"

> A report has reached me that she is "in play", as we say here in HR, and may shortly have an opportunity possibly even more impressive than Jane's, an opportunity to work directly for a senior officer who, among all of RJT's direct reports - excepting, of course, my own incomparable patroness - is perhaps most respected and admired. This is an individual with position, stature, reputation, and prospects. Yet, in spite of all these temptations, let me warn Elizabeth and yourself of what evils you may incur by a precipitate closure with this

executive's proposals, which, of course, you will be inclined to take immediate advantage of.

"Have you any idea, Lizzy, who this individual is? But now it comes out."

My motive for cautioning you is as follows. We have reason to imagine that his aunt, Executive Vice President Catherine de Bourgh, does not look on the hire with a friendly eye.

"You see that the mystery executive is Mr. Darcy! Now, Lizzy, I think I've surprised you. Collins fancies himself well-informed on all such matters, but he certainly missed the mark on this one. I'd expect you're as likely to go to work for Attila the Hun as for Mr. Darcy, whatever his titles and family connections to the sainted Ms. de Bourgh! The rumor I hear is that Darcy was the one responsible for postponing and nearly derailing Jane's opportunity in Claims, and of course we all remember how, when he first arrived, he charmingly referred to you as '*No Einstein*'! Isn't this just vintage Collins, Lizzy?"

Elizabeth liked to share pleasantries with Mr. Bennet, but in this case his wit was not agreeable to her. Still, she was reluctant to stop his fun and explain why. She forced a reluctant smile. "All Collins is vintage Collins. What else does he say?"

After I mentioned the likelihood of this job offer to Ms. de Bourgh recently, she immediately, with her usual transparency, expressed what she felt on the occasion. As it happens, she has had a different candidate in mind for the position in question, and articulated in quite clear and characteristically passionate terms her perspective on the impossibility of Darcy ever offering the position to Elizabeth, and the further impossibility of Elizabeth actually filling the position, and the final impossibility of Ms. de Bourgh ever sanctioning and enabling such a hire. I thought it my duty to give you the advantage of this intelligence as speedily as possible so that - if the rumored offer is actually made, and if I am not too late to influence the response to it - you and Elizabeth can be warned not to run hastily into an opportunity that may sound very favorable on its face, but may, in fact, harbor great peril for all involved.

"Hopefully you're receiving this warning in the nick of time. I know how much you'd enjoy being insulted every day."

Finally, and on a happier note, let me congratulate you on how deftly the shameful business with Lydia was swept under the rug. I think Jane's new position is an eloquent testimony to the fact that you have ridden out the worst of that storm, and that the damage to the career prospects of the team members has not been fatal. I'm only sorry that Lydia and her co-conspirator were invited back at all and treated as if no one cares about what is right or legal. While I strongly believe in the value of second chances, I believe in them only for those who are truly deserving.

"I believe he means to say that he's strongly in favor of second chances for those who don't need them."

Charlotte sends her greetings as well. She is doing very well here, and I hope before the year is out that we may add another to our happy and growing team.

Mr. Bennet turned at last to face her. "But, Lizzy, you look as if you didn't enjoy it. I hope you aren't put off by being gossiped about. This is how we all amuse one another. Ridiculous people gossip about us, and then we in turn make fun of them."

"I'm sorry," said Elizabeth. "It's just so strange."

"Hello? It's a Collins email. Of course it's strange. If he'd imagined you signing on with anyone else, I wouldn't have bothered showing it to you, but the combination of you with Darcy - his indifference and your dislike - makes it, I thought, delightfully absurd! It's emails like this from Mr. Collins that get me through the year. So tell me, Lizzy: when Ms. de Bourgh came by the other day - was she here to blackball you?"

Elizabeth replied only with a laugh, and, as the question had been asked without the least suspicion, she didn't feel the need to make a further answer. She was glad of this, as she wouldn't have known what to say. Did she dislike Darcy? She had certainly, but that was now long in the past. Was Darcy indifferent to her and laughably unlikely to offer her a position? That was a harder call. She was embarrassed and felt some anger towards Mr. Bennet, although she couldn't decide if she was mad at him for being too obtuse or for being too clear-sighted.

CHAPTER 58

An underwriter is a professional worrier. However optimistic the individual may naturally be, the job demands that he or she give thorough consideration to everything that might possibly go wrong, assigning probabilities to the most dire scenarios. It may not be surprising, then, that Elizabeth had pondered the possibility that she would now be shunned and avoided by Darcy, and had even estimated the likelihood of such an outcome as better than even odds. As it happened, however, only a few days later Bingley and Darcy arrived together in the work area near Longbourn, as if it were the most natural thing in the world for two senior officers to pay a social call together on the Pride Team. And maybe it was almost natural - Bingley would presumably have things to discuss with his prospective assistant, and Darcy often spent time with Bingley.

Almost immediately after their arrival, Bingley announced that there was fine weather out in the real world and issued a general invitation for a walk around the grounds. Ms. Nebbit wasn't in the habit of walking, Mr. Bennet was away, and Mary could never spare time, so it was Jane, Elizabeth and Kitty who rose and headed off with the two executives before Ms. Nebbit had the opportunity to fawn over the one or insult the other.

By the time the fivesome emerged from the building, Bingley and Jane were in a serious and detailed conversation about an upcoming Claims departmental meeting. They turned left and walked briskly along the walkway that headed towards Building Three and beyond. The others, seeing no point in trying to be included in that conversation, let them go and turned right. This soon brought them to a fork, with one way leading to the Old Building and the other to the far end of the property. At that point, Kitty - who was too afraid of Darcy to start up any kind of a conversation - excused herself to go visit Charlotte. Darcy and Elizabeth proceeded up the other walkway, the one Elizabeth had walked with Ms. de Bourgh not many days earlier. Elizabeth spoke first.

"I don't believe I ever thanked you properly for all that you did for Lydia. All of us on the Pride Team are tremendously grateful. When I look back on the pushy, unearned, and frankly inappropriate way I begged for that help, I'm deeply embarrassed - and doubly thankful that you didn't just write us all off! I feel that I owe you a great deal."

"You owe me nothing," replied Darcy. "Whatever I did was done in the interest of the company. That's important for me to establish, because I'm looking for a favor from you, and I'm counting on you to say *No* if you like. Fair enough?"

"Fair enough. What's the favor?"

"It's analogous to a Round Robin at an Idea Fair. I'm looking for some quick, creative thinking to answer what, in this case, will be a very vague question. I'm hoping it will help me prepare for an important meeting. How does that sound? Would you be willing to do such a thing?"

Elizabeth could hardly have been more pleased if the favor he wanted to request had involved eating ice cream or sleeping in on a snowy morning.

"Absolutely! I make no guarantees of either quickness or creativity, but I love a good Round Robin, and promise to do the best I can."

"That's what I was hoping. Here's the question: If you were asked to advise the next president of Juniper Re, what are five new initiatives that you'd recommend?"

Elizabeth took a breath and waited a few seconds to indicate respect for the question.

"These won't be in any rank order. Number One: we should create a dedicated new product development unit, meaning not just new structures for reinsurance but actual new products for the primary market. We can't afford to sit around waiting for insurers to need our capacity. We have to give them products that they wouldn't offer on their own without our support. Number Two: our departments are too cut off from each other and our middle managers are stuck in ruts. I think we could make progress on both of those issues with a little musical chairs. Piccolo in the Central RMO is probably the best underwriter in the company and Lee in Underwriting is great with clients. Maybe they could trade places for a while. Harder to roll people into Actuarial or Legal, but there are some actuaries and lawyers who could make great contributions to other departments. Number Three: our reflex is to lobby for less regulation of insurance, but I think we should lobby for more required coverage, particularly on property coverages. Why are flood and earthquake optional coverages? Everyone would be much better off if they were standard coverages. Number Four: I think there's an opportunity for us to mine our data to better understand which of our coverages are inversely related - that is, when one coverage has a bad year the other coverage is likely to have a good year, and vice versa - so that we can use those coverages as natural hedges and take some pressure off our need for retrocessions. What am I up to? Number Five: I think the office of the Special Assistant to the President is shockingly understaffed."

After a short pause, Darcy said, "You're too generous to trifle with me. I promised once not to ask you again. If your feelings are still the same, tell me so at once. My wishes are unchanged, but one word from you will silence me on this subject forever."

Elizabeth, having been as articulate as she could for as long as she was able, now found herself without words. She felt a wave of relief, a weight lifted from her back. None of the dire predictions for her future were going to happen anytime soon: her career was going to be all right, and maybe more than all right. She nodded and smiled and eventually formed a few words to signify that he was in no danger of another angry outburst from her, and then a few more to express the general idea that her sentiments had undergone quite a material change since the last time they'd discussed a job offer from him.

The happiness which this reply produced was readily evident in Darcy. He relaxed, smiled, and began talking with considerable animation about how pleased he was, and what a great thing this would be for the company and for him personally.

They walked on, without knowing in what direction. There was too much to discuss for attention to any other objects. She soon learned that they were indebted for their present good understanding to the efforts of his aunt, who had called on him and related the substance of her conversation with Elizabeth, dwelling emphatically on every expression which, in her apprehension, particularly demonstrated that Elizabeth was unwilling to be a team player. Unluckily for Ms. de Bourgh, her effect was the exact opposite of her goal.

"It taught me to hope," said Darcy. "I know that you'll speak your mind to anyone, but that you don't pick fights for no reason. I figured that if you were irrevocably decided against me, that you would have just said so to her."

Elizabeth laughed. "Yes, you know enough of my frankness to believe me capable of that. After abusing you so abominably to your face, I could have no scruple in abusing you to your aunt or anyone else."

"It was a very important lesson for me. I hated it at the time, of course, but I'm quite grateful for it. Looking back, I wince at my behavior. I needed to be brought down from my high horse."

"I'm the one who should be wincing," said Elizabeth. "I was wrong about every charge that I threw in your face so self-righteously. If you learned any positive lesson from my outburst, it speaks only to your own conscientiousness. But, rather than argue about who deserves the blame, I think we're better off just forgetting the whole thing. We were young and foolish at the time. At a bare minimum, we're now a little less young. But here's something I'm wondering about. Having convinced Bingley in the first place that Jane was in love with him, did you then similarly convince him that she was not?"

"Well, yes, although I don't believe there's any great credit in helping to solve a problem of one's own making. I probably should have acted more quickly. It's not that I haven't learned to trust your word, but I wanted to watch her, particularly when she was around Bingley, to make doubly certain that what you'd reported to me was accurate. And yes, as you could have predicted, I found that she was enthusiastic about Bingley's plans and ideas, but not smitten by him personally. Once I was convinced of this, it was my duty to confess my error to Bingley and encourage him to set right what I'd set wrong. That part of the process was quite easy, as Bingley is uncommonly modest and took little convincing to believe that Jane was not in love with him."

"And what did you think when we bumped into one another after I'd toured Pemberly? I was quite embarrassed at the time. I felt like I'd been caught stalking your past."

"I was surprised to see you there, but pleased. I wanted to show you that I'd taken at least some of your challenging words to heart. Now let me ask you a question. It's about that very long message I sent you the day after the incident we agreed to forget about. I wasn't sure if I should send it or not. Was it helpful, or was it off-putting?"

"Of course it was off-putting at first, but it had a profound effect on me. That message turned me around completely. It took a bit of time for me to absorb it, and I still take some exception to your actions regarding Jane, but that message helped me to understand for the first time who you are and how I'd been misjudging you."

"It felt very awkward at the time. Because I couldn't explain myself in person, I had to ask you to read a treatise justifying my actions."

"Never underestimate the power of the written word. Words that are written down are very patient. I didn't understand your message at first, but it waited for me to come around. Why was I annoyed at first? I think it was because I was reading it hearing a certain voice in my head - a voice that was my very unflattering caricature of your inflections and attitudes. It's my experience, however, that if you read anything closely enough, eventually you hear the words in the right voice, the voice that was intended for them. Actually, if you don't mind, I think it would be a good idea for you to direct all your communications to me in the form of long letters."

They walked for a moment in silence. Elizabeth began to wonder if her little joke had somehow overstepped.

"Well?" she asked.

"You'll have to wait for my answer in tomorrow's tome," he replied. "I'm planning to call it: *War and Peace and Reinsurance*."

CHAPTER 59

In the afternoon, Elizabeth looked in on Jane, who was packing up her things, and said, "Exciting times!"

"Oh, yes!" said Jane. "It almost makes me feel guilty. I'm sure something wonderful will come along for you, too."

"Thank you. And yes, it's on its way."

"That's right. It'll be here before you know it."

"In fact," said Elizabeth, "it'll be here in about two weeks. I just accepted a position reporting to Darcy."

"You're joking, Lizzy. This can't be! Working for Mr. Darcy! No, you won't fool me. I know it to be impossible."

"Clearly, this is going to be a challenge for me to explain. If you don't believe me, how will anyone else?"

Jane looked at her in perplexity. "Of course we won't believe such a story. Yes, you seem to have worked out a truce with him lately, but the two of you have had a longstanding feud. I'm especially skeptical because I happen to know that he offered you job once, and you – by your own description – almost bit his head off."

Elizabeth raised her arms. "So, if it isn't true, why am I saying it?"

Jane, looking to keep pace with the rising intensity of the discussion, raised her arms back at Elizabeth. "I don't know. It's a joke, maybe. I'm not saying it's a joke on me. Maybe you want to tease Mr. Bennet or Ms. Nebbit. Maybe it's a prank on Darcy. Am I getting warm?"

"No, you are not! I'm dead serious and I really need you to take me at my word. I'm going to be the Special Assistant to the Special Assistant to the President, reporting to FWD, Mr. F. William Darcy. And yes, Darcy and I got off to a rocky start when he first joined the company, but we can officially declare that now to be Ancient

History. In cases such as these, a good memory is unpardonable. This is the last time I'll remember it myself."

Upon some further affirmation of these points, and additional assurances that the information was not being offered mischievously or ironically, Jane relented.

"Can it really be so? And yet now I must believe you. My dear Lizzy, I would - I do - congratulate you. But are you certain? Forgive the question - are you quite certain you can be happy reporting to Darcy?"

"I think, actually, that he's the ideal person for me to report to, and that this will be a wonderful opportunity for me. I guarantee you - I assure you - I *reassure* you - that I'll be every bit as happy, fulfilled, and successful as you will be in Claims. So, now are you convinced and are you pleased for me?"

"Yes! I'm surprised but very pleased for you. And for myself - since Darcy and Bingley are such good friends and close colleagues, I expect we'll have plenty of opportunity to keep in close touch with one another."

"I agree."

"And what was it that changed your mind about Darcy?"

"I think maybe it was when I stopped for a moment to consider that he's probably going to be the next president of the company."

They both laughed at this, although it may not have been clear to either of them whether the joke was the unsuitability or the inevitability of such mercenary considerations. After a moment, Elizabeth continued:

"Actually, there's a very romantic story about why he left Cornwallis. He was in love with a woman who reported to him, and he didn't know how she felt about him, but he knew it would be wrong for him to ask her out while he was her boss. So he left the company - just to take the chance and find out if she could love him back. Incidentally, I've met her, she's wonderful, and it seems to be working out for them. Isn't that a great story? The moment it really hit me how much he gave up to take that chance was when I went with Ms. Gardiner to visit the executive offices of Cornwallis, a place called Pemberley. It's the most beautiful office I've ever seen, and it was very clear that he's still loved and admired there. Any ordinary executive would have found an excuse to stay there and try to work something out quietly. That's when I knew: this is a Stand Up Guy."

Jane asked why she hadn't been more open about her high regard for Darcy. She explained that she'd found it difficult to talk about him or acknowledge him because of regret - she felt that her rude and self-righteous rejection of his earlier offer had poisoned her chances to ever have any close working relationship with him.

Later, encouraged by her talk with Jane, Elizabeth looked in on Mr. Bennet. She shut the door of his office behind her and sat down. He looked up with interest.

"I have some important news to share with you," she said.

"You have my complete attention."

"As you know, I've been endeavoring to find a permanent position for myself beyond the Pride Team. I'm happy today to report that I've secured such a position. My prospective boss will be in touch with you shortly to work out the details of my transition."

Mr. Bennet rose and shook her hand. "This is excellent news, indeed! Well done, Lizzy! And who is this perceptive manager?"

"I'll be reporting to Mr. F. William Darcy, Special Assistant to the President."

At this, Mr. Bennet's countenance clouded and he resumed his chair.

"Darcy? And it's quite settled, is it?"

"Oh, yes. Quite."

He paused. "Well, I can see the appeal. Young man on the rise, interesting background, wide portfolio. I worry, however, that you're underestimating the importance of human chemistry, personal compatibility. There are few, if any, people who can affect your daily life more powerfully - for good or for bad - than the person you report to. If you don't get along well with your boss, if you fight or if you're regularly undercut or disrespected by your boss, that will take a toll on you that can't be compensated for by any amount of résumé building or proximity to power."

"I agree with you completely. Please believe me that this is not some mercenary move on my part. I truly believe that Mr. Darcy is - excepting only possibly yourself - the best and most capable manager in the company. It's my experience of him that - having now worked through some initial misunderstandings - we're able to have an open, constructive, and very cheerful working relationship together."

"Well, this is a change. It's my memory that he's been known to speak disparagingly of you in public, and that you've been known to return the favor."

"Guilty, I'm afraid, on both counts - and would that those incidents had been less memorable! But that's all now long in the past. In more recent interactions we've grown boringly accepting and supportive of one another."

"Well, Lizzy," he said, "I have no more to say. If this be the case, he deserves to have you. I couldn't have parted with you to anyone less worthy."

"Thank you. And I hope you'll think better of him going forward. He was instrumental, you know, in working out the resolution to Lydia's situation."

"Yes, I owe him immensely for that. While we're on the subject of my improvement going forward, I'm remembering now that not long ago I made you sit through a recitation of an email from Collins. At the time, I thought it was hilarious because he was suggesting that you might end up reporting to Darcy. I realize now that it wasn't hilarious, and that it must have been hurtful of me to treat the suggestion as a joke. I'm very sorry."

"Yes, that was an awkward moment for me, but you should still feel free to laugh at Mr. Collins's messages for any other reason."

They laughed, and as Elizabeth was leaving Mr. Bennet rose and called out: "If Mary or Kitty want to announce their new positions, please send them in, for I'm quite at leisure!"

At this point, Elizabeth was prepared to seek out the person she anticipated would be the most challenging audience for her news. She found Ms. Nebbit seated at her desk.

"Oh, Lizzy!" she called out. "I have just a small favor to ask. I'm expecting Mr. Bingley to come by again sometime today, and it's very important that Jane have the opportunity to consult with him properly. But, as you probably noticed, when he came by yesterday that disagreeable Mr. Darcy was tagging along with him. I know you find him tiresome - and, really, who doesn't? Mr. High and Mighty!

God's Gift to Reinsurance! But I was very grateful yesterday that you kept him busy for quite a long while so that Jane and Bingley could have a proper meeting. *Taking one for the team*, I call that, and I'm wondering if you'd be kind enough to the same again today - if the unpleasant man happens to show up once again where he isn't wanted."

"I think it's entirely likely that the person to whom you're referring will find his way to this department before the day is out, and I'd be delighted to spend as much time with him as he likes. I do think, however, that you might want to find some friendlier terms of greeting for him, if only for my sake, as I've accepted a very nice position reporting directly to him, Mr. F. William Darcy himself. He'll be speaking with Mr. Bennet about the plan for my transition."

The effect of this announcement on Ms. Nebbit was most extraordinary. On first hearing it, she sat quite still, and was unable to utter a syllable. She began at length to recover, to fidget about in her chair, get up, sit down again, wonder, and bless herself.

"Good gracious! Bless me! Only think! Dear me! Mr. Darcy! Who would have thought it! Oh! My sweetest Lizzy! How rich and how great you'll be! What an expense account you'll have! How people will scurry when you need a report! This is better than Jane's! I didn't think any of you girls would ever do better than Jane reporting to Bingley, but this blows her out of the water! Oh! Ms. Cullis will have a kitten! I am so pleased - so happy! Such a charming man! I've always thought so, even if I didn't express myself very well. *Mr. High and Mighty* I called him. There's nothing bad about that! He is wonderfully high and wonderfully mighty - as you will be, too, my dear! What else? *God's Gift to Reinsurance.* That he definitely is! God's gift to reinsurance and to Juniper Re and to us all! Oh! I'm so happy for you! Ms. Cullis will have a kitten!"

Elizabeth could see that she needn't have worried about Ms. Nebbit's approval. She returned to her desk happy and relieved. Three minutes later, Ms. Nebbit appeared at her side.

"I can't sit down! This is too exciting! He's practically the president! They say he'll be the president eventually! What will that make you? You'll have your picture on the website! You'll have your picture in the back of the annual report! Is he coming here this morning? Should I apologize for things I may have said in the past that might have sounded less cordial than they were intended?"

Elizabeth worried that, where once Ms. Nebbit would embarrass her by her rudeness to Darcy, she would now embarrass her by being obsequious to him. However, when he did stop by later in the day, Ms. Nebbit surprised Elizabeth by being too shy to say anything to him at all.

CHAPTER 60

"So this is really happening?" Elizabeth said to Darcy later that day. "I'm to be your first staff member?"

"My belated first staff member here at Juniper Re, yes. I expect there will be others eventually, but there's no rush. Staff additions are the most important decisions, so there should never be a rush."

"And why me?"

"I'm grateful to have you, and I might just as well ask you the same thing. But, it's a fair question, and I'll try to give you a fair answer. I've seen in you many fine qualities that I think will be very helpful to me and to the organization. Very high on that list are your excellent communication skills - both oral and written. It's a tricky thing in any organization to be able to communicate complicated information in a way that's accurate, but also clear and effective. This is especially important in our business, where we're constantly dealing with very arcane concepts, and where large sums of money can hang on the placement of a semi-colon. Personally, I'm always thinking about accuracy, because I feel the business and moral necessity of it, but too much focus on details means that I'm often neither clear nor effective. I believe you'll be able to help me with that, as well as play your own role in shaping the future of the company. One other thing I'd highlight is our odd personal history, which I see as a plus for us at this point. There's an adage regarding personal relationships that you don't know how strong the relationship is until you've survived a really good fight. I think something similar applies to business relationships. You and I have experienced some pretty intense conflict, and we're both standing, and we're both, I hope, friends. So I'm optimistic that we can work things out, whatever bumps we may have to deal with in the future. Fair answer?"

"Yes, thank you."

"Oh, and one more thing: you're the Einstein who's going to solve all the company's toughest problems."

The following weekend, Elizabeth went out to dinner with Brian Fitzpatrick. They'd finally had their first date a few weeks earlier, and were now seeing each other socially with some regularity. When Elizabeth had first met him, she thought he looked ordinary, but now she was finding his appearance increasingly attractive. Why should this be? Now that she knew him better and appreciated his many good qualities, including his fondness for her, did she see him more or less clearly than she had at their first meeting? Possibly something in their relationship gave her a renewed appreciation that even ordinary-looking people are still actually strikingly attractive. Or maybe she simply decided that she was possessed of sufficient glamour for the two of them.

He asked her: "So, Elizabeth, why did you agree to start going out with me?"

She smiled. "Not quite desperation, but my standards have definitely lowered over the years. Originally, I was holding out for certain movie stars I'd been in love with my whole life, until one day I realized that, not only are they not a part of my life, but they're also getting a little old for me. So then for a while I was fixated on music stars and sports stars - some of whom were at least age-appropriate for me. But still, there was that problem of availability. So we're giving you a shot. But, if you don't mind, it would be helpful if you could become a famous actor, singer or athlete."

"I'll see what I can do."

"I was nervous about going out with you that first time, because of how much you did to help Lydia. I was too grateful. I didn't want our whole relationship to be based on my gratitude. How did you even know about the situation with Lydia and Wickham in the first place?"

"I was put onto the case by your friend, Ms. Gardiner."

"My guardian angel. Well, fortunately for us both, my gratitude has subsided. Oh, and also you're nice, and I like your shoes. Two very important considerations. So now, I need to ask as well. Why did you choose me?"

"I don't know that these things can be boiled down to any one reason. What's not to like? You're quite attractive, of course, and smart and very engaging and fun to be around. But, at the end of the day, the critical element was probably your shoes. I can't take my eyes off them. You do wear shoes, right?"

The following week, Mr. Bennet found time to respond to Mr. Collins:

> Dear Sir: I must trouble you once more for congratulations. Elizabeth will soon be reporting to Mr. Darcy. Console Executive VP de Bourgh as well as you can. No one can doubt your loyalty to her, but personally I'd advise you not to burn any bridges as respect her nephew.
>
> With best regards-

Elizabeth was cleaning out her desk when Mary came by.

"I hope it all works out well for you, Elizabeth," she said. "I should probably let you know that I'm about to leave the company. Do you know Andrei in Actuarial? He left last week, and I'll be joining him soon. We'll be setting up a start-up company - developing some new models for risk transfer. He has a line on some VC funding already. That's Venture Capital. I can't really work on it yet, of course, but I have most of it in my head already, and I'm really looking forward to getting it all documented after we get back from our honeymoon."

"Honeymoon? You're getting married? To Andrei?"

Mary nodded yes.

"Well, congratulations, you crazy romantic, you! You know, the fact that you're leaving the company shouldn't have been the lead piece of information there. Number One is the fact that you and Andrei are getting married. Number Two is that you and Andrei are starting up a new company. The fact that you'll be leaving the company is Number Three at best."

"If you say so. Anyway, I thought I should tell you. I have a project I need to finish."

This exchange left Elizabeth wondering about Kitty, who would apparently soon be the sole remaining member of the Pride Team. Was she feeling left behind? She went over and asked her.

"Oh, not at all," said Kitty. "I think it's great! Now, there was a time when I was quite depressed. That was in the dark days when we were all the co-workers of Lydia the Criminal and nobody seemed to want any of us. Now, we're going like hotcakes! At this point, if someone wants a Pride Team member, I'm the only game in town!"

CHAPTER 61

As our story is now careering towards the finish line, we'll summarize the following year.

Elizabeth settled comfortably into the southwest corner of the third floor - Juniper Re's modest equivalent of Pemberley. She was very busy - dividing her time between assisting Darcy on all his projects and working on projects of her own initiative. She enjoyed her work thoroughly, had a very smooth and cordial working relationship with Darcy, and was widely viewed as a rising young star within the company. Outside of work, she was regularly enjoying the company of Mr. Fitzwilliam, and they were considered a married couple in the eyes of various social media platforms, although, unlike Darcy and Georgiana, they'd not yet become officially engaged. Darcy informed Elizabeth with exaggerated gravity that, if she and Fitzwilliam ever had a child, they should name it *F. William* in his honor, whether the child was a boy or a girl.

Jane proved to be a very capable, efficient, and cheerful assistant to Mr. Bingley. Under his leadership, and with her help, the Claims Department became considerably more professional and more responsive to the needs of those it served. Despite, or possibly because of, her virtues, she had little profile within the organization. This will be a disappointment to those who look to a unit like the Pride Team to produce conspicuous role models, but Jane had little appetite for being a conspicuous anything. It may be some consolation that talented workers willing and able to do challenging work with little or no recognition constitute one of the most critical components of any successful organization.

Kitty took a position in Operations that made good use of her high energy level and positive attitude. She also found herself with a happily settled personal life, which left her working life undistracted by romantic phantoms.

Lydia and Wickham lasted six months in the situation that Fitzwilliam had arranged for them. Technically, they were let go one day short of six months, sparing the company various obligations that would apply once they would have passed that date. Both of them having an impressive aptitude for drawing a pleasing generality from questionable specifics, they found another situation, nearly as promising as the one from which they'd been let go. They'd started their work there, but hadn't yet made it through their probationary period.

Mary was happy at the start-up company she'd helped to found. She enjoyed slicing the traditional rectangles of quota share and excess placements into triangles and other more exotic shapes. Andrei, her partner and husband, had a good head for business, and was surprised and pleased to discover that the right triangle, when combined with an algorithm for calculating a loss corridor, could actually be patented. Mary's models were now licensed to many reinsurers, including Juniper Re. In financial terms, Mary was the most successful of her Pride Team class. Lacking the communication and social skills of her colleagues, she was bringing value to her industry by pursuing ideas that interested her.

Mr. Bennet missed Elizabeth exceedingly. He delighted in visiting her, especially when he was least expected. He remained in control of the Pride Team program - or at least as much in control as he ever had been - and was teaching the basics of reinsurance to a fresh class with, perhaps, a renewed appreciation for the downside risks and upside potential of his charges' nascent careers.

Ms. Nebbit took tremendous pride in the positions and accomplishments of the former Pride Team members, and would regularly find an excuse to look in on Jane or Kitty. However, she rarely ventured to visit Elizabeth, as she was never entirely at ease in the vicinity of Mr. Darcy.

It would be an overstatement to report that the success of so many of her protégées helped to transform Ms. Nebbit into a sensible, prudent, and well-informed employee, one who was able to constructively complement the Pride Team program without undercutting Mr. Bennet, and one who always considered the needs of the organization and her colleagues before her own. When Ms. Gardiner recruited Charlotte to be her assistant and probable successor, Ms. Nebbit took the move as an act of disloyalty against her and the Pride Team. This was despite the fact that Charlotte was a close friend of both Jane and Elizabeth, and that there were no Pride Team members currently available to hire.

Charlotte managed the transition very thoughtfully to accentuate the honor accruing to Mr. Collins for being the catalyst to her career. He was well satisfied with this, although he was left with the task of bestowing her former role on a suitably worthy replacement.

Ms. de Bourgh, seeing there was nothing further to be done about it, resigned herself to Elizabeth's presence on Darcy's staff. She eventually developed a grudging respect for Elizabeth's skills and decided, with the clarity of retrospect, that her efforts to prevent the placement had been good for Elizabeth, testing her resolve and fortitude, and had been intended as such all along.

Finally, a disclaimer is in order. A single year is an insufficient span to enable a complete accounting of the wisdom or folly of the events described in the previous chapters. In particular, judging the success of a relationship – business or personal – can be considered analogous to monitoring the results of a long-tail line of insurance business. A honeymoon period - literal or figurative - is simply an encouraging beginning. The fact that a decision looks good one year later is no guarantee that it will continue to look good two or five or ten years later. Among those who toil in long-tail fields, confidence of success, if it comes at all, builds slowly over time, and is never deemed to be final or absolute.

While some might fear that such a cautious approach could drain a measure of enjoyment from life, happiness shouldn't depend on ignoring downside risk. Some may say that an appreciation of the transitory nature of our joys and successes actually makes them sweeter. In any event, for those committed to a clear-eyed assessment of risk, the honest enjoyment of an encouraging beginning will need to be enough for now.

ACKNOWLEDGEMENTS

Linda is the original and still-champion Pride and Prejudice maven in our household and, for good measure, a copy-editing superhero.

I'm also grateful for feedback from Tina DesRoches, John Espy, Milos Ljeskovac, and Michael Willander.

Finally, my apologies to the reinsurance industry. Needing a setting for a modern, corporate reimagining of the Austen classic, I settled on that business as sufficiently refined and arcane for my purposes. The actual reinsurance industry, as I write this now, is notable for its diversity and conscientiousness.